Will of the Alpha 2

Edited by Rechan and Lafitte

Will of the Alpha 2

Copyright © 2015 by Rechan and Lafitte

Cover artwork by Kadath (www.latenightgrind.com)

Published by FurPlanet Productions
Dallas, Texas
www.furplanet.com

Print ISBN 978-1-61450-280-7
eBook ISBN 978-1-61450-281-4

Printed in the United States of America
First Edition Trade Paperback 2015

TABLE OF CONTENTS

Raddlepated

Whyte Yoté

Olan Chennock sat in a dark corner booth of Aerach's Public House & Inn, and waited.

An unread copy of the *Londonderry Sentinel* lay before him on the table, folded as it had come from the dispenser outside the pub's heavy oaken doors with their twin brass lionhead knockers. The doors, opened for ventilation, also allowed the heavy North Atlantic fog to creep in over ancient flagstones worn smooth and shiny by a century and a half of paws and hooves. Founded in 1850 to serve (and service) the sailors and fishermen who called Greencastle, Ireland home, it now existed like most other things around County Donegal: to wet the whistles of locals and regulars too poor or lazy to make the short drive to Londonderry.

But Olan Chennock liked Aerach's precisely because it *wasn't* Londonderry. None of the business it did could be considered brisk, even on Friday and Saturday nights. And today, on this fog-chilly Tuesday morning when the few who came in were ordering tea and eggs and potatoes and black pudding, the Galway ram was nursing a whiskey.

Kilbeggan (sixteen years old, merely one-quarter Olan's age), straight up, with a single blackberry at the bottom of the glass. Olan stirred slowly with a swizzle stick he'd carved from one of his own horns after he'd lost a brawl in his younger days outside this very same pub. Between his teeth sat a pipe carved from the same horn, unlit and unpacked. Smoking wasn't allowed inside Aerach's, and he hadn't committed to staying long enough to warrant a smoke streetside.

Rory was late, but it was foggy. The ferry would be slow. And Olan was a patient man.

He waited, and drank, and tongued his pipe from one corner of his muzzle to the other. Rearranging his spectacles when they canted too far to one side. Murphy, the stout wolf who owned and operated the pub, absently wiped the bar while just as absently watching a football match on the single television mounted near the ceiling. The Rangers versus some team that wasn't the Rangers. He turned it to BBC2 because they were losing. Swore under his breath and finished wiping the bar. Glanced in Olan's direction, and Olan shook his head. The ram wouldn't have time for another round.

Murphy understood. Murphy knew about Rory. And Murphy didn't care. In fact, Murphy had implied interest, in his own very subtle way. But Murphy didn't have the whole picture.

The ram leaned back until the curve of his horns met the wall, only a few finger-breadths away. Took the glass between thumb and forefinger. Tilted a wee draught onto his tongue, savoring the sweet smoke and false warmth. Swallowed as his phone buzzed; Olan was a conscientious man, even when he was alone.

It was Rory. FOG, the message said, because that was all that needed saying. Whether that meant the border collie had run into it on the way from Coleraine to MacMilligan Prison on the coast, or the ferry had encountered it in the narrow strait between the peninsula and Greencastle proper, the outcome did not change. Rory would be late, and that was fine. Considering this revelation, the ram decided to smoke after all.

Prying his bulky self out of the booth, he donned a worn tweed cap, shrugged on a worn tweed jacket, drained the whiskey and chewed up the blackberry. Pips caught here and there in his teeth, bothersome but necessary when imbibing Kilbeggan, at least to Olan Chennock. He paced to the bar and leant a bit, as if requesting privacy or at least the impression of such.

Tapping the bar twice with his right hand, the fat heather-gem ring punctuating the sound, he whispered loudly to Murphy: "Out for a smoke, be round presently." Ended it with a wink but no smile. "Watch me glass," he deadpanned.

"Right," Murphy grinned.

The R241 outside Aerach's stretched into the murk in either direction, bereft of traffic wheeled or foot. The sounds of the morning, few and far between, were muffled as if by a newly-fallen blanket of thick wet snow. This was September, but the humid chill crept past the ram's jacket and vest, through his plain cotton shirt and down to his skin despite the layer of wool in between. Olan liked it this way, though, because he'd lived on the north coast of Ireland all his life and he would likely die here, on a morning just like this one.

He heard the plaintive call of the ferry just as he touched his match to the bowl of black Cavendish, drawing humid air to stoke it. Wouldn't be more than ten minutes before Rory's arrival. Till then he settled against the old stonework and puffed away, as much a fixture on the footpath as any of the surrounding buildings. Smoke drifted in tendrils around his head, seeping into his wool and clothes. Since the witch-hunt on smokers, the ram had kept his stock in a special flask, absent those awful stickers that remonstrated against the dreaded dangers. All well and good, but Olan had made it to sixty-four and he'd be damned if he'd give up what was as much a Chennock family tradition as Irish Catholicism.

In the name of the Stem and the Bowl and the Holy Leaf, Amen.

A Vauxhall Astra passed by, followed by an ancient diesel Mercedes clattering along, presumably from the ferry. And, a few minutes later, Rory appeared on his bicycle like a wraith, if one could describe a border collie as wraith-like. He rode slowly and rang his bell twice, the sound weak and foreboding like everything else in the fog. When he came to a stop next to the ram he walked the bike up over the curb, leant over the handlebars and grinned. His wearing a wool jumper was not lost on Olan, from whose hide said material had come. It was an ironic nod to their unique relationship.

"Oi." All of Rory Teahan's twenty-four years in one word.

Olan puffed as he talked around his pipe stem. "You're not a punk and ye never will be."

"Suppose not." Leaning the bike against a still-lit streetlamp, Rory bent close and took in a noseful of the ram. He did not move to embrace, though; there were rules around these parts. "Lovely weather, isn't it?"

"Aye. Sure looks it." When the border collie turned to admire the gossamer view, Olan cupped one firm buttock on the sly. "How's the ride?"

"Duller than normal. Nothin' to look at, 'sides fog, fog and more fog. Couldn't even see the prison, it was so thick." Rory was wagging just enough to brush tail to tail with the ram, which was something of a feat. Several months apart would do that to a young pup. Olan, of course, was a patient man.

"I'm surprised you didn't bring your little VW Polo over."

"Exercise is good for me. And Petrol is dear, you know. It's less than thirty kilometers anyway, so." Olan's version of thirty kilometers was much longer than the border collie's.

The ram only nodded. And he couldn't complain. Those thirty kilometers produced that solid round backside he was so fond of. Though no exercise was needed to keep its interior in shape.

"I've got an empty glass inside. D'you fancy I should snuff this pipe and leave it empty?"

"Neh. No reason not to savor another."

Rory stood in silence beside the smoking ram, fairly vibrating with anticipation. Part of the fun was Olan's masterful subtlety, as the ram had found out during a pub crawl two years ago down in Londonderry. At the time he hadn't been looking for a partner as much as simply enjoying a pint or six, since he'd hired a room for the night so he could splurge on drink.

And there the dog'd been, in full Manchester United kit, barking at the bartender because the telly had on the Celtics/Rangers match. Which was a great mistake due to the company in which he had placed himself. Being twenty-two, with a fair amount of reckless abandon thrown in for good measure, he hadn't been prepared for the blowback from the locals.

The only reason Olan had saved his skin was so the ram could drink in relative peace. The two got well into their cups over the next several hours. And, like one of those Internet stories written for wanking as opposed to believing, Olan had offered up his room as a port in the alcoholic storm. It was in the process of holding each other up while they doffed their clothing, once the ram's touch was mistaken for something more (and Olan didn't mind Rory's company) that the border collie had gone to his knees in short order.

What Olan discovered later on that night had been nothing but serendipitous. He was the peg to Rory's hole, so to speak. And that was how they remained.

So the ram smoked until naught was left in the bowl but a few centimeters of char, and after they ambled back inside he nursed a second whiskey while the border collie enjoyed a Beamish Stout in boisterous boycott of Guinness, which he referred to as "piss water". They didn't talk much. They never talked much—talking like men wasn't part of the game—but Olan sensed great contentment from Rory just to be in his presence.

Murphy padded over to them as soon as the ram swallowed down the second blackberry. "Another, or will this be it then?" His amber eyes darted between canine and ovine, inserting sexual tension where none need be. Perhaps, someday in the future, Olan would bring up the concept to Rory. Or, Olan could meet up with the wolf alone, if he hadn't a preference. Murphy was just over half his age. The ram was finding out age didn't matter fuck-all.

"I think we're through. Gotta head home." He knew two pairs of eyes were trained on him, thinking dirty thoughts, while he fished a twenty-euro note out of his pocket. He always paid, more of a convenience thing than age before beauty. Rory carried mostly pounds sterling, being from Northern Ireland just across the way. Nothing said he couldn't carry euros too, but the status quo strengthened their roles during these trysts. "That'll do?"

"I'll owe ya, but yeah," Murphy said. "Lemme get some coins back to you."

"Keep it."

"You sure, Olan? It's more'n two euros."

"Go way outta that, you're fine." And this time Olan *did* add a smile to the wink. Pretty sure he'd end up fucking the wolf by year's end.

"You boys have a great day," Murphy practically drooled, wagging his way back behind the bar.

Rory's paw on his shoulder. "He onto us?"

The ram chuckled, a deep half-bleat. "Boy, he's *been* onto us. Don't fret; he's *into* us as well." A tightening of claws near his neck signified Rory's interest.

"Maybe."

"Maybe. Maybe I should get you home." The border collie whimpered reflexively. "How long's it been?"

"Over a week." That would make Rory good and obedient. He was always more obedient when his bollocks were backed up. He'd gone longer without, but Olan didn't mind as long as the need was there.

Olan brought a hand up to stroke the border collie from forehead to neck. Rory shuddered. "Right, then. Away with us," in his authoritative baritone.

The Toyota Hilux with its mismatched camper shell sat parked behind the pub, and Rory began to pant when he saw the rear door with its little window set up high. "Go on, then," Olan said as he swatted the dog's rump. "It's unlocked for ye." Rory trotted up with his bike, opened the door and wheeled it in, swinging it shut behind him without the benefit of a single word to the ram. Of course, this was perfectly okay as it showed nothing but eagerness.

"Kids," muttered Olan as he stepped into the cab, his gut comfortably warm.

* * *

Baile Ceannach lay up the gentle sloping fields west of the coast and over the crest, on a flat stretch surrounded by a wood planted by Olan's great-great-great grandfather when he had established the place in 1840. Only a shade over thirty hectares, but it belonged to him, and it was home.

Halfway up the slope the fog gave way to bright midday sunshine, so bright the ram squinted until his spectacles tinted down so he could see properly. The truck rolled along, the countryside looking like a patch of heaven above the clouds. Some saw the whole of Ireland that way.

The unnamed paved road the ram took out of Greencastle turned into an unnamed gravel road that zigzagged through scrub and fields and teased along the coast before turning inland again, gently descending into this valley and back up that hillside, where the land was parceled out with stone walls and hedgerows more often than fences.

Turning onto a two-rut track, Olan engaged the four-wheel drive and slowed down so as not to throw his precious cargo into the sides of the camper shell behind him. He passed the only other house on his road, and two kilometers past it the track ended at a metal gate that the ram had to open and close manually. Past the gate the gravel petered out into flat grass, almost blending in with the surrounding terrain.

And at the top of a hillock sat the farmhouse, a two-story spread with more than enough room for one ram to wander a bit. Instead of a whitewash, the family had kept the stone bare over the years, and it had taken on a patina of ivy and moss. It fairly blended in with the scenery, unimposing and revealing nothing of what took place every so often within.

Olan parked out front instead of using the carport he'd attached some thirty years ago. It wouldn't rain today. Rory had picked a banner day to visit.

A scratching came from inside the camper shell, very faint but persistent. Smiling, the ram came round back and turned the handle.

A border collie sat on his haunches, panting, bright-eyed and starkers. Bits of sand and gravel rattled around the bed, propelled by his ceaseless tail. A black leather leash hung loosely in his teeth, attached to a matching collar around his neck. And on blatant display were his goods, waggling and slightly swollen within a sheath locker.

It had begun.

"Well, then," Olan began, scrutinizing the border collie with fingers lifting his chin, "Let's have a look-see. Are you all squared away?"

Rory barked. His junk jumped. The ram, braced against the door frame due to his slight buzz, peered past one floppy ear and saw the pile of crisply-folded clothes in a corner. He pushed off, crossed his arms before his ample chest. Looked Rory square in his emerald eyes. "Good boy."

"Ruff!" said Rory, now incapable of forming words. If all went well, he wouldn't form a single word until the end of the night. He tousled the fur between the dog's ears into a mess of black and white bangs over his eyes.

"Come on, then," the ram said, keeping his tone even and low instead of the singsong one he would otherwise use. "Let's get you fed." A tug on the leash got Rory on all fours and he started leading the way, tail high, hiding nothing. He'd apparently been practicing in the interim. Olan admired his young, lithe body and pined for his halcyon days for exactly one second before remembering leading a twenty-something around on a leash was much more fun than being able to touch one's hooves.

A brass key from his breast pocket turned the old noisy tumblers on the original iron padlock that held the big solid-ash doors shut with a chain. They swung open with little effort on quiet, oiled hinges. Rory trotted through but yipped when Olan held firm on the leash, setting the pace to his liking. Ears flat and tail tucked, the border collie looked balefully back with big, plaintive eyes likely to melt anyone's heart.

The moment their eyes met, it struck Olan that he couldn't tell whether or not the pup was enjoying the reprimand. But they had a word for times when either went too far, or when either became too exhausted to continue. They'd used that word only for the latter thus far.

Nudging the doors closed, the ram tugged the leash as he passed from foyer to kitchen, Rory right on his hocks, sniffing around as if this were some strange, new place. All Olan had done was sweep the floor before driving into town.

Sunlight streamed in through the windows, throwing thick bars through the motes from wall to floor, brightening up the otherwise dark space with its imposing beamed ceilings. Olan didn't use electricity unless he had to, not because of the cost but because the house just didn't feel right with artificial light. Of course, after dusk the point became moot. Though, on nights when Rory stayed over, candles were the order of the evening.

Rory clinked into the kitchen alongside the ram and sat obsequious next to the stainless-steel island with its built-in cook top, the locker's lower band clicking on the stones under his sac.

"Hungry, then?" the ram inquired with a cocked eyebrow. The border collie tail-thumped the sliding glass door behind him. "D'you think ye deserve it?" Rory's face fell as his whine rose, a drawn-out keening he kiboshed when he saw Olan's disapproving stare. His tongue couldn't decide whether to stay in or hang out or lick his lips, so the dog did all three while intently watching the ram bend before a cupboard and take out a small opaque bag. He came back over and poured. Rory snapped at the flow.

"Ep!" Not a word, just a syllable easily uttered, and loudly, with a clear meaning: *Stop doing that, now.* "Bad dog. You know better." Rory *did* know better, too, but he enjoyed pushing boundaries. When his "punishment" was often the most rewarding part of the day, of course he would break a few rules. But he waited, if not exactly patiently, as Olan put away the bag of food (merely some Meatabix cereal, it smelled awful to him, but then again he wasn't a carnivore) and filled the water bowl from the sink.

And there Rory sat, staring at the ram, ears cocked, waiting for the command.

Olan held that moment in suspense, staring the young man down as if challenging him to make a move, to test his luck. But Rory stayed, and when the ram said, "Okay," he dropped to his elbows and proceeded to scarf.

While he watched, the ram marveled at the dog's dedication to their little game. The chastity, of course, served many purposes: heightened sexual energy and willingness to obey commands. But Rory took a much more serious tack with the hunger, sometimes going days without food to trick his brain back into an ancient mode, when the next meal for hunters could be one minute or one week away. Olan Chennock could do many things, difficult things, but he could not go days without food.

But Rory could, and did, and when the food finally came he acted as if it were the last meal he'd ever get. As if he were feral. An ancestor. And that was the whole point.

Rory crawled this way and that, licking up gobs of meal with his tongue, presenting that luscious, tight pink target that sent the ram's hand under his trousers to massage the thickness within. He knew he could kneel down, spit on his cock and take the boy right here, right now, but Rory wouldn't have earned it. And Olan was rarely good for more than one go a night nowadays, so he had to make it count. But he could still rub himself hard and anticipate.

And to think that boy's going to university, he thought, marveling again. *Amazing what lives we lead.* No doubt Rory was smart, working toward double majors in Irish history and Gaelic. It kind of ran in his blood. Once he graduated he wouldn't be able to do much besides teach the history he'd learned, but he seemed satisfied with the idea, the times they'd had conversation post-afterglow. Of course, Rory put his education to good use here on the farm, but that was a pleasant side effect more than a purposeful connection.

The border collie had explained it as "something that just happened, you know?" And Olan understood, because his entire relationship with Rory had "just happened". He knew all about that. You become engrossed in a subject, it takes hold of you more than you thought it would, and suddenly you have a kink.

The sounds that dog had made in the Londonderry hotel room…

After lapping up the last bits of water, Rory plopped back down on his haunches and looked up at Olan. Or at least halfway up; the ram's hand cupped a generous bulge the border collie knew well and couldn't wait to feel. But he would wait, because the waiting made everything better.

And Olan was a patient man.

"Made a right mess, didn't ye?" he asked, frowning in mock disapproval. Morsels of food and water littered the floor around the bowls. "Bad." Rory shrank, tail tucked, though he'd likely done it on purpose. Rory did a lot of things on purpose. The ram entertained the idea of sending him outside, but reconsidered. "Clean it up."

Real apprehension washed over the border collie's features. This was a new thing, an *unexpected* thing. Not entirely out of character for Olan, though; keeping the game fresh kept it interesting.

"Don't try that with me. I brook neither foolishness nor insubordination. Clean. It. Up." He ended with a stiff finger pointed straight at the bowls, his other hand readjusting himself so nothing showed. A double punishment. Rory's eyes fell, a good show, and he slowly turned back to the mess. Tentatively stuck out his tongue. Began to lap. The floor was actually clean enough to eat from, but the boy didn't have to know that. His disgusted expression said it all.

Once the border collie pulled away, licking his lips with a grimace, Olan knelt by the bowls to inspect them. Aside from the sheen of saliva, he found no trace of food or water. He allowed a smile to cross his lips, petted Rory between the ears, and leaned in for a brief nip, enjoying the way the dog fairly melted into him. How he wanted a long, rough lip-lock, but Rory hadn't earned it yet. Plus, it was gauche to shove one's tongue down a pet's throat.

"Out with you." Olan unhooked the leash before standing and sliding open one of the doors that led out to the yard, the field and, beyond it, the woods, which ended at an idyllic stream marking the property line. The canine bounded and ran around the perimeter of the yard, flanked by low stone walls on all sides, sniffing here and there at patches of scent he'd left during visits past. While he lifted a leg and did the best he could with the sheath locker on, the ram divested himself of his jacket. He'd break a sweat quickly in the humid morning, especially with his plans.

Rory trotted around in grass still a bit moist from the morning's dew, exploring as if the enclosure were new to him. A few playthings lay scattered about the turf: a ball here, a Frisbee there, the odd squeaky toy. Olan leant against the wall nearest the patio, crossed his arms and supervised bemusedly.

* * *

Right around the time the ram'd had eager canine lips around his cock, he decided that Rory might be worth keeping round. Not only because the dog went down on him in short order—though it made a strong case—but also because it was the first time anyone had paid him that kind of attention in a very long while. Age, combined with locale, made for slim pickings, and the clubs of Londonderry catered to a crowd forty-some-odd years his junior.

The alcohol—the same whiskey and beer for each, respectively— no doubt had added a certain social lubricant, without which Olan might not have offered up his room at all. And he'd had the border collie's tongue deep in his foreskin, the slime of precum in his whiskers, and an utterly complete willingness to please that the ram rather fancied.

Whether from arousal or impatience, Rory had brushed off the ram's attempts at reciprocation, instead climbing onto the bed and lifting high, desperate for a breeding. And Olan, who had yet to suffer from any sort of erectile dysfunction, climbed up and obliged him.

It wasn't until he'd sunk in all eight inches that the dog bleated, so sudden and out of place that Olan stopped and stared at the small white patch among the black of Rory's back.

"You okay, then?" he panted, winded but nowhere near tired. His hips stilled only for a moment.

"Don't mind me," said the border collie with a clench for good measure. "Just…please, just finish it. Ignore me."

Olan did finish it, with bellowing flair, but he did not ignore Rory's bleats and baa's and murmurings of "I have gone astray, oh good shepherd, reel me in, herd me." Odd as it was, it had no effect on the thorough pounding and seeding he'd given the boy.

Fatigued but very much still inebriated, the questions had come before the ram softened up enough to disengage. And Rory was just as eager to answer as he'd been to give up his tailhole. A history major at University College Dublin, the border collie haltingly but honestly recounted how his studies of Ireland's caste system through the ages had first fascinated him, and then slowly enveloped most aspects of his life.

Transference, he called it. Like the World War II historian who ends up licking jackboots in a scaly club somewhere in Berlin. So it had gone with the ancient shepherds and their sheep, one holding sway over the other because it had always been that way and always would be. How the border collies and sheepdogs and their ilk had kept a kind of indentured servitude over the sources of the textiles they needed. The brandings and clippings and forced pairings. The confinement and long hours of labor for no pay but another day of life.

And somewhere along the line, Rory Teahan had developed an attraction, first out of sympathy and then empathy, for the captives. Starting with a form of pet play, it had evolved in his mind into something much deeper and more servile, with depths he could only explore with a man like the ram.

"Call it a bit of the old 'Self-Hating Border Collie' syndrome," he slurred, doing his best while Olan spooned him and stroked his chest. "'Bout as good as I can explain it. So, I... I saw you across the room like that...and I had to have you." This, despite the fact that the ram had invited Rory up of his own accord. But now that they'd fucked, things were different.

"So, if you don't think me completely daft, I'd like to see you again," offered the dog.

"I don't think you daft at all," Olan murmured, though he hadn't known how he felt about helping out a young dog with his ram-daddy fetish. If it meant more ass around his cock, fine and dandy. The rest he could figure out later. "We'll see what comes of it."

* * *

Of all the objects in the yard, Rory chose a stick that had fallen from the Rowan tree toward the back wall, carrying it up high like a prized trophy. Or a pheasant. He dropped it at Olan's hooves, plopped down and panted expectantly.

"Oh, you think ye deserve a bit of fetch, eh." Of course Rory did. He'd gone on the wall instead of on the grass, he'd not jumped the gate to the field, and he'd not got mud all over the ram's good tweed. In fact, he'd taken care not to get mud anywhere but his pads. "I suppose we could throw a few." He gave a few pats, and then he was waving it over the dog's head.

Rory reared up almost to the point of standing before remembering his place and came back down again, practically squirming. Olan faked a few tosses, then wound up to propel the stick as far as he could.

It amazed the ram how anyone could cavort so freely with a piece of restrictive metal clamped to one's groin, but the border collie made it work and even seemed to enjoy it. There were many things he enjoyed that Olan didn't understand, but he'd learned he didn't need to understand to have a good time.

In between tosses, and Rory's returns, he managed to get his vest off and throw it onto the top of the wall. They'd both be soaked by the end of things, he knew it. A few tosses later his trousers joined the vest, leaving the ram in loose-fitting boxers that accommodated his endowments. Rory became increasingly distracted until, leaping for a high toss, he overshot his mark and came down right in a mud puddle near the rear wall. Suddenly half of him was soaked and brown.

Olan grinned. "C'mere, you." The boy whimpered and crawled his way back to the ram's hooves, eyes baleful, knowing punishment was nigh. Though, the only true punishment for Rory was the denial of his role-play and consequent climax.

Rory looked down at his ruined fur and whined helplessly. Whereas other times he would intentionally make trouble, the puddle incident had been purely accidental. He wasn't sure how to act, so he acted ashamed.

"Hup," barked the ram, and up the dog went, just long enough for Olan to snap the leash back on. "It rained last night," he said in a low voice. "You could see that. D'you know I'm outta dog shampoo; you'll have to rinse under the hose and shower with me."

Rory pretended that this was a horrible prospect.

"Bad dog."

Rory drew down.

"*Baaaaaaaaaad!*" the ram bleated.

Rory started and fell onto his back, limbs splayed in submission, head to the side.

"Mayhap you need a reminder of your place. Mayhap I should start the rinsing myself. Eh? Eh?" Olan turned and walked down the length of the wall until he reached a corner, where three bottles of Guinness sat, open, in the noonday sun. He gathered them and brought them back to the cowering border collie, who knew what was coming.

Rory had an aversion to certain elements of play, and Olan's bladder had a habit of being fickle, so this was as close as they came to a marking ritual.

He may have been whining, but the border collie likely had a chubby inside that sheath locker.

Stepping out of his boxers, the ram gave his foreskin a couple tugs, releasing a cloud of musk trapped since Olan's morning shower. He took the first bottle and straddled Rory about the belly. "This is for your own good," he stated, and turned it over. Hot, flat beer poured down the length of his shaft, trickled off the tip and splashed onto Rory's ruined coat, just the right temperature.

It wasn't the real thing, but it was "piss water" to Rory, and that was enough.

The smell of warm beer scrunched up the canine's nose, and several times he wriggled under the ram's weight, to no avail. After the bottle emptied, Olan rubbed it deep into Rory's belly and stood.

"Hup."

The second bottle went down in much the same fashion, tantalizing the dog with a cock so near his face yet repulsed by the off-putting hoppy-yeasty odor. He bent his head and allowed himself to be marked from tip to tail, held in place by Olan's tight grip on the leash.

"Open." Rory resisted, even pulled back when the ram's fingers worked their way through his lips. "Open or we quit this business right now." The prospect of denial was too much, and the border collie spread his jaw wide enough for Olan's tip and its rancid river. The third bottle's contents traveled down the thick flesh and filled his muzzle to bursting, forcing him to swallow and gag. But soon enough it was over, and he was left a soaked, shivering mess at the hooves of his master.

Olan shook himself off. "You learn your lesson about not goin' where you don't belong?" Legitimately cowed, Rory nodded, and the leash came back off. "Go to the gate and wait for me, if you think you can do that much." With a slow gait, the border collie slunk off to the rear of the yard.

While he would never admit it to the boy, Olan was shaken, if only just a wee bit. He knew their rules—they'd had a long and sometimes awkward discussion at the outset—and the basis for Rory's attractions, but the way he'd looked…

He squinted and took off his specs to rub at his eyes. The lad sat on the far side of the yard, waiting by the gate. They both knew what came next, and Olan was able to work himself half-hard by the time he got halfway across. Rory watched him. Or, at least, he watched what was between the ram's legs as he walked.

Olan lifted the catch on the gate and swung it wide. The dog did not budge. He knew what would happen as soon as he crossed that line, and he wouldn't move until told to. Reeking of brew, he wouldn't risk another reprimand. After this his satisfaction was assured, and he wouldn't arse it up.

Atop the stone wall on the right side of the gate sat a plain white bucket with a lid on. Rory's eyes darted between the bucket and the ram's shapely chest with its slightly less shapely belly below. The ram removed the lid, revealing a wide paintbrush sitting in a slotted tray.

Everything in the bucket was stained a deep brick red from the pigment within. The pigment was raddle.

Raddle had been used in the caste-system days as a way to control the ovid population and breed the best wool producers. Rory had described this in giddy detail on the night they met, while the ram had nodded, having known about the procedure as passed down through generations. The masters would slather pigment onto the chests and groins of horny male tups, and every coupling would be marked for all to see.

This was the kind of marking Rory loved. And after much convincing, Olan had relented. Now it was just part of the game, the culmination of a few hours of vigorous role play, and the thing each looked forward to the most.

Next to the bucket, in an ancient butter tub, sat a whistle. The ram took it out and put it to his lips, blowing three bursts in rapid succession. Rory took off like a shot, running a beeline straight across the field toward the wooded area a hundred or so metres away. When he was halfway to the trees Olan blew in such a way that the note rose and fell again, and the border collie veered off to the right. A long burst from high to low curved him round in a wide semicircle, while a trilled note forced him left.

This was the way they had done it in the ancient times, before the advent of civil society. In the dark ages.

Rory missed a footfall and tumbled a bit before recovering, maintaining his direction until the next command. When Olan felt the boy'd proved his mettle he gave the complex six-note return call, and seconds later he had a puppy at his side, winded but happy as all get-out, chest heaving and tail swishing up a storm.

"Good boy," he said warmly, and Rory's heart looked to just about burst from pride. "I think you've earned your keep for the day." Removing a key from a chink in the stone, he took a knee and gripped the border collie's equipment to get at the sheath locker. One twist and the entire device fell apart, revealing a set of sweaty, and rapidly expanding, genitals. Once free, Rory's first three inches said hello to the Irish sunshine.

Olan stood and took the brush, swirled it round in the raddle to mix it up, and brushed pigment from nipples to cock in broad strokes. It soaked through the first few centimetres of wool but didn't drip, a thick layer that would tell the world just whose bitch the boy was. Rory began to drool, a Pavlovian response he'd developed from the first day the ram had indulged him in raddle play.

"One minute." The ram held up three fingers, then two, then one, and as he made a fist he let out a roaring bleat that echoed off the moors, a relic of the past.

Rory rose to all fours, his bedraggled coat pretty much worse for wear, and responded in kind, as best as his canine vocal cords would allow. And he was off toward the wood in long, bounding leaps reminiscent of the herds of yore. The boy would get a whole minute's worth of head start before Olan came after him.

Sunshine warmed the ram's back, eased his bones and muscles. He wouldn't run; he didn't have to, with the property as small as it was. Just enough for a good game of hide-and-seek before the border collie gave it all up.

Olan Chennock was a patient man. But he was eager to sink his staff.

He counted under his breath. By fourteen Rory'd disappeared in the forest shadows. At twenty-nine Olan cracked his back and knuckles. By forty he'd set his specs on the rock wall and closed up the bucket. And at sixty he trotted off to herd his "ewe".

What the ram didn't have in speed he made up for in stamina, his farm-honed body more than up to the task of covering the ground from farmhouse to creek. He knew every centimetre of the place, and the places where Rory would most likely try to hide. It chuffed the dog that Olan at least played at searching, especially those times when the boy was too horny to try very hard at hiding.

It took only a few minutes to cross the field to the edge of the wood.

Olan slipped between two trees and immediately felt cold. The sun couldn't break through the canopy in most spots, save for a few clearings, and anyplace shaded held the chill of early morning throughout the day. Fifty metres or more in either direction, and at least another sixty til the creek, Rory could be anywhere.

Stumbling through undergrowth and the mossy skeletons of trees long downed, the ram perked his ears up, swiveling to and fro, scanning for sounds of movement other than his own hoofsteps. His neighbor to the rear, an expat Shetland pony, worked in Londonderry and never tended to the creek side of his land, so there was little worry of discovery back here, especially on a weekday. Olan hefted his balls to scratch an itch, pulled on his foreskin and listened.

Not even a bird made its presence known. The coast was still cloaked in fog, the roads were lightly traveled to begin with, and houses were great distances apart. Privacy out in the open, and that's how the ram preferred it.

A stick broke to his right. He turned but saw nothing. No canine scent drifted to his nose in the still air.

And then he saw the tail.

He wouldn't have noticed it but for the twitch. It fairly blended in with the mottled lighting under the canopy, but not even Rory's best efforts could keep it from wagging. The prospect of sex simply excited him too much, and he gave himself away. He was standing erect, hiding behind the thin trunk of a younger tree, the bugger, but he couldn't hide his telltale tail.

Stepping as carefully as he could, Olan closed the distance between them, one hand fluffing himself to hardness. He thought back to Rory eating off the floor, his hole on blatant display, and that got him the rest of the way.

The border collie broke out with only a few metres to go, dropping to all fours again. This time Olan took off after him, agile on hooves that knew the terrain better than anyone. In a straight line on open ground, maybe, Rory might have an advantage, but here his pads slid on dead leaves and mossy soil.

"Cheater!" Olan bellowed between breaths. "Ye hid on two legs! No mercy, boyo!" Sweat broke out on his forehead, sluiced back around his horns. Up ahead, desperately weaving between trees, Rory bleated weakly. The whistle commands had tuckered him out.

Brilliant.

Rory feinted right, then darted left. Olan smiled; the creek was that way and the border collie knew not to cross it. The ram kept a short distance behind, enjoying lungfuls of the lad's trailing scent. It had rained last night, and if Rory did what the ram thought he would do, it was all over.

And that's what Rory did.

Darting between two boles, the lad saw the muddy edge of the water too late and slid onto his side to avoid falling in. Before he could find purchase on solid ground Olan was through the same trees and standing above him, hooves firmly planted in the sandy loam. Forgetting his playacting, Rory yelped and scrambled to no avail. A hand around his neck pinned him down.

"Haven't run like that in donkey's years," the ram gasped. "You're gonna pay for gettin' me dirtier than I already am." Seeing the intimidating piece between Olan's legs, Rory knew the price. "Now, you're gonna stay down like a good boy and take me cock. Okay?"

The border collie nodded furtively, his own erection digging into the mud underneath him.

Olan maintained his hold on Rory's neck even though he didn't need to. It gave him power, and after that chase he had to work off the adrenaline somehow. The black-and-white buttocks, mercifully mud-free, lay before him like twin targets. Leaning down, he stretched one to the side and dived in.

Scent exploded into his muzzle, fresh and youthful and virile, and it infused a certain energy into him that told his joints to take a vacation for the time it took to breed this fine young arse. As usual, Rory had prepped before coming over, and the result was just absolutely delectable. Pre-stretched and clean, the lad was nothing if not considerate.

"Fuckin'-A!" the border collie growled.

Olan pressed harder on the dog's neck. "Ewes don't speak. Do they?"

"Baa," Rory withered.

"On with it, then." Two inches of ovine tongue back and forth, in and out, took away Rory's ability even to bleat. After a minute or so the rapid clenching eased up as the resistance gave way.

Placing a knee on either side of the boy's hips, he drew his leaking tip up and down the valley while he worked up a fair amount of saliva, which he spread in and around before doing the same to his head. He tugged his hood a few times, enjoying the slick feeling, and pressed it down until it met hot resistance before sliding home.

It had felt amazing the first time, when he'd fumbled drunkenly before a series of erratic thrusts that somehow ended up in orgasm. And it felt amazing now, the prize after a fight, the prey after a hunt, the ewe that wasn't a ewe but fancied playing one. With nowhere to go but further down into the muck, Rory had little choice but to lie still under Olan's heavier frame. Which the ram had no problem with whatsoever.

Lifting off the dog's neck to brace himself, Olan rotated his hips down and forward, finding easy travel throughout the length of the border collie's heat. The walls pulsed and grabbed at his foreskin, expertly milking him with the muscle memories of past romps. The ram nudged up against the second ring and stayed there, the shelf of Rory's prostate creating a pleasant pressure along his shaft.

The dog had given up any pretense of bleating and just lay flat, whining out a single long nasal note based not in pain but in something less than pain. His claws made deep furrows in the mud, craving a grip but finding none, as if he would try to get away if he could. They were the motions of a bottom completely and thoroughly taken, the end product of sensation that had nowhere to go but out through the limbs.

"You brought this on yourself," Olan fairly snarled for effect, right down by one flaccid ear, the one with white at the tip. "Feel that on your back? That's me claim. Everyone'll know it once you walk out of here." Of course, they would shower soon after finishing up, and Rory would likely stay the night once they'd drunk enough to warrant a travel moratorium, but in the moment the future wasn't worth thinking about.

"Baa."

"All those years of slavery," the ram continued, accenting every other word with a hard thrust, "this is the least you dogs could do." All tripe, that, but all for Rory. Didn't do Olan a bit of good, but going harder on the dog's hole sure worked.

"Baa-aah!" Air sucked in through Rory's fangs, but the ram didn't bother to worry. He hadn't heard *the word* yet. He pushed back up so he could watch his length disappear between mounds of patchy fur, streamers of bodily fluids greasing up the whole affair. "Ah! Ah! Ah!"

Rory's backside was a mess of matted reddish fur from neck to tail so thick the ram couldn't tell where the black ended and the white began. Besides being easy to see, Rory had once read somewhere that the color supposedly made people hornier. Whether or not it worked, they'd never had trouble and today was no exception. Olan stared at his handiwork and snorted small clouds out of his nostrils on the cool creek bank. The world went on, oblivious to the frantic rutting in the wood.

Three silent minutes later the border collie grabbed pawfuls of mud and moaned into one elbow. Olan's cock suddenly felt as if a vice had grabbed hold of it. He knew what it was, and it surprised him.

"You lose your nut, boyo?"

Rory offered a muffled, "Uh huh."

"Fucked it right outta you, into the mud?"

"Uh huh."

"Right where you belong?"

"Uh huh!"

"Fuckin'-A, uh huh." And he slammed hard, knowing he was shoving the lad's sensitive dick into the mud, rubbing him into his own mess like he would a miscreant puppy. Falling upon the spent body, he held Rory about the chest and growled into his ear until his prodigious sac gave up its contents. Holding in the great bleating bellow in favor of powering through, he held his breath and gritted his flat teeth as the walls around his cock floated away and he held still under threat of over-stimulation.

They both felt the next thirteen shots.

Olan pulled out only when his hip threatened to cramp up. On his back, wheezing, his horns several centimetres deep in creek mud, not a part of either male was anything but a complete shambles. The ram glanced down to Rory's rump and its own creek of seed and he was satisfied.

Presently the border collie managed to roll his mud-and-cum-stained body over to weakly cradle the ram, settling an arm over his raddle-red chest. Olan gave him a couple minutes before he spoke.

"You ready to say it? Because I think I'm shagged for the day."

Rory planted a dirty kiss on the ram's cheek. "Guinness."

"Jesus, Mary and Joseph, thank God. I've got shite in places I don't think I can get to. I'll have to shear some of this off." Still, he chuckled.

"We'll see what the shower can do. *After* the hose."

"Thanks for obliging me."

"Yecch. You smell like wet dog."

"You like wetting dogs."

"That I do, lad." A yawn took hold of Olan's muzzle. "What say we clean up and have a snooze in the house?"

Rory held tighter. "Just a little longer? I want to come down nice and slow."

The ram gazed up at the canopy with its pieces of sunlit sky like stars in the night. It wasn't that cold out there after all. "Sure, boyo. I can wait."

After all, Olan Chennock was a very patient man.

TRAINING KANE

Talon Rihai and Salome Wilde

Master Alain sat at his desk, finishing a last bit of paperwork before closing his laptop. Soon he would head to the marble-tiled foyer to address his servants on the day's duties. First, though, he paused to enjoy a moment of contentment in all he owned, from the perfectly appointed mansion with its traditional Edwardian grandeur and full staff to all the amenities of a truly twenty-first century life. The small gilded clock on his magnificent mahogany desk chimed the hour, and he rose with a determined sigh. It was not his responsibilities as Master of the manor that unsettled him. It was Kane.

His newest possession, the lithe and handsome young purebred he called merely "dog" was sent to his chambers the previous evening to contemplate his misbehavior. Willful and arrogant, Kane had refused an order from a higher servant, claiming he had only to obey Alain. No doubt he had topped many a maid or stable boy in his past. No matter that he might be a true Alpha. He had chosen to serve and he must learn all of what that meant. Despite his irritation, a smile stretched across Alain's proud and distinguished muzzle as he closed his study door behind him. He had grown accustomed to easy and willing obedience. So, while it disrupted his routine, he knew he must see the challenge of breaking him in as an opportunity.

Striding into the vast, high-ceilinged hallway, his thick ebony tail thrashing behind him, Alain admired his well-groomed staff. He valued them all, from those who had belonged to him since he first claimed his Mastery to others who had arrived more recently, begging to serve the renowned canine Master. Only Kane refused him proper obeisance. He easily dismissed the flickering thought that purchasing Kane from Mistress Naomi was a mistake. The dog overestimated his value—and Alain must ensure he understood this. Naomi would likely have presented him as a gift, had Alain asked. But he knew she could use the money, so he made it a purchase. Kane, when told of his forthcoming change of venue and ownership, seemed to like it far too much. Did he know of Naomi's financial problems? Was she happy to be rid of the troublesome creature? No matter. He pushed the worrisome idea away with a flick of a black furred ear.

Concern returned, however, as Alain dispensed his orders for the day, from meals to be prepared and draperies to be cleaned to flowers to be planted and a dungeon party to be planned, and Kane was still not present by the conclusion. All stood at quiet, patient attention while Alain strove to control his tail, which longed to thrash. Alain wondered (not for the first time) whether it had a mind of its own. He strode the hall, boots clacking on the tile, scrutinizing his servants. He looked in vain for a button unfastened or a tuft of fur out of place. Though he saw none, he pointed at the white patent-leather stilettos of the pretty Siberian bitch Natalia. Usually, the shoes offered a pleasant contrast to the matte white and gray of her fur. "Did you polish your shoes this morning?" he queried.

Her eyes grew large and her pointed ears drooped. "Yes, Master," she answered, abashed.

The sound of her voice was pleasing. Its twined notes of humility and deference spoke to the Alpha in him.

"Then you did so poorly," concluded Master Alain, and pointed toward the servants' wing, where she could repair her inadequate presentation.

"Yes, Master," replied Natalia with a deep, straight-backed curtsey. High shoes clacking lightly, she hastened from the room.

At last Kane appeared, hustling himself to the end of the line. He stood tall, properly dressed if not adequately neat, head slightly bowed. His breathing was rapid as he waited for Master Alain to address him. Even more unacceptably, his slender, pointed tail was up when it should have been down. Surely Kane knew it.

"Dog," Alain said quietly, "your tail."

The appendage dropped.

"Perhaps you'd like to tell your fellow servants what so delayed you that you could not present yourself at the time specified."

Kane raised his amber eyes. "I have neither adequate explanation nor excuse, Master," he said, voice a humble, sensual thrum.

"I see." Alain could smell the cocky grin even if Kane's lips did not curl. "Kindly make your apologies to all who have been kept waiting in your absence."

"Master?" Kane looked around the room.

"You feel you are above the other servants?" If the dog wished to have his day, Alain was ready to oblige.

"No, Master." The words were a lie. No others were forthcoming.

Alain stepped closer, dominance rising in his scent and body language. "I await your proper words of apology for wasting the valuable time of my most worthy servants." He gestured to the dozen staff members, all of whom remained obediently still. For the one or two who smelled of smugness, they would be dealt with later. With canines, obedience training was not only about words and deeds. Master Alain did not settle for less than complete submission.

Kane flushed. "I regret that anyone has been kept waiting for my presence, Master."

Kane's frustration was palpable. Alain breathed it in with pleasure. "And now, what of wasting *my* time?"

"I apologize, Master."

Alain curled a lip, showing the barest hint of fang. "Pitiful words, dog. Your apology to me will not be so easy…or so painless."

"Forgive me, Master, for my failure," Kane answered.

The game was afoot. Kane wanted punishment, though it was clear by the stirring in his trousers that what he expected was what Alain would call reward. At most, he likely envisioned some trivial degradation, like being told to expose and present his scruffy neck. He must know that his disobedience was compounded by speaking once again without permission. This boy needed a serious correction, promptly.

"Dog," said Alain, striding down the hall, "you *could* be a good servant." His boots offered a punctuating thud to his words, spoken with implacable calm. "You are intelligent and strong. You have focus and determination, even a hint of discipline—when you choose to exercise it." He turned sharply on a heel and walked back. "Your poor choices and lack of true humility, however, show your inadequacy." Arriving directly opposite Kane on the final word, he gripped the young servant by the muzzle, eyes boring into his. He bared his teeth and rumbled low.

Kane trembled and fell to his knees. It was easy to see he had never been spoken to in such a fashion, no matter how sorely he needed it. Alain inhaled the heady mixture of fear, resentment, adoration, and need. "Remove your garments, dog," he commanded.

Kane knelt, frozen. His scent and posture were, at least for the moment, free of disobedience. Yet, he did not obey. It seemed incredible that he had belonged to Naomi and another Master before her, but had never been made to truly serve. "Are you challenging my order?" asked Alain.

"No, Master," Kane replied, voice firm.

Alain tipped Kane's beautiful face up once more. Did he fear seeming weak before his peers, before his Master, even? Did he truly not understand that submission gave one strength? Alain himself had learned this lesson early and well, serving others as part of his own training for dominance.

The word "Please" seemed to be forming on Kane's lips. Alain narrowed his eyes, and the unformed syllable vanished. Slowly, Kane rose and began to undress himself. He kept his head down, perhaps imagining that he was alone with Alain, something the experienced Master had not yet permitted. Perhaps that was what stuck in the dog's craw. Though calling him "inadequate" was an overstatement, in this moment Alain realized fully that "indulged" was not.

"Good boy," Alain encouraged, more to embarrass than to praise. He was taken with the purebred, no question. Indeed, Kane's Alpha pride was no small attraction. But he would not let this draw him from maintenance of perfect procedure, of effective ownership. He came around to draw his nails down Kane's exposed back and watched him shiver when he did so. "Now the rest," he demanded into a high, glossy ear.

Alain had, of course, seen his dark, sleekly furred body before purchasing Kane. Naomi, more interested in sexual control than what Alain would call true dominance, had allowed Kane to show himself off, oiled and posing like a pretty bitch in heat… with his ample erection proudly on display. Alain had demanded proper decorum, and Naomi acquiesced. Kane was ordered to drop his head, his whip-like tail, and his cock. The latter instantly flagged, evidence of some training, at least. Tall and slender, fit and smoothly short-haired, lush-mouthed and almond-eyed, the seductive canine had stood at attention while Alain circled him in silence, forcing down even the slightest hint of his own arousal. If like spoke to like, there would be no controlling him.

Now, despite his efforts to control the potential Alpha nature in Kane, all had come to this: a public display of dominance. Kane was unclothed and without pretense, finally truly bared before his Master.

Alain slowly retrieved the black leather gloves that always hung from his belt. He liked them for formal occasions, and what was this if not formal?

At the sight, Kane's cock bobbed and rose.

"Are you hard for your Master, Kane?" Alain taunted.

Kane whined softly. Alain sniffed the air pointedly to ensure the sound was genuine. It seemed this was indeed what the servant required, what he had always needed. A feeling of absolute authority washed over Alain, something he had not felt in too long.

"Yes, Master," breathed Kane.

Alain gripped the gloves, but did not put them on. Could he trust his instincts with this whelp? He called to mind his long-ago youth in Paris and the wise words of Maître Henri and Maîtresse Angelique, the silver wolf couple from whom he had learned the true source of dominance in the depths of submission. "An Alpha Master relies on his instincts," advised Maître Henri. "Trust them and grow stronger," counseled Maîtresse Angelique. The lesson served him well, and suited Kane's needs, too.

Supple glove held tightly in his fist, he raised his arm. One of the other servants suddenly coughed. He turned and narrowed his eyes at the offender, the bulky mutt Charles. An astonishing workhorse of a man, Charles never disobeyed. Was this outburst action or reaction? Was Charles jealous of the attention his Master was paying the new pedigree, or evidence only of a momentary lack of control? Regardless, his glare restored the propriety he required to begin the punishment proper.

He struck Kane across the muzzle with a quick whip of the glove. "You were tardy." Kane's wince evinced a flick of delight from Alain's tail. Next, he backhanded Kane across the nub of a small tan nipple. A sharp intake of breath was the dog's only response. "You can offer no reason for your behavior to me or your peers." Alain began to circle slowly, basking in the tangible aura of Kane's efforts to keep obediently still. "This shows me you hold your position in little regard." Without warning, he struck again, this time just above the base of Kane's tail. He heard Kane's jaw clench. "Now, you force me to question whether you belong in this household." Coming to stand before his prey once more, Alain raised both gloves and slapped at Kane's cock and balls, alternating whipping blows in quick succession. By the sixth, Kane whined softly; by the tenth, his body shook with strain; and at the thirteenth, his knees gave out and he dropped to the floor. Steadying his breath, Alain observed the fruits of his Alpha labor, of his protective and demanding dominance. As Kane panted harshly, he tucked his gloves away.

"To whom do you submit?" Alain demanded.

Kane struggled to find his voice. All that emerged was a long whimper.

"That will not do, dog," replied Alain, though the sound was sweet to his ears.

Kane straightened his back, but kept his eyes lowered. "To my Lord and Master, Alain."

"I will assure the truth in those words," answered Alain, as he moved to stand behind Kane. He admired the well-abused cock, still hard and flush with blood, jutting between Kane's thighs. With a firm hand between his shoulder blades, he firmly pushed the servant down to all-fours, kicked his knees apart, and then raised his boot to press into Kane's back, producing a perfectly raised ass, with tail properly tucked.

From the servants that watched, he could smell a rich mixture of shock and arousal, distaste and envy. He felt the prickling of his thick ruff as the hairs along it rose and his tail lifted high. He neatly withdrew his massive cock from within his leather pants. "Lubricant," he barked. The pale, curly-maned Lizzie stepped forward, ever prepared, and pressed a small tube into his hand. He could not remember how long it had been since he had told this long-held and deliciously butch poodle to always be prepared for his bodily needs, but he treasured now how seriously she had taken his commandment.

Coolly, he allowed Lizzie to prepare him, pouring ample lube over his thick, blunt-headed cock and smoothing it in. To truly teach the servant a lesson, he might have taken him dry, but after all, this was a lesson, not a call for blood. As she worked the gel over his heavy shaft, his powerful gaze met every eye in the room, and every eye lowered. "Dog," he snarled. "Who commands you?"

Kane gasped and tilted his head. In the sound and his apprehensive scent, Alain suddenly knew for certain that Kane had never been claimed. No doubt Naomi had ridden his prick and spanked him prettily. And he had likely performed like the purebred he was, fucking every servant and anyone else from whom he attained permission. Alain knew the sort of parties at which Kane could be ideally displayed and exploited. But it was clear Kane had never fully belonged to anyone.

"You command me, my Master." Kane returned his gaze to the floor.

So, it's "My *Master,*" thought Alain with possessive delight as he moved Kane's tail and parted his cheeks. Smoothly, he bent to cover Kane with his body and pressed the head of his cock to the small, tight entrance. Salivating thickly, he took the slender neck in his jaws.

Alain worked slowly, letting Kane relax around his impressive girth. He embraced the boy's conflicting desire: to submit to his Master while still giving off the vestiges of an Alpha scent. Kane desired his Master's approval, even more than maintenance of his own pride. This business of dominance and submission, of leading and being led, Alain had learned it and Kane would, too. This was the truest canine tradition, borne in the blood. As he slowly withdrew and pressed in again, there was barely a whimper from his prey.

Alain had to fight back sounds of his own as his rigid cock was nearly strangled by the tightness into which it bore. Alain knew both sides of this equation well. He remembered vividly the painful stretching at his own long-ago claiming by Maître Henri, another vital lesson in his own path to Mastery. There was a fiery surface sting and a dark, deep ache, all surrounded by the overwhelming reek of Henri's dominance.

When Alain was at last balls deep, he knew the panting young beast beneath him was no longer able to speak. And as he began to fuck him in earnest, he knew Kane was equally unable to think. He could now only react, to trust his own instincts and Alain's dominance. Alain resisted the desire to reach a strong hand down to stroke from beneath, down the lightly furred, flat-muscled chest to close around his straining cock. Kane was learning, publicly, that he owned nothing of himself anymore, wanted for nothing, and was made of nothing but surrender.

Alain chose to pause for several moments, teeth still clamped as his eyes quickly surveyed the line of servants. He enjoyed how his musk dominated all others so easily, as it should be. He growled softly into Kane's neck, evincing a tightening of the servant's muscles around him. With a slow, deep breath he drove home again, rejoicing in filling Kane with each determined lunge, while holding him still in his grasp and rich Alpha aura. Each thrust was made of dominance, care, and warning, not only to Kane but to each and every person in attendance. Kane belonged to this Master. Inside he smiled, thinking of a relationship that he had not imagined before this moment, before the welcoming aroma of Kane's true submission as he was fucked with devoted mercilessness. *Feel your insignificance before me*, thought Alain. *Yield everything and I will show you your true self.*

Kane shifted suddenly, seeming to grasp all this moment meant. His body stiffened and a low sound of panic escaped from between his clenched teeth. Alain acted, quickly and decisively, to retain control over the body he had bought, the mind that had allowed that body to be sold for service. He released his bite and drew a hand out to wrap Kane's slender throat, to stretch and hold his proud neck. "Be still," he hissed. Then, he lowered his voice to a calm, confident whisper: "Don't struggle against what you most desire. Let yourself belong to me."

"Master," whimpered Kane, centered entirely on his Master. He controlled his breathing and obeyed entirely.

Alain knew he had won his prize. Neither natural-born omega nor even beta, Kane was that most rare of beings, an Alpha drawn to service. Alain alone, it seemed, had seen the truth in the young canine, and was wise enough to bring him to his destiny.

Taking Kane now was entirely enjoyable. If the servants watched even more eagerly, Alain doubted they fully understood the significance of the moment. How could they? And why should they? He owned Kane entirely now, and knew he would climax soon because of it—and the grip of that tight, virgin ass. Alain gloried in every breath, every hard thrust. *You are mine, Kane*, he said to himself. *And I will never let you go.*

Thoughts of their future as Master and servant flooded Alain's mind. He rocked their bodies with his powerful cock, imagining orders, punishments, and even the possibility of rewards. Perhaps Kane would one day seek more, would desire a servant of his own, or more than one, for there was no denying the Alpha side of him. But now and always, Alain knew with certainty, he would belong to his one true Master.

Kane pressed back into Alain's relentless fuck, and Alain no longer wished to hold back. Kane would not be permitted to climax this day—and likely not for many weeks or even months to come—but Alain would not deny himself the gratification he had earned. As he reached the precipice, images of cock cages, straps, and depravation of privacy danced before his tight-shut eyes. He gave a satisfying howl when at last he filled his newly precious servant with his thick, ample seed.

Withdrawing with purposeful suddenness, he demanded a cursory cleaning from Terrance, a reward for the slack-jawed boot boy, and ordered Kane to his room. He knew he would have one of his betas give Kane his orders for the rest of the day—perhaps longer. By the next summons, he contemplated as Terrance got to work, Kane would ache for his Master's merest glance or a single sound from his mouth. He made a mental note to decide when he should first shift from calling him "dog" to using his name. It would likely be sooner than Maître Henri or Maîtresse Angelique would have.

Turning away, he heard but did not watch as Kane rose, grabbed his garments, and padded from the room. He still smelled absolutely delicious. "Good enough," he told Terrance, ruffling his tatty fur, waving him away before tucking his slack prick into his trousers. "Now, get to work, everyone," he said brusquely. "We're already running late, and this house won't run itself."

A Peculiar Case of Symbiosis

Friday Donnelly

Time's passage is barely relevant in The Osprey. The only ways to measure the passing seconds are the beats of the music that pulse around me and the throbbing light show just above the dance floor.

All around, fish of bright neon colors shimmer on the dance floor, fin-like hands raised above their heads. Some of them hold their beer cans above the crowd, the occasional drop of beer escaping the confines of the tin and floating through the water into the shaft of a strobe light. It's almost impossible to distinguish any one body. Around the edges of the dance floor, guys are tugged along on leashes or by halters.

The crowd of fish swirling through the club mesmerizes me for so long that I'm not sure exactly when I first spot him. He's a shark; lean, all muscle, grey skin occasionally turned purple or green by an errant strobe. Some half-empty glass on the bar beside him contains a purple liquid and a—a glass straw? I can't tell from here.

So I move closer. His black pits of eyes are roaming the crowd, searching for something or someone. Whoever he's looking for, it's not urgent. Each sweep is slow and aimless.

There's a space at the bar beside him if I squeeze.

"What's your poison?" I shout.

He turns to look at me; until I'd yelled in his ear he'd been pointedly ignoring me.

"I don't have one," he replies. "Not just one, anyways. If you're looking to buy me a drink, a martini wouldn't go awry."

I nod and signal the bar tender. "Martini," I say, tapping the space beside the shark.

"What's your name?" I ask.

"Marvin," is what I think he replies, but the music's loud.

"Marvin?"

"Martin!"

"Sorry," I reply. "I'm Anthony."

I want him. He's exactly my type: a bit of muscle, but not too much; casual clothes and a ripped t-shirt that tells me he doesn't take his appearance too seriously; and a quiet, calm demeanor.

"Let me guess," he shouts, serrated teeth showing as white dots along his lips, "You're gonna ask if I want to *wrassel*."

It takes me a moment to catch the pun on my species. I thought it was just a sudden accent. "Oh, I get it. Because I'm a wrasse. No, I'm not that lame." I'm sure he doesn't think much of me, just another twinky bluestreak cleaner wrasse in the crowded bar. Probably expects me to start showing the yellow skin under my shirt and running my blue hands up and down his forearm all while flirting and giving him black-lined smiles.

"Good," he replies. He turns to stare at me, his black eyes emotionless and predatory. I have to suppress a shiver. That feeling like I'm being sized up, as if he's deciding if I'm more useful providing him a service or as prey… it's delightful.

"How much are you willing to give?" he shouts.

I don't think I heard him correctly. "What?"

The martini slides into place beside him. He shakes his head. "Never mind."

I'm at a loss for what to say. Like usual, I'm trying to make it clear I want him to take the lead. I don't get the feeling he's uninterested in me, but he's not exactly pursuing me either. I don't quite know what to do. "Enjoying yourself?" I ask, for lack of anything better.

"More so thanks to this," he says, tipping the martini towards me and downing it with a single gulp.

"What are you looking for?" I ask.

"Characters."

"The music's too loud," I shout back. "I can't hear anything you're saying."

He leans in, dangerous mouth inches from my ear hole, and shouts: "Characters!"

"Oh," I say. "I guess I did hear you right. Characters?"

He nods. "I'm a writer."

"Journalist?"

"No, fiction. I write… well, erotica, porn, smut, whatever you want to call it."

"Writing a BDSM story?" It's the only reason I could think of for him to be looking for character inspiration in The Osprey.

"Always," he replies.

"Oh!" I say. He's hot and a porn writer, too? That sounds like the most exciting opportunity I'll have all evening.

"It's rather hard to talk in here, don't you think? Want to go someplace quieter?" I flash a smile at him. Bluestreak cleaner wrasses like me have the best smiles; the black streak running from the corners of our lips down our bodies moves with the expression, allowing our whole bodies to show the grin.

A jolt of excitement hits my stomach as he puts his arm around my shoulders. "Sure," he says. The grip is strong, only a few pounds of pressure away from being painful. "I know a little restaurant just down the block. Quiet enough to talk, loud enough to do so privately."

"Jalento's?" I ask.

He nods. "Sound good?"

"Sounds great," I reply.

Jalento's is a tiny Mexican restaurant in a nearby alley. It's no more than a two minute walk of dodging drunks. It doesn't look like much, but the food is good and cheap and it's open all night. I've been here more than a few times before with guys I met at The Osprey. After we find a dark booth the problem of him not talking returns.

Struggling for something, the best topic I can find is, "So, you said you were looking for characters. See anything inspirational?"

He fiddles with a wide leather bracelet on his wrist. "Sort of."

I wait for him to elaborate. He doesn't. "How do you mean?"

"I dunno. Writing characters isn't… it's not a eureka thing. Not normally. They grow, like coral."

"Ah," I reply.

"It's difficult." That's the first information he's volunteered, and I decide to wait for him to follow it up. He doesn't.

"How long does it take for a character to grow?"

"From conception to the start of a story? It depends. Inside the story? Sixty-thousand words, ideally. That puts it long enough to be searched up on sites as a novel, which is all people ever want. That and lots of raunchy sex."

"Are you good at the raunchy sex part?" I ask, voice on the lower side for risk of being overheard by the more normal patrons of the restaurant.

"Good enough," he replies.

The cashier calls his name. He comes back with both our orders. "Yours was ready so I grabbed it."

Eating and talking has never been my strong suit. As much as I'd like to hold a pleasant conversation over the food it's just beyond my capability. Since Martin seems content in silence, I don't force it.

He finishes his meal first. It's gone in nearly three bites. The rest of the time he spends staring at me.

It's hard to meet the gaze of a shark. Most people don't even try. The black abysses of their eyes are very Nietzschean. Staring long into them ends with the sensation of saying a word so often you forget what it means, only regarding who you are and what you're doing.

Still, I look up occasionally and smile. I want him to know his gaze is welcome.

At least, I'm pretty sure he's staring at me. With no pupils, it's a bit hard to tell exactly where he's looking. But I'm pretty sure I'm what has his attention.

I don't let his gaze distract me too much. In the silence, I try to decide what I should ask him and how direct I should be. Since he's not offering any information, I figure it's my prerogative.

"So," I say, swallowing the last bite of my burrito. "Would you like to go back to my place?"

"I'd prefer mine."

I frown. He's staring me down, and of course he'll win that contest—and I want him to. The aggression is perfect; not scary, just commanding. Like he wants me to challenge him so he can show me where I belong.

"I... I'd feel safer going to my place."

"You don't want safe. You want dangerous. You live on dangerous." He smiles, showing all of his teeth. From just a few inches away each serration is easy to see, slightly uneven like the edge of a slab of concrete. "My place is more convenient for me, but if you insist I can work out going to yours."

I take a leap of faith, letting the exhilaration take me. "Your call."

"Mine," he answers immediately.

It turns out that he doesn't live far. Several apartment complexes abut the commercial district that The Osprey resides in. It's an eight-story building of red brick and green glass, an old-fashioned building with a modern finish.

His apartment is surprising. It's clean and simple, made of wooden floors, brick, and a loft area where I presume the bed is. A couple terrariums line the walls.

"I was expecting some slings and whips, maybe chains, straight-jackets," I joke.

"They're in the closet," he replies, and I can't tell if he's joking.

One corner is a window. A desk sits in it, computer monitor glowing against the city skyline beyond.

"So, what do you like?" he asks.

"Uhm…" It's not that I don't know, it's just disappeared from my mind at the question's presence.

"Pain? Bondage? Humiliation? Subservience?"

"Yes, yes, no, yes," I respond.

"Orgasm denial?"

"Yes."

"Good," he replies. "How about I string you up while I write a bit? I need to get some words in. Every time you distract me, I teach you a lesson. Sound good?"

I think over it as he stands nearby, shifting his weight from one foot to another. "How long are we talking?" I ask.

"An hour or so, unless you want longer. If I'm satisfied… there might be some fun afterwards. Sound good?" He licks his lips. Maybe they just itch, but I have to suppress a quiver all the same.

"Yeah," I say, looking down.

"How much pain are you okay with? I've been complimented before for my slapping… but it'll leave a mark for a few days. Blood, likely."

"If slapping's your specialty," I say with a grin, "I'd hate to pass it up."

He crosses his arms and his bicep stands out nicely. Unable to resist now that I have a bit of permission, I reach out to run my fingers down it.

Just as my fingers touch his skin, his other hand shifts and grabs my wrist. "No. You don't have permission to do that yet. Apologize."

Trying to suppress a blush, I look down. "Sorry."

"You seem ready to get started." It's as much a question as a statement.

"Sure," I reply. "I'd like to look around a bit first, though."

"Suit yourself," he says. I walk over to examine the terrariums. "While you're doing that we can talk about payment."

I stand up straight, alarmed. "Payment?"

"You want sex. I don't. Payment seems fair."

"You don't think I'm... attractive? Why did you..." I stammer out.

"Sex isn't my thing."

"But you're a porn writer!" I shout.

"Money is money. Writing smut makes me a living while I work on writing what I actually want to. Domming does the same. A hundred seems fair to me; I can tell you're obsessed with me." As he speaks, a mocking smile spreads over his face. I can't help imagining those teeth near my flesh, ready to rip into me if I do something wrong... It's not fair.

I look over at the terrarium as I debate. Inside, an orange coral of some sort is growing on a bit of fertilizer. I'm already hard from just talking about what we were going to do. A hundred is steep, but not exactly the most expensive thing I've bought recently. But I don't want it to be an act, a business transaction. I want him to be acting on a carefully restrained desire to own my body and my will. I want him to want me.

"I guess I'll just head back to The Osprey, then," I say.

"Sure," he says.

I leave his apartment and turn the corner of the hallway, waiting for him to come running after me.

When he doesn't, I sigh. A porn writer. A BDSM porn writer Dom. A BDSM porn writer dom shark who looks like that. I slap the wall—gently, since its brick—but enough to vent some of my anger.

I can do a hundred.

He lets me back in when I knock. *It's a shame I'm not into humiliation*, I find myself thinking as my cheeks burn.

"A hundred?" I ask. "How do I know you're not some sort of cop?"

He looks around. "Accidentally drop the cash somewhere in my sight. It's not 'payment' in that case. Legally."

"Do you do this often?"

"As often as it comes up. I have a few fans and the occasional person like you."

I shake my head and take five twenties out of my wallet and drop them on top of one of the terrariums. This had better be worth it. It would be hard for it not to be… but still.

"Whoops," I say, motioning towards the money.

"Good. Would you prefer to be clothed or naked for this?" he asks, taking two lengths of rope and a metal weight from the closet.

"Uhm."

"Naked it is," he says. "Take 'em off."

He stares at me as I undress. I feel his gaze move down the black stripe, from my cheek down my arms, along my side, and down to the soles of my feet. "I didn't realize so much of your body would be yellow," he says.

"Yeah, we get that a lot."

"Probably because most of what's not covered by clothes is blue," he replies. He stares pointedly at my crotch when he says 'most.'

The apartment feels cold. The cool water is especially noticeable around my groin.

"Put your hands together," he says.

"Uhm, what's the safe word?"

"You tell me," he says, motioning to my hands.

"Abyss," I reply.

"Abyss it is," he says, and loops the rope around my hands.

He's experienced. The rope is tight, but not too tight. "Feel this?" he says, putting an end of rope in my hand. "If you pull it, the knot will come loose. In case something happens."

I nod.

"Now." He grabs the rope and swims up to the loft. I can't help but admire his rounded ass through his khakis. One sweep of his bladed tail and he's gone. There's a railing on the loft area, and he hoists the rope up until I'm floating about a foot off the ground. With a few tugs of the rope, it's tied down. And just like that my stomach drops out. What if there isn't actually a way to untie the rope? What if he was lying? I could be completely at his mercy. I shiver slightly at the thought.

Being the slut I am, though, I know that's just a fantasy.

"Good," he says, viewing his handiwork.

And then he's down on the main level taking off his shirt, allowing me a moment's glance at his beautiful upper body—less apparent abs than I'd like, but still fine—and then tying my feet to the metal weight. I'm trapped now. Then he sits down at his chair to write.

I can't tell what he's writing from here. The screen's too far away. He types in short bursts, occasionally flicking the backspace key dozens of times until a blank page stares at him. Even for a writer, I think, he writes fast. Within a few turns of the second hand of his clock, he's already gone through several pages.

I remember what he said about being punished. Fear holds my tongue for only a few moments. "What are you writing about?"

He jerks his head up like he's seeing me for the first time. Even with those emotionless eyes, I can see anger in his expression. "What did I tell you about keeping quiet?" he asks, standing.

"I—"

He advances on me, palm raised. His closed hand is long and pointed, the fingers sealing together nearly perfectly into a fin. It sweeps towards me like a chop, cutting easily through the water, and angles up at the last second to scrape against my skin.

Slap.

The first blow is to my cheek. It's not as strong as I'd expected, but it stings more. It takes me a few moments to realize why. He used the outside of his hand, the sandpapery part of his skin. I'm probably bleeding.

He sniffs a few times towards my cheek, his nose dangerously close to my neck…

I struggle, the metal weight scraping the floor slightly. I'm actually scared. I pull away as far as the rope allows, his mouth opens…

And his tongue caresses my cheek, cooling the burning for a second.

Then he turns and goes back to the computer.

I sigh and try to contain my panting. My erection is throbbing, and part of me wants to slip my hands free to attend to it. But I don't. The fun's only just starting and I don't want to spoil it.

I decide not to be too rude and let him get a bit of work done before speaking again. He said an hour, and I make it to fifteen minutes before I speak again. "Are you writing something like what we're doing right now?"

He stands up suddenly, his chair rolling away a few feet. A growl escapes from his snarling lips, and a significant number of his teeth are showing. With no words he simply slaps me again, this time on the other cheek. Rather than lick the blood, instead he caresses the wound gently. The rubbing only adds to the pain. After a moment, he withdraws his hand and licks the blood off.

My self-given goal is to make it to the half-hour mark before pestering him again, but my erection is flagging at the twenty-minute mark, and by twenty-five I speak again.

"Could you let me down? This is starting to hurt..." The words are true, but I'm relishing the achy pain in my shoulders and wrists.

This time he stands up slowly, stretches, cracks his neck, and turns to me. I have a full view of his gorgeous chest and arms, the muscles gently traced against his grey skin. "It's gonna start hurting a lot more," he replies.

This time, it's two blows. Each lands on my side, stinging. The strikes sweep up at the end like the rest, so I'm not worried about him causing any permanent damage by hitting me there. As I look down, I can see where the scales have fallen off and blood is speckled, dark red on faint cream. It's a scrape, just like the kind I'd get falling off my bike. He moves slowly, setting his mouth around the first wound. If he closes his mouth, a chunk of me will just be gone. I'd bleed to death in a matter of minutes. But once again, all I feel is the faint caress of his tongue. When he moves away, the red is gone... though it begins to show again even as I watch.

He does the same for the other side.

"Now," he says, "the next time you speak up... the blows will be lower. Don't say I didn't warn you."

He strides back to his chair, but stops short mid-way. He reaches down, and to my intense excitement I hear him unzip his pants. The shorts and boxers fall away. There are only a few lights on in the apartment, fewer than I'd like. While I can't see everything perfectly, I can still see cords of muscle along his back, the bones too. I can see the roundness of his ass, even somewhat covered as it is by his tail.

He looks so natural naked. Like his clothes were scraps of cloth pinned haphazardly to a Greek sculpture, cluttering it up. As he sits, he keeps his torso facing out towards the skyline, but turns his hips so his legs are out perpendicular, one crossed over the other—and I can see that he's erect, both white cocks rising in a V. Behind them, the city glitters in red and white dots. He traces one length errantly until he reaches the tip, and then resumes typing.

I want to ask if he prefers one over the other, or if he strokes both off, or if there's a difference in sensation between the two, which one he comes out of, and so many other questions. But I keep quiet… for now.

As he types, his tail sweeps slowly left and right, as if he were swimming, looking for prey.

Forty-five minutes and I'm getting blue balls—metaphorically.

"Which has more sensation, the left one or the right one?" I ask.

He stops.

The keyboard quits clattering under his fingers, his tail stops swinging, even his breathing.

He stands up. "I think I've waited long enough," he says.

As he strides over, I can see he's no longer aroused.

He walks by me, and as I try to turn to track him…

Whack.

Pain explodes from my rear. I feel something slide down my leg. At first I think it's blood, but then I realize it's his tail, sliding down from the site of its impact with my body.

"You gonna… lick that too?" I try to say with a sneer, but my breathing gets away from me halfway through and I gasp.

"No," he replies.

The next thing I feel is his paddle-like hands on my sides, gripping me from behind. "You haven't done a good enough job exciting me, so you don't get this," he says, pushing his lengths against my rear. "I will let you down so you can suck me off, though, whore."

I smile, but immediately try to hide the excitement.

The ropes come loose and I stumble a bit, falling forward onto my knees. Martin walks past me and sits down at his desk, resuming the pose from before. One after another, as he teases them, his cocks rise.

"Hurry up," he says, and returns to typing.

I crawl over, staying on all fours in hopes that it pleases him, and situate myself between his legs. I stare up at the spires of cock, then past them. Each shaft is long, a slight ridge on the outside of either one. The two holes at the tip of each are just visible from the angle I'm at. Martin's eyes are, I think, fixated on the screen as he types.

Beginning with light pecks all over them, I consider how I'm going to do this.

I get a bit of an answer when he stops typing long enough to grab my head and force me down over the right one. His own hand goes to the other.

"You can make a mess here," he growls.

I figure that's the closest I'll get to permission to cum, so I take it. One hand is necessary to prop myself up as I kneel, but I use the other on myself as I bob on his length. I work my tongue along the edges of his right cock a bit, flicking the ridge as I go. The flesh heats up from slightly cold to warm as a dark stone in the morning sun. The texture of his skin is similar to stone too, but not so rough that my mouth is in danger of bleeding.

He still hasn't let go of my head. The inside of his hand is much smoother than the outside, so the way he's rubbing the back of my skull isn't leaving abrasions. That's probably a good thing, considering it'll be hard enough to explain the scrapes on my cheeks tomorrow.

Glancing to the side, the other cock is so close to my eye that it dwarfs the skyscrapers behind it. It almost fits right in, only a bit more round and of course pale white rather than black with sparkling windows. Glancing up, I can see he's thrown his large head back some and his mouth is open, panting. I speed up the pace to try to match his hand.

His leg shifts, stiffening. His tail flicks back and forth, forcing him forward into my mouth. I don't resist.

A hot liquid gushes into my mouth as he grunts. I time my swallows to match the ejaculations as best I can. After a few moments, his hand withdraws.

I slip off and sit back, still rubbing myself.

He rolls his chair away. "I'll get a siphon," he states.

The pain flares up as I think about it, the burning sensation all over my cheeks and sides, and the jerking motion exacerbates the ache in my shoulders and arms. If that wasn't already enough to bring me over the edge, his dismissive attitude and retreating ass would have done it. I've been on edge for hours and my body doesn't let me take very long. As he's walking back in from the small kitchen area, siphon in hand, I make a mess. The release is somewhat painful. I've been aroused for too long. But it also feels amazing, an endorphin rush almost strong enough to make me forget how much I paid for this. I want to just close my eyes and drift, rise to the ceiling, basking in the warmth of it.

Something bumps into my chest. I look up and see the siphon ricocheting into the living room area. I grab it..

"Sexy," I reply.

"Sorry. I don't like messes."

"Get a lot of work done, I suppose?" I ask as I suck the semen out of the water..

"Enough."

"Sexy enough that next time I won't have to pay?" I ask hopefully.

"If you want to do this again, a hundred. Something else might be more, might be less."

"You're basically just a prostitute," I say, feeling bolder now that I've gotten what I wanted and nothing is on the line.

He shrugs. "It's business. Everyone's gotta make money somehow."

"What about enjoyment? Where does that factor in?"

"Sex sells. Real life or stories… it's all the same. People pay me money for it because I'm good. I just enjoy getting paid."

I don't understand and it's suddenly maddening how obtuse he's being. "You just use people for sex?" I shout. "That's all it is to you? A tool?"

He shrugs again. "What is it to you?"

"It's about… about joy and pleasure and feeling good!"

"So for you it's a tool to feel good. For me it's a tool to feel good. I don't understand the problem."

"Whatever," I reply. "Fuck you."

Martin shrugs a final time. "It's probably time for you to leave."

"I think so too."

"Martin is my pen name, by the way. Martin Bitely. If you ever want to look up my stuff. And you know my apartment number if you feel like coming around again. I spend most of my day writing. Evenings too. Just knock."

"Fuck you," I spit as I gather up my clothes and put them on. Luckily the bleeding has stopped enough that the blood won't stain them.

I take the swim shaft over the elevator. I need to move, and not just because I spent the past forty-five minutes strung up. Anger energizes me. He's such a prick, using people like that. It was hot when I thought it was just an attitude he affected to be more in-charge, but now I'm just angry. And I want my money back, too. Not that it wasn't worth it, I just don't want him to have it.

As I burst out of the exit at the bottom of the stairs, the cool night current hits me. My car is in a parking deck a few blocks away, and I begin walking. I feel used. It sucks.

Part of me wants to turn back, go back up and yell at him.

The other part of me is wrestling with the fact that what he said is right.

He used me. I went in there hoping to use him. It wasn't that he used me that I'm having a problem with, it's what he was using me for. It feels shitty because I wanted just me to be enough.

It's stupid. I'm creating a problem where there shouldn't be one. If we're both getting what we want... I guess I could keep doing that. Not that I'm ready to admit that yet.

The road turns into a steep incline, and for a few steps I have the city's skyline stretched before me. Lights glitter, drowning out the stars above.

As I walk, I pull out my phone and search the internet for "Martin Bitely." I guess it wouldn't hurt to pick up one of his books.

Maybe I'll enjoy it as much as I enjoyed that.

A LESSON TO BE LEARNED

Tarl "Voice" Hoch

Leah and I had another fight. Need to talk! Coming over.

Raven stared at the text.

Holly came up behind him and wrapped her arms around him. "Kai?"

The panther sighed. Frowning at the phone in his black paw, he tucked it into his pocket. "Yeah. They're at it again. What are we going to do with them?"

"They're young," his wife said, the jaguar sliding along the couch so she could look into his eyes. "We were that bad once, remember?"

Raven chuckled, raising his free paw to caress Holly's whiskers before moving his palm-pad to her cheek. "Were we ever this bad though?"

Holly's ears lowered and she grinned, flashing one shining canine. "Remember our first play party at the Anderson's?"

Her husband's ears dropped and his tail lashed behind him. "Oh, right... yeah. Any word from Leah as to what they fought about?"

"You'll just have to find out. Kai should be here soon." She grinned, her tail playfully dancing behind her.

"Tease."

"You know it!" Holly giggled and danced away from her husband, doing a small twirl in their living room. "And if you're good, you may get a reward when you get home."

Raven came to her and lifted her muzzle to his. Their kiss spoke of a familiarity only years of marriage could create.

An angry buzz broke their embrace. Raven pulled the phone from his pocket and swiped it on.

A few blocks away.

"I should go love." Raven gave her a quick lick on the nose. He turned and grabbed his jacket from a nearby chair back. "I hopefully won't be long."

"Take all the time you need sweetheart. I'll be here."

* * *

Raven let out a sigh while he carefully closed and locked the back door. Turning, he stepped off the back porch and took a moment to stare up at the sky. A clear night, he could just make out a scatting of stars above, those not drowned out by the city lights. Taking a deep breath, he pulled in the winter air. The crispness stung the panther's nose and he smiled. Raven loved the winter.

The Christmas lights he had put up a week before blinked and twinkled like multi-coloured stars around the eves of his house, and he took a moment to admire his handy work. If there was one thing he liked more than winter, it was Christmas. Family, friends, and good food. That made him happy. Especially the food.

The panther's ears flashed up when he heard a car door slam from the alley. Already he could make out Kai's distinct muttered cursing, something the young vulpine had picked up since the birth of his child. Raven was secretly hoping it would pass with time, but right now he tried to put himself in the vulpine's mindset. What could have he and the red panda fought over?

Raven reached the fence before Kai and pulled the gate open to the fox's shocked expression. As usual, the youth looked gorgeous, if a little frazzled. Kai's short, russet hair was more ruffled than its usual styled chaos, though it only made Raven want to run his fingers through it that much more. Where Raven was all defined muscles from a daily workout routine, Kai was slight and feminine. Even in a navy parka, he made things tighten beneath the panther's onyx chest fur.

"Hey, Kai." Raven moved forward, forcing the fox backwards and pulling the gate closed behind him. "Let's go for a walk and you can tell me what's up."

"I was kinda hoping to come in, maybe talk to Holly." He met Raven's gaze with eyes almost as golden as the panther's.

Raven shook his head again. "Not tonight, kiddo. Holly's busy."

Guiding the vulpine with a paw to his back, Raven started down the alleyway. He could feel the youth's lean muscles even through the down-filled fabric. Kai was one of the few men that Raven could imagine other men questioning their sexuality over. A unique mix of masculine and femininity combined to create a very tempting treat. The panther forced himself to remember why he was there. "How's Leah doing?"

At the mention of the red panda, Kai let out a puffed cloud of air. "We had a fight."

"Your text said as much."

"Right, right." The vulpine muttered something Raven couldn't hear before looking upwards to the larger male. "You and Holly ever fight?"

Raven chuckled. "We did when we first started dating. She's always been the more adventurous of us and though I was curious about the things she talked about, I wasn't as into it as she was."

"Like what?"

"Well, take men for example. Before I met Holly, I wasn't into guys. Not one bit. But over time I came to understand *how* I could like men. I may not be very far along the slider bar of homosexuality, but I now understand what makes a man attractive to me." He winked at Kai.

"What changed? I mean, you two seem so cool."

The panther blew out through his teeth while he considered the vulpine's question. "I guess I got okay with it. I mean, you do something enough times and it starts to feel normal. Stop doing it, and it starts to feel awkward again."

"Getting to have sex with different girls probably helps."

"And guys, don't forget." Raven reached out to ruffle Kai's hair. It felt like silk against his paw-pads. "It does, but it's never as good as it is with Holly, because she's my number one."

Kai kicked a piece of gravel with the toe of his boot, sending it skittering across the flattened snow of the alley. "I hope Leah and I can get there at some point. I mean, she's all gung-ho and that, but…"

They came to the end of the alley and Raven turned out onto the street. Christmas lights of all sorts combined and inflatable decorations greeted them as they started down the middle of the road. The night was pleasantly silent but for the sound the soles of their boots made on the car-smoothed snow. It was late enough that there would be little to no traffic on the streets and they would have some privacy.

"But?"

"What do you do if you're uncomfortable with something?"

Raven's ears perked up while he glanced sideways at Kai. "Well, generally I talk to Holly about it, make my opinion known, and then we see if we can compromise. It also helps to pick your battles when it comes to things you don't like."

Kai huffed out a cloud of air. The panther took the moment to admire one of the houses done up with frosted lights before nudging the vulpine. "What's she asking you to do?"

"It's silly." Kai's ears lowered, his tail curling against the back of his legs. "It's just… She says I'm not dominant enough in bed."

Raven remembered his first meeting with the red panda and nodded to himself. Leah was fairly headstrong and very well versed in getting what she wanted. The young adult was no stranger to the power a sub had over their dominant, something she wouldn't be able to enjoy if Kai wasn't stepping up to the role. When she had first called Raven 'Daddy'…

"You okay, Raven? You're shivering."

The panther blinked and shook himself. "Just a chill, that's all," he lied.

"I wanted to talk to Holly, but Leah said I should talk to you about it." It was hard for Raven not to notice the gleam of the fox's teeth when his lips curled back. "Like you were an expert or something."

Raven reached out and pulled the vulpine against him, halting their walk. Lowering his gaze, his nose almost brushed the fox's. The panther swore he could feel the rapid beating of Kai's heart, even through all the layers of winter clothing. It matched his own pulse. Quick and steady. Their whiskers brushed and their muzzles met a moment later. Kai's tongue was long, longer than Holly or Leah's, and it found and caressed Raven's. The fox made a noise high in his throat and pressed himself against Raven, the flies of their jeans brushing against each other.

It was the panther that broke the kiss first, their mingled breath plumbs thick and heavy.

"There is no room for jealously in a poly relationship, Kai." Raven's voice sounded like the rumble of a volcano. "You take that route and you will lose Leah, Holly, and myself. It will be faster than you can blink. I know they don't want that… I don't want that."

"But—"

"No," Raven shook his head. "No buts. Listen to me, Kai. You clearly want to work through this, which is why you're here talking to me. If you are feeling jealous of my time with Leah, then talk to Leah about it. Don't you think I get jealous of your time with Holly?"

"Do you?" The fox's breath was a ghost against Raven's whiskers.

The panther smiled. "Here and there. You're a young lad in his prime. You can outlast me, do it far more often than I can without rest, and there are certain things to be said for a knot."

Kai's eyes widened and Raven's smile turned into a laugh. They broke apart and Raven patted the vulpine on the shoulder. "Look, when I feel jealous I talk to Holly, and she reminds me that I am still her first, her primary. She reminds me how much she loves me and the fact we decided to spend our life together. If she ever gets jealous of Leah and me, she's never told me or she's never been."

"She's a special woman." Kai gave Raven a sidelong look.

"That she is. But so are you and Leah." Raven turned down another side street, seemingly at random. A few light snowflakes danced on a gentle breeze. Unlike the previous streets, one side was dark where it gave away to a wooded area. "Now, Leah wants you to be more dominant, eh? Has she tried to goad you into doing things?"

Kai gave a half-shrug without pulling his paws out of his jacket pockets. "She keeps telling me to bite her neck. Pull her hair. Spank her."

"Do you?"

Another shrug. "Sometimes. But it's hard to keep that in mind when you're not really thinking with your upper head, you know?"

The panther's tail flicked sharply. "And therein lies the problem. Now follow me." Turning, Raven struck out off the sidewalk, cutting a furrow through the fresh, unbroken snow towards a small clearing nestled among a crescent of trees. "You see, like anything, experience makes you better at it. You know how Leah calls me Daddy?" The fox nodded and Raven continued. "That took some getting used to. I wasn't comfortable with Daddy/Daughter roleplaying, especially when she first pulled it on me mid-coitus. But the more I did it, the better I got at it, and the more I enjoyed it. I don't even think about it now."

Kai made a sound behind the panther. "I don't think I could do that."

"If she hasn't suggested it at this point, she probably doesn't want that kind of play from you. The whole biting, spanking, and hair pulling thing is a nice place to start, but in themselves aren't really dominating her, though they are aspects to a degree. Has she suggested anything beyond that?" Raven sat on a bench facing the snow-shrouded playground, ears turned to follow Kai's approach.

The fox's jacket whispered while he shrugged. "No."

Raven highly doubted that. Leah was many things, subtle wasn't really one of them. "Collars? Ropes?"

"Yeah, both of those." Kai reached the bench and Raven scooted over. When the fox sat their knees brushed. Kai rested his elbows on his thighs and hung his head, eyes on the snow between his feet. "I just don't know what to do with them though. I mean, when we first started dating, it was all wham, blam, thank you ma'am. She'd see me naked, or I her, and we'd be on each other a moment later. Now, now I'm expected to put actual work into it…"

There was a zip and leather whispered against the jacket's material. Raven shoved his paw under Kai's nose, something dark curled in his fingers. The panther watched as the smaller male realized what it was and pulled it from Raven's paw.

"Wha?"

"It's a collar. My collar actually." Raven's ears lowered a fraction. The fox turned the worked leather over in his paws, the moonlight catching the silver studs that ran along its length. A small bell tinkled and Kai ran his thumb-pad over it. Finally the fox turned to meet the panther's gaze, ears raising and lowering in indecisive flicks.

"Am I supposed to wear it?"

"No. I am."

"You carry your collar in your jacket pocket?" The fox tilted his head.

"You never know when you'll need a collar."

Raven took the collar from the fox and with practiced paws, clasped it shut around his neck. After turning it so the small bell was centered in the front, the panther placed both of his paws in his lap. "I am yours now, I will do whatever you want me to."

"Anything?" Kai's tail wagged, thumping against the bench.

The edge of Raven's mouth curled upwards and one of his fangs peeked over his bottom lip. When he spoke, it was slow and measured. "Anything."

Kai rested his paw on the top of the Raven's thigh. The panther leaned over until his nose nearly touched the youth's ear. "Think of all the things you could make me do, all the things you could do to me. Ask me to be your footstool, and I will. Ask me to tie myself to the trees, and I will."

The younger male swallowed and turned his gaze to the panther's. Their breaths mingled. The vulpine's paw moved higher, sliding along Raven's pants.

Raven whispered, "Ask me to put on a school girl uniform and let you span—"

The youth's muzzle pressed against the panther's, a quick dart that turned into something deeper a heartbeat later. Raven opened his muzzle when Kai's tongue slid between his lips. Their whiskers brushed, sending quivers along the feline's spine. The fox tasted of cola and pineapple.

Kai pulled back, ears flagging up and down. His paw flew from where it had come to rest against a hardness in Raven's pants. "Shit! I'm sorry, so sorry. I should have waited!"

"No," Raven purred. "That was perfect. That feeling, that's what you want. Remember, I did say you could do anything you wanted. You are allowed to take it, at least until I say the safeword." He grabbed Kai's paw and placed it back where it had been. "You want this?" The panther whispered.

The youth made a high-pitched noise, his fingers gently massaging the bulge, finding the contours of a familiar shape. "It's so thick already…"

"If you want it," Raven whispered, leaning closer to the fox. "You'll have to take it."

Kai snickered and the panther rolled his eyes.

"I'm trying to be serious here…" Raven started to turn away when Kai's paw grabbed the larger man's coat and pulled him closer. Their muzzles met and the panther forced his mouth to open wide when the fox's tongue pushed its way between his teeth with a fury.

Raven's paws moved to Kai's shoulders, pulling him closer while their kiss deepened. The fox's paw moved from the panther's chest to the back of his head. Blunt claws dug into the short fur there and Raven let out a gasp into Kai's muzzle. The other paw continued to massage the large bulge, tracing its length while it filled the front of his pants.

When the kiss broke, Kai eyed the panther's pants. He licked his chops. "I want to taste you."

"No."

Kai's ears lowered and he started to pull away. Raven stopped him, claws pricking the fox's jacket. He met the panther's gaze with raised ears.

"What do you *really* want to do? Do you really want to suck my cock?" Raven's paw moved to the youth's jacket zipper and tugged it down slowly. The hiss of the fabric coming undone was loud in the winter air. Kai squirmed slightly when the zipper finished its travel and the jacket hung open. Raven reached out and traced a fingertip down the vulpine's chest to his inner thigh. It was hard not to notice that the young man was enjoying himself.

"Or do you want me to lick you?" Raven grinned.

"You've… you've never done that. Ever." Kai glanced around them, only the empty park and field meeting his gaze. "We could get caught. What if we get caught?"

Raven's ears flattened against his head, until Kai turned back to face him, head nodding up and down like the beat of a hummingbird's wings. "Yes. I… Oh God… yes! I want you to suck my cock."

"Then make me…" Raven dared the youth, lips sliding back from his fangs.

Kai's paw moved back to the panther's head, tracing against the man's cheek before grabbing the collar and pulling his head downwards. Following the movement, Raven moved off the bench and onto his knees until he was sitting between the youth's legs.

"Yes," Raven purred. His palm's pad rubbed over the vulpine's bulge, making the youth chirp above him. He could smell the fox's arousal, a lighter, almost flowery smell when compared to the sharp tang of his own.

A second zipper echoed in the night.

It took a moment of shifting for Raven to pull Kai's member from where it laid awakening. The vulpine winced as the cold air touched it, but also managed to keep one paw on the back of Raven's head, pulling his short muzzle towards the bright red length. A single, perfect pearl of pre sat reflecting moonlight just below his pointed tip.

"What do you want me to do, Master?" Raven whispered, his breath tracing along the fox's bared flesh.

"I've wanted this for so long. Shit, are you sure?"

Raven sighed, tail lashing the snow behind him. Slowly he leaned in, letting his breath out against the naked member, tracing along its length from tip to base.

The youth jumped, then half-growled, half-whimpered, "Please lick it."

"If it helps, think of a nick name to use with me."

"Lick me… lick, my little kitty."

Raven made a noise deep in his throat. His tongue crept from between his lips, the tip sliding along the underside of the fox's member from base to tip. The pressure of the claws at the back of his head increased while Kai let out a high pitched bark above him. A shiver ran through the fox, the thump of his tail against the bench quickening. Raven gazed upwards for a moment to meet Kai's gaze, lust bold on his face. "Your barbs. God damn! Holly never uses them like that!"

A second lick and Kai's other paw joined the one on the back of Raven's head, making the feline's tail dance behind him. Raven deepened his third lick, his tongue curling around the shaft. He could feel the veins thickening where they pushed against the agile muscle.

"Yes, oh God yes. Fuck." Kai's voice was deeper; deeper than Raven had ever heard it before. He was about to say as much when his head was shoved down, forced to widen his muzzle for fear of catching the fox's sensitive tip on one of his fangs.

Down and down the paws forced his muzzle while the feline closed his mouth around the hard flesh. Another shiver quaked along Kai's thighs to pass under Raven's paw, hard enough he felt it through the flesh of the fox's member. Yet still the paws kept pushing until the tip brushed the back of the panther's throat.

Raven's head shot up, a cough shattering the stillness of the night. A second cough followed and a dry heave. A tear ran down Raven's cheek.

"Oh shit, I'm sorry!" Kai reached out only to have his paw batted away.

"I'm okay." Raven let out another pair of coughs before scooping up a handful of snow and shoving it into his muzzle. Kai started to shove himself back into his pants until Raven grabbed the youth's paw and shook his head. "No, no! You were doing well. That was just too much." Another cough. "Part of dominating is knowing how much your partner can take. Despite what you may think, I haven't sucked as much cock as you."

"But I hurt you…"

"I like a little pain." Raven rolled his shoulders and moved back over Kai's shrunken length. Leaning down he traced his tongue along it, slowly coaxing life back into it. Within three licks it was standing proud. Raising his gaze to where the fox looked down at him, muzzle open in a pant, Raven grinned. "Pay attention to how your sub is acting. Don't just react with your cock. Doing so could very easily lead to you hurting your sub as you just saw. Now where were we?"

The fox's yelp seemed to echo among the trees when the panther's muzzle encircled the throbbing length. Raven rested his paws on the younger man's thighs, tracing circles with his thumbs while he lightly bobbed his head. Kai's paws returned to the top of the panther's head, fingers brushing through the short fur there. At points Raven would pause, forcing Kai to make him continue by applying pressure to the feline's scruff. The collar's bell chimed with each downward thrust.

The young man's pre tasted sweet, no doubt from some sort of fruit-based diet Leah had forced upon her mate, probably why the kiss had tasted of pineapple. Not that Raven was complaining. Out of all his experiences, only half had been pleasant enough to want to remember. Yet the fox's pre was sweet enough that Raven let it linger on his taste buds before swirling his tongue around the younger man's length.

Kai twitched under the panther's paws. "For someone that hasn't sucked a lot of—"

The fox jumped as if an electric shock had shot through him as the panther sunk the vulpine's entire length into his throat. Kai's paws moved to the bench, causing it to creak. Raven chuckled, moving one paw to cup the fox's knot, which had grown to a surprising handful. Sliding off of the member, he grinned upwards while wiping away thick threads of saliva and pre. "You liked that did you, Master?"

Kai looked down at the panther, dazed.

"See, if you wait for your partner to be ready and keep it in mind, things can get quite pleasurable for you. Well done."

A growl rose from the vulpine's chest and Raven started to jerk back only to find himself held by both of Kai's paws. Slowly the feline's muzzle was pulled back towards the fox's gleaming member, its tip crested with a large pearl of pre. Kai's voice was a snarl of need. "Is this okay? I'm not pushing too hard am I? Damn, I need more."

The fox threw back his head with a gasp when Raven's muzzle covered the moist length in answer to his question. Kai paused, his paws almost leaving the feline's head. Raven started to move his muzzle along the vulpine's shaft, and hesitantly Kai took control, forcing the older male's muzzle up and down with quickening motions. Each downward thrust pressed the cock deeper into the panther's muzzle. Raven was careful not to let the barbs on his tongue backslide each time the younger man forced his head upwards.

All Raven could smell now was the fox, the scent flooding his senses. High-pitched yips pierced the night, and from the way the fox was breathing – each breath a ragged draw and exhale – Raven could tell the man was close. Gently the panther moved his paw from the fox's knot to the heavy sac underneath. Sure enough, it was tight against his paw-pad. Gently he caressed it with his fingers, earning the feline a yip and a tightening of the claws on his head.

"Yes, kitty. Yes." Kai panted. Raven could feel the man's balls shift a moment before the first spurt splashed across the feline's tongue with a cry. Raven's paw caressed the throbbing sac while he sucked at each pulse of Kai's member. It was deliciously sweet with a hint of salty after taste and he drank it down with heavy swallows.

Slowly the gushes of hot seed faded, then stopped. Kai released Raven's head and gently pulled himself up off the softening length. A thick strand hung from Raven's muzzle and he licked it up with a delicate flick of his tongue before meeting the fox's gaze.

"For someone who doesn't suck a lot of cock," Kai took a deep breath and let it out in a plume of hot air, "you certainly do a damned good job."

Raven licked his muzzle again, the taste of the vulpine's semen strong on his taste buds. He made a mental note to include more pineapple in his diet. "I'm glad you enjoyed it." He reached out, running a palm-pad across the young male's cheek, caressing the white fur there. "But we're not done. That was only lesson one."

The fox's ears shot skywards. "Another lesson?"

"Oral's one thing. It's easy to control someone while they've got their head buried in your crotch. You've got to stop asking so many questions, stop darting between taking control and then stepping back. You're hot or cold, but never in the Goldilocks zone."

Kai nodded, the inside of his ears flushing. Raven rose. "So how are you feeling?"

"Pretty good." The fox's tail flicked behind him. Reaching out, he traced the front of Raven's collar. The panther watched the movement until a single finger wrapped around the loop in the front. Raven grunted when Kai tugged it.

"You like this, don't you?"

Raven chuckled.

"I never would have figured you for a sub," Kai said while he pulled on the collar again. "Not after all our times together."

"I'm full of surpri—" Raven's reply cut off when Kai yanked again, pulling the panthers muzzle to his own. The kiss was rougher this time, more forced. As if the vulpine was hungry to taste his own seed in the panther's muzzle.

When the kiss parted, Raven grinned at the look in Kai's gaze. The naked lust there sent a trail of excitement tingling down his spine, his tail lashing the snow behind him.

"What does it feel like for you?" Kai tugged at the collar again.

Raven groaned, his eyes sliding closed and open slowly. "It feels good… a way to let go."

"But I thought you liked being in control."

"I do." The panther chuckled. "But drink the same latte every day and eventually you crave a change."

"So I'm your venti maple macchiato?"

"Damn it, Kai." Raven flattened his ears while rolling his eyes. The fox giggled, making the panther let out a heavy sigh. "When I said you needed to slow down and think, I didn't mean this…"

"I know, I know." Kai brushed his paw along Raven's whiskers, dusting some snow from them. "But you have to know that seeing you sub is just… well it's hot."

Raven's gaze moved to where the fox's member was slowly regaining its glory, waving slightly with the fox's heartbeat. The panther motioned to it. "See, this is what I am talking about. It would have taken me twice as long to get back up. Youth." He laughed. "What isn't there to be jealous of?"

Kai's ears lowered and he turned his gaze away until Raven reached out his paw. Taking it, the fox was pulled to his feet where he quickly pulled his pants up.

"Okay, some things to take note of. One, you shouldn't have let me stand up without being told. That's my fault, but you should have caught it and punished me somehow. Two, since you're still excited, we can continue without a break."

Soft ropes were placed into Kai's paw and the panther chuckled when the vulpine's ears shot skyward. "You have bondage ropes in your jacket too?"

Raven shrugged. "You've met Holly, right?" He stuck his tongue out and Kai giggled. "Now what are you going to do with them?"

Kai's tail swayed behind him as his gaze moved from the ropes to Raven and back again. Slowly he started to circle the feline who remained facing forward, mentally reminding himself not to move despite the almost inherent curiosity driving him to follow the vulpine's movements.

The footsteps paused behind Raven, and his tail flicked when his arms were pulled behind him. Soon the panther stood with his arms firmly secured behind him and the fox before him. The fox's ears were raised and Raven nodded slightly, causing Kai's tail to wag.

Licking his muzzle, Kai tilted his head. "So now what?"

Raven's ears lowered. "If I were Leah, what would you do now?"

"I'd fuck her."

The panther's tail lashed. "Which is why we're here."

Kai lowered his gaze and Raven sighed. "I'm your slave, or pet. Tell me what you want me to do."

The fox raised his eyes, ears slightly perked. "On… on your knees."

Raven dropped, the cold ground hard. He was going to feel it in the morning. Kai started to walk around the panther again, stopping once he was behind the larger male.

"I want you to lean forward."

Shifting, Raven managed to fall onto his left shoulder, his muzzle blowing snow clear of his nose when he huffed at the impact. Despite the cold and the ache of his shoulder, Raven grinned. He felt vulnerable in the position, and thoughts of what Kai could do flashed in his mind's eye. With a look over his shoulder, his tail tracing slowly back and forth, he flashed his teeth at the vulpine. Heavy snow now fell around them, a light blanket between them and the rest of the world.

"Oh my God." Kai's voice came a moment before a flurry of steps. Paws traced the hard, taut muscles of Raven's rear. They were careful, hesitant touches. "I've always admired your ass."

Raven closed his eyes, shifting on his knees, letting the fox feel the play of the rock hard muscles under his paw-pads. A shuddering breath from Kai rewarded Raven. The paws slid along the panther's sides before finding the buttons to his fly, undoing the top one and practically tearing the rest open. The jeans and boxers slid down and the cold air bit at the glistening tip of Raven's cock where it peeked from its sheath.

Kai's first lick brought a soft moan from Raven, and he shivered as another lick followed. Then another. Each one caressing the midnight black fur from the bottom of his tight globe to the base of his swaying tail. Despite the back-combing, Raven purred deep in his throat. Yet Kai was avoiding the one thing Raven wanted to feel. But damn it felt good when the appendage finally brushed, then plunged against the feline's puckered ring. A plume of snow scattered from the feline's muzzle as he gasped, eyes closing tight. From behind he felt the play of warmth circle around his tail-hole before testing his eagerness to be entered. Again and again the tongue tested him, each time sliding slightly deeper when Raven started to relax.

"Right there, keep working it. Now grab my tail, Kai."

"I thought I was in control." Kai laughed. It was a giddy sound.

"Good."

A slap cracked across the flat of the feline's ass and he let out a snarl. Claws dug into the firm flesh, forcing Raven's head towards the snow.

"That wasn't too hard was it?" Kai rubbed the spot he had slapped. Another crack cut off his response and sent shivers racing down Raven's spine. After squeezing his eyes shut he heard a chuckle from the fox.

"That's quite fine, Kai." Another slap of Kai's paw made the feline wince, the pain starting to turn into a slow burn that had his member braving the cold.

"Do you like it?"

"I'll tell you if I don't like it." Raven wiggled his ass, earning him another smack, this time with more claw dug in after. The panther's tail danced above his tail-hole. A lick turned what had been a cooling circle of flesh into a hot center of need. Raven wiggled his hips as

Kai's tongue dug deeper past the feline's ring. One of the youth's paws caressed along the larger male's inner thigh before travelling higher, sliding along the bared skin of Raven's arousal.

"You're so thick." Kai's voice was low, his breath teasing along the soaked fur along Raven's crack. "I want you to take me so bad right now... I want to feel you inside me."

"No!" Raven snarled, the mood shattered. He glared back at the vulpine with his ears flat against his head. "God damn it, Kai!"

With a growl of his own, Kai's ears mirrored Raven's and his muzzle darted down. Teeth flashed. Raven let out a cry as the vulpine's fangs sunk into the wet fur of the larger male's rear. The feline gasped, trying to rise while Kai's paw shoved him further into the snow, his knees forcing the panther's knees apart. Kai's pants being re-opened brought Raven's ears up. The shattered pleasure from before returned and the panther lowered his rear, conscious of the fact that Kai was smaller than he was. When the impossible heat of the vulpine's length slid along his bum's fur, Raven huffed into the snow.

"Do you like this, my kitty?" Kai snarled from above Raven's body while he massaged his cock along the panther's ass-crack. The other dug into the feline's back, holding his face in the snow. "I'm going to stuff this deep inside you!"

A gob of warm spit landing on the panther's asshole stole his reply away. His eyes closed as a finger massaged it gently around his entrance, teasing it open with a blunt claw point. A bolt of pleasure raced down his spine before fading with the claw point's retreat. A sigh escaped when the slick tip of vulpine heat touched his button and started to push in slowly.

"Kai..." Raven whispered, trying to relax while the fleshy intruder pushed further and further into him. The heated sting made his eyes roll back, the vulpine's pointed tip seeking to fill him deeper and deeper. Raven considered saying something, but bit his bottom lip instead. His own cock was evidence enough at how much he enjoyed it, throbbing in the night air, the tip cold as his pre-cum stole away the raging heat that filled its length.

"Kitty like that?" Kai paused, then with a quiver in his voice continued. "Does he like having a cock in him?"

Raven let out a mew when he felt the pressure of Kai's knot touch his tender ring. The fox leaned over, tracing both his paws along the feline's fur until his stomach rested along the curve of Raven's back. Fingers hooked into the back of his collar, tugging, causing Raven to gasp. "Damn, you feel good. I've got to be careful or you'll make me cum before I can fuck your little hole."

The fox's cock pulsed inside Raven and the panther's inner muscles clenched back, making the youth squirm. "Damn," Raven whispered. His legs tensed and started to push him back before he stopped himself. Kai pulled back harder on the collar and the tightness around Raven's throat made him gasp. His cock pulsed while a drop of pre fell to the snow.

Rising and letting go of the collar, Kai's claws dug into Raven's sides. Slowly his shaft slid out of Raven's pucker, the feeling of skin sliding against skin making them both shiver. The vulpine took himself almost completely out before pushing back in, his knot bumping against the panther's hole once, twice. Raven's breath was coming fast with each brush of the vulpine's knot as it pushed against his entrance. Each one felt as if the hard globe of flesh would gain entrance before it slid away, only to return with slightly more need.

Kai paused and Raven snarled. "Why did you stop?"

"Close. This is so fucking hot!"

Raven chuckled and started to push back only to feel Kai's dull claws scrape down his back, making him arch and gasp. Kai made a tsking noise. "No, you wait my kitty."

With a violent thrust, the vulpine's shaft hammered back into Raven, the knot spreading him wider, almost gaining entrance. Raven called out, his torso raising before dropping his face back into the snow. His ass felt like it was on fire, but in a way that made him want to push it farther, to feel just how hot he could take it. "Damn it, uhnn. Your... ugh... knot."

Another thrust slammed the knot against Raven's tail-hole, the panther pushing back against the thrust with one of his own. Kai's body shivered against Raven's ass. His voice was high. "I... I can't hold back much longer."

"Then take me, Master, pound your little kitty." Raven pushed his face into the snow, forcing it to retreat when faced with the heat of his panting. Snowflakes coated his whiskers and he shook his head. Glancing over his shoulder, he met Kai's gaze. "Bite me or pull on my collar... please. I need it. I need it to let go. I need it to cum!"

A snarl cut through the air behind the panther. Kai's claws dug into Raven's hips. The vulpine's thrusts were mad with need as each one hammered against Raven's ass, the knot beating a tempo against the panther's ring. Each thrust caused the bell on Raven's collar to ring, echoed by the panther's grunts. Raven closed his eyes against the burn that ran through his body sending lances of electricity racing along his spine.

Need pulsed through him, just out of reach. His breath was ragged, but the last traces of his control held on. Raven mewed, ready to beg, ready to do anything to get Kai to bite him or pull his collar.

Raven opened his eyes for a moment, staring along the underside of his body where he could see Kai's balls and hips rock back and forth as they slammed into him. His own swollen member, pink and engorged with need bounced with each thrust. The snow below melted by thick ropes of clear pre that traced like spider webs from his tip to the ground.

The vulpine shivered again, his body's pace losing its rhythm. Raven closed his eyes and pushed back when he felt the fox's length push back into him. Warmth stretched him, filled him, and suddenly his anus touched Kai's pelvis as the knot slid all the way in.

Raven roared at the feeling of being filled completely, the cry barely muffled by the snow.

Kai came with a cry of his own.

Heat flooded Raven's lower half as Kai's seed filled him with hard, violent bursts. Each one made the panther snarl and wiggle his ass, but the knot kept him and the young vulpine locked together. Pulse after pulse of heat swirled inside Raven, trapped there by a fleshy plug, expanding him with the youth's seed.

Kai's body came to rest on Raven's back. His breath was hot against the panther's fur while he sucked in great lungful's of chilled air. "That was, wow. I mean… wow." The vulpine's arm curved around the feline's body, trailing along his stomach until it came to encircle Raven's shaft.

"Wow, someone's excited."

"You didn't bite me." Raven's voice was barely a whisper. Anger bit at its edge. "I wanted to cum with you."

"My kitty wants his release?"

"This isn't a joke, Kai."

"Did I learn my lesson?"

Raven hissed.

The paw around Raven's member let go and the weight across the panther's back vanished. This shifting of the knot in his ass made the panther mew and Kai chuckled. "I'm sorry, I just got so caught up in it."

"What?" Raven's snarled while his ears shot up. Trying to turn, his bound arms only allowed him to move so much. The knot pressed against something inside him and Raven squeezed his eyes closed until he could control his body against the roaring of need that beat against his self-control.

Fingers slid through the back of Raven's collar and yanked hard upwards, forcing the panther to arch his back. "I should have listened to you."

Raven couldn't help but laugh, the sound weak through his constricted throat. "Yes."

Kai gave a short bark and the panther jumped when the fox's paw resumed stroking his length. Kai's breath ghosted across the back of Raven's ear with a harsh whisper. "Does my kitty want to cum?"

"Please, Master. Bite me."

The youth's paw burst into a flurry of motion along Raven's shaft, making the larger man buck against the knot locked in his ass, shifting it against things deep within him. When the vulpine's teeth sank into Raven's neck ruff, it was the final straw.

Raven's roar sent snowflakes scattering when the panther released his pent up passion into the snow in long ropy strands. Kai let go of the man's collar, Raven immediately gasping for breath.

It took long minutes before either could speak. When Kai finally was able to slide himself free of the panther, a small waterfall of cum following in his member's wake. He sat back on the snow, rubbing a paw along the top of his muzzle and then through his hair. It was only when Raven gave a cough that the vulpine seemed to realize he had forgotten about the older male. Dexterous paws undid the panther's restraints and Raven rolled onto his side so he faced the fox.

"So?" he grinned while trying to massage feeling back into his wrists.

Kai laughed, looking down at his own member while it leaked out the last of his cum. His gaze shifted to Raven's own semen-shrouded length and smiled at the panther. "I think I get it, wouldn't you say? Think I can borrow the ropes?"

Raven's laugh echoed through the trees. "Yes you can. You didn't do too badly for your first session. You just need to pay more attention to giving your partner pleasure over your own. Yes, being dominant is about getting your own rocks off, but you are responsible for your partner, and they come first. That's the power of the submissive. You already know how to suck dick or eat a woman out, just think of the whole collar pulling and commanding as part of the same toolbox. When you're with Leah, keep that in mind."

"Mix in the dirty talk, commanding and collar pulling with the fur petting, love bites and scratching, right?"

"Right. We'll have to practice again, but you show some promise."

The fox cocked an eyebrow. "Practice again?" His tail gave a wag behind him. He started to undo Raven's bonds. Another laugh shook the panther's frame. When the last rope fell free, he pulled his boxers up, followed by his pants. Kai dressed quickly and started to follow the panther as he packed up his stuff and started towards the street.

"What do you mean by 'practice again'? That means I did well, right? Right?"

When the fox finally caught up to him, Raven turned and pulled the small vulpine into an embrace, his muzzle finding the youth's. After a few minutes they broke apart, breath steaming in the air in heavy pants. It was all Raven could do not to push Kai back into the snow and see what the smaller male could do.

"It means I think you have potential," he winked at Kai. "What you did there, I think it warrants exploring. I've never really ever been able to let go like that and I liked it. A lot actually. I want to see just what you can do, and I think we should practice again. If you're okay with that?"

"I would like that a lot. I like being with you." Kai whispered before his muzzle sought out Raven's.

"Just listen to what I say in regards to what turns me on. The more pleasure you give me, the more I will give to you."

"Yes sir!

Raven couldn't help but feel that perhaps Christmas had come early.

METHOD ACTING

Lafitte

Please don't let me get an erection… Julian thought as the boy's thighs pushed his wooly legs apart.

In the back of his mind, whispering traitorously, another voice longed for the erection to form. Deep down he wanted the handsome okapi to feel his shaft and desire the little sheep, but seeing the nervous shame in Amal's emerald eyes, hope was much weaker than fear.

Julian blushed, turned his head to the side and let out a slight whimper of fear. At the sound he felt Amal's grip on his own arms slacken, and those strong hands trembled. The hips between Julian's legs froze, then drew back just slightly.

"Just stop, for fuck's sake!" The director shouted, throwing a copy of the script to the floor. The aging lemur rubbed his brow theatrically before turning toward Grace, sitting just to his side. "I shouldn't have trusted you, bitch."

"Calm down, Mabatha…" Grace lilted calmly, looking up at him with the unnervingly steady gaze of a border collie, eyes eternally framed in a black mask that obscured her emotions. "Staged sex scenes are always hard in rehearsal. But if you're that worried then why don't we make the scene easier? We could use silhouettes or put a sheet over them."

Mabatha dismissed the suggestions with a wave as profound as a shriek. "Idiotic. Without the sex we don't sell tickets; no one goes to the theater for love of the art anymore. We must be…" His drawn face exaggerated his exasperated scowl into something unnervingly cartoonish.

"Risqué." Grace shook her head. "You speak French. How could that one be hard?"

"In the Ivory Coast, we do not speak French when we're not speaking French." Mabatha fumed, turning to storm out of the theater, suit-coat tossed over his shoulder. "Deal with this." The door slamming behind him echoed ghostly through the near empty theatre.

Amal was still in position, holding the sheep's arms down firmly. Julian had to wonder, did Amal remain in position out of fear of reprimand? He looked down their tight bodies, still somewhat clothed but disheveled to look like they were actually having sex in their garments. Amal's suit was barely functional, really only good for the stage, with unbuttoned shirt exposing his well-defined chest and his trousers undone to let his underwear-clad package rub at Julian; only the necessities of keeping up appearances really occurred on stage.

Julian's dress, on the other hand, was very functional. Grace had made it for him especially, dressing him up like a Victorian doll in black. His skirts were drawn all the way up to the base of his chest, exposing his midriff and slender-if-wooly legs. His gaffs, crossdressing undergarments that tucked the penis out of view, had only the thinnest string so his fur would hide them from the audience, making him appear naked under the skirt from the side. His actual panties had already been pulled up for the scene, hanging off of one ankle like a flag to excite the viewers.

Julian realized, with deep embarrassment, that in his distraction an erection had indeed formed. The gaffs were tight enough to keep his shaft from working free and tenting, but the bulging ridge would be easy to see if his acting partner looked down. Luckily, Amal was too distracted to notice.

Grace sighed and gathered Mabatha's script from the aisle floor. "He's right, though. That was awful. You seriously need to start being actors and get over whatever is going on." She watched them steadily, darkly. "Maybe you two should just fuck for real?"

Julian's embarrassment was matched only by Amal's, who finally pulled away, mortified. The other actors laughed off-stage at their reactions, Amal's ears folding back in further shame.

The okapi recovered quickly, putting on what attempted to be a winning smile for Grace. "I'd do a lot better with you up here, miss." His attempt at being suave fell flat, though even that endeared him to Julian. It may have gone better, of course, if his pants weren't still bunched around his hooves.

Grace bared her teeth in a predatory grin. "If I was up there I would be holding a whip, making you hump Julie faster. But just my luck to cast the one actor that doesn't like boys, for fuck's sake!"

Julian bit his lip, hoping no one noticed she'd called him by the "female" name they only used at home, or when she took him out in drag. Luckily no one seemed to question it; Grace's anger was a far stronger draw of attention.

At the nervous silence that followed, the canine sighed and shook her head. "I don't think we'd be allowed to show real sex anyway. Just get down from there. We won't solve your problem by having you two fumble awkwardly." She shuffled the script, looking for another scene to practice. "Xuan, Molly, get out there!" Julian couldn't look up at the otter and cocker spaniel as they passed, only watch Molly's toeless, heeled shoes click across the stage while he felt her disgusted eyes on him.

"You should have girls play girls!" Molly shouted out to Grace, though the barb was really meant for Julian. Her long, fluffy ears flipped as she gestured toward Julian with glove-clad arms. "At least the important roles."

"Oh, shut up," Grace snapped uncharacteristically. She had no need to be nice to the actors but, even so, it wasn't like her to abuse the privilege. "Girls get embarrassed in these scenes, too. Now worry about not fucking up your own role."

As Amal and Julian passed behind the curtain, the sheep whispered, "I'm sorry." Amal looked like he was about to respond but, as the other actors gathered around them, he shut his mouth.

* * *

"It really was bad, lamb chop." Grace had been mostly silent the whole drive home and for some time after. The collie had opted for lounging on the couch with a book, reading glasses perched on her long, thin muzzle. Hours thinking about the disastrous rehearsal and this was all she had come up with to say. "Both of you. I guess Amal is finding it hard because of what's between your legs, but you… what's the deal? It hasn't been that long since you've been with a man, has it?"

Julian bleated softly, confusion welling up in him. He sought words but fumbled with them, staring at the ceiling from where he lay naked on the floor beneath her paws; Grace had forbidden him from using furniture or clothes in the house until he could do better. These little, demeaning punishments were her preference for enforcing obedience. Today, he was so worthless that she used him as furniture. The pet names were much the same; on a good day he was Julie, her little girl, but on a bad day she would tease that he might be better used as food.

It had been several months since Julian and Grace met. An aspiring actor hooking up with a stage producer was a bit scandalous, though there had been no intent to exploit the relationship. Julian wasn't seeking a sex change but he had only ever felt really comfortable with a female identity, and had spent his attempted acting career struggling to attain female roles; not crossdressers, not pretty boys, but women. He certainly could pull off the appearance, and his startlingly feminine features had drawn the older woman to him, but the only favor she'd ever done for him was convincing the director, Mabatha, to let him audition. He'd earned the role himself.

If anyone was taking advantage of the relationship it was Grace, what with demanding Julian take part in her bondage and dominance games, a scene he'd never been involved with before. If he was being honest he was quite happy with the arrangement, though; without her constant bullying and demands he wouldn't have the courage to overcome a lifetime in the closet, too fearful to admit to any of his secret longings. The bondage was simply a more physical version of the same interaction to the sheep.

At his prolonged silence, Grace turned to look at Julian over the rims of her reading glasses. "You have had sex with a man before, haven't you? I sometimes forget how young you are."

Julian blushed again, "I... not really." He laid an arm over his eyes, hiding from her gaze. "I haven't had much experience with men. Or anyone. Too shy, I guess."

"A little is something, mutton." Grace pressed her footpaws down into Julian's stomach. "Are you holding back from me? I can hardly believe you got to be so delightfully girly without ever getting manhandled."

Julian snickered despite himself. "I wasn't even crossdressing when you met me. I guess I was kind of androgynous but I was too shy to even do casual women's wear. Do you forget that you were the one who pushed me into that?"

Grace scoffed. "Pushed? You, my little sheep, have loved every minute of it! You just needed to be... corralled before you could find your way. So are you admitting to being a 'virgin' as far as men are concerned? That would certainly explain why you've been so afraid to let that stud between your legs. I expected you to be thrilled!"

"It's not that I'm afraid to get close to a boy, though." Julian's heart felt like it would beat its way through his ribs. "I don't think he likes boys. I can see how nervous and ashamed he gets and it feels like I'm molesting him or something. I don't want to make him upset, so I don't want to actually get aroused. I'm trying to act like I'm only acting like I want him and that's really hard!"

Grace cocked half a grin—the half lacking mirth. "That sounds like his problem. You two are actors and at least one of you has to start fitting your role; the other will fall into place after, and I have a lot more control over you so that's where I'm focusing my efforts. But know this… I won't let you two ruin this play. Now tell me about what you've done with men."

Julian raised his arm from his eyes, giving Grace a simpering look. "But… that would be so embarrassing! Besides, how would that help?"

"This isn't a request." Grace had leaned forward, paws pressing all the harder into the sheep's stomach, and from somewhere she'd materialized a crop that she spun between her fingers.

Julian eyed the leather wand nervously; pain was one part of BDSM he'd never enjoyed, though he'd put up with anything Grace did to him. Honestly, though, he wanted her to embarrass him. He only complained to draw that sadistic side out of her, baiting her into bullying him. He wasn't sure if she realized that or not.

"Alright. I was at a party a couple years ago. Still in high school. The party wasn't in my home town, though. A friend dragged me off to it, thought I needed to be more social. I pretty much just sat on a couch with an empty beer cup all night." Julian kept an annoyed tone in his voice but inwardly he smiled, thinking back to it. "Then someone came up behind me, started rubbing my shoulders. I looked up and there was this pretty panda boy there, kind of punk and kind of fem… and he just leaned down and kissed me."

Julian felt himself growing hard remembering it. "I followed him up to an empty bedroom. We locked the door and I went down on him. He didn't reciprocate, and then I never saw him again. If it hadn't been a party where no one knew me but my one friend I would have been too afraid of word getting out."

"That's it?" Grace's words pulled Julian sharply back to reality. He shifted his legs as if he could still hide the towering erection he was pointing at the ceiling and realized he'd already leaked quite a bit over his belly. He desperately wished Grace would do something about it, but lately she'd be more likely to punish him. "Surely there's been something since? I know plenty of men who would have taken you for a ride, lamb chop."

Julian shook his head and shrugged, "Shy. I was too afraid in high school. Then I went to college and didn't know anyone. A few months later you met me. I didn't really get the chance, though I probably would have still been too shy anyway."

Grace lifted a footpaw, stretching her leg out and using it to ruffle Julian's long, curly hair. Sometimes he didn't deserve the attention of her hands. "You poor little thing. Maybe I should tie you down and let a man have his way with you?"

Julian bleated in shock, pulling away from her footpaw. "But… but I'm yours, mistress!"

Grace giggled a little. "Oh dear… I'm afraid I've never prized monogamy too highly. Is that a surprise to you?"

"Well," Julian had to admit, "not really. But I thought you would want to keep me to yourself, even if you weren't just for me."

Grace considered that a moment before answering, "To an extent. You're mine, most certainly, and I won't give you up. But I can give permission. I think I might even rather like to watch a man ravage you." Grace shook her head at the look of something hurt and fearful in Julian's eyes. "But no, some anonymous and forced encounter for your first time would be terrible. Don't worry, Julian, I wouldn't do that to you."

In the quiet moment that followed Grace took notice of the sheep's erection and cracked it with her riding crop. Julian yelped in shock, hands shooting down, too late to guard the organ. As his shaft throbbed in pain it slowly deflated. "You are not to get off. At all. If I even suspect you are, I'll put your cock in a cage. No rewards until you manage your scene, lamb chop."

Julian whimpered on the floor, staring up at Grace with a mixture of hurt and fear that she might not be done. Pain meant this wasn't a game. She was very serious now.

Grace slipped off of the couch, padding across the room while his eyes followed her. She paid him no mind, but he knew from experience his every twitch was seen anyway. He dare not move without permission.

She bent before a cupboard, innocuous looking to company but it required a key to open. While the drawer's lock clicked her pants fell to the floor, revealing sheer black panties beneath. She pulled a harness from the drawer and buckled it around her waist, stepping out of the crumpled slacks left behind on the floor. Grace turned to him with one of her largest dildos belted to her crotch. It bobbed, black and stiff, while she grinned at him.

"Get in position, actress. We're going to rehearse this scene." Then she set a cock-cage down on the mantle. "And afterward, you'll wear this until you've pulled off your scene."

* * *

"Can't we just give him boner pills or something?" Mabatha was rubbing his temples in frustration. Somehow he always felt throwing tantrums was the best way to manage his stress.

"No, Mabatha…" Grace mimicked the gesture, "you can't just go into a drug store and buy those things."

"Bullshit! I've heard all about it!" Mabatha seemed to just be yelling whatever came to his mind now, striped tail flipping about with exaggerated emotions. "You Americans just take one every time you go on a date! I've seen it in my e-mails!"

"If we give an actor a controlled substance for our play we will go to jail." Grace was reorganizing her script notes just for something to do. "You have to handle your actors in the old fashioned way: by directing them. You know, like a fucking theater!" Mabatha's anger was usual, but Grace's open hostility had shocked the actors into silence.

"You find a way to get them to act, you tell me about it." Mabatha began walking away again.

"You're the director!" Grace called uselessly after him, "That's your job. You can't keep walking out on your own play."

Grace turned back to the stage, Julian's stocking-clad legs wrapped around Amal's hips tightly while he lounged back over a couch. Even if Amal didn't want him, for the sake of the play Julian had tried to convince himself otherwise. At least the cock-cage took away the fear of sprouting an erection, though the way it rubbed through his fur was terribly uncomfortable. Especially in the gaff undergarments those metal ribs were uncomfortable.

"Everyone get out of here." Grace waved her hand to the small gaggle of actors and actresses, "Everyone but Julian and Amal, of course." They began filing out of the hall, Molly casting superior glances back the whole way.

It had become their habit to keep the sex scene for last in rehearsal, not only because it was giving them so much trouble but because it put everyone in such a bad mood. Typically the other scenes went fine, even when Julian had them with Molly, but today everything was a mess. The perpetual bad moods of the director and stage manager had worn everyone down, and if anything their moods were even worse today. Mabatha seemed to be close to making a drastic decision.

Molly turned off the stage at the last minute to head over to Grace for a whispered conversation; whatever it was had the collie laughing, and Molly stormed off grumpily. After everyone was finally gone, the spaniel being the last, Grace clambered up to the stage.

"She was trying to proposition me for your job. Said she could share the role with you, take the sex scenes." She shook her head, tail wagging in sadistic mirth. "Some actresses, huh?"

Julian offered a weak smile, knowing soon the complaints would be directed his way. "Seeing me, maybe she just figures you like girls."

Grace gave him an appraising look. "Looking to get the same deal, huh? Too bad for her our relationship isn't as exploitative as the gossip no doubt would have her believe."

Amal cleared his throat as he got up from Julian, the sheep missing the warmth of his body. On the upside there didn't seem to be anymore shame, like Amal had forgotten what he and the sheep had been miming for the scene. "It's not as if she's the only one up here that's interested in you, ma'am."

Julian offered only a shrug for his opinion, beginning to rise as well. Grace lifted her leg and planted a heeled boot on his chest, pressing him back across the couch. "We have things to discuss still, lamb chop. You wanted a chance at the stage and now I damn well expect you to work for it. This isn't a free ride."

Julian's ears folded back nervously. He wanted to tell her he didn't expect a free ride but he knew that would only irritate her. He didn't want to make things worse. Usually he would secretly delight in this treatment but the consequences of her anger were growing all too real. This was no longer a game of domination. He could lose her respect.

Her boot dragged down his chest and stomach, the dress pulled up to expose his midriff, and slid over the frilly panties concealing his member. There was no danger of an errant erection this time, caged as he was, but it didn't stop his eager little cock from trying… and it was terribly uncomfortable having it so driven and thwarted at the same time.

Julian bleated, squirming on the couch while the pointed toe of her boot pressed firmly down on his constrained manhood. "You did a little better, I guess, but it seems like you lost your nerve after a bit. Can't you just close your eyes and imagine it's me with a strap-on? I'm sure you'd show plenty of excitement for that, my little ewe. You only need to pretend for the scene, and then it's all over." She drew her foot back slightly and slipped the toe under Julian's gaffs, pressing into the crotch just above his shaft. "Or is there more to it? You don't imagine me because, deep down, you do want him… right? So you care how he'll feel after the play is over, too?"

Julian trembled, tried to hold back, but denying her the truth was impossible. He couldn't hold anything back from her when she asked directly. She'd never demanded it of him, yet it was a rule of submission important to him; too much of his life outside of her was about deceit and cover stories. He nodded his head.

Amal looked away, blushing at the confession. He brushed his hand through his tousled mane and over his knobby horns in an obviously nervous gesture. "I'd much rather pleasure you, Grace."

She drew back her boot with a smile. "If you want to please me, you'll let me put a collar around your neck and follow my orders. And my orders have been pretty consistent; get on top of Julie and act like you want him! Even if you'd rather… 'pleasure me.'"

Amal glanced around nervously and swallowed, "I, uh… I can't say I'm not interested, miss Grace. I just… I'm not sure. About that sort of thing." After a moment he blushed and added, "Bondage, that is."

Grace nodded, walking over to him and patting his head like a child's. "Think about it, Amal. I'm not kidding about the collar. You're a nice boy. A bit clumsy with your flirting but I could train you into a real sweet thing. But if anything were to happen, it would have to happen with Julie here, too. Not just because of the play but because of our relationship."

The okapi looked down at Julian, and though the familiar shame was still in those green eyes there was nothing of the disgust the sheep had expected. Amal smiled at the sheep and gave a nervous laugh. "It's not that I'm not interested in that sort of thing, either. It's just… I've never done it before. I look up chicks with dicks online sometimes, but it's never gone further than a fantasy. I don't know if I'd like it for real."

The laughter Grace let loose made Amal jump. "Are you serious? Both of you little idiots are having the same issue? At least Julie here knows he wants it, but you won't even try a fantasy with it laid out in front of you on a silver platter?"

Amal's ears drooped and he grumbled, "Getting pushed into it with hundreds of eyes on me is a little high pressure for exploration. I could just act through it if I didn't care. But if I do too well, will you get jealous? Or if Julian can tell I'm getting into it, will things get weird? And if it all works out, but then I can't actually get into it, you know… physically, it'll be all the worse!"

Grace lifted the toe of her shoe, still under the rim of Julian's undergarments, and gave a hard yank. The thin strings on the sides, meant only to hide under his wool, snapped and left his hips stinging. The metal of the cock-cage glinted in the heavy stage lights, the small brass lock hanging from the tip like an exotic piercing.

"This is what you're so afraid of?" Grace finally returned her foot to the ground and gestured to Julian's crotch, the sheep blushing deeply but remaining obediently still. If not for the cage all of this embarrassment would have given him one hell of a hard-on.

Amal coughed nervously, averting his eyes. "I, uh… don't know what you're trying to do here. Or what that is all about."

"This is your fear, laid out bare." Grace moved her hand to gesture to the whole sheep. "You've been with women before, from the way you talk. And you don't mind the sight of a dick, at least on a feminine enough form. So why fear it being there? You're not even being asked to spread your ass for little Julian here, are you? So come here and face your fear."

Amal glanced over, nervously, and gave a hard swallow. He took a step forward and looked directly at Julian's body, down his bare chest and to his hooves. The sheep had spent enough time looking in the mirror to know what sort of figure he made; white wool carefully clipped in a classic style, long on the forearms and shins but short most everywhere else. Long, curly locks of golden hair and big, blue eyes. His makeup was overdone for the stage and looked a bit whore-ish, but there was nothing to be done for that.

He smiled up at Amal, trying to be enticing. He arched his back, the tight and soft curve of his trim stomach giving way to broad hips; he'd often been jokingly told he had "child-bearing" hips. If not for the cage nestled between his thighs, he'd look like a shapely, flat-chested girl.

"Touch it." Grace patted the okapi on the shoulder reassuringly. "It's okay. I won't be jealous. I'll be pleased to see it. Find out that there's nothing to fear."

Amal swallowed again, then shook his head. "I'm sorry, this is all happening a little fast. I need to think about this."

Grace sighed and shook her head. "Then go. Think about what you really want to happen here."

Amal nodded smartly and headed out the door. Grace turned back to Julian, arms folded and fingers tapping her forearm. "But what to do with you... there must be some way to get you over this. He might be more adventurous if you didn't lay there like a frightened victim." She turned away, pacing the stage. "But I can't think of a solution right now. Head on out. I need to finish some things here." For the entire time it took Julian to gather his things and leave, she never turned around. The weight of that denial dragged on him. He was beginning to fear these professional problems were going to hurt their relationship.

Slipping out as quietly as he could, Julian shut the heavy back door gently. Even a loud noise could break Grace's calm these days. He was going to have to wait outside until she was done since she'd driven him to the theater. Yet another little punishment.

Just as the door closed Amal's hand clamped around Julian's arm and spun him around. Before he could make so much as a noise of surprise Amal's lips were pressed against his, drawing the sheep into a long kiss. The okapi's thick lips pushed Julian's thin, glossed ones open and his broad tongue dove in, exploring the girly sheep's muzzle. By the time Amal drew back, Julian's heart was hammering so hard his chest hurt.

Amal looked deep into Julian's eyes, confusion and excitement dancing in the jade globes. "I'm sorry, Julian. I don't know how to handle these feelings. You're so beautiful but… I don't think I'm gay. I want you, I really do, but I keep thinking about what's down there and I get scared of what it means about me."

Julian just nodded slowly, trying to understand. The mix of desires and uncertainties in Amal's breathy words were familiar to Julian, though the experience was entirely different. He had, after all, spent years trying to reconcile his own desire to be feminine with wanting to keep his penis. He knew how confusing it could be to balance between categories. One day this okapi thought he had a handle on his own sexuality, even if he needed some odd excuses to justify his online browsing habits, but then Julian came along and threw a monkey wrench into the whole thing.

The okapi's broad hands were running all over Julian's shoulders and arms, over his cheeks, fingers brushing his lips. Julian playfully licked the hoof-tipped fingers. "I understand how you feel, really. Just stop worrying about the labels. What you want is just what you want. Just be honest with yourself about it and don't worry about what it might make you." Julian kissed the back of Amal's hand. "It can't make you anything."

Brow furrowing in confusion, it was clear Amal wasn't really convinced. The idea never made sense until you had it for yourself. Amal was trying, though. His arms encircled Julian in a tight hug, burying the sheep's head in his chest. "For now, can I just pretend you're a girl?"

Julian took a quick look around; the area behind the theater was lightly wooded with no other businesses nearby. They had used the back door, of course, where no one had any business outside. They weren't really exposed at all.

Slipping out from Amal's arms, Julian gave him a warm smile, then knelt down, hands fumbling at the boy's pants. He tried to push Julian away, assuring him there was no need, but the sheep was insistent. In a moment the okapi's cock and heavy balls flopped out through the open zipper of his pants. The sheep pressed his nose against the loose sack, taking in a deep breath of Amal's scent, the heavy shaft laid lazily atop his muzzle. He'd dreamed many nights about this, wondering how it would smell and what it would look like.

He kissed the tip of Amal's shaft, slipping his tongue into the domed flesh of his foreskin before using his lips to push the loose skin back. It was Julian's first experience with an uncircumcised man, though only his second with a man at all, and the musky flavor within surprised him. Amal moaned needfully above him, hands clasping the back of Julian's head, all pretense of resistance gone.

Stroking Amal's balls in one hand, he engulfed the growing shaft in his muzzle. When he could fit no more he kept going anyway, the boy's sizable shaft sinking down Julian's throat, tight and hot around his swelling member. Try as he might, Julian couldn't hold back his gag reflex any longer and released the cock, gasping as it popped from his throat, but in a moment he was again suckling on the throbbing organ.

They couldn't really keep track of time in the dim lights of the building's exterior, with the sun already long set. Julian only knew it'd been long enough for his jaw to begin to ache, so he slowed down. Whenever the soreness subsided he'd bring up the speed again, bobbing his muzzle fast and sucking in hard as long as he could manage, massaging Amal's heavy sack the whole time. There was no way he would give up on this opportunity.

Amal moaned in the deep reverberating way that meant the end of their encounter was approaching. Julian could feel the pulsing in the okapi's cock as the orgasm built and pulled his head back suddenly. He shut his eyes tight and let the boy's semen spray over his face, ropes of thick fluid stretching across his skin and soaking into his wool. He opened his mouth wide, catching all of the okapi's flavor that he could manage on his tongue. The orgasm seemed to last forever, the poor boy obviously as pent up as Julian had been. When it ebbed, Julian closed his lips around the shaft again, milking the last bits of seed from it. He kept it up even after the okapi had gone soft, savoring the all-too-rare experience.

When Julian finally drew his muzzle from the spent organ, Amal took his wooly cheeks in his palms, kneeling down to kiss Julian longingly. After drawing back he whispered, "But now you're all a mess."

Julian smiled despite his blushing, "I thought you'd enjoy seeing it, though."

Still holding Julian's cheeks in his strong palms, the okapi began to lick his own seed from the sheep's face. When he'd finished cleaning Julian up as much as possible, Amal pressed his lips back to Julian's, the sharp tang of semen washing over their entwined tongues.

"I didn't expect that," Julian admitted, still breathing heavily.

Amal shrugged. "Some straight guys swallow their own cum." He stroked Julian's shoulders. "But then, maybe I'm not as straight as I thought."

Julian shrugged. "Straight and gay are just words. Not all of us fit into them."

Amal looked down at Julian a while and smiled. "Like how I wanted to call you a girl? Or how you're obviously into men and women even though you seem so… super gay?"

The sheep had to hide his face for a moment to stifle his laughter, "You know, Grace calls me a girl sometimes, too. It's totally fine. I'm not sure I really believe in gender, like, as an internal thing. I definitely don't think what's between my legs should determine how I act and dress."

Amal let one hand stroke over Julian's ass. "I can't really complain. If you'd been a girl I don't know if I would have gotten so… obsessed with you."

"So… what do you think about Grace's offer?" Julian laid his face into Amal's chest, sighing at the warmth he felt in there.

"I think I'll take it." Amal stroked his fingers through Julian's curly hair. "If you don't mind."

"Good." Grace spoke from behind the door. "Because your first order is no more sex before the show. I need you two to still want each other on stage!" She pushed the theater door open with her car keys spinning around a fingertip. Before Amal could ashamedly cover himself up she gave his soft cock, still hanging out of his fly, an appraising look. "I hope you didn't have any plans tonight. There's going to be some… extra rehearsal."

* * *

"Anything else for you?" The waiter, a trim red panda in a tight-fitting uniform, gave Julian a slight grin before adding, "Miss."

The sheep blushed deeply and shook his head. He heard giggling but didn't look up to see whom it had been. Nearly the whole play's cast had shown up for their dinner, celebrating the final night of rehearsal before opening night. Four tables linked end-to-end made it hard to distinguish any voices that weren't very close.

Grace handed her credit card over to the panda without even looking up. "We're done ordering, thank you. We'll just be hanging out for a bit."

86

Julian watched the panda depart with a shy smile. He'd definitely been teased, but had it been flirty teasing or mocking teasing? It was often hard to tell. It hadn't sounded spiteful, at least, and that alone was usually good enough for the sheep.

After the play he'd slipped into the changing rooms to get back into his regular clothing, a first for the rehearsals. Grace enjoyed making him go out in public dressed up in ridiculously fancy outfits, and the play had been a perfect opportunity, but most of the time his regalia was much less exaggerated. With the dinner after the rehearsal Grace had allowed him a respite from stage clothing, however; far too much danger of a stain the night before curtains opened.

Tonight he'd donned a tight halter-top that molded his flat chest, with a hoodie and capris to complete the outfit. This was the first time any of the cast had seen him in street clothes and he'd caught several bits of gossip about it, not to mention a few overlong stares. Surprisingly, many of those stares had come from Molly, as well as a surprising lack of gossip.

"So, are we celebrating our last rehearsal, or our first flawless rehearsal?" Molly snickered and a few of her friends offered laughs as well. Julian tried to convince himself the comment wasn't meant specifically for him. It was hard to remember, sometimes, that he hadn't been the only actor having trouble. Molly herself had a surprisingly difficult time projecting her voice.

"Sort of an 'about time' dinner, then?" Xuan added in, his cheerfulness banishing any spite in the girl's joke. "I hope we can all be proud of this play, right? Even you, Molly?"

The cocker spaniel glared at the otter, "And why, pray tell, wouldn't I be proud of our little play?"

Grace's glass clinked to the table, hard as a gavel. "We'll stop this joke before it gets too bad-natured. Don't pretend you haven't been angry through the whole rehearsal, Molly. We all know how you feel about the casting."

Someone at the far end of the table coughed, and the word "jealous" could be clearly heard amidst it. Molly's head swung around, searching for the speaker with a growl.

"I'm not fucking jealous of him!" The canine fumed, paws slamming into the tabletop. "Women don't get a whole lot of quality roles on stage. I resent seeing one of them go to a damned boy, let alone her boy-toy!"

Grace cocked her head at the response. "Really? That's your whole complaint? Well shit, I can't control the casting and I certainly can't make that old bastard Mabatha do what I want. If I'd had my way the whole play would have been crossdressed, every single role! But I think it'd have less impact than this does."

Molly stared at Grace, waiting for the collie to elaborate. Instead the older woman just took a sip of water and stared back. Chewing her lip, Molly finally asked, "What impact?"

Grace accepted the check and pen from the waiter with a nod before she responded. "Simple. It's hard to get folks to go see plays these days. It's a money losing venture. But if you do something that gets people talking, well, then maybe you don't lose money. So we have a staged sex scene between two boys, one crossdressing. The word-of-mouth this generates could be very good for us."

Molly glared between Grace and Julian, chewing on her words.

Amal laughed, patting Julian on the shoulder. "A dangerous plan, miss. I'm glad it worked out, for my sake if nothing else."

The sheep gave Amal a wry smile and leaned in close to whisper, "Hasn't worked out for you quite yet. Wait till tonight."

Amal snickered, then Julian realized everyone at the table was staring at him curiously. He gave them all a big smile. "If I'd wanted to share with you all then I wouldn't have whispered."

"Why do you always call her 'miss' and stuff, man?" Xuan leaned over the table to poke Amal's arm. "No one else does."

Amal swatted the poking finger away and said, "Because my mother raised me to have respect. I think you all have the problem here."

"I refer to her respectfully, too." Julian leaned against Grace's arm and smiled at a cat-call from the far end of the table.

"So, you crossdress even outside of the play." Molly poked around at the remnants of her meal with her fork, an oddly fidgety gesture for the brash girl. "I had you figured for a fetishist or something."

Julian glanced at Grace for a moment and decided to leave out her part in his clothing habits. "No, I crossdress all the time now if I can. I'm not a transsexual, but I still only feel comfortable like this."

"Why?" Molly's fork had stopped and her gaze was locked on Julian. He had the unnerving feeling her opinion of him was teetering on his next words. "Why would you appropriate women's identity when you don't want to be one?"

He sighed and took a drink of water to calm his nerves. Explanations were always surprisingly hard. "I don't think in terms of gender, I guess. I like feminine things, and I like to be treated like a feminine person, but my physical body doesn't really have anything to do with that. The idea that some clothes are for boys or girls, or that some behaviors are, well… doesn't that seem sexist to you?"

Molly gave him a long look, even after others began speaking again.

"At least you're dressed like a real person now." Xuan gave a stifled yawn before continuing. "All those frilly dresses were a little too drag-queen for my tastes. I mean, not that you are my taste. I prefer my men to at least look like men. Like Amal there."

Julian barely bit back his laughter, disguising it as a cough. "What a tragedy, huh? But honestly, I prefer my men to be a bit manlier than you, too."

Xuan scoffed in mock offense, gesturing to his body broadly. "What could be manlier than this sexy pile of otter parts? I think you meant that you prefer men more 'straight-acting.'"

He hooked his ankle around Amal's under the table, hooves clinking, and they both smiled. "Straight-acting, huh? Maybe."

The actors were starting to filter out, heading home for the night. They would all need to be well-rested for opening night tomorrow, and many of them had day jobs to work first. The life of an actor was never easy, at least not on the stage.

As the group grew tighter and tighter Molly finally stood, eyes leaving Julian for the first time since he'd responded to her, though only to gather her belongings. "I understand what you're saying, Julian, but you have to understand that you're making these choices within a social context. The way you dress sends certain messages."

Grace laughed openly at her. The collie was the only person Julian had met that Molly couldn't intimidate. Even Mabatha would leave rather than argue with the fiery canine. With a shake of the head, Grace responded, "Little girl, these clothes put him at greater risk than they do you. Now get home and get some sleep. And for goodness sake, worry more about what messages you're sending people instead."

Molly blinked in shock and almost responded, but the collie's steady gaze seemed to unnerve her. With a nod, the spaniel left for home.

Only Xuan remained, slapping his cheeks to keep awake. "I think I'd better get out of here, too. Thank goodness I don't have to work before the play tomorrow! See you all there and thanks for dinner."

Finally alone, Grace turned to Julian and her new pet. "Time to bring you into the fold then, Amal. I must figure out some good nicknames for you, though. If you have any more questions about the rules of our relationship you can ask in the car."

"Why didn't Mabatha join us?" Amal offered his hand to Julian like a gentleman; he seemed to delight in playing their role out.

Grace laughed again, slipping a stack of bills onto the table for a tip. "That's your first question? I didn't invite Mabatha, that's why. And for your next question, I didn't invite him because I'm not a masochist. You two can put up with his shit on your own time if you want it that badly."

* * *

Amal knelt on the floor, naked and bashful. The room was dimly lit, the occasional stripes of headlights through window blinds playing over his white stripes and chocolate pelt. He kept his head down and eyes low, though Julian could see his eyes track Grace's bare paws.

Amal had said that he'd never been involved in this kind of relationship before. Julian hadn't really, either, but it came somewhat naturally to him in a way that it didn't for Amal. Or so the sheep presumed; it might be a mistake to assume dominance would come naturally to Amal merely because he was more masculine. He remembered how different real bondage had been from the assumptions he'd always had, though, and could only imagine the okapi expected the same things.

Grace clipped a blue-and-black collar around Amal's neck, barely managing to get it around the broad trunk on the loosest setting. Even with his wiry build, a thick neck was just part of Amal's species. After tightening the strap behind his neck Grace affixed the buckle with a lock. Amal coughed a little and turned his head side to side; it was obviously tighter than he'd expected but he was wise enough not to complain.

"Until you've properly learned your place you'll not be able to take the collar off. I don't know if you fully appreciate just how big of a deal collaring is for our community, but it won't be coming off until you do. If you must go somewhere that you can't wear it then I will take it off for you." She twirled a key around her finger. "I'll only stop locking it when I no longer need to."

Amal nodded and leaned forward, pressing his muzzle into her crotch deferentially, trying to stimulate her through her pants. She reached down, the motion so swift she must have anticipated what the okapi would do. Julian was surprised at her reflexes and realized he hadn't been much of a challenge to break. She took hold of Amal's mane and tugged his head back, eliciting a yelp of surprise, followed by a foot on his chest shoving him to his back. Amal tumbled over, squirming in surprise and alarm. She planted her foot on his chest and he attempted to lick her toes submissively.

"No." The sharpness of her voice froze the okapi. "You don't understand how this works. You've seen some porn or something, with men on their knees working to please cruel women? But those films were made for the viewer, and the viewer wishes to be in control still. You will have no control here."

"I… I don't understand." Amal looked over to Julian for some sort of help. "I'm just trying to please you. I mean, please my mistress?"

"You are my pet, not I yours." Grace lifted her foot from him and began circling his prone form like she was corralling a sheep, cutting off his escape. "I'm not a cruel Domme but I do expect obedience. If I want you to do something for me I will tell you, or just make you do it. It will be on my terms. Never attempt to please me of your own accord."

Amal seemed unsure what he had done wrong. Like many he had a skewed idea of what it meant to serve and obey. His lips trembled. "Then what do you want of me?" He barely whispered the words.

"What do I want?" Grace circled the boy once more, eyes steady on him, before settling into her recliner. Julian knelt patiently on the floor to its side, still wearing his dress from the play rehearsal. Her fingers twisted through his hair, stroking idly. "I think normally I'd teach you obedience. Make you wait. Deny you the privilege of orgasming and make you sleep in a cage until you deserved to cum."

Amal swallowed hard and looked around nervously, like he was seeking a route of escape. Julian feared he was changing his mind; Amal had come for sexual thrills, after all, not the exact opposite.

"But…" Grace cut off his line of thought, "there's something better available now. In the play, without telling anyone else, you two will really have sex."

Julian's eyes met Amal's and they were both shocked, uncertain... and excited. "But, that's not now. What do you want of me now?"

Her lips twisted into a toothy, wicked grin. "Preparation. You're still nervous about that girly little dick hiding between this little ewe's thighs. I'm going to get you over that."

Amal's ears fell. "I'm not against that, but... I wanted to serve you, Grace. To pleasure you."

"That's a harder prize to earn." She crossed her legs, leaning back into the cushioned seat. "For now you'll prove you're worth giving prizes to. Now return Julian's favor from earlier. And dear... convince me you want it or you'll be wearing a butt plug up on stage."

Amal looked terrified up at the stage manager, only finally learning how readily she would use the control he'd handed over to her. Both the punishments and rewards would be meted out without hesitation. Finally, he nodded. Seeing the resignation that followed, Julian got up onto his hands and knees.

The sheep bit his lip in excitement as Grace lifted his skirt and tugged his panties down to expose the cock-cage. The older canine took hold of the metal frame that had imprisoned his shaft for what felt like years, though he was pretty sure it was only a couple of days. Even as the metal fell away he was growing hard, and Grace gave his cock a quick brush of her fingers. "Remember, this isn't something you earned, lamb chop. You'll have to pay for it later." Ears drooping, the sheep nodded, attempting to hide his excitement under a glum facade. Finally he moved, crawling forward on his hands and knees toward Amal.

"You know, I've never had anyone go down on me before." The little sheep giggled nervously. "Grace thinks it's too submissive a position for herself."

Julian jumped as a switch struck his ass, wincing at the lingering sting. "Don't you ever speak for me, mutton! Say another word tonight and you wear a ball gag till morning!"

Julian hung his head in shame, but hidden from Grace a smile crossed his lips. Seeing it, Amal felt relaxed and with relaxation some measure of his desire returned. He licked his lips as Julian slipped his panties down from under the skirt. "I don't know if I'm going to like this, mistress, but I'll try it."

"I didn't ask what you like." Grace spun the switch between her fingers. Amal's ears dropped again.

Julian knelt before Amal and stroked his cheek. "She'll be really good to you if you stop fighting." Amal continued looking glum. "You're going to hurt my feelings if you don't start acting like you want me."

Amal finally smiled, seeming to take some pleasure from Julian's pouting, and raised himself up. "I hope I'm sufficient. This is my first time, you know. With a… girl. With a penis, that is."

Julian leaned in, rubbing his cheek to the boy's before kissing him. "On stage it'll my first time. Taking. A penis. Remember?"

The larger boy's eyes twinkled at that and Julian shivered, feeling like a special prize under that gaze. Amal's big hands rubbed over Julian's hips, the sheep bleating while the okapi's snout lifted his skirt, snuffling blindly at his crotch.

Amal's hands slid up over Julian's flat chest, stroking heavily, rubbing through the sheer cloth at his pert nipples. Julian planted his hands on Amal's shoulders, legs trembling as he moaned. He felt Amal's chin press into the tip of his shaft and felt embarrassed again.

"I'm sorry you won't be able to pretend I'm a girl now." Julian groaned at the bristly fur against his erection. "I hope it doesn't make the scene too hard."

"Shhh," Amal responded under the ruffles of skirt draping his muzzle. "You are a girl. Just let me explore." His muzzle twisted to the side, nuzzling his way under Julian's erection and licking tenderly at his balls. The sheep fell to his back, lifting his hips up with hooves planted firmly on the floor. His skirts tumbled over his stomach, revealing Amal to Grace's sight, still suckling on the sheep's balls with a slim shaft against his nose.

Amal released the orbs, looking up at Grace while he pressed his thick lips to the tip of Julian's shaft, cradling the tip there like a prolonged kiss. When Amal's thick, pebbly tongue slid out over him, Julian cried out in surprise. And then the sight of his erection was gone, the whole length easily contained in Amal's long muzzle, though the unseen activity within left the sheep writhing and moaning on the floor.

Amal pinched Julian's nipples, the sheep gasping at the pleasure and pain and trembling against the urge to thrust up into those lips. With such intense sensations, Julian wasn't sure how long he could hold out.

"Slow down." Grace was leaning forward in her recliner, watching intently with paws folded under her chin. "You should draw this out slowly. Don't let him orgasm until he's begging for it… and even then make him wait."

Amal stopped cold, the throbbing shaft held still his muzzle, and locked eyes with Julian. Starting back up carefully, he stroked his tongue over the boy's cock gently. His fingers now only rubbed gently at the sheep's nipples.

"Better. But don't let him get bored, there. The trick is to keep him on the edge so long it drives him mad." She pulled out from some secreted stash a pair of handcuffs. "Controlling his position should help out. Here, catch."

Julian's cock popped out of the okapi's muzzle as Amal reached up to catch the restraints, looking them over curiously. Grace had risen from the chair and was drawing more implements from her locked cabinet. "I think you may make a good Dom, too, Amal. I'll direct you and see how it goes. To start, lock his wrists behind his back."

Julian helpfully arched his back from the floor; normally he'd not cooperate so well, but Amal didn't need this to be any harder for him. When the manacles clicked around his wrists he tested them, seeing if he could slip his hands through the holes. "This ought to be interesting."

Grace appeared over him, a ball gag stretched between her paws. "I said no more talking, lamb chop." She pressed the ball into his muzzle, undeterred by his momentary resistance. Once he relented the rubber ball shoved his jaws open and he tested its firmness with his teeth; he'd have to get used to it until morning. His pillowcase was going to need washing with how much he'd be drooling.

Then she reached down for the base of his cock, squeezing it and his balls so she could wrap a leather ring around them. He heard a click and looked down curiously to see a thin chain connecting the cock ring to Amal's collar, giving no more than a foot of space. The okapi looked downright worried.

Finally she clipped a pair of ankle cuffs around Julian's waist with long ropes tied into their rings, and carried the ends of those ropes back to her recliner. She pulled them taut, lifting and spreading the sheep's legs wide just in front of the okapi's muzzle. She gestured to the pair, keeping both of the ropes in one paw. "Proceed."

Amal got back to work immediately and Julian had to wonder if he was enjoying this far more than he'd expected, or if it was merely to impress Grace. Either way, he was certainly stretching it out more now. He licked over the long shaft and balls without taking them into his muzzle for some time. He rubbed the sheep's nipples between thumb and forefinger slowly, only occasionally giving them a sharp pinch that made Julian bite hard on the ball gag. Even when the okapi did get his lips around that cock again, it was slow and gentle, only growing intense when Julian grew softer.

Every now and then Grace would give Julian's legs a tug, stretching them out, or relax her grip, letting the sheep settle against Amal's strong support. Whenever he felt too comfortable one way or the other, she would force him to shift his weight. It didn't seem like he would ever manage to reach his climax when he couldn't remain comfortable.

Then Amal stopped drawing back, sucking hard and firm at Julian's cock. He pressed up with his tongue firmly, wedging the crown of the sheep's dick into the roof of his muzzle, and bobbed his head in long strokes. The sudden flash of intensity left Julian crying uselessly against the ball gag, and it wasn't long before he came, nipples sore from the continued pinching and cock pulsing against Amal's thick tongue. The okapi swallowed Julian's seed without a sound of complaint. Then he let the spent cock flop against the sheep's belly and grinned playfully down at his partner.

"Very good." Grace not so subtly pulled her paw from between her thighs, cleaning it with a tissue. "And how did you like it?"

Amal gave Julian a quizzical look before responding nervously, "I thought you didn't care what I liked."

"I said I didn't ask. Now I have." She tossed the tissue aside with visible annoyance. "And never make me repeat myself again."

"Of course, mistress." Amal bowed his head. "It wasn't bad at all. I don't think I'd like it so much with a man that was, well, manly... but I enjoyed it with Julian."

"Good. You only need to enjoy it with him." Grace settled back in her recliner, stretching out her legs. "Now you may kiss my paws. But don't get too adventurous, they are the only part you've earned the right to kiss."

* * *

"But… this is so wrong!" Julian turned his head to the side with downcast eyes, facing the shadowed audience he pretended wasn't there. "My husband—"

"He doesn't appreciate you," Amal's eyes burned hungrily. "And he never will. Not the way I do."

Julian felt a tear at the edge of his eye and blinked, surprised. He gave a nod. An unrealistically extreme nod so that even those in the back rows would see it. The woman he was at this moment thought to herself, *my life may never be more than it is now, but I can have this, this one secret mistake, to remind me that I tried.*

The line wasn't in the play, though. Instead the script contained only the note: simulate sex.

No one shared the stage with them, though actors watched from the sides, and Julian had no idea how many seats were filled with unknowing eyes. Would they be suspicious eyes? Too late to worry about that.

Amal's pants were already down as he pressed in between the sheep's raised legs. Julian lifted his panties, sliding them up the boy's stomach as they stretched to near tearing. The okapi pushed down his own underwear in the front, letting his straining erection free. Julian had a single-use packet of lube hidden in his palm, already stealthily torn, and he stroked it quickly over Amal's cock, then dribbling the last between his cheeks. He let the packet fall to the couch. When the stage was cleaned, what would the cleaners make of it?

In theory this should be easy for the sheep; he may have never taken a real cock but plenty of things, very large things, had been inside his ass: butt plugs, strap-ons, stretchers and the odd improvised toy. Yet when the tip of the okapi's member touched his pucker, it clenched tight. He gasped, loud, and arched his back. Though unplanned he could hear the stir of excitement in the audience.

He closed his eyes, concentrating, and managed to relax. With another moment he was pushing back and the head of Amal's cock slid in. Julian bleated, a dark blush rising in his cheeks, and his thighs squeezed the boy's hips. Amal, unperturbed, let his settling weight drive the thick rod in. Julian's arms wrapped around his shoulders. His legs trembled. His breath caught.

Julian heard a low, faint electric crackle and Amal was suddenly shocked out of the tender embrace; boring for the audience. Amal's hand flinched toward the shock collar wrapped around his forearm, but he caught himself and followed the silent instruction. His hips launched into motion, pounding against Julian's ass.

Over the audience's applause and murmuring Julian cried out, shocked at how different it was than a dildo or even a strap-on. The subtle give and pulse of flesh against his anal muscles was far more engaging, and the boy's strong hips sent each thrust through Julian's whole body. He supposed that, without the feedback of nerves, Grace's use of a strap-on just didn't bring her whole body in on the act in the same way.

Then there was the heat. As if the stage lights weren't hot enough, the fire of another body overflowing with the heat of arousal made Julian feel like he'd burst into flames if he weren't sweating so much. Yet he could hardly think about that with how every muscle in his body wanted to curl around the handsome boy ravaging him.

A sudden vibration deep inside his anal cavity shocked him back to the present, and he could see that Amal had felt it too; another 'stage direction' fail-safe, an egg vibrator left in Julian's ass since before the play. After long enough even it, and the cable running out to a battery pack taped to his inner thigh, could come to feel usual. This one reminded them to keep the sex hidden; Amal took hold of Julian's leg and glanced to the side, ensuring the raised limb hid his thrusting cock from view.

Their first time had an audience of witless observers. Quite a unique first time. And beneath all of that, the woman Julian pretended to be whispered in his head of long held yearnings, desires and fears. Dreams of being taken away by a prince, pubescent fantasies of being ravaged by a handsome wanderer and secret, dark desires for the very things she feared; discovery, illegitimate pregnancy, obsession till she ran away... an end to the monotony of safety. In this secret sin she was unleashed. Freed from all the invisible bonds society could shackle to her mind.

Another shock made Amal wince, and then the vibration in Julian's ass activated, and stayed on. The scene was nearing its time limit. The vibration would stimulate Amal, and the shock let him know he needed to finish. The boy closed his eyes, pressed his lips firmly to

Julian's, and he thrust as hard and fast as he could. Julian grabbed his ankles and concentrated on clenching down tight, hard as it was with the unending stimulation behind his prostate.

The sheep wasn't sure which of them orgasmed first, just that they both were. Wisely Julian had put on a condom and taped it down along his inner thigh, so it could grow without pulling the tape free and the semen could be contained. All of that torture to his prostate was simply more than the poor organ could handle even without the okapi's thick cock pumping through his "virgin" ass, finally giving him the feeling of a real man inside of him.

The two lay against each other, hips locked tight, delirious in the afterglow of their first time together. Panting, sweating, limbs weak and shaking... and then the shock. Amal jumped a little, reached between them to pull his cock back into his underwear and Julian reached between their bellies to push his panties down.

It wasn't for the audience; the scene had ended. Over a mixture of applause and cat calls the lights went out. The curtain dropped. And their garments were fixed only seconds before crew and actors were around them. Between preparation for the next scene and congratulations Julian thought his heart would explode; there were so many ways they could be discovered.

As Xuan passed by them, getting into position for the next scene, he stopped and sniffed the air. The others had been in too much of a hurry to think about it, but the otter had been too attentive. He gave the sheep a look, and then Amal, before breaking out in a grin. "You two really did get into it. I've got to admit, though, you pulled off the role well. No wonder he came in his pants."

Julian choked a moment. "Uh, thanks. I think."

Xuan shrugged and waved them away. "Credit where credit's due."

As Amal hurried him off stage on unsteady legs, Julian finally breathed a sigh of relief. A sigh that caught in his throat when he saw Molly standing in front of him. The spaniel regarded him quizzically for a moment. Then she nodded.

"You did well. Very well. I almost thought it was real. I don't know why you couldn't do that during rehearsal but I guess you did deserve the part after all. But for gods sake, clean up before your next scene! I can smell it from here." And with that she walked onto the stage. They would have at least one scene before they had to be out again.

Grace and Mabatha appeared, the collie with bottles of water for them both. Grace guided them out of sight with a big smile. "Barely on time, but you two got it! Congratulations!"

Mabatha nodded curtly. "Adequate. Now do it every night that well. We have to build hype, not lose it, so don't you dare backslide!" And then he moved on to berate the next actors he could find.

The pair took the water bottles and drank desperately. In their newfound privacy Grace leaned in. "Good job. I guess I can give you a treat."

Amal spit his water out. "You mean…?"

She shook her head with a wicked laugh. "No. I mean I'll stop locking your collar. Do that well at every single showing and maybe you'll get a better reward."

Julian patted the disappointed boy's shoulder. "Your plan worked, I guess."

"Plan?" Grace laughed again. "This wasn't to make you act better! This was for my own amusement. As if I'd let you cheat at acting for anything less than my own selfishness."

She left the two boys alone, huddled together in the dark. Amal leaned in close to Julian. "If this is how things start… does she get worse than this?"

Julian nodded.

Amal chewed his lip. "Maybe we should run away?"

"Sure." Julian cuddled up against Amal, head on his shoulder. "She'd have so much fun chasing us down!"

TWINS APART

Ross Whitlock

Two black-clad men walked Beck into the cell, holding his biceps. They bound him with a nylon rope. One of his captors wound it around his wrists and made a sturdy knot. The rest of the rope went through a dangling ring over his head, and the smallest of the men, the fennec fox, tied it off to another ring on the wall. Beck had enough slack to move his arms around a bit, but he still had to stand in one place. They didn't gag him, and he stayed quiet.

As Beck's handlers finished, more came in, hauling Traveler's unconscious form. Beck stifled a whimper of concern. At least they weren't handling Traveler like a sack of potatoes; two large, muscular men bore him with care, as if he were a hospital patient. Traveler was plenty buff himself, but they showed no strain.

Beck watched as they put Traveler up against the wall. They cuffed each of his wrists to a shackle and tied his ankles to a floor ring. Later, Beck would try counting all the rings set in the floor, walls, and ceiling, and come up with thirty-two. Overkill, maybe.

Beck's own captors checked over his restraints. Focused as he was on Traveler, Beck almost didn't hear when the fennec muttered, "The safeword is 'peaches.'" Two seconds later, Beck grasped the words. He blinked and replied, "Uh. Thanks?" but they were already leaving.

The door slammed and locked.

Traveler slumped in his bonds. Him, they'd gagged. Tight leather straps went around his muzzle and buckled behind his head. Otherwise, he wore only black underwear. Beck, too, had been stripped to his skivvies, a pair of dark blue boxer briefs. He was relieved. This would be so much weirder if they were naked.

Beck shifted from footpaw to footpaw and tried to decide how the hell he was going to explain this to his twin brother.

* * *

Events Were Set In Motion. That was how Beck thought of it, with the dry internal eye-roll of a lifelong writer. Events Were Set In Motion, and he still couldn't believe it had begun in a tiny used bookstore, except it really went back further. If Traveler hadn't…

Well.

Traveler had been depressed for months. He flat-out refused to admit it, obnoxiously stoic as ever. He spent hours at the gym, getting bigger and stronger until strangers assumed Beck was the little brother. ("I am. By about seventeen seconds.") Beck tried to join in, tried to make Traveler react to anything at all. Most of the time, it was like talking to a bowling ball. Dammit, why?

Traveler had never really gotten over their dad's death, four years gone. Their mother had gotten on with things. Beck had, at the time, cried till he was parched, but the grief had run its course and now he mostly just felt a gentle ache. But Traveler drew inside himself. He'd had support from his boyfriend, Will, but Will left the scene rather abruptly. Traveler made it clear the subject was not to be discussed. Since then, he'd worked his grunt-level job at the print-and-copy warehouse, hit the gym, watched TV, and further calcified. Beck, meanwhile, got his amateur foodie blog noticed by an online magazine, was now being paid to write, and was maybe going to get a book deal. Basically, his dreams coming true.

Except, because Traveler was stuck in place, Beck felt his control slipping. They shared the telepathy of twins, and Traveler's largely unexplained sadness became an ache in Beck's chest, a roiling in his gut. He tried to be with Traveler but got only silence, and it hurt so much that Beck fled from everyone and did things alone. Parties and social gatherings were torture. "And this is your brother? Irish setters? So… from Ireland? Kinda quiet, aren't you? Hello?" People flirted with Traveler because his body was to die for, and people flirted with Beck because he was the "cute" one and it seemed like he might be rich one day. It made Traveler more stony, and it made Beck spend more and more time alone.

And then the used bookstore.

Beck loved the place. Tiny, but with so many shelves crammed in that they seemed to create a fifth-dimensional space. Newcomers got lost. Beck went in, shaking off the late-November slush, and browsed the food books, as he always did. Then, on a whim, he investigated the psychology section. Maybe the experts knew something about Traveler that he didn't.

A title caught his eye. <u>Twins Together, Twins Apart</u>. He pulled the ragged-jacketed book from the shelf and flipped through it. It seemed to be about the emotional bonds between twins, and how they influenced life. He backtracked to the table of contents. Chapter seven was entitled, "When One Twin Hurts."

Beck sighed at his own desperation, then flipped to the chapter. Tucked between the pages was a small slip of paper. It bore a neatly typed message:

WHEN ONE TWIN HURTS, BOTH SUFFER. THEY
BUILD THEIR OWN PRISON. BUT THERE ARE BETTER,
FANCIER CAGES. IF THIS IS YOU, PERHAPS WE CAN HELP.
BUY THIS BOOK AND KEEP THE RECEIPT.

Beneath this was a small red symbol that could have been a leaf, or a flame.

Beck stood stock still, feeling a stripe of backfur stand on end. He felt he'd pried open some sort of window into the mechanisms of the universe. But he knew who'd put the note in the book, more or less.

CityScape.

Everyone who spent any time on the internet knew about CityScape. It was an alternate reality game, an ARG, and possibly the biggest and most grandiose of them all. Its players were more like religious zealots, spending all their free time scouring the city, following strange clues, calculating, triangulating, researching… and for what, exactly? Those who'd penetrated deep into the game were made to do things they didn't talk about, claiming they'd been sworn to utmost secrecy. Legions of hackers couldn't get through the outer shell of the CityScape website. All this implied that powerful people ran the game, and whoever they were, they refused to reveal what happened when you won. If you even could.

A billion dollars. A date with the president. A tour of Willy Wonka's freaking chocolate factory. Players spun a million theories about the "goal" or "prize" at the end of the CityScape labyrinth. It made Beck chuckle. To think people devoted their lives to something so intangible.

Now here he was, holding a strange message with the CityScape logo on it, and it said it could help him with Traveler. Obviously they couldn't know who he was. How long had this clue sat in this book, waiting for an unhappy twin to find it? Was this how CityScape worked? A thousand random scraps of paper cast to the winds on the hope that some few would find the right recipient?

"Fucking stupid," Beck said to himself, and then he bought the book.

The owner of the store was a plump little rabbit named Mr. Charles who chortled a lot. He gave Beck the receipt and said, "Hope it's what you were looking for."

Beck went home and combed through the book for more clues. He read chapter seven and found it to be a string of unhelpful platitudes. He even held it under his blacklight. Nothing. Finally, the exact wording of the message kicked in and he looked closely at the receipt. At the bottom, he found a URL.

So chortling Mr. Charles was somehow involved in CityScape? Again, that glimpse of machinery behind the scenes.

Beck tried the URL, which took him to a black screen where red text asked him to input the title, author, and publication date of the book he'd just bought. Then he had to play a weird little Flash game where the goal was to align rows of symbols. After that, he entered a bare-bones chatroom. Seconds later, someone joined him.

The other user was called "LordZephyr". They politely asked Beck why he was here. Beck's instincts told him to turn and flee, because this was how bad things happened to people online. He asked his faceless companion why he should tell them anything. They replied, "You shouldn't. I'm obviously a creeper." That made Beck chuckle despite himself, and he stayed. He and LordZephyr traded witty remarks, which somehow turned into Beck explaining his recent unhappiness, and Traveler's. His new friend was sympathetic and wise, putting Beck in mind of a therapist. The whole time, he told himself, *I'll leave the moment they ask me a question I don't like.*

Finally, LordZephyr typed, "I know you have no reason to trust me, but I think CityScape can help you. We just need your address, and your brother's."

Beck laughed out loud. "Sorry," he typed, "but I'm not an idiot."

"Fair enough," came the reply. "I'll still be here if you change your mind."

Beck left the chatroom. He made dinner and ate it while editing his latest column. After awhile, the words became meaningless. He tried calling Traveler and got voicemail. He played a video game, showered, and went to bed, but not to sleep.

At ten PM, he got up, opened his laptop, and returned to the chatroom. He had another conversation.

The knock on his door came two hours later.

* * *

Traveler had stopped dreaming lately. The void between midnight and dawn was another warning siren, blaring behind his ears, telling him to get help. He ignored it like the others.

His mind skipped from wakefulness to wakefulness. One minute, the man in black laughed as Traveler bent his head to the bowl of incense and inhaled. The next minute, he felt plaster under his butt and against his shoulder blades. Something held his arms in place. Something else held his muzzle shut.

Traveler opened his eyes. His brother smiled anxiously back.

"Hey, Trav," Beck said quietly. "I, uh, want to apologize. That we're in a dungeon."

Traveler wondered if he should be angry. Anger was hard to come by these days; his emotions seemed buried under invisible, suffocating wool. He remembered the invasion of his bedroom, the laughing man, and the incense. In truth... well... back when he'd had dreams, he'd dreamed of this.

Did Beck know that?

Traveler gave a questioning grunt around the gag.

He could tell Beck was trying to collect his thoughts. "Okay," his brother said at last. "What's going on is, we're inside CityScape. The game? I found a... clue... that led me to someone who offered to, I guess, capture us."

"Why?" Traveler asked, or tried to. "Wmmph?"

"You know why," Beck said quietly. He tugged at the rope around his wrists. "I found the CityScape clue inside a book about twins." His voice rose a bit. "Seriously, Trav, I am reduced to looking in books for some fucking idea of how to deal with you."

The guilt came washing over Traveler, icy-cold. He wanted to yell, "You think I don't know, Beck? This goes both ways. I hate what I'm doing to you and I hate myself. If I knew, if I understood…"

He was hollow. A golem. It wasn't just Dad's death. Traveler ached with restlessness but had nowhere to go. He filled his days with repetitive activity but none of it had purpose. The only spark came when he stood naked before the mirror, admired the results of his intense gym regimen, and thought, *Someone else should be here. Seeing and touching my body. But not to worship. Not to submit. To…*

To something.

"They told me what's gonna happen," Beck was saying. "You and I are prisoners and we have to do whatever we're told. We'll be punished otherwise. Not in a bad way… I don't think." He chuckled. "The safeword is 'peaches.'"

Safeword. Hearing it made Traveler tingle. He let out a sound of desire.

"I knew it!" Beck cried. "I was right!" He calmed himself. "Sorry. I was just thinking… remember when we were pups and you always wanted me to tie you up?"

Traveler glared. A faint blush rose to his cheeks. He was not ready to talk about such things, and certainly not with his brother.

"I told that to the guy I met online. He said, maybe a bit of captivity is what you need. You've trapped yourself in your own prison, but…" Beck wrinkled his reddish-brown muzzle. "A true prison will liberate you, something something. It was really pretentious. I went along with it because… I'll try anything at this point."

Traveler tested his bonds. They held firm. He wished he wasn't muzzled, although it felt nice to be. This one-sided conversation was getting them nowhere.

To his relief, the cell door opened and a man came in.

He was simian, some kind of tamarin monkey, with glossy black fur, terra cotta eyes, and hands and feet the color of mustard. He wore a dapper gray vest and slacks and carried a tablet. He also wore an expression that Traveler associated with tax collectors from old silent films.

The monkey sighed. "Right," he said. He studied the tablet, glancing occasionally at one or the other canine, for several minutes.

Finally, Beck cleared his throat and asked, "What—?"

"No talking," their captor barked. "You're the defiant one. Of course. Extra headache for me. Lord Georgio might want you, but you wouldn't enjoy that. And you." He rounded on Traveler. "Do you have any idea how many muscleheads I have to process? Dime a dozen. I suppose it's Lord Sturm for you, at least to begin with."

"Hey, asshole," Beck said. Traveler winced at his brother's tone.

The monkey flared his nostrils. "Either you're a masochist, or..."

"Punish me if you want," Beck retorted. "But don't act like we're not here. I didn't sign us up for this so we could be treated like furniture."

The monkey barked a laugh. "You have no idea where you are or what this whole experience entails, boy. And for the record, it's quite possible you will be placed in a latex suit with a lamp balanced on your head and made to, in fact, be furniture."

"That your kink?" Beck asked puckishly.

The monkey marched up to him and poked him in the chest. "Boy, if you knew my kinks, you would piss yourself. If it weren't imperative to leave your handsome russet body unmarked, I'd have you regretting every insolent word of the past few minutes. I am Lord Atticus and I am not even the worst of our lot. Now. Be. Quiet."

Beck shut up. Lord Atticus fiddled with the tablet for another moment, then sighed and stretched. "Ye gods." He turned to the door and called, "Alright, people. The big one goes to Lord Sturm. The mouthy one stays for now."

Two black-clad attendants came in, one male, one female. They removed Traveler from his bonds and stood him up, then immediately cuffed his hands behind his back with metal handcuffs. He didn't resist. He just looked at Beck in a way that said, *You got us into this. Don't whine at me later.*

"You can't just leave me here," Beck complained.

Lord Atticus rubbed his temple in irritation. "Boy, this is not some sort of high-end bordello. You do not call the shots. Pray one of my siblings notices you soon. The safeword is 'waterfall.'" He marched out.

"I thought it was..." Beck closed his muzzle, baffled. They led Traveler away, slamming the door behind them.

Traveler decided they were in some kind of manor. As his handlers walked him down various hallways, he took in the classical architecture, the fake gas lamps, the thick red carpet under his footpaws. He caught glimpses of other people moving here and there. Most wore simple black, like his captors. Others had kinkier attire. Was that a figure on a leash? And was *that* a bare bosom over there?

Light snow fell outside the windows.

They took Traveler down a very long spiral stairway, then a gloomy stone hall, and finally, a very large, dark, low-ceilinged room. Traveler's hackles rose. The chamber was lined with… devices. In the dimness, he couldn't see them very well. They lurked like giant insects, each a tangle of metal and rubber. Some were occupied. He could make out the slow, tormented movement of naked muscle and heaving flesh. He heard faint groans and whimpers. He smelled sweat and semen.

In the room's center, a single light illuminated a series of metal frames, each no more than a simple square, two vertical bars and one overhead. The handlers moved Traveler under a frame. They freed his arms and muzzle, then pulled off his underwear.

"Hey," Traveler protested. He had a partial erection, the tip of his dark pink cock visible through the soft russet curls covering his sheath and groin.

"Grab hold of the bar above you," ordered one of them, a caracal.

Traveler obeyed.

"Lord Sturm will be here shortly. Don't speak unless spoken to. Do *not* try and goad him. And if you can, don't flinch." The caracal wore a slightly pained expression, as if he'd been in Traveler's place once, and made the wrong choices. "The safeword is 'satin.'"

They left. Traveler stood in place, footpaws planted, hands gripping the cool metal overhead. He studied his own erection, which had grown in size a bit. He couldn't pretend he wasn't turned on by his captivity. Leave it to Beck to guess what he truly needed.

Was this what Beck needed, though? Or was he just here on Traveler's behalf?

A few minutes went by, and Traveler's mind wandered. He remembered how they'd caught him.

They'd quite simply broken in. He'd come awake to find three men standing around his bed. They wore black silk hoods that concealed their features.

"Who the fuck—?"

One man spoke. "The safeword is 'alchemy'. We're here for you, Traveler. Are you going to resist us?"

And he hadn't. His senses had been ignited by the man's tone, and by the way their hidden gaze had seemed to crawl over his half-naked form, appreciative and possessive. He knew what "safeword" meant. He spent plenty of time lurking on certain websites, though something, some inner feeling of dread or shame, held him back from reaching out to the BDSM community. Lingering trauma from how his last relationship had ended, perhaps.

This was different. These men seemed to know.

They had ordered him to inhale aromatic smoke from a wooden bowl. He'd obeyed, and the scent had taken him away, relieved him of all senses, as the man with the bowl laughed.

Back in the here and now, a door opened. Traveler cleared his mind and watched as a large silhouette approached.

The man moved into the light. Another monkey like Lord Atticus, with the same dark fur and mustard-yellow hands and feet, but bigger, more heavily muscled. Lord Sturm. He wore a thick leather harness, belt, and thong. Furless scars marked his body here and there. His dark eyes glared under a low brow. Just the kind of dom Traveler would expect in a place like this. He held a long bullwhip.

"What's your name, dog?" he asked in a low, rough voice.

"Traveler... sir."

"Flattery," Lord Sturm grunted in contempt. Without warning, his arm flashed and the whip cracked. Traveler yelped and twitched. One hand let go of the bar. He saw anger in Lord Sturm's eyes and grabbed it again. The whip hadn't touched him, but he'd felt the wind of its passing.

"I don't want some simpering bitch," Lord Sturm snapped. "Are you a man, dog?"

"I... yes. Yes."

CRACK. The whip made Traveler's fur ruffle. This time, he didn't let go of the bar. Or flinch.

"Do you think your muscles make you special?"

"No."

"Liar."

"I'm not lying!" Traveler protested.

CRACK.

The whip touched his chest. No. No, it hadn't actually lashed him, but for an instant, his skin stung as if it had. Lord Sturm's hand came down on Traveler's ass, smacking it firmly, and that really did sting.

Traveler fought the urge to shield his body. His arms stayed above his head, clutching the bar.

"Did that feel good, dog?" Lord Sturm demanded.

"Yes," Traveler said through gritted teeth.

"Do you want another?"

Traveler didn't answer.

Lord Sturm studied him for a moment. Then he put the handle of the whip under Traveler's chin and forced his head up. "Arrogant dog."

Traveler held his tongue.

"You don't need to be so stoic," Lord Sturm hissed. "Doesn't it hurt?"

"Yes," Traveler said evenly. "It smarts."

"Aren't you going to get angry?"

"Why should I?" Traveler asked. "I'm yours. I'm here for your enjoyment."

Lord Sturm tilted his head. "I don't enjoy this."

"Then why are you doing it?"

"I ask the questions!" Lord Sturm snapped. But then he went on. "See the men around you, dog? In my machines? See them moan and squirm? Most of them have been here for days. I'm breaking them, bit by bit. Because they insulted me, they talked back to me, they struggled and protested and refused to obey. They *made* me punish them. Do you understand now?"

Traveler didn't understand. He didn't get it. Was he supposed to be defiant, or submissive? It had to be one or the other.

Lord Sturm stepped back and cracked the whip again. Traveler felt the phantom sting across both his thighs, dangerously close to his balls. All his instincts told him to bring his legs together, to protect his tender bits from the cruel lash. But he'd become skilled at ignoring his instincts. He stood still, exposed. He looked calmly at Lord Sturm, not daring, merely curious as to what would come next.

Lord Sturm snarled.

"Oh, for heaven's sake, brother, enough!"

Someone new had entered the room. Even in the dark, the approaching figure glittered and twinkled.

"Lord Harlequin," Lord Sturm said murderously. "Aren't you afraid of getting your precious clothes dirty?"

Lord Harlequin tittered. Another monkey, of course, this one clad in garish silk attire, purple and green and pink. A large, diamond-patterned cape swept out behind him. Press-on jewels ringed his purple-lined eyes and glittered on each fingernail.

"My poor, poor Lord Sturm. I do believe this boy's beyond your limited comprehension."

"Do you want me to break your fucking limbs, brother?" Lord Sturm asked.

Lord Harlequin showed no fear. "Language, Lord Sturm. As soon as I read up on this one, I knew he wasn't yours. Lord Atticus is such a delightful bigot, isn't he. Not every musclebound lad belongs in your grim and grisly dungeon, you know."

"He's defying me!" Lord Sturm snapped.

"He is not, my dear. You don't want to admit that you haven't a clue how to handle him."

"I suppose you want him, then."

Traveler couldn't believe how much he enjoyed this. Standing here and listening to others discuss him as if he were an object up for auction. It felt amazing. It felt… liberating. Every time either of them looked at him, he wanted to whine in happiness. Yes. Look at my naked body. Examine it.

"I can put him to work," Lord Harlequin murmured. He moved to Traveler and touched his chest. One finger circled a nipple, then pinched it lightly. Traveler moaned. The hand slid further down, traced his abs, toyed with the curling pubic fur.

"Oh, you like that, don't you," Lord Harlequin said, giving Traveler a huge wink. "I have a leash for you, handsome pup. I'm throwing an absolutely to-die-for party, to which my unpleasant brother is not invited. And I need… shall we say… servers."

"I'll do whatever you like, my lord," Traveler replied quietly. Just addressing a man as "my lord" made him shiver in enjoyment.

"Oh, I love him!" Lord Harlequin rounded on Lord Sturm. "You would have whipped him into oblivion and it wouldn't have done a damn thing, you philistine. Go tend to your silly machines. Leave this boy to me."

Lord Sturm looked furious, but he nodded and stomped away into the darkness, toward his strange gallery of imprisoned, tormented men.

"You can't blame him, really," Lord Harlequin sighed. "To be fair, all of those poor brutes are getting exactly what they wanted, even if they don't know it. But you're quite special…Traveler, is it? I have some truly shocking ideas for what to do with you."

"Lead on, my lord!" Traveler said. For the first time in… weeks? Months? He smiled.

* * *

Time passed and Beck wished he'd never started this.

No one came for him. His legs ached to sit down. The rope on his wrists was no longer sexy, just tiresome. Had he failed some sort of test? They'd taken Traveler away on some grand S&M adventure while Beck got to languish. He was horny and bored.

Well, he'd done this for Traveler, hadn't he? Yes, but during the second of their conversations, "LordZephyr" had implied that untold sexual delights awaited Beck as well. Or had he imagined that?

He was about to try yelling "Waterfall!" when the cell door finally opened. A middle-aged hare came in, dressed in the usual black. He untied Beck's arms, producing a sigh of relief. Then he took Beck's shoulders with gentle insistence and led him from the cell.

"Nice place," Beck said, taking in the classical aesthetic. The hare said nothing.

Beck allowed himself to be guided down hallways and stairs, through some kind of dimly-lit library, to a small foyer. The hare stopped him, then handed him a small envelope.

"The garden is through those doors," he said, gesturing. "Deliver this to Lady Foxglove. You'll know her when you see her. Be polite." He headed back the way they'd come.

"Wait!" Beck said. The hare paused. "What's the safeword?"

The hare looked at him for a moment. "You won't need one," he said quietly.

Beck sighed and went through the wrought-iron doors.

The garden looked immense, a labyrinth of hedges, trees, flower beds. Much of it resembled a wild wood, but Beck could make out order amid the chaos, subtle patterns. His footpaws touched soft grass. Snowflakes alit on his fur. Some hidden environmental control kept the garden warm even as the snow fell.

Beck ventured forth, turning to regard the immense manor. The blindfolded car ride from his apartment had taken less than an hour;

this must be one of the estates on the side of Mt. Jamieson. Reclusive rich folk—who else would have the means for all this?

The trees swallowed Beck. He wondered how he'd find this Lady Foxglove. Calling her name seemed inappropriate. He listened and heard nothing. The first major sound was his own yelp of terror as he came face to face with a large dark figure. It took him a few heartbeats to realize he'd found a statue, not made of stone, but of… rubber? He touched its smooth, cool surface. It depicted a powerful stallion in an Atlas pose, a sphere balanced on his shoulders. The statue had a massive erection. Beck flicked the rubber cock and chuckled, shaking his head.

He spotted a few more sexualized rubber statues, male and female, as he forged on. Eventually, he broke through the trees and onto a wide lawn ringed by hedges. Gaps in the shrubbery led in all directions. Stone benches ringed a central pool choked with large white lotuses. Their scent teased Beck's nose as he spun slowly in place, wondering which path to take.

Near one end of the pool, another rubber statue stood, a muscular male elephant. Out in the open, the light from the tall hanging lamps played over its glossy black surfaces. As he approached, Beck was unsettled to notice that the statue had real ivory tusks. Donated willingly, he hoped. He sat on a bench and sighed.

"What now?" he mumbled. "This sucks."

Something moved at the corner of his vision. He turned sharply but saw only the elephant statue. Then he really focused. Muscle shifted beneath the rubber surface. He looked at the statue's face and saw living eyes—stormy eyes, gray with flecks of gold—that quickly looked away.

"Whoa. Hey!" Beck stood up. "You're real!"

Up close, it was more obvious. The elephant wore a skintight rubber suit that hugged his nude form tight, defining each muscle, with openings for tusks, eyes, and all orifices. He'd been standing stock still, posing. He said nothing.

"Oh, come on," Beck said. He poked the elephant lightly in his firm, rounded belly. "You don't need to keep up the act."

"Please don't," the elephant whispered urgently. His stormy eyes darted around.

"Why not? Aren't you bored? What's your name?"

"I... I'm Phillip. But, please, I'm not supposed to move. Lord Cesare said..."

"Whatever," Beck interrupted. "I don't see any Lord Cesare. How'd you get here? CityScape?"

Phillip nodded slowly. "My little brother talked me into it. He found some clue or something."

"Hey, I'm here with my brother too! Huh." Beck sat back down. "I'm Beck. Don't you think it's weird that they make us do this stuff? It's like they're messing with our heads. Or our libidos..." He glanced at Phillip's crotch. The elephant was quite well-endowed, and his rubber-covered cock looked a bit stiff between his meaty thighs. Phillip saw him looking and gulped.

"I like it," he mumbled. "Being turned into a statue. Ordered to stand still. Lord Cesare said I'm perfect for his... collection."

"Whatever turns you on," Beck chuckled. "You do look good in rubber." His eyes kept straying to Phillip's cock. He wanted to touch it. Why not? He was still horny, and wasn't this whole place some sort of Caligulan pleasure palace?

"Thanks," Phillip replied shyly. "You, uh, look good in undies."

Beck laughed softly. Then he slipped his boxer briefs down his legs. He stretched, leaning back on the bench.

"Why'd you take them off?" Phillip asked.

Beck smiled. "Well, you're naked. Kind of. Honestly, Phillip, I've been blue-balled since I got here." He scratched his pubic fur, shivering at the small contact with his sheath. His cocktip peeked out, signaling its need.

"Are you being seductive?" Phillip demanded, sounding amused. "Pretty sure we both have jobs to do."

Beck glanced at the envelope he was supposed to be delivering. Then he shrugged, stood, and lightly pressed himself to Phillip, his flat tummy against the elephant's warm musclegut. He rested his hands on Phillip's chest. Phillip sighed softly and let his trunk drape over Beck's shoulder.

"Call this a work break," Beck murmured. "If you like, that is."

"I... I like."

They kissed. Phillip's lips felt full and warm. Their tongues touched, greeting. Beck rather liked the feel of the smooth rubber with bodily warmth beneath. His hands massaged Phillip's pecs in slow circles.

Phillip rumbled, a musical trumpet-note in his throat. The end of his trunk rubbed at Beck's upper back, warm air blowing through the nostril holes.

This is more like what I signed up for, Beck thought.

His cock slid free. Tapered and dark pink, it frotted against Phillip's larger shaft. Beck was amazed at how the suit moved with Phillip, barely any folds or wrinkles. As his dick hardened fully, the rubber stretched over the shaft and head, defining each ridge, each vein. Below the root, heavy round balls throbbed gently. Beck reached down and felt over the cock and balls, and Phillip moaned.

"Doesn't it make you less sensitive?" Beck asked.

"Not... really," Phillip panted. "Ahh..." His thick fingers dug into Beck's hips, then slid back to massage his ass. Beck yipped happily as he felt his buttocks get kneaded, then spread. A finger ran up and down his cleft and toyed with the curly russet fur on his tail.

"Guess we know what you want," he breathed, kissing Phillip firmly.

"I'm... kinda big..." Phillip replied, words muffled by their locked lips.

"I can take you, big guy." Beck squeezed Phillip's shaft firmly.

"Please."

Beck stepped back, then laid himself across the stone bench. He smiled up at his new friend, one hand rubbing over his own chest. "Lift my legs, babe."

Phillip crouched over him, grinning. He took Beck's ankles and slid them over his broad shoulders. Beck gripped the bench as he felt that thick organ rub under his fuzzy balls and find the sweet spot. His pucker was tight... it had been awhile since he'd been properly mounted like this. He welcomed it, gently letting his anal muscles relax.

"Ready?"

"Mmhmm."

Phillip pushed. Beck could feel his strength and his restraint. Phillip's cock began to spread him. He whimpered, grimacing for a moment, then further relaxing. Another inch. Its rubber coating felt better than any condom. Phillip grunted and thrust, and his shaft vanished halfway into the setter's butt.

"Ahh..." Beck arched his back. His cock bobbed and dripped over his tummy. Phillip trumpeted softly in pleasure. He drew his dick back out, then buried it all the way in. Beck's toes curled and his tail wagged rapidly.

Stormy gray eyes gazed down into Beck's as the two men began to mate in earnest. Phillip's hips flexed and his shaft penetrated deep. It felt so good. Beck panted, tongue hanging out, mumbling soft, sexy words of encouragement. Phillip's trunk caressed his cheek. He felt its delicate movements, nuanced, the powerful muscle touching him so sweetly. He stroked the trunk with one hand while the other clutched the bench. His body rocked with each powerful thrust. Phillip had obviously been pent up. Even in his lust, he didn't lose control. He fucked Beck with care, never rough. Beck had always treasured that in a lover.

"Cum in me, Phillip," he whispered.

"Yes!"

Phillip's thrusting grew faster, harder. Beck clenched his cheeks around the rubbery shaft, waiting for that explosion. He wanted to feel the elephant's body flexing and quaking in orgasm. He wanted to hear Phillip trumpet, wanted that delighted sound to shatter this silly place and all its silly games…

And then, "Shit," Beck gasped. "Shit shit shit. Stop. Phillip, stop!"

Phillip blinked dazedly and slowed his thrusts. "What's wrong?"

"Uh…" Beck jerked his head to one side.

A small female monkey stood watching them, looking highly amused. She wore a simple white blouse and jeans, and gardening gloves hid her yellow hands. Beck couldn't tell her age.

"Oh, dear," she sighed. "I suppose I should have let you boys finish. However, I'd rather not have orgiastic screaming in my garden."

"Lady Foxglove?" Beck asked weakly.

She dipped her head. "I've been expecting a letter. Are you Beck?"

"Y-yes. Ma'am. Sorry about this."

Lady Foxglove laughed. "Oh, it's fine, honey. My garden tends to inspire erotic stirrings." Her gaze traveled to Beck's companion. "Phillip, I believe? Normally I don't interfere in the games of my family, but Lord Cesare, well… if he found you disobeying him, he'd be very unhappy. And…" Her eyes clouded briefly. "Some punishments you wouldn't enjoy. Neither would your little brother."

Phillip swallowed and pulled himself free. Beck winced as the elephant's cock popped from his anus. Phillip quickly moved back to where he'd been standing and tried to recreate his pose from before.

"That's not fair!" Beck complained. "I'm the one who made him break the rules."

"It's okay, Beck," Phillip said softly. He smiled. "Thank you for the work break. I'll be fine."

"I hope your brother's okay," Beck said.

"Yeah. Yours too."

Lady Foxglove touched Beck's arm. "You're a sweet boy. Why don't you make yourself modest and come with me."

Beck put his boxer briefs back on and followed Lady Foxglove toward one of the garden's many pathways. He glanced back to see Phillip motionless, a statue once again. Phillip's stormy eyes locked with his in momentary farewell.

* * *

"You want me to wear *F*, my lord?" Traveler asked. His cheeks burned.

"My dear pup," Lord Harlequin replied. "Wanting has nothing to do with it. You're going to wear that."

When he'd pictured himself serving drinks at a party, Traveler had assumed he'd be in some kind of Chippendales-inspired costume: bow tie, little black shorts, maybe a cummerbund. No. The outfit brandished by Lord Harlequin consisted of a black corset with red laces, panties of sheer black lace, long fishnet gloves, and matching stockings.

"They're all your size," Lord Harlequin said. "I've femmed up bigger studs than you. Now, don't be a prude. My guests are practically at the doorstep."

Traveler took the armful of humiliating garb and began to dress himself. They were in an anteroom near the large dining chamber where the party would take place. This was to be Traveler's base of operations: drinks and hors d'oeuvres would arrive from the kitchen, and he'd circumnavigate the dining room, offering platters and topping glasses. He had three other servers helping him, but they were dressed in simple black.

The fishnet hugged his limbs perfectly. The panties defined his package and were see-through enough to be scandalous. They also left his buttocks mostly bare. He slipped uncertainly into the corset, and Lord Harlequin sashayed behind him to help with the laces.

"Don't you look divine!" the monkey chirped. "They're all going to want to eat you up."

"I don't look… silly, my lord?"

"Heh. Trust me, pup, I know when a male looks good in quasi-drag. Your masculine physique is not undermined but accentuated by the feminine attire. All you need to do is wear it with confidence. No shyness allowed!"

"Yes, my lord," Traveler murmured. He could hardly refuse. Lord Harlequin had been very kind—giving him food and water, letting him use the bathroom. At the same time, he was overbearing and domineering, but not in a bad way. "You look amazing," Traveler added.

"Why, thank you!" Lord Harlequin twirled. His upper half was so puffy-sleeved and high-collared that it resembled a giant muffin made mostly from gold lamé and intricate red ribbons. From the waist down, he wore only a gold chain-link posing pouch and lace-up sandals. Traveler figured he'd gotten off easy in the outrageous costume department.

Lord Harlequin finished securing the corset and gave Traveler's butt an appreciative fondle. "I must go meet and greet. This party could get devilish, so expect anything. The safeword is 'croquembouche.'"

"I dunno if I can pronounce that, my lord."

"Just wing it," Lord Harlequin giggled, and left.

Traveler waited with the other three servers, all of whom seemed unwilling to chat. Traveler didn't feel like talking, anyway. His girly outfit felt so strange. He tried to make himself at home in the corset and fishnet. He didn't want to disappoint Lord Harlequin. Not after he'd finally been given a sense of, well… purpose.

Soon enough, the drinks and hors d'oeuvres began to arrive through a door, borne by cooks in white coats. Traveler took a platter with some kind of shrimp-and-cheese concoction, and followed the others into the dining room.

The guests stood here and there, chatting. Lord Harlequin's laughter rang out. Traveler kept his eyes down demurely, but couldn't help shooting glances at the partygoers. An eclectic bunch, men and women alike (though a couple seemed to defy gender), some dressed formally, others as flamboyant as their host. He moved here and there, silently offering. Fingers with glittering claws and bejeweled rings plucked at the shrimps and lifted them to painted and sequined lips. And they paid him in words.

"Thank you, pup. Such a lovely boy you are!"

"Oh, you're a treasure. Wherever did Harlequin find you?"

"I'd pay big for you, boy. Put you in my bedroom to admire every night."

Traveler tingled with pleasure from the praise. This was what he craved, not mindless compliments about his muscles, but words of dominance. Ownership.

"Cheers, pup," said a chubby little rabbit in a pink silk shirt, taking a shrimp and winking. He looked vaguely familiar. Was he from that used bookstore Beck loved so much?

Traveler returned to the anteroom with an empty platter and returned with a new delicacy. Guests kept waving him over, and he had to work harder to circulate the food. Everybody had glasses of wine, brandy, or cognac, and the alcohol seemed to be working its magic. Now, besides offering words, they rubbed Traveler's arm, smacked his rump lightly, ran his tail through their hand. One lizard even kissed Traveler on the lips. Their talk grew more perverse.

"... bend you over and spank that perfect ass..."

"... put you on all fours..."

"... cage the mighty beast... make you howl..."

Traveler got a brief respite when Lord Harlequin rang a silver bell and summoned his guests to the table. They took their seats, still raucous, as Traveler and the other servers began to bring out the first courses. The soup and appetizer smelled amazing. As the guests ate, Traveler topped off their glasses from an expansive liquor cabinet. He felt at ease now. He basked in their gaze, their lewd smiles. When he went to get a bottle of expensive single-malt, he bent over and let them take a good look. Someone wolf-whistled, and Lord Harlequin laughed merrily. Traveler spun and made a little bow.

Then a set of double doors banged open, and a small army of chefs wheeled out a large dolly.

"Ahhhh!" Lord Harlequin beamed. "Our main course!"

Traveler was momentarily forgotten. On the dolly sat an enormous platter, and on the platter lay a nude male elephant. He reclined with his arms behind his head and his legs butterflied. His short, stocky body was covered in food: strips of salmon, stuffed grape leaves, little arrangements of caviar and paté, anchovies, starfruit, melon balls wrapped in prosciutto, dates and figs. And morsels that Traveler didn't even recognize, all arranged artfully over the elephant's body. He'd become a work of art. Even his penis was lined with mounds of savory jelly.

"His name is Rowan," Lord Harlequin said, "and if he moves, I have promised to make him watch while I inflict inspired torments upon his elder brother. So feel free to tease him!"

The elephant blinked his deep blue eyes, obviously nervous, but stayed perfectly still as the chefs maneuvered his platter onto the table. The diners grabbed for their long-handled forks, eyes gleaming with more than one kind of hunger.

The following meal was almost ritualistic. They skewered and plucked food off Rowan, transferring directly into their mouths. Traveler watched in fascination. Rowan didn't move, even when they pinched his nipples, prodded his thighs and ribs with their forks, tickled his balls. His gray body trembled, but that was all. Traveler wondered if the young elephant was living his own greatest fantasy. To be a meal, or merely a medium for a meal?

One of the other servers, a female civet, handed Traveler a small glass of red liquor. "It's only gonna get lewder in here," she whispered. "This'll help."

"Are we allowed?" Traveler whispered back.

"I'm not. But I'm not the one who'll be up on that table next." She gave him a wry look.

Traveler drank the liquor. It burned his throat, sweet and smoky.

By the time the guests had mostly cleared Rowan's body of food, they'd entered a mild frenzy. Any moment, it seemed, someone might mount the table and try to mount the elephant. Lord Harlequin rang his bell again, and the chefs returned and carted Rowan away, to loud applause. Traveler briefly caught Rowan's eye in passing. One glance was enough to confirm that Rowan had loved every minute of this.

Alcohol flowed. Voices raised in wild laughter and jubilance. A chef beckoned Traveler into the anteroom, where they presented him with a cart laden with decadent bowls of trifle, each one overflowing with fruit and cream. He wheeled the dessert out and began to circle the table, but he didn't get far. The guests grabbed at the bowls. One man collected a spoonful of cream and then plopped it onto Traveler's chest. It ran down his fur. His mind buzzed pleasantly. Across the table, Lord Harlequin grinned, his painted face like a Joker card. He made a sign with his hand. Traveler understood.

He climbed up onto the table, striking an inviting pose on all fours. The guests roared. They demanded more. Traveler got up on his knees and flexed his arms and chest. They loved it. Their shouts ran together. He caught the occasional command. Show your ass. Grab your crotch. Turn this way. He obeyed each one. At some point, he found that his panties had ripped. He pulled them off, exposing his body more. They told him to pleasure himself. He stroked his sheath, displayed his erection. He spun about, pointing his dick at various guests. Their hands grasped it, stroked it. Cupped his balls. Pinched his nipples.

Then someone ordered him to cum.

Traveler's mind reeled in delight. Yes. He wanted to cum for these people like a good pup. He leaned back, bracing himself with one arm. The other hand stroked his dick, up and down, fingers digging in. Dollops of cream and syrup-drenched berries hit him from all directions. He'd become the dessert.

He wasn't drunk. No. Only one glass. He was high on pleasure, on excitement. He didn't want this to end. He pawed off harder, panting, smiling, raising his voice in escalating barks and howls of pleasure. A tamed beast. Muscle and beauty, and they owned it. They owned him. Yes. Yes.

He came. The explosion of semen painted the corset and ran over his crotch and thighs. So long, so long since he'd last gotten off. He fell back and lay, panting, near-mindless. Hands began to touch him, to grope him, but Lord Harlequin's voice rose, firmly forbidding more molestation. He cut through their booze-induced lust and they relented.

Things quieted down a bit. Traveler rested, half-listening to the sounds of the guests taking their leave. Bidding their host farewell, yawning, drifting away. Leaving only the clink of plates and silverware being cleared.

Lord Harlequin appeared, beaming down at Traveler. "Well, pup, you have exceeded all my expectations. Well done."

"Thank you, my lord," Traveler murmured. "Thank you."

"You need a shower."

"Yes, my lord." Traveler sat up slowly. "My lord, I... I..." He struggled for the words.

"Yes, sweetie?" Lord Harlequin asked gently.

"I can't say it," Traveler mumbled. "Something… something's happening to me. I want… I want…" He groaned.

Lord Harlequin kissed him on the lips. "Hush. Take a shower, drink some water, clear your head. I know what you're trying to say. Once you're recovered a bit, we'll talk more."

He knew. Traveler's heart leaped. And in that moment, suddenly, guiltily, he remembered Beck.

Where was Beck in all this?

* * *

A small, naked jerboa burst from the underbrush and skidded to a halt, panting. He stared at Beck and Lady Foxglove, eyes wide and giddy, cock bobbing. Then he let out a nervous giggle and kept running. Beck glimpsed pink marks striping his back and rump. He'd looked eighteen years old, barely.

"That'll be Lord Sade," sighed Lady Foxglove. "He likes the thrill of the hunt."

They'd been gardening, nothing more. Lady Foxglove had led Beck to a plot of, yes, foxgloves, pink and purple. She was transplanting a few, and made Beck stand by and hand her various tools. It actually felt nice, doing something simple and productive. They worked in silence while Beck wondered if he dared submit any of his numerous questions. Now the ice was broken.

"How many of you are there, lady?"

"Plenty," she said dryly. "We're an expansive dynasty, but you won't have seen us in *Forbes*. We're private."

"Except for CityScape, right? I mean… and tell me if I'm being rude… but you invented CityScape?"

"More or less. CityScape was originally a collaboration between two of my brothers and a cousin. A whim. It's grown quite a bit, hasn't it."

"I'll say, my lady." Beck flung his arms up. "This goes way beyond following clues."

Lady Foxglove laughed. "Oh, honey, none of this is CityScape. CityScape is the shell that keeps most of the players occupied. There are deeper levels. The people in black, who ferry you boys from place to place, they're all former CityScape players. They gained access to the next level, 'Chessmen'. Tidy, isn't it?" She rolled her eyes. "Their 'play' amounts to free servitude for us."

"Am I a Chessman?" Beck asked.

"No," she replied softly. "You and your brother, and that nice elephant of yours, are deeper still. The third level is 'Pantheon'. That's where things get kinky. Newcomers are passed from Lord to Lady to Lord, until they find a place where they can best submit and serve."

"But I wasn't a CityScape player. I just happened to find a clue. How come I got bumped to Pantheon?"

"Don't ask me," Lady Foxglove said. "I barely participate in all this. It's mostly for wilder types than I."

"So you don't, y'know... indulge?"

"Oh," she murmured, "I have my private games." She smiled, and her smile unsettled Beck. He suddenly remembered that foxgloves were poisonous.

"So..." He bit his lip. "Well... isn't it all kind of silly? The ritual of it. Messing with people's heads. What's the point? Just to make a bunch of rich idiots feel superior? No offense."

"None taken. I imagine that's part of it. But it's not just for us. Why did you come here, Beck? Why did you entrust your body, your freedom, to us?"

Before Beck could answer, another monkey strode from the bushes. This one was no older than twenty, in a gray suit, leather gloves, and shiny boots. He twirled a riding crop in his fingers. When he saw them, he paused, looking annoyed.

"Hello, Lord Sade," Lady Foxglove said politely.

"Yes, hello." His voice dripped arrogance. "Did you see a boy run by here?"

"A few minutes ago. He could be anywhere."

Lord Sade sneered. "Typical. I suppose I'll take that pup of yours, if you're not using him."

"Nobody's using me," Beck said.

Lord Sade flared his nostrils. "Impudent boy! You'll feel the sting of this crop, and more. Come here."

"No. I'm helping Lady Foxglove."

"You will do as ordered!"

"Really, boys," Lady Foxglove said. "My garden isn't for contests of machismo."

"Stay out of this," Lord Sade snapped.

Then he froze, as though realizing he'd made a huge mistake. Lady Foxglove stood and looked at him calmly, arms folded. Amazing, Beck thought, how someone so petite could radiate such terror.

"Stephen," she said. "You're being very rude to me. Very, very rude."

"I… I'm sorry, my lady," Lord Sade said, trying to maintain his facade. "I was simply frustrated. I'll leave you be."

Suddenly, Beck made up his mind. He was through with this place, with these crazy monkeys and their sexual games, their fake personas. He wanted to find Traveler and get out.

"It's okay, lady," he said. "I'll go with him."

Lady Foxglove raised her eyebrows. "Are you sure, honey? You won't like it much."

"We'll see," Beck said, staring down Lord Sade

She shrugged. "All right. Thank you for helping me. I hope you find what you're looking for."

An exit, Beck thought. *I'm looking for a fucking exit.* Lord Sade jerked his head impatiently, and Beck went with him.

They walked in silence, Lord Sade leading the way. The manor loomed overhead. They went up a set of stairs and through a door. As soon as they were inside, Lord Sade seized Beck's arm and raised his riding crop. "Let me show you what happens to pups who humiliate me!"

Beck grabbed the crop, yanked it away, and flung it down the hall. "I want to leave," he growled. "I want to leave with my brother. Whatever the fucking safeword is, I just said it."

"You don't get to decide anything!" Lord Sade snapped.

Beck laughed. "I'm supposed to be afraid of you, *Stephen*? You're not even old enough to drink. Your nickname is stupid. Where's Lord Atticus? I want to talk to an adult."

"Stop it!" Lord Sade cried. "You're breaking the rules!" He took a deep breath and lowered his voice a little. "We… dammit, we work so hard for you people. Giving you what you want."

"What I want? None of this was what I wanted. Maybe some guys like being chased around by a brat with a riding crop, but I…" He faltered. "This isn't my place. I can't put myself in the right role. Please. All I want is my brother, Traveler. And a door to the outside."

Lord Sade shook his head, glaring. "You asked for this. You don't get to change your mind."

"Then I'll find my own way out."

Beck whirled and stomped off down the corridor. He heard Lord Sade yelling for aid. He picked up his pace and ran, but he didn't get far. Footsteps pounded behind him. He glanced over his shoulder to see large men in black. Chessmen, playing their own game. They knew the manor and he didn't. They caught him and hauled him back to Lord Sade.

"This insolent whelp needs some time in the oubliette," the young monkey sneered.

Beck cursed, yelled, struggled. But they were stronger. They dragged him down many stairways, into dimmer and dimmer places underground. Finally, they reached a low-ceilinged stone passage lined with little wooden doors. Lord Sade had picked up a ring of keys somewhere, and he unlocked one door and swung it open. Beck's handlers tossed him into the room. The door slammed. At the last second, Beck heard Lord Sade say, "The safeword is 'Jupiter.'"

Beck flailed about in the pitch blackness. His limbs connected with stone—above, below, all sides. The cell was too small to stand up in, a tiny box, deep underground.

"No. No! Let me out! Fucking let me out!"

He screamed. Red lines of panic danced before his blind eyeballs. He clawed at the door. No sound came from the other side. They'd left him to rot. Starve. Suffocate.

No.

No. One thing made it through his panic. Safeword. There was a safeword.

This was still the game, all part of the game. Everything that happened was for someone's benefit. The cells around him held people who wanted to be here. To be deprived of light and senses. That was what the game did. Whatever you desired, to be locked up or bound, flogged, hunted like prey, dressed in leather or latex, even treated like scum.

And there was always, always, always a safeword.

"Jupiter," Beck said. Then he said it louder. "Jupiter. Jupiter. Jupiter!"

And the door opened. They let him out. A black-clad cow held his arms, almost tenderly, and led him from that place.

"Where's my brother?" Beck asked weakly. "Please. Where is he?"

The cow didn't answer. She took Beck back up to the warm, lighted places, to a small room with chairs and sofas, and a fire in the fireplace. She sat Beck down, held up a finger as if to say, "Wait a moment," and left.

Beck sat, feeling lonely and vulnerable in his underwear. After a few minutes more, a member of the family came in.

He looked a lot like Lord Atticus. He had the same height and build, similar clothing. But the friendly smile on his simian face didn't match.

"Hello, Beck," he said. "I'm sorry things didn't work out for you. But it's nice to meet you outside the digital realm."

"The..." Beck's brain put things together. "Lord Zephyr?"

"Yes. I must apologize for Lord Sade. He has a lot to learn."

"About what? What in all the fucks is this whole thing *for*?"

"Tricky question." Lord Zephyr chuckled. "It's for us. For you. For anyone who needs it. My brother, Atticus, and I both hold doctorates in psychology. When people come to us, through CityScape or, like you, through random chance, we profile you and try to determine what you need. Powerful businessmen need to spend time as a slave or pet, free of cares. Unhappy partners need something to spice up their relationship. A man might have some odd sexual fetish, buried and never realized, that'll tear him up if he doesn't live it in the flesh. We do all that."

"You did nothing for me," Beck said coldly.

Lord Zephyr sighed. "Mistakes happen, and I am truly sorry. But if it makes you feel better, we did a great deal for your brother. And isn't that why you came to us?"

"Traveler. Where is he? I want to see him!"

"Of course."

Lord Zephyr took Beck deep into the manor, and into a large white room with high ceilings. It seemed to be a place for relaxation... and recovery. Its occupants reclined on large sofas and napped on simple cots. Beck realized how tired he was. It had to be past six AM. So much had happened in one night.

Traveler sat on a sofa, nude, talking quietly to a young elephant. As Beck approached, the elephant moved away. Traveler saw Beck and smiled.

"You're a jerk, Beck," he said, eyes twinkling.

"Fuck, Trav, I'm sorry about all this. I thought it was gonna be so amazing. Want to get out of here?"

Traveler was quiet for a moment. Then he said, "I've decided to stay."

"You... what?" Beck blinked. "Stay?"

"Yeah. They don't make you stay... but they don't make you leave, either. I've talked to Lord Zephyr and some of the others. They want me."

Beck felt like the world was unmoored, twisting painfully. "But, but you can't just live here. You have a place, a job..."

"I can deal with all that. Beck, come on." Traveler stood and squeezed his twin's hand. "What's out there? For me? Nothing I care about but you and Mom. And it's not like I'll never see you guys again. I can leave here whenever. But I'm choosing to stay. To be their property."

"I don't understand," Beck mumbled.

"Beck, you remember Will? My old boyfriend?"

"Of course."

"We broke up because... one day he came home from work, and I was on the couch, naked. I'd gagged myself and handcuffed my arms behind my back. That was how I decided to show him what I really wanted. I hoped... I hoped he'd smile and undress and take me. Own me. But he didn't. That wasn't his thing at all. It was just awkward, and stupid, and when he left me, I didn't blame him. I was disgusted with myself, so I tried to ignore how much I wanted... this. All this." Traveler opened his arms wide. "I'm so happy you found it for me, Beck. I want to belong to them."

His eyes moved upwards. Beck followed his gaze. High up on one wall, figures moved behind a broad window, gazing down, observing their willing slaves. He saw Lord Atticus, Lord Sade, and others. One monkey was covered entirely in latex and a gas mask. Another wore scars and a grim scowl. A willowy female sported jodhpurs and bare breasts. They came in all shapes, sizes, and fetishes.

"Pantheon," Beck muttered. "I get it." He turned back to his brother. "You really want this."

"More than anything."

Beck gulped. He had to say it, the selfish thing. The thing that ached. "Trav. I... I've been looking out for you. I can't be happy if you're not. But... what do I do without you? You're my twin. My other half. Out there, without you..." His eyes dropped.

Traveler hugged him tight. "Beck. I love you. I know how you feel. But if you want to be happy, to be Beck, you should let me go." He chuckled softly. "It's okay to."

Beck didn't think he agreed. But Traveler was so happy, so at peace. All Beck could do was nod and try to smile, and then leave. Before he thought of more arguments.

Lord Zephyr gave Beck a shirt and pants, then walked him to the front door of the manor. A car waited to take him home. Before he got in, Lord Zephyr handed him a card with the red sigil of CityScape.

"Whenever you want to come back, use this URL. We'll send someone to fetch you. Once you've been in Pantheon, you're always welcome."

"You better not corrupt my brother too badly," Beck said. "I don't want to find out that he's been teleported into some deeper level of the game."

Lord Zephyr chuckled. "Pantheon is the deepest level… so far. But we've got some ideas."

"Well, thanks, but leave me out of it. I'm glad Traveler found what he needed. But I didn't."

"Are you sure?" Lord Zephyr asked softly. With those words, he turned and vanished back into his strange, erotic world.

*　*　*

A week later, snow fell with force. Beck sat on a bench in his favorite park, observing three people who were trying to measure the dimensions of the central, pyramidal war monument. They kept slipping all over the place. Playing CityScape, of course. Searching for clues toward the mysterious, intangible goal.

Beck felt empty, hollow. He knew he needed to get back to his blog, his articles, his friends. Life. But Traveler was gone. He was back in that manor, eagerly serving and being served by his new masters, happy and fulfilled. And what did Beck have now?

He needed to be glad for his twin. It was selfish not to be. But didn't he have the right to be selfish? Pantheon had given everything to Traveler and taken everything from Beck, or so it felt.

He stood and left the park. The Christmas shopping season had begun. People swirled by, swathed in their coats. Their scarves and mufflers turned them as faceless as Beck felt. He'd go home, stare at his computer screen, write nothing, force himself to eat and sleep. This wasn't living.

The snow fell heavier. Beck started down the sidewalk, numbly avoiding the other pedestrians. He almost bumped into a large, shuffling person in a black coat. Stumbling slightly, Beck paused. He glanced back at the slump-shouldered, melancholy figure, then sighed and kept walking. So many sad people in the city. Guess he would be one of them forever now. They'd look at him and know he'd lost something, or someone...

Wait.

Beck turned again, slowly, not daring to breathe. The large, sad, shuffling figure was gone in the snow.

Beck began to walk. Then to run. Snowflakes flew everywhere, blinding him, erasing the world. But he felt warmth, warmth in his bones, his toes, like the warmth of a garden where flowers bloomed and snow fell, both at once. The one place in that damn game where he'd been happy. Because he hadn't been alone.

His paws pounded the snow. Up ahead, the sad figure rematerialized. Beck flung himself forward before the snow could swallow everything up again. He reached out, words stuck behind his open lips. He saw a large, limp hand and took it in his own, squeezed it desperately tight, and the figure turned, and the warmth exploded outward as Beck looked up into a pair of startled, stormy eyes.

TEAMWORK

Tym Greene

Barry Ecklin sat in his office, dreaming of black rubber. He leaned back in his executive desk chair, feeling the counterplay of springs and mesh accepting his bulk. "Tell me again," he sighed, massaging the top of his beak, "what the trouble is."

His new secretary, Miranda, glanced nervously at her folder, then handed the papers to him with a grimace. Even in this day and age, paper was still indispensable.

The peregrine falcon groaned; he'd seen all this before. At first glance, it seemed like only the time-stamp on the data had changed. It was the same underperforming department with the same low results and the same at-issue employees. He sat forward, resting his elbows on the cultured mahogany of his desk, golden predatory eyes staring directly at the doe.

"The t-team leaders, sir. They blame Johnson. They say he's disrespectful and unmotivated…"

Barry resisted the sudden impulse to fire them all. This sort of thing ought to have been handled several levels down, closer to the source of the issue. "Look, Miranda, I'm leaving soon for my vacation. I will be completely unreachable for the next week. The building could be on fire, and I wouldn't find out about it until I get back on the twenty-sixth. So you tell those team managers that they have until then to resolve the problem." He glanced up at the clock and smiled. "And now it's time for me to leave."

He stood, picked up his valise, and with his coat draped over his arm headed for the elevators. Executive parking was right by the main entrance, and though he usually parked in the farthest corner of the lot, today he had neither the time nor patience for a long, healthy walk. He wouldn't need the exercise in the coming days anyway. He took off his jacket and placed it in the back with his luggage: one small bag with his toiletries and a bottle of thick lube.

Barry activated the car's autopilot—as he usually did when in the city—and sang along with the radio's oldies station: "I want your drama, the touch of your hand. I want your leather-studded kiss in the sand..." He smiled: that had lately been one of his favorite lines.

Soon the bustling city streets thinned to a light suburb. A thumb-claw pressed to the console and toggled off the autopilot as the steering yoke rose obediently to meet his touch. This was the start of the ritual.

The falcon shut off his satellite radio as the last master-planned subdivision rolled by, opening the window to let air ruffle through his feathers.

"Ahh..." He could smell it now. Dirt. Dirt and mud and trees and fertilizer. There was a crispness in the rushing wind, too. He could taste the tang of first-rain-on-asphalt, and it made him happy.

It must have rained recently.

As he pulled off the main road he reminded himself, as he always tried to do, that he had a choice. He could turn around right then, head home, and use his week's vacation some other way.

He kept driving.

Struck by a sudden similarity, he realized that this must be the way some of his employees felt; the illusion of a choice. Barry could remember being young and hungry and afraid, taunted by the idea of just walking out, of quitting what seemed to be a dead-end job, and knowing at the same time that he couldn't. Knowing that he had to stay and be responsible.

"I *am* responsible," he said out loud, lightly pounding the armrest, keeping his talons away from the leather. "I've earned this, and Zeb is counting on me." Taking a deep breath, he calmed himself, scaled palms flat against the steering yoke.

It's the office, he thought. *I don't trust them to pull their own weight.* He wanted to dig out his phone, connect to the car's uplink back to the office, and get back in control again. On any other trip he might have. Just as his will was flagging, however, he pulled up to the gate.

The rusted iron was devoid of any name or symbol, save the faded "595" stenciled on the plastic mail bin. Feeling slightly giddy and slightly relieved, he began the usual dance: out of car, open gate, pull car forward, close gate, back in car. As he closed the door he could smell the mud he'd tracked onto the floormats.

He drove slowly through the farm, toward the main structure hunkered in the middle of the property. The farmhouse and barn were connected by a covered walkway, a barrier he had never crossed and likely never would. Beside the house was a carport, but next to the antique green jeep, in the spot where Barry himself normally parked, was another car. It was a new BMW. As he parked next to it, he could see mud splatters drying on the paint.

Snorting, Barry got out of his own car. "That's no way to treat a machine," he grumbled as he stripped down in the crisp air. Folding his clothes, he placed them squarely in the middle of the driver's seat. He paused for a moment, enjoying the feel of air on his nethers, stretching after the long drive. A few gentle touches got him respectably hard. Then, with the toiletries bag in one hand and lube and car keys in the other, Barry Ecklin trotted out from under the carport. Zeb was waiting for him.

The grey-muzzled Clydesdale stood on his house's broad porch, thumbs tucked behind the straps of his overalls. The falcon stopped at the foot of the steps, looking up at Zebediah.

"Hello Ecks," he drawled, the rich soft timbre of his voice setting Barry's feathers on end. The falcon nickered softly in reply, standing poised, like a showhorse.

"Good boy. We got plenty of fields to do, but not today." Zeb clicked his tongue, making the well-trained bird come to attention. They walked in tandem to the barn, Barry staring at the horse's rump swaying before him with each easy step.

His usual stall awaited him, door open, with fresh hay on the floor and tack hanging from nails in the wall. Barry—already thinking of himself as "Ecks" now—handed over the few items he held. The draft horse placed them on a shelf outside the stall, where previous generations of drafters had displayed trophies and ribbons. This was just another part of the ceremony for him; anyone walking by could take his keys. No one would.

His trust in Zeb was unshakable, forged over years of this shared ritual, as regular as the seasons. Ecks stood, hands curled before his chest, waiting. As he stood there, he thought he heard something— breathing perhaps—but before he could think about it further, the sound of clinking metal overwhelmed all else. The last stage of his transformation was at hand...*at hoof*, he thought wryly, cock throbbing down below.

Rubber and plastic blackness first enclosed his left hand, then his right. Buckles tightened as fingers found their well-worn indentations. The weight pulled at his wrists, forcing him to tuck them up against the feathers of his chest.

Zeb saw this and chuckled. "You've missed it, eh Ecks?"

The falcon tossed his head and snorted. Just as some people wore fake paws to immobilize their hands when playing at being canines, and others strapped fake wings over their arms, the hoof-gloves were an aspect of the mimicry not based in reality. Of course horses had hands, but the addition of hoof-gloves did wonders for one's mentality.

"I thought so. Now hold still and let me shoe you." The horse tapped Ecks' left knee and the leg lifted, muscles bulging under bright yellow scales. Another tap on the knee a minute later and he planted a broad hoof-boot in the stall's hay. Once his talons were seated in the other boot as well, he stood, finding his balance. A rough hand stroked along his back.

The hoof-boots shifted his posture, making him stick his rump out to counterbalance. The hand continued moving back, thick blunt nails raking through downy feathers, finding his hole. Barry Ecklin had several horse-shaped toys back home at his loft. Just the thought of them made Ecks' tail lift a little higher, giving Zeb easy access.

The pre-lubed horsetail buttplug popped in easily, causing Ecks to let out a very un-equine *"kree!"* Zeb fiddled around with the plug's settings, making it swell up to fill his hole, warming and vibrating gently. Ecks shuddered, stamping a hoof at the sheer pleasure of it; his cock fully emerging and dripping a slow stream of precum. He panted from the anticipation, not certain what was to come next.

Every visit was different depending on the season, how early Barry could get out to the farm, and what mood Zebediah was in. Ecks savored the strength in the older man's body, his passion and need. Sometimes they had gotten down to business right away, other times the falcon had been tethered to a fence post or left in his stall. With a heavy thud that broke his reverie, a thick padded collar dropped around his shoulders.

Tack jingled as a bridle and blinders were wrapped around his head, and suddenly he felt as though he had blinders *in* his head too, blocking off thoughts beyond what was directly before him. The rubber bit slipped into his beak, tasting like dried familiarity. Straps were tightened and adjusted to better fit Ecks' body; Barry had been working out more lately and had reaped the results of his usual dedication and focus. Ever since that visit when Zeb had said in an offhanded way that Ecks might make a good drafter, the falcon had been trying to build up bulk. A small part of himself, peeking around the mental blinders, wanted the Clydesdale to praise him, to comment on the improved physique. He tried to push that thought back; praise didn't matter.

With a pat to the ersatz horse's flank, Zeb tugged the reins and led him out to the main part of the barn. There was a buggy, waiting in the middle of the packed-dirt floor. Waiting for two horses, judging by the single pole sticking out from the front. With skill born of long years of practice, Zeb hitched Ecks to the left side of the carriage.

When Zeb left, Ecks wondered for a split second if the Clydesdale was going to harness himself up as well. But it was two pairs of hooves that returned, moments later, and Ecks remembered the sound he had heard from the stall next to his. Well-trained, he did not look over as the tack was pulled and hitched, connecting the stranger to him and the buggy.

Zebediah appeared before him, stroking his beak above the nose-strap. "This is Cherry, Ecks. She's on loan to me from a friend." That likely meant this new "horse" was unable to go to her usual farm due to a scheduling conflict, Barry thought from deep inside Ecks. There were, after all, other farms; remnants of a past era when sweat and muscle were needed, instead of GPS and bio-diesel. Barry would never have gone to another one, though, if he could help it, and Ecks couldn't have imagined hands other than Zeb's holding his reins.

"Cherry," Zeb continued, moving out from between the falcon's blinders, "this is Ecks. He's been working my farm for almost a decade now. You trust him, ya hear? Follow his lead." A heavy snort answered his admonition, along with the tug and rattle of harness that suggested Cherry was nodding. Wood creaked behind them and with a flick of the reins and a click of his tongue, Zeb coaxed his two drafters into an easy trot.

Before too long, Ecks realized where they were going. Years ago, back when he was new to the scene, Zeb had used him as merely a light cart horse. They had gone this way many times, so he barely needed the gentle tug of reins to guide him along the trail circling the main fields.

It was easy going, though he couldn't tell if that was due to his recent successes in the gym or to Cherry's presence beside him. From the way the other breathing sounded, and the dense flanks that brushed against his with each step, she must have a powerlifter's build. Then they rounded a stand of rangy pine trees and stopped in their tracks.

Arrayed before the trio was the vast Central Coast panorama; rolling tawny hills, sprinkled with pine and oak, flowing down to the distant ocean, and all of it dyed purple and orange by the setting sun.

"Oh, wow," murmured the voice to his right, the contrabass rumble hindered by a thick rubber bit.

Farmer Zeb, however, was having none of it. "Ey," he said sharply, flicking the reins, "gee-up, there." He knew, and Ecks knew—and apparently Cherry did not—that drafters did not talk. The rest of the ride was an uneasy silence. Ecks waited as Zeb unhitched Cherry, back at the barn, and tried to quell his anxiety.

The week is ruined kept repeating in the back of his mind. He wondered, with an ill humor, if this was how only children felt on being informed that mommy was expecting. *He'll spend the whole time with that dumb mare,* he thought, champing his bit in consternation, shifting from hoof to hoof. *And I'll have spent all that money on a wasted week. Why couldn't Zeb have told me? Maybe I should have gone to Aruba instead.* But he knew he was being silly even while he fretted.

His tongue found a worn spot on his bit and he rubbed it, letting his horse-mind take control once more. The money didn't *really* matter, he knew, and if he had gone to Aruba, he would have missed this. In his fancy loft's fancy bed he had dreamt of the feeling of tack and bit and blinders, the weight of collar and hooves, and the reward of a day's hard labor in the fields. He clenched around his plug, waking his cock up just a little. That's why he had no gear at home; these four weeks out of the year had to stay special. Sacred.

By the time Zeb returned to unhitch him and lead him back to his stall, Ecks once more felt like the drafter he was. With steady hands, the farmer removed all of the falcon's gear, apart from the hoof-boots. Then he patted his beak and shut the stall door, switching out the main lights as he went. Ecks used the composting toilet tucked into the corner of his stall, then curled up on the hay. He drifted to sleep, comfortable as any bird in a nest, listening to the sounds of Cherry settling down on the other side of the wood paneling.

* * *

The next morning Ecks woke at dawn, as he always did on Zeb's farm. Stretching, he brushed hay from his feathers, unable to resist a little preening. From the sound of it Cherry was taking her time in waking up. All too soon, however, the quiet of the barn was broken.

"Good morning," came a rather bovine yawn from the next stall. Established custom held that draft horses spoke only in their stalls or in emergencies. Ecks could imagine Zeb's father, and mother, and grandfather, and on down the line, all standing silent in the fields or murmuring softly in the barn that still smelled faintly of their sweat and hair. There was no need to fill the air with idle chatter.

Their traditionally monk-like life of hard work and quiet contemplation held appeal for many, Barry Ecklin included. The feel of the tack on his muscles, the hooves encasing his talons, even the odor of earth and hay, all drove him to silence. He had expected nothing less from this trip.

In reply, he produced with practiced ease a very equine snort. His neighbor did not take the hint.

"Did you sleep well?" Cherry said, with a very un-ladylike grunt, as though stiff from a night on the ground. Ecks tried to ignore the invasion of his sanctuary, and instead clopped over to the trough in the main area of the barn, against the far wall. He dipped his beak into the dawn-cold water and splashed around, further waking himself.

He did not hear the hoofsteps as the barn's other occupant approached him. The hand on his back made him spin around, nearly losing his balance when his hoof-boot slipped in a muddy puddle. The arms that caught him were strong.

Beak and snout faced one another as Ecks looked up at Cherry.

"You're male," Ecks stated with flatness, despite his double-disorientation. Still shaken from nearly cracking his skull on the floor, he let his eyes roam down the bull's thickset chest, his black hide mussed and dull from a restless night, and glanced further southward. He looked up, noticing that the bull had been dehorned—though polling was currently in vogue and therefore no obvious clue to the bull's proclivities.

Standing once more, he turned to the bull. "I must have misheard: I thought Zebediah had called you 'her.'"

"He did."

"I…see," the peregrine falcon said hesitantly, stepping back to give the bull access to the trough. Hanging back, he watched the heavy rump, the powerful thighs occasionally allowing a brief glance of pendulous sac. Then he saw the brand.

It was still slightly pink—relatively new, Ecks surmised—but still stood out against Cherry's black hide nonetheless. The mark was a stylized C, with what looked to be a stem and leaves growing out of the top. In short, a cherry of seared flesh. Taken aback, Ecks returned to his stall in silence to await Zeb and the start of the day.

They plowed that day. Even with two strong bodies pulling, the trio barely finished the acre by sunset. Ecks was drenched, not from sweat like Cherry, but from the water Zeb kept spraying on him to keep the falcon from overheating. Panting, he shook himself, enjoying the apparent lightness of unyoked shoulders. He had toiled in stoic silence, letting their labors overwhelm any thoughts: work, money, and the enigma that was Cherry.

But now they had finished their feedbags, their hoof-gloves had been removed to allow some freedom, and Zeb was eating his own dinner in the farmhouse. Now they were free to talk.

"You've been ignoring me all day," Cherry said, looking up from where he sat on a hay bale, tightening the straps of his boots. Ecks noted that they fit tightly around the bull's hooves, custom made, turning his cloven hoof into a fair simulation of a horse's single digit. From the look of the hand-tooled brass and thick, polished rubber, they must have been very expensive.

Ecks remained silent, stalling for time and making a show of adjusting his own gear. Tucking errant feathers back under the chest strap. Before he could say anything, however, there was a rattle as the barn's side door opened.

Wearing the same worn overalls he'd had on all day, Zeb had left his dingy white shirt behind him in the farmhouse. Despite his age, a lifetime of plow work had left the draft horse with a thick solidness that Ecks had always found appealing. He wanted to run his fingers over that chestnut hide, feel the heat and shift of the muscles beneath. That was not ordinarily a part of these trips, however. Many times he had gone the whole week without any relief. It was, he often reflected, hard to jack off with hooves for hands. Once, just once, Zeb had milked him, just as might be done with any breeding stallion unwilling to form emotional attachments. Just thinking about the firmness of those fingers gripping him, the rubber of the collection tube, the efficient manner of the farmer, all conspired to make the falcon erect and breathless.

Zeb patted Ecks' flank. "Looks like you're taking an interest in our new mare, eh boy?" Fingers gripped Ecks' slender shaft. Beak slack, he could only pant silently. He wanted to respond, to tell the farmer that he wished the interloper would just leave. But the introspective silence of a draft horse was one of the things he most prized about his quarterly vacations, so he kept quiet. The hand on his cock felt too good.

"Cherry, girl, you still want this?" Zeb asked the bull without a break in his strokes. Trying to stand motionless, to resist the urge to hump into that hand, Ecks saw the black, hornless head nod. "Go on then, gee-up."

Leaping to booted hooves, the bull trotted back to her stall. Zeb, meanwhile, left off his manhandling and turned to a cabinet. He returned and, before the falcon could move, swiped a finger across Ecks' beak. Thick pungent gel dripped into his nostrils.

He blinked. His sharp surprised intake of breath had pulled the substance in, setting off fireworks behind his eyes. It smelled like him, of course, but utterly female. It smelled like sex and eggs and chicks, of downy feathers and smooth glossy scales and…hay? Hay and horse sweat and winking black velvet holes. There was even a hint of the scent that lingered around Ecks' own shaft from the hand that had been there only moments before.

Zeb stood close, once more caressing the falcon's shaft. Ecks felt a cold breath of wind as the gel on the horse's fingers evaporated onto his cock's taut skin, chemicals flooding into his blood. He gasped, and somehow stayed still, planted on his hooves.

"Pheromones," the farmer said. "Special blend," he added with a wink and a squeeze. His own lip was starting to curl, flehmening, and Ecks thought he glimpsed a pulsing in the front of those overalls.

Is this it? Is he going to—his thought was interrupted by a sharp tug at his groin. Docilely, he let himself be led to his stall. Bit and blinders were strapped on, as were the heavy hoof-gloves. In his state of pheromonally-induced arousal, the tightening of buckles and tug of rubber felt even more erotic than Zeb's hand had. Then that hand returned to his shaft, slickening it. A tug on his bridle and he clopped out of his stall…and into Cherry's.

They were greeted with a singular sight; two ebony globes dangling between meaty thighs and beneath a pulsing hole and swishing tail. Ecks watched them lift and bounce, their cords visible behind thin smooth skin. Cherry was straddling a blanket-draped hay bale, four rubber horse hooves planted on the barn floor. Zeb stepped forward, running a hand along the curved black back.

"You ready, girl?" A nod. "Good. I've got your stud ready for you." He turned to the falcon, for whom the visual fireworks had faded to a glowing white aura around most objects. "You've still got work to do, Ecks. This mare needs breeding."

After that, there was no more talking. Zeb bent forward, with one hand pulling the falcon's bridle, coaxing him, and with the other guiding his tip towards the waiting, glistening hole. It slid in easily, the slender length spreading Cherry open with ease.

Ecks took a deep breath at the sensation of hot bovine engulfing him and pulled in another lungful of concentrated blended musk. At that moment, Barry Ecklin faded from existence. Taking his place was Ecks, the Clydesdale. It was horsehide, not feathers, that clad his flanks. Real hooves pawed the floor as rubber harnesses creaked and stretched across his powerful muscles.

What and who he was mounting no longer mattered to Ecks. Cherry needed breeding and he was going to make sure she got what she needed. He bent forward, nuzzling her broad, strong neck. He could taste the sweat and dust on her. Male sweat. Bull sweat.

His vision flickered, his worldview momentarily shifting, before the pheromone cocktail once more asserted its own reality. Glancing to one side, Ecks could see another stallion, leaning against the stall partition.

Zeb had shucked his overalls, allowing them to puddle around his hooves. The dusky grey sheath had already begun to unfurl as Ecks watched. Three horses in a barn, enjoying one another. Ecks half wished the other horse would come closer, close enough for him to reach out and touch the farmer's body, stroke the well-honed muscles as they shifted and pulsed. He wanted to share in the moment, but that would distract him from his mare.

Ecks hooked one hoof around a strap of Cherry's harness, wedging it in between rubber and hide. With the other he caressed her broad flank. The eponymous brand caught lightly on the tip of his horseshoe; smooth, hard, solid amid the fat and muscle, and he let it rest there, anchored for the moment. He needed those anchors of rubber and skin, as the rest of his being seemed focused solely on his cock.

Cherry was tight but flexed and gripped around him masterfully, her shoulders and back rippling with the effort of bracing against the stallion's thrusts. She moaned, a deep lowing sound that only spurred Ecks to further depths. His whole length pistoned through her now, and he had to spread his own hooves wider in the straw and dirt of the floor. He could imagine how she felt, the hay bale unyielding on her belly, his weight atop her.

He ducked his head again, biting her shoulder, letting his hooves slip to either side of her hips. No longer rational, he had allowed his hindbrain to take control as he envisioned foam beginning to fleck his hide, his balls starting to tense. This mare was his mate, his to pleasure, his to breed. She bucked beneath him, moaning frantically now, her deep voice rumbling his core. He plunged deeper, his sheath and belly tucked up under her tail, his shaft rigid, pulsing.

A droplet of moisture touched his leg and he glanced up, eyes wild. Zeb had shot one thick rope of cum clear across the stall, a line of white in the straw pointing straight at him. Even as he watched, the old farmer came again. The third spurt barely cleared the pile of denim below.

Meanwhile, Cherry had stopped bucking and was now panting and blowing. The occasional shudder sent ripples across her broad back and spasms fluttering around Ecks' shaft. He was so close. He dropped his head one last time, biting onto his mare's harness. He screwed his eyes shut and inhaled deeply, scenting not only the pheromones drying on his snout but also Zeb's fresh musk. There was also the taste of bull, but Ecks was too far gone to even notice.

He came, letting out a very un-equine creel, his jaw releasing its grip on Cherry's harness. Two hard thrusts were all it took to finish, pumping the last of his seed into her, and then he collapsed across her back. The three stayed that way for a few minutes, Zeb slumped against the wall, Cherry easily bearing Ecks' weight atop her on the bale.

After a few moments, he was able to blink the stars from his vision. The farmer had already stepped out of the overalls and was gathering up a few rags. Ecks propped himself up, the pressure from his hoofed hands making Cherry moan again. Once more, the only horse in the barn was Zeb.

"That," the falcon said hesitantly, still loathe to break his habitual silence, "was some trick."

Zeb bent, pulling Ecks' shaft out of the bull and giving it a wipe-down before tending to Cherry's hole. "Well, you needed to let go," was all he said by way of explanation before giving both men rump pats and leaving the stall with his overalls draped across his arm. The falcon watched him go, remaining there until Cherry started to squirm, bringing him back to the present.

He leaped back and reached out with one hoofed-hand to offer assistance. Cherry waved it away and pushed up from the blanketed hay bale, revealing a large puddle of cum on the floor.

"So, are you going to talk to me now?" he asked. "Or do I need to borrow some of Zeb's little trick?"

Ecks felt his tail feathers draw together, his tail and beak dipping in a blush. He *had* been unfair and quick to judge. The bull stood there, arms crossed over a chest still spangled with strands of hay. "No, you're right. We're here for...fantasy." *There, I said it.* He tried not to worry about ruining the magic of the week with his declaration, as though speaking the word could make it all unravel. "So if you want to be treated like a mare, who am I to deny you that?" He walked back towards his own stall, trying to hide a shudder of remembered pleasure. "You make a pretty good mare," he admitted.

With the lingering taste of combined falcon, horse, and bull phero-mones slowly fading from his senses, he bedded down in his stall, too exhausted to even think about the days to come. It was nothing he needed to worry about. Zeb would take care of everything.

INTERCHANGEABLE PARTS

George Squares

The monolithic stadium curled under the city skyline, pale-stoned with colosseum arches. Instead of natural light shining through the gaps, advert upon advert for chips and drinks and cellular phones blinked hotter than the stars above, drowning them out in the deluge of light pollution. The rat stood huddled in a middle section of the colosseum that had a cold, blue-brown hand railing instead of seating. There were too many bodies and tails and talkative twits to keep track of in the muddled mess of an audience, even with all the cameras everywhere, scuttling across the rails like tripod viruses with bulging lenses for capsids. For once the cameras were focused on the field, more interested in the football game than surveilling the citizens. He didn't want to wait for the field goal kicks. Dent just wanted the results of the game and get out of here.

Dent chuckled to himself, shivering, wondering whether or not he could flip off the camera without anybody taking notice. This city had to have more cameras than eyes. Could they really be watching at all when there was too much to see? The thought was fun but thoroughly stupid. Even if some folks got a laugh out of public spectacle, he didn't want to be a prick to some poor wage-slave on security. He was more considerate than that, really. Regardless, the fantasy was a more amusing bet than the one he had taken from the bookie. Dent liked crowds because they were one of the few places he didn't stand out. It didn't matter that the rat didn't particularly like watching the football game starting on the field below.

Icy wind bit at the rat's disk-shaped ears like angry gnats, and the chill snaked past the holes of the piebald patches sewn onto his old hoodie. The temperature read 20 degrees Fahrenheit on Dent's phone. His digits were warmly cupped together.

The rat clutched a ticket in his paw, which he ought to be holding tighter, considering the entirety of his rent money wound up in the coarse construction paper, but the numbness that started from the tip of his twitchy fingers ran through his arm into the socket of his shoulder.

He peeped at the field below, squinting. The crowded rumble of spectators carried through the cold air, cacophonous and indiscernible, but high in spirit. Light refracted off of the sides of skyscrapers, steel-blue, looking like icebergs or the ships they had sunk, nose-up.

Dent turned up his collar, enveloping his neck in the soft cotton, and he hid his oblong nose in the cloth of his shirt. Wracked with cold, his body gave an involuntary shiver, nearly shaking free the knitted cozy keeping his naked tail warm. The exposed slip of his pink tail set him shivering, and it reflexively hit the arm of a dog whose drink was almost knocked out of his hand.

"Watch it, sewer sucker," said a grizzled beagle in black who glared down at him. The dog's free fist clenched.

"Sorry," he stammered, not particularly sorry, but he resolved to curl his tail around himself, holding it tight as it shook. He had been called worse things by dogs before. Once, Dent had applied to an accounting position at a local firm. The Pomeranian conducting the interview had told him they didn't need any janitors. When Dent had reminded her that he was qualified, and had a degree in accounting, he was met with an icy "I know." That felt meaner than any insult could feel.

"Dent!" He heard the reedy voice of Bircham, another rat, call out from behind. "Goddamn it Dent, is that you?"

He had been unlucky plenty enough, but had never been so unlucky as to run into his landlord a few hours before he could pay off his ticket. The money was technically already overdue, but he could pay it in full if he just had more time—he was certain the new kicker would make two field goals. A man on an intercom stifled the noise of the stadium with a bold and choppy voice. Dent retreated further into the crowd, his heart struggling to keep steady beat. Panic's first kick of adrenaline had set in. His thin lips pulled into a grimace while he scampered through the rows of standing people.

Maybe his situation was shit, sure, but at least his life was interesting. If a rat was good at anything, it was making money. Bircham's cries followed him as Dent escaped, happy for once that he was small. "Get back here! Un-fucking believable, you're doing it again!" Rent would put him back 700, but a game would put him 1400 ahead. He'd won plenty before, so he was sure this week would pay out. The flight fired him up, warming Dent with his own body heat. God, he felt fresh.

The fanfare roared like a cresting wave, breaking into a discordant rumble as Dent squeezed the metal hand railing and hurdled feet-first past another row of people. Looking back for the other rat's befuddled face, Dent saw he wasn't followed. His bated breaths formed smoke signals, causing him to cover his mouth with his cold paws. They smelled like loose change. Dent rounded on the field, scuttling between a wolf and a tiger, face smushing against a fuzzy arm that peppered his nose when he tried to get a better look. The tiger looked down, scoffing; it prompted an embarrassed apology from the rat.

The players appeared on the field, flickering into position. Dent thought he had read somewhere a long time ago that the football players used to be real, living people before the sport was banned due to too many players developing brain trauma in their fifties. The star players were now the opposing coaches, who *were* real, and who still designed their own stratagems to pit against one another.

A player's main stats were set from the beginning of a season, and players lasted two seasons before they were deleted. Popular players could return as mascots in the hall of fame to interact with children, immortalized and beloved. Physical health, field conditions and developing skill were still factors—random stats put into the machine's algorithm. This close, Dent could see sweat rolled off the player's noses, as if they were expending energy, which looked real until you noticed all the players had the same sweat patterns in identical locations on their faces. The golden eye of the rat punter Dent had placed his bet on even blinked.

A group of three husky puppies wagged their tails, chattering and pointing at the players. They ate popcorn from colorful cardboard boxes. One snapped pictures of the characters, his finger pushing down madly on a camera phone. "Think I can turn these into football cards, mommy? We don't even need to buy the stupid things. They're just pictures on paper and I took these myself!" Dent liked that child the best, and he caught himself smiling.

Impatiently, Dent hopped from foot to foot, mulling over his wager's odds in his head again. After performing two seasons, the home team's punter was replaced. The new character, the rat, had the name James Feldspar. He had white fur, broad shoulders and a daring expression. Dent thought the character was very handsome for a rat, something a few had said about himself, too, which he supposed was a compliment.

All this punter would have to do was make two field goals and Dent would be paid back, two-fold. In the first quarter, the first kick had been made by the home team. James didn't *seem* bad (his accuracy rating, at least) although it was still too early to tell. He made his first goal from twenty-five yards, which seemed very good.

By the third quarter, James had another attempt from thirty yards. It missed, leaving Dent with a dull, uncomfortable sensation in the pit of his stomach. Could have been that the wind factor had a bizarre calculation. Could have been an unlucky roll from the punter's random number generator.

He had another chance in the final quarter. James made it from 49 yards. It wasn't a record, but it likely affirmed this player was good considering the probability of him making the goal. Dent smoothed down the fluff on his neck, peeling away from the noise of the crowd and the cold, a grin screwing up his exasperated face.

* * *

The Doberman bookie took a hard look at him. "Sorry kid. Two kicks from at least thirty-five yards."

"That's not right," he repeated, irritation edging into his tone. "There's no yard limit on the ticket. Two field goals. Double the input. I won my bet, and I'm due 1400. The bet's on my ticket, too."

The Doberman took the ticket from his hands, held it up, and nodded. "It's legitimate, sure, but the yard limit's stated on the board before you buy the ticket. Always has been. Haven't you gambled here before?"

"Listen buddy. I know for a fact that an implicit limit has never been the case—"

"—sorry, boy, but there's not much I can do for you but give you a good sulk. I've about thirty sob stories to run through before the day's over." The Doberman looked over his shoulder, the same nervous expression reflected in his own as his eyes met what had to be an impatient line of people behind him.

Dent slammed his paw on the counter. "Hey—I'm fine with losing. Hell, I wouldn't have put this kind of money down if I didn't think the terms were so ambiguous. Two thirty-five yarders is hard probability for a new kicker with unseen stats. But this just isn't an honest loss."

"Sorry," repeated the bookie, a bit irate. "But you did lose. Ain't my fault if you're unfamiliar with procedures and fine print and all—"

"I have the fine print," he spat, taking the ticket back with trembling paws and placing it on the counter. "That was rent money and I'm out 500 because you're a bunch of damned crooks."

"Nothing illegal about reading comprehension," sneered the Doberman. He turned the ticket over and pointed out a thin line of text at the bottom. Dent sounded it out slowly in his head, and then his ears burned bright red, feeling equal parts a victim and an asshole.

"I'm sorry," squeaked Dent.

"Look." The Doberman's voice softened. "If you're that strapped for cash, you could make 500 easy with a walk down to Hard Street."

Dent stammered a bit. "I need seven hundred."

"You can make that too! It's just... going to be a little bit crazier than the usual."

"The usual, huh?" He had performed before. Prostitution wasn't the right word, because prostitution was illegal in this country. But Hard Street was the sex-industry's response. Performers had to sign a waiver for onlookers to give them commands. They were paid by the hour, and could be granted a tip, too. There was no actual sex, supposedly implemented for safety regulations, but the workers knew that the rules could be bent. Sometimes the injuries were permanent.

"Well, you just look the type. You are a rat, after all." The Doberman sized him up, tipping his nose and scanning him over with his eyes. He lowered his voice to a rumble. "Rats are dirty. You can play that up and probably make a lot extra."

Feeling both embarrassed and harassed, he gave the dog the middle finger and ran away from the line before any strangers could laugh or yell at him today. The Doberman just shook his head, saying "next."

* * *

Dent sat in his apartment alone, grumbling as he looked through temp job listings on his phone. The rumbling bass of electronica vibrated against his thin walls often, so he had to wear headphones to drown out the noise. They were the nicest birthday gift he'd received. His phone was good too. It had lasted four years, and he could still use it as a hand-held computer. There wasn't much space for a computer, considering he had only two rooms, and much of the area was taken up by a wardrobe and a sink. He shared a bathroom and a kitchen with the other floor tenants, who weren't always considerate or tidy.

Would things have been the same if he stayed somewhere more rural? Could he grow his own food and pay for his own home, or was he merely kidding himself? He didn't need for his life to be easy, but he didn't see the point in making it difficult for no reason.

He sighed, and looked out of his apartment's one square window and wondered if the city was worth it, or making him another part of its inefficient machine. Nobody had hired him as an accountant after all of the humiliating interviews, but he felt an accountant's work wasn't a titillating goal, either. His brain needed some kind of challenge. He lived in a society progressive enough to mass produce its own food, yet still paid workers next-to-nothing to move thousands of boxes of car parts. It was something an assembly line robot could do faster, probably even cheaper over a longer period of time. Were the useless jobs just there to make *them* feel useful? The perception of rats was already poor. He was already familiar with the surprise expressed when he told people he went to a university.

Dogs were usually given the best jobs, or played the heroic roles in action movies. Sometimes rats were side-kicks. Usually villains. He didn't think he was one of those. He didn't steal, and gambling was legal. He had a job, and he rented an apartment, after all.

A rap sounded on his door. No slamming. No yelling. Just a little pitter-patter on the aluminum, familiar to the ears. Rising, Dent plucked the headphones from the sides of his ears and plodded to the door.

He opened and Bircham moseyed his way in, looking about the apartment, nodding fondly at nothing in particular. Most of the other tenants were rats too. There happened to be a few mice. A weasel or two. Rumor had it that there was a badger somewhere, but Dent had never seen him. There wasn't a single dog renting here, not even a mutt.

Bircham was the kind of rat Dent didn't want to ever be. He had a dumpy, sad little face and a reedy, high-pitched voice that quavered and sounded nothing like Dent's, which he had been told was deep and confident. Bircham's posture was ruined, bent over by the gravity of his shortcomings.

Bircham plucked an electronic cigarette from his pocket and sucked on it, inhaling and letting out some vapors. "Glad to see the extra time I gave you to pay off rent was spent on a good day at the game."

Dent's neck jerked, head tilting out of the way of the vapors and he reached behind himself, rubbing his shoulder. "I don't usually lose. I've never been late on a payment before this."

Bircham put the electronic cigarette in the pocket of his cheap shirt and placed his arms akimbo, letting out a sigh. "Usually? Damn it Dent, did you toss my money in the pisser?"

Dent narrowed his eyes. "I get that it's *gonna* be your money—"

"Shit—I mean, you only just make the payments at last minute's notice and I was expecting the rent tonight. I can't account for unexpected things like this when I have to pay for everybody's bills and feed myself too. I can't afford to cover for some kinda bum."

"So the difference between a bum and a businessman is one exchange? I gotcha." Dent crossed his arms.

"Really, 'cos gambling away things you can't afford sounds like something a bum does. Take care of your basics first, then spend your extras on whatever you want."

"I'm not reckless with my bets," Dent snapped, making Birchim flinch and his nose tremble. "And I couldn't afford to bet at all if I put the money towards rent first. Hell, I've been paying off the last three months with bet money and I get to buy food that doesn't make me feel sick. You telling me there's something wrong with that, all the while you smoke that crap?"

Bircham's eyes watered, his voice sounding wounded. He walked past Dent, big belly brushing him out of the way when he took a turn, standing near the stone slab with high shelves that sandwiched the sink and the cinder block walls near the door. "I didn't say I was perfect. I didn't say I was the healthiest rat either. But I have to make ends meet or else thirty families have to find new homes." He pulled out a chair at the counter and took a seat. "You're not the only person who scares me with possibility that you might not pay rent, sometimes. Yeah, I use a few luxury products that get me through the day. But I can afford these things when my system works, and it works with the bare minimum of monthly rent. I can try to accommodate as best as I can but I have to know ahead of time so the payments work out. Last month I almost thought you wouldn't pay at all, considering your car broke down."

Dent wasn't interested in having a one-to-one chat with his landlord when he knew it was eventually going to come down to the same scummy thing. "Something bad just happened to me. Has something bad ever happened to you?"

"Yeah, lots of things. I'm probably looking at another," he said shortly. "If you don't have that money in one day I'm going to have to put up an eviction notice. I'm at my wit's end, and you don't want to listen to me when I try to work things through. I don't give a damn what you do with your money if you just give the minimum that you owe to me for bills. But that doesn't seem to deter you."

"One day," Dent echoed, and then nodded. "Okay. I'll have the money by then."

"Don't fuck me," said Bircham calmly. He stood up, quietly pushed the stool under the counter, and stepped out the door with his tail dragging. The door snapped shut, and Dent smacked the counter. He kicked over the trash can, let out a snarl and slumped, trying to think. He looked forward, seeing himself reflected from a mirror hanging on the bedroom door. He supposed he wasn't bad to look at even when he did feel screwed. The Doberman's advice played through his head. Thinking back to his time at Hard Street, he'd get 100 from a thirty minute strip tease. He'd take off his pants, touch himself. Trace the outline of his dick in his boxers until it swelled. Dent knew he was a bit of a grower, so the audience members in the camera room always got happy about that.

But he didn't have the time for that. There were rooms that paid more. Rooms with conditions. With waivers. Rooms where bad stuff could happen, and it was all legal.

Twisting his whiskers with his back paw, he winked at himself, getting butterflies. He really did have a handsome face. He wouldn't let them ruin it, but he'd have to earn more than 100 per show.

* * *

Despite its name, Hard Street looked more like a row of warehouses or a chain of electronic stores than a seedy brothel district. Even the sex industry had been streamlined. Dent remembered a time when he was younger and hornier, and he had wanted to see another male naked for the first time. He had stared at a screen from an undisclosed location while a stark naked otter with broad shoulders stared back into the camera, and a menu similar to a fast food diner blinked up for him on the screen.

He had options like stretching, squats, sit ups, jogging in place. To get more options, two things had to happen: you had to pay more, and the performer would have to consent to the pay bracket before he or she was subjected to whatever the user might choose. There was an option that said jizz or no jizz (he picked jizz every time) and the performer was paid for his performance.

In later years, when Dent found himself on the opposite side of the screen, Hard Street felt less exciting. Less taboo. Just another service to earn a paycheck. He would stand in the performance line with his clothes in his paws, waiting to be inspected by young women who assigned him a waiting booth until his order was taken. The steel walls of the industry line were made of the same material and bolt pattern of the clothing warehouse he worked in. It was just another factory.

He had always consented to the easiest work. He'd get a free workout, strip off his clothes, and jerk off without even seeing who was watching him. Easy. But this time, he wasn't consenting to easy. His performance tonight was called Blue. There were higher settings that gave exorbitant amounts of money. One was called Red. Another was called Black. Both of those options required a death waiver so the company couldn't be sued if things went wrong. Lawyers made it too good in this city for that not to be a risk.

When Dent entered his assigned room, he noticed the walls were an immaculate black chrome. Something like a dentist's chair sat in the center. He slid his smooth tail through the loop at the back, and settled in, waiting for whoever watched from the outside. The metal arm rests were cold to the touch, and had straps for the place where his paws would go.

When he sat back against the seat's curvature, the sound of somebody's voice came from the other side of the intercom. "Bit battle-scarred, but it looks like I made a good choice," said a honeyed male voice. It carried a confident kind of lilt to it. Husky, certainly sonorous to the ear. "You're something nice to look at, I think. Handsome devil."

Dent looked around the empty room, no sight of any camera in view. He stroked his groin, groping his pants a little compulsively, pressing his paw to his package when the voice interrupted him. "There's no need for that now. Not right now, anyway." Dent imagined he could hear a grin exposing perfect teeth, and he stopped touching himself.

So maybe whoever was watching didn't want a show of his privates after all. Maybe he just wanted something weird and goofy. "Just testing the waters, ratty." Dent nodded in no particular direction, biting the inside of his lip softly. A cutesy pet name felt a little too forward.

"You don't need to pet your cock unless I tell you to. I know it feels nice, though," he cooed, sounding more interested and a little more gruff. "This isn't just a peep show you know. I didn't pay just to watch a cam whore play with himself." Not *just* to play with himself. Dent smirked. Clearly, whoever was behind the intercom wasn't impressed. "No, I have some things I'd like to do to you. And I have a short time to do it, so I feel we should get started."

"Augh!" Dent covered his eyes with his paws, blinded by a bright light that shone from the ceiling. The sides of room were built from many panels, or segments with interchangeable parts, looking like the shards of an obsidian disco ball when they shifted, made from much more expensive and elaborate robotics than the easy rooms. "Sit back," the voice commanded. Dent nodded, slowly, and wrist clamps from the mechanical chair clasped into place and tightened mechanically. They weren't too tight but they strapped in good. He couldn't much move his paws.

Below him, a mechanical whirring sounded, and he felt a part of the seat cover vanish when cold air hit his rear. The chair was more like an amusement park ride, and used robotics to transform different parts of itself into appendages that he could not see, but rather *feel*. Something soft that felt like warm rubber rolled over him with a textured, bumpy sensation against the bottom of his nethers, getting a bit of blood flowing to his groin, making him swell. "God damn," said the voice behind the intercom, a little satisfied. "That didn't take long, did it? You should see your face. Is this for me, or is this for you?" Dent shivered. That wasn't the most complicated question.

"It's for you—"

"Damn right," replied the male. "I don't mind you enjoying this a bit. You aren't going to enjoy everything."

Yeah, your attitude is a little grating.

"Your clothes are just awful."

"Oh," said Dent. "I forgot to take them off before the chair tied me down." He tried to pull his arms free to unbutton himself, but the straps were too tight.

"Just awful. You're better off without clothes."

"Wait, no, this is the only shirt I came with—"

Rip. Graspers had extended from the side of the wall, ripping the white sleeves right off Dent's arms. "Oh, come on!" They dropped the tattered cotton on the floor and gripped again. Dent's eye's widened when they pulled, ruthless, and he could hear the clicking sounds of buttons falling to the floor.

"Now let's wreck those shitty pants."

"Stop!" Dent tried to kick the appendages away. He got a good kick in, but a second set of straps clamped down on his legs, holding them to the foot rest. The mechanical graspers deftly undid the belt clasp with dexterous plucks and grabbed at the sides of Dent's jeans. The pull was slower this time. Stronger. Dent groaned when he heard the tearing denim. His legs were still covered, but his groin area was completely exposed.

"Now let's get that underwear."

"What the hell is your problem!" Dent shrieked. This tool had no respect for his things, even if it was a performance.

"Don't worry about your clothes, ratty. You look better without them."

Dent squirmed his hips when the apparatus snagged his boxers, tearing them too and giving him a horrible wedgie. When his underwear finally tore, it was dropped to the floor, now a useless rag. His dick and balls hung out in the cold air, limp while he heard the voice over the intercom laugh.

"Much cuter."

The bumpiness that rolled beneath him touched his naked taint now, and rolled across it like a plastic, fleshy paint roller slathering the bottom of his groin with warm wetness. Dent shivered, feeling his cock get hard even though he was too upset about his clothes to speak.

"You know, I picked a rat because I know they have a pretty foul reputation. Turns out you're no exception, huh?"

Dent resented that, growling. He would have pegged the man over the intercom as the bookie, but his voice was lighter. There were plenty of ways to get dirty. Paying to shoot a sitting duck in a barrel didn't seem like the most ethical thing to him, anyway. Maybe that's why the payoff for these things was so damn good. Put up with enough losers and sociopaths so they can get their paws off of their cocks and back to their keyboards. The cogs are put into place, and the machine keeps working. Dent's throat rumbled as he felt the first surge of pre dribble out of his cock.

For now, an entirely different machine was working on Dent. A lovely machine that was warm to the touch and pressed into him with the same calculated firmness over and over again. "You seem ready to be fucked now," said the voice again, still a little bored.

Dent jerked up. "That's… a bit dicey for me. I thought penetration isn't allowed on this setting."

"Are you hamming this up?" said the voice dismissively, surprised, and a little joy even crept into his tone. "You're telling me you've never done this before? You read over the setting description, surely? *You're in a fuck machine.*"

"I mean…" Dent's voice trailed off as the machine still rolled his taint. He felt a little tense. He knew these places were risky. Dangerous, even, but he didn't expect the machine parts would go *into* him. Blue setting mentioned some pain. That's all he remembered. "I'm sorry, I just…"

"You're okay? I'll leave you new clothes after." said the voice again. For a moment, the machismo was gone, and there was a warble of concern. Even if Dent did feel dirty, and even if he did feel like a deviant, he did sign up for this, and there was a person on the other side of the computer who seemed concerned. Dent didn't have to like this guy… but maybe he could like the experience. Or try to.

"Yeah," Dent decided. "I'm alright." There was a whirring sound, like the groan of a motor and a slick, warm piece of what seemed to be metal pressed underneath him. It vibrated, burning the inside of the rat's ears bright red as he moaned. "I… haven't had one of these things up me," he confessed, tugging on his bonds, ropey tail trying to thrash but held in place by the mold of the chair.

"It's just a douche." There was a fatherly softness to it that bothered Dent. It didn't fit the youthfulness of that timbre. "Time to get clean." His chest heaved as something spread him, and he felt a sharp pinch when something tapered and smooth worked its way inside of his tail hole. A whistling sound went off, and warm water shot up his bowels, making him shout. The runoff splashed underneath him, dripping off of his fur and down a drain anchored at the room's concave center. "There. Now the prostate stimulator will go in easier. I'll get a nice video shot of it sliding around inside you."

Dent cursed as warm metal pushed against his bum, feeling this edge was round and thick. Gel with a silky texture squirted into him, and the massager rubbed against him in a circular fashion, working him gently. He felt some new sensation when it pressed against him. His legs shook, and the fur on his arm stood on its end as he felt his pucker spread. The round head pushed inside slowly with what seemed a good minute worth of testing. The spread came with a pinch, causing him to screw up his face. More gel pumped into him, warming from the center out. The round piece curved, pressing inside toward the direction of his cock, and the rat looked up, sucking in air. Dent thought the touch was much similar to two previous sensations he knew: the first was like touching a pressure point on his thumb to relieve a bad headache. The second was like when he lost control while he stroked himself off, and he couldn't stop the milky jizz from welling up all over his black paw.

"You don't have to stay quiet," said the man on the intercom, panting like a dog. "That's probably the closest thing to a cock you've felt inside of your virgin asshole, isn't it? The vents let me smell you. You're working up a nice stink."

"Shut the hell up," Dent stammered. He'd had enough of this guy. "I don't smell."

"Then why's my cock is so hard," said the voice again, tongue audibly lolling. Dent was certain it was some sort of canid when he heard him lick his chops. "But speaking of smells, here's the part you're not gonna like. Hint—it's not the dildo going up your ass."

The lights in the room went out, leaving Dent only with the squelching sounds of the smooth, warm metal now churning into his rear, forcing liquid from the tip of his cock and groans from his mouth. Something whirred on the ceiling, and Dent's ear's jerked. Before he knew it, his snout was entrapped in a soft, padded cage, forcing his jaw open with a rounded shape. The cage was similar to an eye doctor's oculus, the sides of him strapped in. To top it off, a pungent cloth covered his long nose. It smelled like the subway, full of dogs on a rainy day. He squirmed, stuck in place. What the hell was this thing? He tried to speak, but all he could do was gag and sputter.

"Told you, you wouldn't like it," lilted the voice. "Those are the underpants I've been sweating in for the last few hours. Did a little work out, so they're fresh as opposed to foul." He punctuated the last word. "You're gonna be sniffing these until you come."

"The hell would you make me smell your underwear?" he tried to say, speech garbled. The scent was sharp and damp, and very male. Definitely doggy, but a little sharper… and a little cleaner than most he smelled.

"You really should get familiar with the smell of my groin before you drink my jizz."

Dent shivered. "What did you say?" The lights turned on again. He could see that whatever had his mouth propped open had a narrow tube slipped inside of it and disappeared into the ceiling. Sticky pads adhered to his abs and groin by mechanical rods, seeping into his fur and cooling his sensitive flesh. "Just take a deep breath."

"Wait." His heart skipped a beat. He shouted out of the side of his mouth. Shocks went through his body, lighting his neurons on fire, bathing him in both pain and pleasure simultaneously as the shaft inside of him stopped pumping, pressed firmly against him and buzzed. The heavy sounds of the dog's pant covered his own. His dick was jerking, covered in its own slick while it dripped down to the base of his balls.

"Almost," said the voice. This turned into a mantra, echoes of 'almost' drowning out the sound of Dent's pulse. The dog barked out a trail of long, low groans, and another momentary shock went to Dent's abs. His whole body shook in the chair. He was wet from every end now, electricity still running through his muscles.

The scent and sound of the dog clouded his mind as he looked above, startled. The tube connected to his mouth filled with a cloudy, opaque white liquid, which he knew could only be the dog's jizz. He closed his eyes, feeling the tube in his mouth, pretending the mouth piece was just his water bottle. He had no idea how it would taste, only knowing the flow would inevitably get to him. When it seeped out the opposite end, too much of it filled him, cramming the pockets of his cheeks, warm and murky with a thick texture. When another electric shock was applied, he gurgled through the scream. The smell, the taste, the sound and the feel of sex washed over him, forcing the pressure in his balls to build up, push out the end of his cock and splatter thickly on his black belly.

He sat in silence, damp and sweating. The apparatus holding his head in place disassembled, freeing him from its clamps and his wrist and leg straps opened. The rod sticking into him pulled out with a gentle retraction, making him gasp. *850 credits for 45 minutes* read the blinking screen on the wall in neon green letters.

Warm mist filled the room, tingling his fur and his bum until they suddenly stopped. His sticky pads melted away, running off the sides. He was grateful that he wouldn't be ripping them off with large clumps of his chest fur. The exit sign on the opposite side of the room directed him back to a bunk, where he whimpered, unsure how to get home without any clothes.

Within minutes, a young rabbit knocked on his door, providing a white shirt and black sweatpants in a clear bag. She also pressed a note into his paw and left him quickly without a word. The clothes were simple but soft, and slowly, sorely, he dressed himself, then put his credit card into a slot to collect his pay.

He pulled the note from its envelope, reading over the words as a card fell from the folded paper and clattered to the ground.

Now that you're clean, you ought to dress like it. Buy something better for next time.

There was a tip: 500.

* * *

After Dent gave the money to Bircham, he thought that it would be the end of his troubles and he could go on with his life. He'd bet at less crooked establishments from what excess he could make after bills were capped, and he wouldn't have to save himself from debt last minute ever again. But he found that he couldn't sleep as well at night.

When he smelled a dog around the corner, or opened the door

for one, he felt a twitch in his abs, and his groin tingled. On one of the harder work days before the holiday season, a burly mutt had built up a sweat. It wasn't the same smell as the boxers that were pinned to his nose that night at Hard Street. More sour. More smoky. But he found himself in the bathroom, shaky paws running up the sides of his pink length, hearing the pants of the dog. *Are you okay?* His jizz shot off like a bottle rocket, splattering against the porcelain in the bathroom. He even heard somebody mumble "guess somebody hadn't taken a piss in a while," embarrassing him.

Rats are dirty.

He stood up in the stall, taking a coarse slip of industrial toilet paper and cleaning off the milky dribbles pearling on his tip. More beaded there, and he wiped it away again. He wiped for about ten minutes until he was sure it was all gone. He mussed the fluff on his head in the mirror, trying to make the short, jagged fur into something smart and professional looking, but he couldn't shake off the scruffy pot head look that peeped back at him in the mirror with reddened, sleepless eyes.

Once work was over, Dent walked through the snow. Flecks of it landed on his black fur and tie, looking like dandruff. He cut around an office building and held his long, naked tail in his paw so it didn't touch the snow. He passed the front of a banking firm, then stood in place. He wasn't just smelling any male dog this time. He remembered the chair, and the underwear. Even from a distance he could recognize the pungent, slightly sweet and sweaty scent.

The bank had a black mansard roof with dormers, and a gable supported by thick, sandstone columns that sat squat on raised steps. It had a dated look, but it was still properly managed by somebody wealthy. The door opened and a vixen dressed in white wandered out, closing the door casually behind her. She sniffed the air, catching Dent's glance as she passed him, and then eyed him carefully, as if something was amiss, but she kept on tromping. A bit of that smell clung to her too, but it didn't linger. Dent grabbed the handle, took a deep breath and walked through the door, watching the snow flake off of him from the shivers. Hot air licked his face from a blazing fireplace, leaving him damp with the melting snow. He walked up to the front desk, placing his paws on it, tapped gently and leaned forward.

The black teller's window at the marble counters hid every face, but he could hear their clacking keyboards. "Excuse me, I'm, uh, looking for somebody."

"Are you?" said a voice he knew. The electronic slats in the window turned upward, and a surly arctic fox with a long muzzle stared back at him. He looked surprised and embarrassed, but a small smirk wiped that away. "Are you interested in opening an account with us... sir?"

"I had considered it," said Dent, carefully. "I might need to be convinced. Maybe you ought to talk with me in private."

The fox tapped the desk, pinching the bridge of his nose with his other paw. He really didn't seem much older than twenty-something. His name tag said Russ. "Well I'm, ah... okay. Let me do that for you. There's a conference room where we could open up a bond." His elbow knocked over a magnetic pen on a chain that neatly reorganized itself, and his fluffy tail curled in on himself as he stood.

Russ led him down a hallway, almost pacing, briskly leading onwards. He had big paws and wide shoulders, but a formal posture. Stuffy came to mind. That changed when Russ grabbed Dent's paw and flew through the hallway, acting more like a hunter on the chase than a bank teller. "Hurry," he whispered without looking back. He led Dent to a conference room with chairs, a table, and no windows. The fox closed the door, locking it behind, then turned on his heels, clapping his paws together in a single smack. "You're here. Good job. I see you got better clothes." A coy smile curled up the side of his face.

"So my nose wasn't wrong," said Dent, smelling the fox's sweat heavy in the air. He already had a boner, but he wasn't going to show any weakness. "I wasn't sure it was you, you know, but then again... your smell isn't easy to forget. Or your voice. You caused a bit of a problem for me. I know we're not supposed to seek out clients after anything, but hell, I didn't even mean to find you on purpose."

The fox's nose tilted with his gaze, looking him up and down, freezing for a moment at the area of Dent's groin. He belligerently sniffed the air, and then gave the innocent kind of shrug that defense attorneys give when faced with incriminating evidence. "But you did find me," said the fox, bereft of the insecurity in his voice mere seconds ago.

Dent nodded, feeling a little bit stupid for following his nose, but the stiffy in his pants and the memories of drinking come from a tube reminded him of what had been impressed onto him. "Yeah. Your smell."

The fox held his palm to his forehead, eyebrows slightly raised. His eyelids formed a slit. A crooked, sloppy smile spread up his cheek as sickeningly sweet as his lilting tone. "Yeah. You know... I really wanted to try that one. Scent immersion."

"Immersion," echoed Dent, tone as hard as his leaky cock while the fox's oily smell filled the room. The fox wore the expression that said *this will be easy.*

Russ let his fluffy tail spin to his front and held it in front of his vest. "Yeah. You make somebody sniff you long enough when they're bothered and they can't get enough of you. You associate my smell with sex and, well, you're just that much easier to mold. I didn't think you'd get hooked the first time."

Dent dragged a wooden chair from the polished conference table and took a seat, sighing. "Well, I had never been fucked. Or swallowed come, either."

"I kinda got that," said the fox a little too quickly, then chuckled. "But then again, I haven't either." Dent wasn't sure if that was a lie, or if it even mattered.

A puddle of pre started leaking through Dent's jeans. He was horny and angry and still felt a little bit left in the dark. Dent noticed that this Russ wasn't quite the same in person as he was behind the intercom... but the possessive nature of his personality still showed. Was that why it didn't feel real? "Okay. So this scent thing worked on me a little too well. Is there a way to stop it? It's hard to lift car parts when I work with sweaty dogs all day and what you did to me is stuck in my head."

Russ picked up on that and stepped a little closer. "So you're un-questionably hooked, huh?" He let go of his tail, and it swished back and forth, a bit like a pendulum.

"Have you been listening to me at all?" Dent slapped the table with his spread paw.

The change in the fox was sudden and predatory. He didn't sound like an oily banker anymore. His lip curled, showing a sharp tooth, and there were wrinkles in his snout and brow.

"Yeah. You sound angry and desperate. Why's that my problem? You tasted my jizz before. What's a second time?"

Dent folded his arms, shaking his whiskers. "Sorry, but that was an exchange of currency. Not passion."

"Maybe not then," said Russ, shrugging. "But what about now? I could let you suck me off again. Smell me. That might make things normal for you again. But if not, well… by all means, we both know you're not opening an account here." He waved his paw, offering the door.

Dent didn't move a muscle. Russ slid back his chair. He rose and took a little stroll while he dragged his padded digits on the table, swaying his hips until they were in front of the rat's face. Russ smelled strong, like a specific kind of overpowering perfume, and it made Dent remember how loud he squealed, trapped, with every hole wet and sticky and full of slick.

"I could hurt you," Dent growled, staring at the fox's groin, probably inches from his face. Dent turned his face, and a soft squeak escaped his throat.

"Would that solve anything?" cooed Russ. He didn't sound so much like a young adult anymore, but that was his work personality behind the desk. Like himself, Russ didn't seem to have much power over his life as a bank teller. But here, Russ had a lot of power. He wondered if Russ knew how naked he looked right now. The fox had utter power over Dent's arousal, but it was a transparent domination. It was difficult to think of him as a nobody when he was so viscerally close. After all, Dent was sitting in the younger man's shadow, and he could smell his dick this close to his face.

"You have a girlfriend," said Dent, watching the snowy paw freeze on its pants zipper. "I could smell you on her."

Russ growled. "So fucking what? She's not here. She didn't come searching for me like a thirsty bitch in heat." There was jingling noise, then the soft unzip. Dent almost shuddered, smelling the sickly scent of what had dripped its way down his throat and settled in his belly weeks ago.

"You're going to suck my cock for free, now, aren't you? I could see your fucking boner for the last ten minutes."

The fox's red tip pushed out of its sheath, pre well on its way to the point, presenting itself. Dent couldn't decide if the liquid looked more like honey or gasoline.

"I'd be lying if I said I didn't want to," muttered Dent, the inside of his ears blushing.

"If you want to, then why not just go for it?" Russ said. He slipped out of his sheath, moist and musky, dangling himself like a prize in front of the rat.

"Because I don't think I want to give you that kind of satisfaction," he said. Dent took the fox's cock into his paw, rolled it, and then opened his mouth, dipping in deep. He licked away the sweat and stickiness. A single bead of pre gravitated down his throat, slow and sluggish even after his gullet put in the work. Then he pulled away, looking up. "This is for me. Maybe there isn't much power in a fantasy when I'm through with the real thing."

"Whatever you fucking say," said the fox, eyes half-lidded, hinging on his haunches as Dent felt his warm length thrust at the opening of his throat. "Either way you're still sucking my cock, right? And doing a damn good job with it, too. Pity you aren't allowed to be a real slut. I'd tell every fucking pervert about you and you'd make enough to put a down payment on a mansion."

"Quiet," Dent muttered. The damp dick was warm under his paw. He pulled the skin back tight and stared, and could barely fit his grip around its circumference. This was the closest he'd ever been to a male, but he'd already swallowed come. He was holding his first dick to suck, feeling it pulse from the rush of blood. More dewy liquid oozed from the tip. Deep throats were supposed to feel good, and he wanted to see if he could pull it off. The tapered length fit neatly into his oblong muzzle, and he let it slide along the top of his tongue until it rubbed at the back of his throat. Dent remembered hearing from the man he *wanted* to lose his virginity to that you had to try and swallow, even though you couldn't actually down it all. He nearly choked, but, gauging from the fox's elated squeal, succeeded.

With a yowl that warbled high in pitch, then lowered to a bestial, guttural moan, Russ' hips thrusted, rubbing against the sides of Dent's cheeks. The familiar pant sounded in the room, and Dent remembered *almost* on a loop wheezing out of the intercom. "Damn, slut. Your mouth is tighter than my girl's cunt is." Dent squeezed the base of him, which swelled into a knot. Each fresh, messy pulse of pre that squirted down his throat was swallowed, but he had to breathe through his nose when the fox grabbed the back of his head with a burly paw and slammed down to the base of his groin. A muffled squeak followed by a gurgle echoed in the room until Dent was violently pushed off, leaving a trail of spit and pre mixed with phlegm that dribbled down the canid's plump bollocks.

Suddenly, the fox was handling his groin with greedy paws, unzipped the rat's trousers and sifting through his damp boxers. Russ tugged Dent's trousers off, exposing the rat's pink cock as it bobbed in the air from the force. He surprised Dent as he went down too, greedy for dick, lapping on the rat's dark balls with his strong, flexible tongue that felt warm, spongy and filled the room with wet, sloppy sounds. Dent's chest heaved as the fox hauled him from the chair, forcing him to the ground with a grunt, supine, with his strong white paws holding the rat's waist still. The fox's long, narrow snout sucked hard on Dent's shaft, undulating his tongue as he growled. After edging for so long, Dent couldn't help but come, and the fox drank him down, not spilling a drop.

After he was done, Russ raised his head, smiling. "See? You finished first. You like this."

Dent groaned, still caught in the afterglow, and cocked an eyebrow. "I like having my life disrupted by a brat who couldn't just flog me for fair pay or whatever other kinky shit you could choose from the menu?"

Russ tsked. "You like being my little fuck boy. As for pain, I'm sure I can electrocute you another round. I think you're cute when you scream, and when you're being warmed from the inside out. You're going to finish my cock off and swallow it all again." The fox's huge paw grasped at the scruff of his neck while he wrestled Dent's nose into his groin, still hard, still leaky. Dent took a deep breath through his nose, smelling body odor and something pissy as he opened his mouth, going down. Russ bucked at the back of Dent's throat, making it burn. Hot tears welled up and rolled down Dent's cheeks, though his expression remained focused, concentrating on the scent of the fox. Russ's thick body heaved beneath the bunched up shirt and shiny vest that looked like wrapping paper. His vulpine face crinkled and he whined as Dent tasted him again, attentive to his body and his smell, no longer a distant concept but right here before him. Weaker. Wonderful. A hot, familiar murk pumped into his mouth, similar in taste, new in context. Dent swallowed, and when he pulled away, the fox's cock bobbed below him, still stiff, dragging a trail of slick across his cheek.

They sat for a while, spent and warm, silence punctuated only by the ticking of the display of the electric clock on the wall, programmed to make tiny mechanical sounds for the passing seconds.

Russ pawed at his chest, and Dent squeezed his palm before letting it hang loose on the floor. "Your smell's a bit different, I think," said Dent. "I uh… thank you." They sat in silence as the fox crawled up to him and wrapped his tail around the rat, looking unfit to graduate prep school, much less sell somebody a banking account.

"Well, I'm sure I could fix that again," said the fox, smirking.

"No," said Dent, shaking his head. "You don't understand. That time at Hard Street… it was just a desperate moment. I don't think I'll need that kind of money anymore. I won't run out of rent again. I'm not really a regular, there. Or for the Blue setting."

"Desperate moment," mocked Russ. "Was it really a desperate moment, or just an itch you couldn't scratch?"

He smoothed out the ruffles in the vest of the fox. "Desperate moment. You were my first, you know? I never really went for guys. Or anybody." Dent sighed. "I'm not a private fuck boy or a call rat or whatever you want to think of me as. I can guarantee you that I'm not that whimsical or exotic. You say I'm the one who needed an itch scratched—but, well, maybe your fleas were just contagious. I don't want to make this a regular thing."

The fox's ears flattened. He let out a one-note laugh, then a scoff. "I mean… I love my girlfriend. She's really the best, you know? She cooks for me, and she cuddles when we watch movies, and… well, she doesn't feel comfortable with some of the things I like. She thinks it's weird. Hell, I know it's weird, but fuck it if it doesn't feel great. And I need to have somebody who knows how that feels."

"Yeah," said Dent. "And I think that's what scared me a little. You know… maybe this is just my body talking again, but there's a part of me that wants you. Maybe there was something deep down that said, 'yeah, you like what you are, and you like being treated like filth.' But that's not really true. Deep down I know I want to find somebody who treats me like a person."

The fox rolled his eyes. "I don't mean everything that I say when I fuck. You can't be a whore, and then tell me I'm not politically correct for treating you like a whore. You think you can just move along after Blue setting sex?" Russ said, sounding even younger than he had before. His voice was bordering on a tantrum, now. "There was something so very satisfying there. It felt right… and I'm certain it felt right to you, too. Didn't it feel right to you?"

Dent shrugged. "Well... you know, for what it's worth, I did like the things you did to me. I didn't think they were weird. They were frightening, but they felt good. I don't dislike the sex so much as I dislike the way you think. You can treat me like a service when I'm providing that service, but I get to go home after. You're not home."

The fox shook his head and sat up, using his tail for leverage. "You're telling me you could last a few days without a dick in your mouth? I know what your type crave."

Dent nodded. The white-hot anger that bored itself into his center had petered out. "I wasn't lying. You were actually my first. I know what your type crave, too. You don't fool me. I know you don't just want sex. You sound like you want somebody to love. That's not a product up for purchase." Dent took a good look around himself. The conference room was so devoid of detail or personal touch that it just felt like a hotel room. He didn't want to be used for... whatever kind of emotional need this was. He wasn't storage Russ could put away and then take out when he had insecurities. "I have to make my own life work." Dent stuffed his cock into his boxers, pulled up his trousers and buckled his belt. Then he sat up, still feeling a bit of vertigo, but the fox grabbed his paw.

"But can't you just try?" said the fox, his tone softer. "I love how you whine and squeal and it's so hard to get into somebody's head like that. Do you know how rare that is? How hard to find? I know you way too goddamn well for you to just walk out of here—"

"You don't know my name," said Dent. He pulled away again, stood up, paced over to the door and put his hand on the knob when the fox put his hands on both of his shoulders. He was so fleet, Dent hadn't even heard him move. The canid's hot breath was on his ear, and he whispered.

"Well, I paid for conditioning. It's sequential. If you ever do choose Blue setting, I'll get a call and I'll know. Your profile is programmed to please me if you ever want to use an extreme setting. You don't get to throw me away. I get to throw *you* away if I ever so chose, and I won't ever do that. I won't."

Dent nodded. "I thought as much." The hair prickled on the back of his neck. A memory distracted him. He thought about himself, five years ago, when he first left home and met some friends for a graduation party. Dent had his first kiss there. It was on top of a skyscraper.

He never had the chance to follow up on the guy. His name was Frank, and he was a deer who wanted to live somewhere green. Dent had never been kissed before in a place that was green, so he asked Frank to spare the romanticism, but the buck just kissed him again, and he could taste the piney gin on his lips. He never found out if Frank found his way to a forest, but his antlers felt like tree bark anyway.

Dent put his paw on the door handle. The cold metal bit at his skin. "Alright then. I guess if I do need emergency money, I'll use the Red setting."

The fox barked out a laugh, mocking him. "That's stupid. You know how many people get maimed that way? You'd lose a fucking hand. Then what would your piece of shit car job be worth? I'd like to fucking know."

"Well. Guess I better not resort to any fuck machines again." Dent gave a massive shrug. Russ looked humiliated, but he held up his paw to make a point, like he had a slam dunk point to make in a debate that would knock the audience dead.

"You're poor, and you're a rat. There's no doubt in my mind you'll be back at Hard Street, and if you are, you'll damn well not do anything crazy."

"Guess that's a bet," Dent said.

He wiped the jizz off his mouth and closed the door on the fox.

UNMANNED

Kjorteo Kalante

Keith had the ball and the chance to redeem himself. He needed only to reach the other end of the court. That should have been easy for the red-tailed hawk. His thick, powerful legs carried him to the halfway mark in seconds. The opposing net was in sight. *Could this be the day?*

Before he could answer that, a gray blur was upon him.

Kody. The mouse was easy to overlook, even as he tried to grab the ball and missed. If it were anyone else, that would have been Keith's opportunity to advance. Against Kody, though, the opening itself was a trap. Even when the mouse fell for a feint, he was always quick enough to recover and strike again.

The hawk took off laterally instead, faking right before running left. He was at least sixty pounds heavier than his opponent, all of it muscle. With it, he exploded across the court. He only had a second before Kody was on him again, but a second was all he needed.

He leapt straight up, arms over his head, and shot.

Kody tipped the ball.

Keith gaped. He was over a foot taller with arm length to match, and had taken a high jump shot while wide open. How in the world had the mouse even caught up with him, let alone leapt high enough to block anything?

The ball wobbled through the air like an unsteady bird; wounded, yet still determined to reach its destination. It might have gone through had the trajectory been more stable and just a little longer. Instead, it hit the front rim and bounced away.

Half buried on the nearby bench amongst keys, water bottles, and discarded shirts, a cell phone went off. Its timer signified the end of the game.

Keith let out a screech. Kody had found a way to outlast him *again,* though it had come at a cost. The mouse leaned forward, doubling over and panting hard enough to hyperventilate. Soon, he was on his hands and knees.

"You all right, squeak?" Keith had wanted to beat his rival, not kill him.

"Kody," the mouse corrected sharply, then coughed. "You can call me any name you want when you beat me, but not until then."

"Kody, sorry." Keith raised his hands as if he were under arrest. *Touchy.* Bad enough he had to deal with impossible customers all day. Were his weekends on the court destined to end in impotent frustration, too? Probably, so long as Kody kept playing every little pickup game as if it were a world championship. Theirs was supposed to be a *friendly* rivalry. The mouse still remembered that, right?

"Come on, let's go home." Keith knelt and reached to help his fallen opponent up.

"You're good at this." Kody wouldn't take Keith's hand, but he did take the bird's forearm, and was soon on his feet again. Standing next to each other, the mouse only came up to Keith's collarbone after one counted his big, round ears.

"You're better," the hawk mumbled. He waited for Kody to let go, but it appeared the mouse had become a permanent attachment. That was all right. Kody wobbled with every step, so the need for support was understandable.

"Aw, don't be like that," Kody consoled as though *Keith* were the one taking the game too seriously. "I needed to give it everything I had just to keep up. No one makes me work for it like you do. You'll get me one of these times for sure."

"Maybe next time?" Keith suggested, though he somehow wasn't hopeful.

"Maybe." Kody grinned proudly, as if he *weren't* also gasping and dying between words. "I won't make it easy for you, though."

Keith couldn't help but laugh. "You never do, squeak. Kody. Sorry."

* * *

Kody's apartment was already small, but with all he had apparently done to keep Keith away, it seemed even smaller. They had showered separately, changed separately, even eaten separately before retreating to their respective rooms. There had been a time when Kody had only kept one dresser drawer locked and hidden from the hawk. Now, it was the entire bedroom. Keith had to make do with a bedroll on the living room floor.

It wasn't as though Keith had expected to get any action. They hadn't been a couple in years, after all. He wasn't trying to spoon naked in Kody's bed anymore. Still, something bothered him about the mouse's coldly professional treatment, as if the two were nothing more than roommates... or even coworkers. As if their entire relationship had never happened.

Keith rolled onto his side and sighed. He should consider himself lucky that their relationship had ended as well as it had, he supposed. Many exes never so much as spoke to one another, but Kody still invited him over on weekends so both of them could get away from their respective day jobs. That was at least something... or was it? Kody had fought on the court as if it were an actual battle and shown distant courtesy the rest of the evening. Keith worked retail in a clothing store; he knew the feigned customer service platitudes when he heard them. Was Kody punishing him? That seemed needlessly petty, but why else would the mouse bother to have him over only to act like this?

Or was Keith the one being petty? He wouldn't admit it, but the loss still stung. If only he could come out on top *somewhere*. Retail work meant subservience despite his size and strength. The hawk could have tossed half his customers like pizza dough, an especially tempting fantasy whenever they were being rude or difficult. Instead, he had to serve them with the least menacing beak-smile he could manage. He flew remote-control helicopters and drones as a hobby in his leisure time, but *true* flight was something only his feral ancestors could attain. They still had wings, after all. Venting his aggression on the court might have helped, but there he couldn't even beat a hot-blooded mouse half his size. Was there no recourse for him?

A noise interrupted him from his musing. Several noises, actually, though all were coming from Kody's room.

Moans.

Oh, was *that* why Kody had kept his door closed? Was the mouse pleasuring himself to the thought of his latest victory? Rubbing it in by rubbing one out? *Well, good for him, the smug little show-off.* He rolled onto his side and folded his pillow over his ear holes.

The mouse had always acted as if he had something to prove,

which explained his refusal to lose. That was what had drawn Keith to him long ago, but it was also what had doomed their young relationship. Kody had been defensive, stubborn, and prone to lashing out, as if the entire world—even his boyfriend—were his enemy. *Some things never change.*

Still, try as he might, the hawk couldn't quite tune Kody out. Something about those noises bothered him. Something about them felt wrong, somehow…

Those aren't pleasured moans.

The sounds were fearful. Distressed. Pleading for help.

Well, that changed things. Keith cursed, wriggling out of the bedroll and grabbing his boxers. Kody had been a pain in his tail since high school but, damn him, the hawk still *cared*.

Keith entered Kody's bedroom and found the mouse in the midst of a fitful sleep. Sheets and blankets lay strewn everywhere except the bed, all casualties of Kody's tossing and turning. The mouse himself, now exposed, had clearly been keeping himself in shape. His gray-furred body was too small even for a swimmer's build, yet what little he had was toned and athletic. Kody whined and shifted, apparently still trying to run from the monsters in his dream. His narrow yet solid legs twitched and moved through a slow striding motion, as if attempting to jog underwater.

"Kody," Keith called. "Hey, Ko—"

The mouse rolled onto his back, his legs spread, chest rising and falling in ragged gasps. The sight shouldn't have been anything shocking to Keith, but it was. *Well, that's new.*

Kody didn't have a penis.

The mouse's scrotum was still there, but above it was nothing but a small stub. Rumpled folds covered and coated it, as if a petaled flower had bloomed between his legs. It almost looked like overhanging foreskin, but it was far too short for that. It could have been a sheath, like what canines had, except for the fact that Kody was a mouse. Besides, Keith had seen Kody's penis countless times before. It had never retracted into anything, sheath or otherwise. It had always hung exposed and unhidden, low, loose, and free. *Had.* It was gone, now.

Something must have happened while they'd been apart. It must have been after they had split up and moved, before they had reunited. The folds likely covered a stump with a long-faded scar from whenever the injury had occurred. That was Keith's theory, at least, but the coating of skin was too thick and too complete to see whatever might or might not have been underneath it.

"Kody?" the hawk repeated, much more hesitantly than before.

Kody gave one more fitful whimper, and then his eyes opened. "Keith?" His voice was faint, tired, as if he had just run a marathon. "Good, it's only you. I thought—"

The mouse's next words died in his throat. All color drained from his inner ears. Even his gray-furred face somehow seemed paler. "Oh, no," he said, the last of the dream fog lifting from his voice. He was awake, yet he looked even more terrified than he had during his nightmare. "No, no, *no!*"

"Relax, it's just—"

"*No!*" A pillow flew toward Keith like a missile. The hawk caught it, but only as it smashed into his feathered chest. By then Kody had already amassed a small pile of blankets and buried himself beneath them like a young child hiding from the monsters beneath his bed. "No!" he repeated, as if denying reality loudly enough would make it go away.

The lump beneath the blankets flattened and Kody dropped low, as if he were attempting to sink into the mattress and disappear. As if hiding would make Keith forget what he had seen. The hawk was used to Kody being stubborn, but never before had he witnessed that much of a blind, desperate panic.

"Kody, listen." Keith sat on the corner of the bed like a weary parent. The blanket-monster mouse let out a loud, alarmed squeak, and started to thrash and flail his way toward the opposite corner. Keith sighed. "I said *listen*. I'm not going to hurt you, all right? Stop that."

"Please don't tell anyone." Kody stopped struggling but sank lower again. His voice was quiet and broken. It was very much unlike the person Keith had usually faced. The hawk had never been able to beat Kody before, even after six attempts. In that moment, though, the mouse was surrendering and Keith wasn't even attempting to fight. "I'll do anything," Kody rasped, sounding close to tears. "I'll... I'll pay you. I have some money saved up. Not much, but I'll give you as much as I—"

"*Slow down.*" Keith put his hand over the mound of blankets, not even attempting to guess what part of Kody he was touching. He tried to make the gesture as sympathetic as he could, regardless. "You think I want to *blackmail* you? Hell's sake, Kody, I'm not *that* bitter."

Kody lessened his struggling. His ragged breathing grew slower and quieter. "What do you want, then?" His voice was so soft that Keith almost hadn't heard it, especially through the blankets.

"Nothing," Keith answered as warmly as he could manage. "Maybe to know what happened, but mostly nothing. I wasn't trying to confront you, or unmask you, or anything like that. You were having a nightmare and I was worried. The goal was to make you *less* scared."

"I'm not scared." Kody finally poked his head out from under the blankets. He surveyed the room cautiously, like a soldier in a trench. Even his ears were flat, tucked back, as if trying to stay hidden.

"Well, then." Keith spoke flatly, his arms folded, though his teasing beak-smile betrayed his amusement. "Perhaps you're brave enough to explain what I saw?"

Kody's eyes shot open and he retreated beneath the blankets again.

"Was it a disease?" Keith asked. "Infection? Something where it had to be amputated?"

"No."

"An accident, then?"

"No! Nothing like that."

In his attempts to deny everything, Kody had given himself away. *If it wasn't an accident…* He squeaked and flattened himself against the mattress. Keith tried his best not to laugh; this was the warrior who had bested him every time they'd met.

"Come on, squeak," the hawk said. "There's nothing to fear."

"My name is *Kody*, and I'm *not* afraid." The mouse rose to his knees and cast the blankets aside. He even puffed out his chest. "You haven't beaten me yet, you don't get to… to…" As if waking from another dream and realizing what he'd done, Kody once again looked down at his own exposed body. He sighed, defeated. "Damn it." He pulled a blanket over his lap, at least, though they both knew the secret was already out. "All right, you win. Just… please don't tell anyone."

Even as exes and rivals, Keith couldn't bear to see the mouse fall apart like that. "Your secret is safe with me," he promised. He put a taloned hand on Kody's shoulder, rubbing with a thumb as the mouse sniffled.

"Thank you," Kody uttered weakly.

"Shh." The bird's voice was deep but soft, as gentle as he could manage. "I just want to know what's going on, all right? That was why things didn't work between us before. I wanted to help you, but you never trusted me enough to let me try. I still care about you, you know. I..." *I still love you,* he almost said, but caught himself. "I still want what's best for you. But you have to *let me in.*"

Kody reached forward to hug Keith but leaned back, apparently changing his mind. He swayed like a seasick passenger on a churning boat, the storm and waves almost too much to bear. Finally, he gave in and held Keith's arm as if it were a guardrail, keeping him from falling overboard.

"All right," the mouse forced out, despite his small voice. "Thank you."

* * *

Kody couldn't get out of the car just yet. One moment. He needed at least one moment, first. *Not that it will help. This is still the stupidest thing I've ever done.*

His mind had been in constant turmoil ever since the previous weekend, when Keith had uncovered his secret. A part of him had wanted to reveal everything immediately, if only because he knew what the waiting would do to him. Besides, if his life was over anyway then postponing his execution wasn't helping anyone.

However, as much as he had wanted to get it over with, he couldn't. The words had refused to come. He'd tried repeatedly to write his confession after Keith had left, only to change his mind less than a sentence later with each attempt. *Keith deserves to hear it in person,* he had told himself, pretending the thought wasn't an excuse to keep hiding and procrastinating. Even when the weekend had come again and he had parked in the bird's driveway, he still hesitated. He needed to catch his breath, gather at least some semblance of courage and wits, and *then* he could face his doom.

Keith had been sending him concerned texts all week. The hawk had been making plans, arranging dates, but mostly just checking on him, and the worrying had only made the week even more agonizing. Yes, Kody was all right, nightmares aside. No, he hadn't been the victim of some hideous crime. No, he wasn't heartbroken over the loss, as he was sure most men would be. Yes, he was doing well.

The hawk was only worried about him, of course, and he did appreciate the gesture. Still, every reassurance he was fine only further incriminated him. He wished he *wasn't* fine. If Keith's fears had been true, if some horrible fate had befallen him, if some criminal had kidnapped him and done this to him, it at least would have been easier to explain. He didn't want to be a victim, really, but it would have been nice to be innocent.

Still, whether Keith had suspected him or not, he had stayed true to his word. There were no obvious traps, at least that Kody could see from his car. No news vans in his driveway or prank show personalities lurking about. Was it safe? Kody dared to hope that Keith had kept his secret after all.

The mouse grabbed his backpack and stepped out of the car, walking as if marching off to war. He held his breath the entire way, and squeezed the pack's straps so hard that his claws dug into his palms. Every instinct screamed at him to turn around, go back, but instead he knocked on Keith's door. He wanted to run, but he held still and waited.

After a few seconds that felt like years, Keith opened the door. At least, he assumed it was Keith. Kody wasn't brave enough to look up, so he had settled for staring at the ground.

"Hey," came the bird's voice, after Kody had failed to speak. "Glad you made it. You all right?"

"Oh!" Kody jumped, surprised, as if he had forgotten that he was supposed to be talking. "Thanks. Yeah."

"Care to come in?"

No! "Sure."

Kody shuffled inside, led by the sights of Keith's white carpet, the pieces of fluff and feathery down that adorned it—someone hadn't vacuumed recently—the legs and wheels of a few nearby chairs and, of course, Keith's feet. Yellow scales, black talons, and massive size, just like his hands. Staring at them was easier than making eye contact.

He did eventually tear his eyes away, though, and he saw the rest of Keith. The hawk wore beige shorts with a black belt, a gray tee serving as an undershirt, and a thin tan button-up shirt over it. The undershirt was tucked in, but the shirt over it was loose and unbuttoned. For someone who worked in a clothing store, Keith's dress was oddly mild. Kody had dressed down as well, but even his simple white tee and jeans felt loud in comparison. That Keith was barefoot was the most adventurous thing about him, and even that only meant so much inside his own home.

The room's furniture was similarly nondescript: an ordinary wooden bookshelf, a medium-sized television, a couch opposite a bare glass coffee table, and landscape paintings that appeared to have come from thrift stores. It looked like the default setting of a living room, as if Keith lived in some sort of basic example world, the stock photo that came with the frame. Along with his outfit, it was all far too dull to match how nervous Kody felt. Was that the idea? Had Keith sensed Kody's fear, and attempted to dress and decorate to make himself less threatening? If so, had—

The sound of the door closing behind him startled Kody out of his contemplation. He couldn't decide whether the *click* of the lock made him feel more safe, or less. "You keep saying you're fine, and I believe you," the hawk said with a look that suggested he didn't. "I just worry, though. Especially with your nightmares. You said those are a regular thing for you?"

Kody hadn't expected that to be Keith's first question. Surely the bird had wanted to know what had happened between his legs. "Yeah," he answered, while looking for a place to sit. Keith had claimed the couch, and Kody wasn't quite bold enough to sit next to him. Instead, he wordlessly pulled the coffee table backward until there was ample room between them. *There.* The table was big enough for the mouse and his backpack. It wasn't particularly comfortable, but then, neither was Kody.

"Sorry to hear that," the bird said. "What sorts of things do you dream about?"

"Standard stuff. Being chased, mostly. Monsters coming to get me, that sort of thing."

"Having to hide?"

Kody clenched his jaw. He knew where the hawk's questions were going. It was a good guess, and probably correct, but still... "Probably just stress," he answered instead. He certainly had no shortage of that in his life. Then again, if that were true then the stress itself had been his undoing. It had led to the nightmare, which had led to Keith discovering him. Would his secret still be secure if he hadn't feared so much for its security?

Either way, it had happened. As a result, his new biggest worry was the discussion he *knew* was coming, but that they'd both been agonizingly slow to bring about. Kody had never imagined he'd be the one to broach the subject, but the self-imposed wait had driven him close to madness. He needed to *be done with it*, which meant speaking up, as he should have done that night in his bed. He cleared his throat and braced himself. "I thought you were going to ask me about my penis."

The look Keith gave was equal parts puzzlement and alarm. What had he expected, though? Had Kody's question been that out of line? That *was* why they were there, was it not?

"Well, it did give me quite the surprise," Keith said hesitantly, grasping for words. As if giving up on any other way to express his thoughts, he silently moved over to one side of the couch and patted the now-empty seat next to him.

"I know." Kody swallowed. He was afraid of being too close to Keith, but he was even more afraid of being in front of him. The glass seat was growing harder and more painful by the moment, but more importantly, Kody couldn't stand Keith looking at him like that, like there was a spotlight on him, like Keith was the audience for some play of which Kody was the star. He reluctantly accepted the invitation and moved to the couch, if only to escape that stare. Part of him wanted to cling to Keith like they were still a couple, while the rest wanted to shy away.

"If you really are fine, though," Keith said, "then you're taking this better than just about anyone else would. I mean, you really don't... you know, miss it?" Keith clenched his beak shut tightly and, for a moment, he almost looked as uncomfortable as Kody.

The mouse smiled. He knew even without asking what Keith's discomfort must have been. The bird was trying to be euphemistic, as if Kody had suffered some horrible loss and asking about it would dig up painful memories. *So many guys seem to love that thing. No one can live without it, so how could I? That's what he wants to know, but he's afraid to say it.*

He shouldn't have found it so amusing. It was another piece of evidence against him. The fact that he wasn't like the others was a sign, a clue, something that could give him away if investigated deeply enough. He couldn't help it, though; it was funny. Keith had brought up the one subject wherein Kody *was* comfortable, so let the bird be the one squirming for once.

"Miss it? Not really," Kody finally answered, after a long enough pause to savor the reversal.

Keith stroked his beak. "How long has it been?"

"A couple years, I think." For an event that significant, his memory wasn't as good as Keith likely expected.

"What happened?"

So it was back to that again. "I knew a guy who knew a guy," Kody tried, continuing to force a mask of nonchalance. Inwardly, though, his nerve started to falter after he realized what he had said.

Wrong answer.

He had meant to be casually dismissive, as if that question were beneath him. Instead, he accidentally admitted that his decision had been deliberate and purposeful. "Knowing someone" implied that he had sought this person out for the sole purpose of getting it done.

"Why?" Keith asked.

Kody huffed, his chest pushing out defensively. "Because I didn't need it anymore." All of his momentum had disappeared as quickly as he had acquired it. He had only held the edge for a moment, but he already missed it.

Keith didn't say anything, but he gave Kody a tired, wounded look. *I thought you were going to open up to me,* the bird's eyes seemed to say even if his beak didn't. Or was that Kody's guilt talking? Whether the mouse had wanted to confess his secrets or not, he had made an agreement, and he normally wasn't one to back down on his word. The prickly walls were his instinctive first reaction, and they had served him well for many years, but Keith was right; the time had come for Kody to tear them down.

"Sorry," the mouse uttered awkwardly. "It's … well. A lot of it is my job, but this started before that. It's the *world*." He spat out that word as if it were a curse. "I went from sports teams in high school to working in a factory. My whole life, almost everyone around me has come straight out of a beer commercial. Muscle cars and pickup trucks, competition, catcalls, chauvinism. I've been applying for jobs and trying to save up for *years*, but until I can escape this place, I have to pretend I'm one of the guys. And I hate it! I hate acting like boys don't cry and empathy and intellect give you cooties. I hate guy culture. It's not who I am. It's not *what* I am."

"So what are you?" A pause, then, "Trans?"

"No, I don't think so." Kody blushed at the insinuation, but then thought about it further. "Well, maybe. Probably not. It depends on your definition, I guess?" He took Keith's blank stare as a sign that, yes, he would definitely need to explain himself. He sighed. "What I did wasn't transitioning. It wasn't any kind of official, recognized treatment for anything. There were no hospitals or doctors, just some shady guy in a back room with a knife. I wasn't trying to be a woman, or I don't think I was anyway. I was just trying to be... girly." He swallowed. Even though Keith had already seen his empty crotch, there was still anxiousness, a sense of irreversible finality about admitting it. *No turning back now.* "You always wanted to see inside my drawer, right?"

"Yeah?"

Kody inhaled, bracing himself, and unzipped the backpack. He had never shown his bedroom drawer's contents to *anyone*, and that had included his boyfriend. The secrecy had been a sore subject with both of them even after they'd split up. The bird had always felt wronged for being shut out, but what about the mouse's privacy? Keith was finally getting his way, and it was easy to resent that, but Kody would have to swallow his pride to get through this.

He set every item on the coffee table delicately, reverently, as if they were priceless antiques. The bottle of glittery pink nail polish was the first to emerge. A tiara was next, its single shade of faux gold contrasting the multicolored translucent bead necklace that followed it. The tiny plush unicorn oversaw the rest of the items, including, perhaps most scandalously, a pair of lacy pink silk panties.

The silence terrified Kody the most. Keith should have judged him, or gloated over finally getting to see, or *something*. The hawk's eyes widened and his beak partially opened, but he betrayed no visible or vocal reaction beyond the obvious surprise. Was he struggling to wrap his head around what he was seeing? Was it that bad?

"This is what I am," Kody explained before the moment could grow any more awkward. He arranged everything in a perfect symmetrical row, mostly just to give his hands something to do. "Just a timid little mouse who likes girly things."

"Timid?" Keith had recovered, and it was his turn to smile. "You're not timid on the court. Or anywhere else I've ever seen you."

"I'm not timid at work, either. That's all a cover. A front." *A lie,* he almost said, but then changed it to, "A… face I put on for the others. I like dollhouses and lace. Flowers and butterflies. All the things actual women would probably consider trying too hard. Now do you see why I couldn't show anyone? Those guys at the factory would beat me senseless if they knew. It's high school all over again."

"High school." Keith closed his eyes and balled his fists. "Too many secrets. We were only a couple when no one was looking. Even when we were alone, there were things you wouldn't tell me. You kept this from me the whole time."

Kody hung his head. Whether the shame he felt was from the secret itself or what he had done to hide it, he couldn't say. "Yes. Well, the sentiment that eventually led up to it, anyway."

"Yeah." Keith chuckled, opening his eyes again. "Obviously, the actual cutting came later. I've seen your cock enough to remember you used to have one." He beak-grinned at Kody, whose short fur failed to hide his blush.

"It was my way of fighting back." Kody faced straight forward with a scowl. "In my job, the guys call you a dickless femme, something less than a real man, if you so much as root for the wrong sports team and your guys don't knock the other guys' heads off hard enough. Well, I *am* a dickless femme, I don't *want* to be a real man, and I've outworked, outperformed, and outright beaten every single one of them. So what does that make them?" Not that he would dare ask that to their faces, of course.

Keith's grin disappeared, as did any semblance of amusement or playfulness from his voice. "You're not happy, though."

Kody blinked. "Excuse me?"

"This didn't culminate with you getting your penis removed. It didn't culminate at all. It's still going on. You got the procedure done, sure, but you've been carrying on like this ever since. You cover it up well enough with your straight-acting competitiveness, but look how hard you're trying to maintain that image."

Kody felt his defenses starting to return. "If you knew—"

"I *do* know. I've dealt with 'real men' flaunting their masculinity, too. I was on the same teams you were, remember? I can still picture all those guys who bragged as they played, like the points they scored reflected the size of their… worth as a man." Keith coughed awkwardly. "Still, what do you think you're doing now? Your pride is every bit as fragile as theirs."

"Hey, it's not like that. I've never been happier with who and what I am. It's pretending to be something else that's the hard part." Kody puffed out his chest again. He sat straighter, and even spread his legs. He was still clothed, but the gesture conveyed slowly returning confidence. He was tired of being ashamed of his body... around Keith, at least.

Keith ran his claws against his beak, considering. "Afraid of discovery, then?"

"Yeah. And you're right; that's probably what's causing my nightmares." The wrong person finding Kody's secret could ruin him, and he could only guess who was or was not the wrong person. For all he knew, even Keith could have been like the others, full of swagger and obsessed with his dick. Any other guy in those locker rooms would have loved to shame and torment him, especially after he beat them all. Could Keith be out for revenge, too? The mouse's voice grew low and quiet and his body slumped, like a balloon losing its air. "It's easy to be strong and fearless on the outside. Showing weakness is what gets you in trouble. So I hide my vulnerability from everyone."

"And you do a fine job of it." More beak-scratching, more pondering. Kody could almost *hear* the gears turning in the hawk's head. Judging him, perhaps? "That's not what you need, though," the bird finally offered.

"What do I need, then?"

"To submit."

"What?"

Keith looked at Kody, unblinking, with a predatory grin. The bird seemed even taller somehow, his figure blocking more and more of Kody's view. The smaller mouse felt compelled to shrink from the giant hawk, but Kody met the gaze even while receding from it. It intimidated yet compelled him, as hypnotic as it was fearsome. *I have felt this sense of dark allure before*, he realized. *In that room, the stranger and his knife beckoning me closer. And I followed...*

"You know what you are, or at least what you want to be." Keith's movements were subtle yet insistent. The mouse hadn't even realized Keith was advancing until their bodies almost touched, feathers brushing against fur. The bird's voice was low but sharp, a bass-filled thrum that resonated deep within Kody's core. "You can be tough and strong when you need to, but that's not what you want. What you *want* is to be a pretty little girl who likes pretty little things, including the pretty little stump where her dick used to be. So why don't you give in?" the hawk asked quietly, expectantly.

Kody tried to shift backward, and lean so far away that he almost fell onto the couch's arm, but there was nowhere else for him to go. Keith loomed over him, imposing and impressive, like a true bird of prey come to take him away. *Being a girl...* The words danced in his head, flooding and overwhelming his senses. He could become drunk on the hawk's mental images if he wasn't careful. Finding an answer proved difficult. "I... I can't..."

"Oh, I'm not asking you to show up to work in a dress or anything like that." Keith remained in front of Kody. The mouse could see nothing but those eyes, which somehow captured him even when he tried to look away. The mouse was almost on his back, the bird inches away from lying down on top of him, and it still wasn't enough. "You just need to treat yourself, is all. But you already do that, don't you? That's why you have these." He gestured at the items Kody had left on the table, his secret stash of femininity. "You just need someone to play with you. Someone who can keep your secrets while indulging them." There was no mystery surrounding which 'someone' Keith had meant; the glint in his eye, the way he licked his beak, and his ever-advancing lean made his hinting all too obvious.

"Keith, I... ah..."

"Kody, would you like to submit to me?" Keith's voice took on a sudden sultriness.

"Would I... what?" Kody wasn't an idiot but it was impossible to think in the heat of the moment. Words came to him slowly, as if his entire mind had fallen underwater.

"I can give you what you want," Keith whispered. There was concern in his eyes to match his confidence, love as well as lust, sympathy as well as hunger; his was the gaze of a compassionate predator. "You can share your vulnerability with me, and I won't judge you for it. Let go, squeak."

Warning bells rang loudly in Kody's head until he couldn't hear his own thoughts over them. Keith's offer represented everything he had tried to hide, every urge he had been denying ever since the procedure. And yet...

The mouse regarded the hawk with fear, but also longing. He sought refuge, an escape from the world that had assailed him, and he found it in Keith's piercing gaze and sturdy arms. Keith wasn't one of those conceited jocks from high school, the mouse decided, nor was he a narrow-minded brute from the factory. Keith was his friend, his partner, his onetime lover. Perhaps again…?

"I… all right. Yes." Kody finally allowed himself to fall. His head landed softly on the arm of the couch—or he thought it did, but then he felt claws poking gently into his hair, along with the scales of Keith's palm. That was all the mouse needed. He closed his eyes and sighed in relief.

"Good. Now, what's the safeword? We need something for if you get too uncomfortable."

The mouse was entering a world that was exciting and new and he was eager to explore it all. Keith's pointed claws had become the best feeling he had ever experienced, like scratching an itch he hadn't even realized was there. He *wanted* to be uncomfortable. Still, there was no harm in being careful, and he appreciated Keith looking out for him. He just needed something far from his mind, a relic of the world he was leaving behind…

"Factory," he answered.

"Good." There was Keith's grin again. The bird lowered himself almost close enough for beak and snout to touch, teasing a kiss. The memories of how it had felt all returned at once—the way his hard beak dug just slightly into the mouse's soft lips, the smooth dryness of the avian tongue. Kody closed his eyes expecting to feel it all again, but instead Keith sat back up. He set Kody's head down and pulled his hand away. "Strip," he ordered.

As if to demonstrate the concept, Keith then slipped out of both of his shirts and cast them aside. Compared to the dullness of his clothing, the hawk's autumn-feathered body was vibrant and wild, as if his upper half had caught fire. Feathers partially concealed the lines and ridges of his physique, but he still radiated power even through them. Kody was used to the sight of Keith's chest from all their shirtless pickup games. When the bird's shorts and underwear followed, though, *that* was something the mouse hadn't seen in years.

"Keith—"

"Stand before me, little mouse. Let me see all of you."

Little mouse. Kody's ears tucked back. His name was *Kody.* That was something to which he clung tightly, fiercely, like any other facet of his public identity. A pet name only compromised his defenses; he was no one's pet. But this wasn't the court or the factory. This was a safe place. For once in his life, he actually *could* be a little mouse if he wanted to. And he did want to. The name bounced around in his head to his surprised delight, like his first time hearing what would become a new favorite song.

He rose from the couch and removed his clothing, as ordered. His socks and shoes were the first to go, followed quickly by shirt and pants. That left him in his underwear; tight, padded briefs packed with an artificial bulge. Wearing those, the mouse almost looked normal.

"Oh my." Keith clacked his beak in a *tsk-tsk* motion. "This will never do. You went to all that trouble to make yourself feminine. Why hide it now? Let me see the *real* you."

As tempting as it was to cower behind the illusion, Kody held his breath, bit his lip, and pulled his waistband down. Briefs and packer alike fell to the ground as the emasculated mouse revealed himself.

Kody's crotch was the same emptiness Keith had seen before, but this time he allowed a much closer and more intimate view. There were no blankets, no hands in the way, no panicked attempts to cover himself. He held still and allowed Keith as thorough an examination as the bird could want.

"You did this," Keith cooed as his hand found Kody's stub. "You found that person, reached out, went to him, had this done. You *wanted* this."

"Yes," Kody said, with a small gasp. Keith's touch was gentle, even with sharp talons adorning his scaled fingertips. They traced around his root with unexpected care, making the mouse shiver. The touch wasn't quite as intense as it would have felt with a full cock to grope, but he didn't mind. What remained of him could still feel and respond.

"And such a pretty little thing it is," the hawk mused. His claw-tips glided over its every fold. "It suits you. But what good does it do to keep it to yourself? Surely it must feel good when I appreciate your beauty."

"It... does," Kody admitted. He'd have been happy enough if Keith had *put up with* his modification. If he had merely accepted it without panicking or running away. However, Keith had *appreciated* it. Called it pretty. Called him beautiful. The praise was as wonderful as it was unexpected, and he was quickly becoming lost in it.

"Then you know what you *should* be wearing. No more lies, now."

Kody had never worn his panties in front of anyone else before. He had scarcely even worn them in front of himself. Comfort was not a familiar sensation to the mouse, even when he was alone with his mirror. The panties were a powerful fantasy when off and locked away, but too embarrassing to wield more than a few times a year. Stepping into them in full view of the hawk, he was worse than naked.

"There, see?" Keith leaned forward. "Those ones fit much better, especially without that pesky bulge in the way. Now, the jewelry."

With costume beads around his neck and a fake crown atop his head, the mouse looked like a little girl dreaming of becoming a princess for her birthday party. His face burned as if he had a fever and he couldn't make eye contact to save his life.

Keith remained sitting on the couch while standing Kody up to straddle his legs. He leaned forward, drawing closer to the mouse's silk-covered root until the fabric almost brushed against his beak. Kody looked down and Keith looked back up—to the mouse's surprise, the hawk seemed to stare into his eyes more than at his crotch. The gaze was that of a hungry bird of prey and Kody's legs grew weaker the more he stared into it.

"Are you happy like this?" Keith asked. "Do you like being a girl?"

"I'm not a..." Kody stopped and thought about it. "Yes," he admitted, with a small, uncomfortable whine.

"Good girl."

Keith's voice was deep but quiet, at the edge of Kody's hearing and so very, very soothing. Almost singsong in tone, the hawk whispered in a way that made Kody melt like an ice cube in the calming warmth of a gentle sun.

Keith pulled Kody's hips and the mouse fell forward, his hands finding the hawk's massive shoulders for support. "What have we here?" the bird asked with a wicked grin. His large, scaled hands wrapped around Kody's tiny wrists and lifted them away. He then brought his catch lower, setting the hands atop his broad avian hips instead.

The feeling of Keith's thick, downy feathers between Kody's slender fingers was familiar, nostalgic, yet every bit as exhilarating as the first time he'd felt it. *Strong,* Kody thought as he tried to squeeze Keith's legs.

The hawk's thighs were much bigger than Kody's hands, and even what little he could grasp was thick and solid. Keith's legs were like those of a granite statue draped within a fluffy coating of soft feathers.

Far more captivating than the bird's legs, though, was the wet pink tendril that slowly emerged from his genital slit. Keith's penis, unlike Kody's, was exactly as the mouse had remembered it; a reddish length, wavy, almost fluid, its thick base tapering along its flexible shaft toward the narrow, pointed tip. A simple slit held the organ when not in use, just as it housed his internal testes at all times. Once, long ago, Kody had envied Keith's ability to hide his masculine parts.

Kody's head was already low enough for Keith's shaft to meet it. A twitch, a flex, and the hawk's tip kissed the mouse's lips as if moving under its own power and desire. Kody had only to open his mouth and he would reunite with the old, familiar taste of the bird's manhood.

"Careful with the teeth, now," Keith said as Kody started to take in his length. "Sharp things down there would be your kink, not mine."

The mouse's cheeks blushed so hotly that, for a moment, he wondered whether Keith could feel the heat through his shaft. The bird must have known that his warning was unnecessary; Kody had more than enough practice to know what he was doing. Either Keith was accusing him of being rusty, or it was a cruel tease.

As experienced as Kody was with Keith, though, this time felt different. They had once pleasured each other as equals, each working the other's length in turn, or even simultaneously. Yet at this moment, the hawk's attitude and tone reflected a shift in power, an element of dominance. Kody now pleasured him on command, a pet servicing his master.

Keith's shaft, thin at the tip, fit deep within Kody's maw. The little mouse took it all the way to the back of his throat, just as he always had. No, maybe not *just* like that—the same actions somehow felt different to the newly subservient pet. More debasing, somehow. They shouldn't have been; it was just a cock, after all. Just one guy pleasuring another. There was nothing inherently wrong with that, right?

No, it was the submission. He had tried so hard to stay on top of the world, had defeated Keith six times in a row, yet there he was, servicing him like he was paying off a lost wager.

It felt good.

Fighting was easy but unfulfilling. Giving in was more like a roller coaster, terrifying but with a thrill to it. The blowjob felt debasing because Kody *wanted* it to. Keith could have treated him as an equal, with all the care in the world—Kody had only to speak the safeword and the humiliation would end in an instant. But no, he wouldn't do that. He didn't want the humiliation to end. There was too much power in it. With that realization the fire in his cheeks turned to fire in his loins.

Said fire was smaller physically than what a whole man could boast, of course, but it burned every bit as hot. Even hotter with the way his secret desires came to life around him. The leftover stub of his cock twitched and bulged in what would have been a powerful and intense erection had the rest of his shaft been there to support it.

"That's it," Keith murmured. "You've been dreaming about pleasuring a cock ever since you gave up yours, haven't you? Go ahead. Use your hands and that pretty mouth of yours. Show me how much you've wanted this. Good girl."

Kody whimpered. Taking orders was unfamiliar yet somehow welcoming, like his first walk through what would eventually be a new home. Very well, then. If Keith wanted to guide Kody as if the mouse had never done this before, then Kody would allow himself to be so guided. He would do whatever Keith asked of him. After all, his master deserved a reward. *Good girl*, the hawk had said. Kody loved it. He began to lick at the avian shaft, his enthusiasm bolstered by what his actions represented. He suckled devotedly because he wanted Keith to know how devoted he was. He was eager to be eager.

"That's it," Keith crooned. "Just like that…"

Keith wouldn't last long; Kody was still too good at what he did to allow it. As if to prove he hadn't lost his touch over the years, he brought back every old trick he remembered about what Keith liked. Every sensitive spot, every favorite tongue motion, they all came back to him as if they had never left. He even remembered Keith's little tells: the twitches and spasms of the bird's shaft, the erratic and unfocused thrusts from his hips, the way he would string sentence fragments together at random when he was almost—

"Ah, yes… that's… such a… pretty… you're so… oh, God… going…"

Perfect.

Keith screamed and screeched as if unable to decide between the two. Whichever vocalization he used, though, it all ended in twitching, throbbing, and a mouthful of avian semen. The mouse swallowed without hesitation. He had come too far to reject Keith's offering now. Besides, accepting it sat well with him, especially as it slid down his throat and warmed his insides.

As the intensity of Keith's climax faded, Kody let go of his master's shaft and pulled his head away, only to press his snout into the bird's soft feathers. How he had missed that smell, like chalk dust warmed in the afternoon sun.

Keith rested his foot on Kody's thigh, shifting his weight back and forth to make a small rubbing motion. The mouse mistook it for fatigue, a sign that Keith was tired, and therefore willing to settle for a half-hearted foot-nuzzle while he rested. However, he quickly realized that the rubbing was anything but lazy. Dexterous and controlled, Keith's talons traveled as gracefully as the claws on his fingertips had. His toes and soles moved with as much fluidity as his shaft, and soon his foot made its way inward and upward.

"Little mouse," Keith said, his first words since his orgasm. His voice was quiet, strained, but only slightly. The climax had sapped some of his strength but he had more to spare. "Can you still get off?"

Kody whimpered, more from the pet name than the personal question or rubbing, though all were effective in their own ways. "Yes. It's harder now, and it takes longer to reach climax, but it can still be done. I've... I've done it myself. The touches are duller but they still feel good." He smiled weakly. Even just a few minutes ago, he would have been mortified to admit his private bedroom habits, but now... "I just have to be so lost in the mood, so turned on, that even that dull rubbing is enough."

Keith grinned, then pressed his foot more firmly against Kody's thigh. "Pull down your panties."

Kody blinked, not sure what Keith had in mind but willing to obey. The waistband lowered easily enough and the mouse's stub was soon exposed again. He pulled the panties down to his thighs, where Keith's foot still rested. He tried to unfurl his legs and he expected the hawk to move out of the way as he did, but instead Keith's foot pressed down hard. Heavy weight bore down on his folded leg while talons dug into his fur, making him yelp in surprise and pain.

"I said *down,* not off." Keith scowled, his eyes as sharp as his claws. "Leave them there. Sit back."

Keith still didn't move his foot, but he allowed Kody to try spreading out anyway. Was that part of the command? Something he threw at the mouse to watch his pet squirm?

Bare rodent hands sunk into the white carpet as Kody struggled into position in front of the towering bird. His legs faced forward in what would have been a spread V shape, though his panties narrowed the angle. His balls rested on the ground, and above them his... well, whatever was left to be bared.

"You were staring at these earlier." Keith raised a leg, one foot in the air between them while his other resumed its journey toward Kody's crotch. "Did you like what you saw? Perhaps you need a closer inspection."

Keith's plantigrade heel bore a vestigial toe extending backward, ostensibly opposable, yet too short to control or grip anything. A scaled sole extended forward, separating the toughened heel and ball. At the front, his three forward-facing toes were long and powerful. The talons adorning each were also big, impressively so, yet they came to fine, needle-like tips.

The raised foot found its way to Kody's muzzle before the mouse could respond. The hawk's front toes were long and flexible, and by scrunching them he could make a perfectly serviceable cover over Kody's snout.

Kody gasped, or at least tried to, though Keith's foot made it more difficult to take in air. The curled toes felt like they could crush stones in their grasp, and the scales were similarly tough, thick, unyielding... *hard.* Keith's feet were as strong as the rest of him. Like a feral predator and prey, the hawk had caught the mouse and held him in his inescapably powerful talons.

While one foot held Kody still, the other found its way between his legs. Keith worked along the folded-over root of Kody's shaft, alternating between lazily stroking it like a pet cat and grinding against it as if putting out a cigarette. He was gentle on the upstroke, when the flat topsides of his talons traced along Kody's fur almost delicately. He was much more firm when his foot moved back down, dragging claw tips along Kody's skin. The scratches were gentle yet frightening, never harming the mouse but always threatening to.

"Such a good pet," the hawk whispered. "Good girl. Yes. Good girl..."

Kody couldn't take the teasing anymore. He leaned forward and grabbed the foot pressing against his muzzle, burying his nose even deeper in the avian sole. His hands clutched the topside of the foot partially for support, as if it were a rope to keep him from falling. Beyond that, though, he did it as tribute, even worship. The mouse was taking his rightful place beneath the hawk. Keith offered protection and, in exchange, Kody offered service.

"That's my girl," Keith said warmly, as Kody held his foot. "Look at you. So shy, so timid, yet so eager. Beautiful. This is what you've always wanted it, isn't it, pet?"

"Yes," Kody attempted to utter.

"Yes, *sir*." Keith drove his foot hard, pushing Kody back. Only by holding on with all his might did the mouse not fall. The more gravity threatened him, the more tightly he clung to his master's foot. "Say it like a girl," Keith added before pulling back his leg, returning the mouse to a safer angle as if he were pulling a drowning man ashore.

"Yes, sir." Kody's voice was even weaker after the chastisement, and what little strength it had went into softening its tone so the mouse could sound more effeminate. The words themselves were muffled. Fearing his attempt might not have been heard, he instead kissed his master's sole as one would kiss a newlywed spouse.

"Much better. And when my sweet little girl is being good, she gets what she wants." Keith's other foot drove its toe against Kody's stub. The talon lightly poked just above where the shaft would have been, while the toe itself rubbed insistently against the folds of the root.

Kody moaned, from the words even more than the sensations. The names, the affectionate tone, even the use of "she" all melted his heart and took him to heights he had never reached before... even when he had been "whole". He basked in his newfound femininity and let it cover him like a soft, pink blanket. One that nurtured him, protected him from the chill of the outside world, and kept him cozy within its embrace.

"That's it," Keith encouraged while continuing to rub the mouse's crotch. "You love this. You love the fact that you love this. This is who you are. You are a girl, *my* girl, and what a pretty one you are..."

Those words overwhelmed Kody, and the rubbing was a perfect conduit for his intoxicating need. Even dulled as the sensations were, in that state it was enough to drive him half-feral with lustful bliss. It

189

was like listening to a hauntingly elegant symphony through a door, muffled but still beautiful.

Kody squeezed the avian foot tight against his muzzle, clinging as if for dear life, and then buried his head lower. He had to get closer. Even the length of his own snout was too far away. He looked down toward at his chest and allowed his head to fall forward so that Keith's heel ran along the length of his muzzle bridge, the small opposable covering his nose. The ball rested directly between his eyes, half-covering them. The toes dislodged his crown, sending it falling to the ground below, and the talons dug into his hair as if threatening to pull him up like captured prey. He tried to breathe and almost failed, the air barely managing to get around Keith's sole. The threat of asphyxiation only made him gasp harder, moan louder, and push his hips forward so powerfully that Keith's other talons dug into his skin. Kody winced and whined, but moaned again.

"My girl wants more, I see." With Keith's foot in the way Kody couldn't see whether the bird was grinning. Still, the smug and amused tone told him all he needed to know.

"Yes, sir…"

"Then beg for it, girl."

Kody's mind flashed to the last time he had heard those words. For a moment, he was back in that dark room. *Beg for it, girl.* He had considered fleeing for the hundredth time; even standing his ground and quietly allowing it to happen was almost too much to ask, let alone begging for it. Yet the words danced in his head…

"Please," Kody uttered. "I want this. I *need* this."

"Good girl."

Keith clenched down hard with both sets of talons. One foot ground against Kody's root, digging insistently into his fur. The other pressed down, putting more of the hawk's considerable weight on Kody's snout.

The mouse's mind grew fuzzy. Every breath through his constricted nose was a labor. The air was almost too difficult to take in to be worth the energy spent acquiring it. Every hard-fought breath he did claim carried essence of Keith's foot. It was like being anesthetized; the foot was a mask and every breath Kody took through it pulled him further from reality, deeper and deeper into the throes of addled pleasure.

One set of talons dug into Kody's scalp, the other into the fur above his root. Both sensations were sharp, painful—had Keith finally punctured him? He would have to check whether he was bleeding later, when his mind was less frenzied. For now, let the cuts and scratches come. He wanted more. He *needed* more. He had to explore the world into which Keith had brought him. He had come too far, flown too high to turn back.

"My greedy girl." Keith's voice was so deep Kody felt it more than he heard it, through the contact between scaled feet and furred skin. Keith ground both soles against him roughly, as though he were the doormat after coming in from the snow. A broad toe teased the folds of Kody's root as if trying to work its way inside to touch whatever was left to touch.

Like his master, Kody lost control of himself as his climax approached. His breathing came in quick, ragged gasps, each punctuated with a quivering hip thrust. His moans grew louder and higher in pitch, building up to the moment of his release.

"Cum for me, little mouse." Keith must have known how close Kody was. He teased, encouraged, used his voice as that final push over the edge. "You are my girl, my lovely princess. Show me how good it feels to know that."

Kody gave himself completely to the sensations, to his role and his own desires. His orgasm was the means by which he accepted it all, his assent, his signature on the contract that officially made him Keith's girl.

"That's it," the hawk said softly, accepting the mouse's unspoken declaration.

Kody thrust his hips forward, well beyond caring about the damage from Keith's talons. He didn't shoot his seed so much as leaked it, but the intensity was still there. Fur and foot alike became a mess, as if the bird had stepped on a water balloon. The foot on Kody's face pressed firmly but not firmly enough. The mouse wanted more and he squeezed with all his strength to get it. His empty crotch continued its flowing release, like the gentle output of a faucet. Entire years of his life poured out in that stream; years of school and work, years of hiding in false masculinity, years of intensity and competitiveness and stubborn defensiveness, years of denying who and what he was. It was like the final, long-anticipated draining of a wound, one that had plagued Kody since he was young, long before the two lovers had ever drifted apart.

Seconds felt like years as Kody struggled to descend back toward reality. After touching the stars the ground seemed so very far away. Still, after pulling Keith's foot away and taking in a few unobstructed breaths, the living room slowly returned to view. There they were again, with the now-messy foot and thighs and carpet.

"My good girl," the hawk cooed. "My beautiful girl. Here, come sit on the couch."

Keith scooted over and then stood up entirely, freeing the entire couch for the mouse's use. Standing up without making a further mess was a challenge, but fortunately Kody didn't need to hobble very far.

"That's it." There was warmth in Keith's voice. "Stay there. Hold still."

By the time Kody had regained enough awareness to understand what Keith was up to, the bird had already left and returned carrying paper towels and two small spray bottles. The carpet received a few squirts of cleaner, but most of Keith's attention went to his mouse. He wiped away the white mess Kody's release had made, and dabbed at the red spots his talons had pierced. "There we go. All better." Keith's voice was nurturing and affectionate yet proud, like an owner polishing his new car.

Kody tried and failed to find words for what seemed like ages before he finally uttered a weak, "I wasn't expecting that."

"I'll bet." Keith chucked. "How are you feeling?"

"Um…" As the last of the euphoric cobwebs left Kody's brain he took a moment to assess himself. He looked down at his waist and saw a few small spots of red forming in his fur. Keith had drawn blood, but nothing serious; the scratches were comparable to paper cuts, at worst. The panties would easily cover them. He stood to pull them up and retrieve his tiara, then returned to his seat on the couch as Keith had ordered—no, *invited*. The domination was over.

Not even everything they had shared could make sitting there any less awkward for the gussied-up mouse. However, Keith had returned to being friendly and casual, as if there were nothing at all unusual to see. He went from teasing Kody for his stub and attire to treating them with respect, if he even acknowledged them at all. He didn't even look down again after he had finished his cleaning and grooming.

"Good," Kody finally answered. "I'm feeling… good. Thank you."

"Of course." Keith wrapped his arm around Kody, pulling him in, and before the mouse knew it the two were pressed against each other. Kody was all too happy to fall into Keith's embrace. The bird's chest and midsection were as big as ever, and when he wrapped his equally large arms around the smaller mouse it was as if Kody's entire world had been engulfed in warm feathers.

"I missed this," Kody said as memories of cuddling with his beloved bird slowly returned to him. He wasn't even sure if he had spoken aloud until Keith responded.

"It was nice, wasn't it?" Keith removed the tiara and gently traced his claws along the back of Kody's head, gliding them expertly through his hair and drawing pleasured groans for his effort. "You ever think about getting back together?"

The thought hadn't crossed Kody's mind until that day, but the submission had made him reconsider a great many things. It had been wonderful, even magical. More importantly, it had removed the deep, dark secret that had made him push the world away. Keith knew what Kody was and still accepted him. Still loved him, perhaps? He dared to hope.

"Yeah," Kody finally responded, even more blissfully than before.

"You have to trust me this time, though. Can you do that?"

Kody had been guarded and suspicious enough to drive off the one person who truly cared for him, yet Keith had never truly left. Armed with the mouse's newly uncovered secret, the hawk had every opportunity to ruin him and no reason in the world not to. Yet rather than do so, Keith had remained loyal, supportive, and respectful. If that hadn't earned Kody's trust, then nothing ever would.

"I think I can," the mouse admitted. It felt nice to lean on someone. Scary, but nice. *Like submission.*

"Good." Keith smiled and moved his hands to Kody's ears, giving each a gentle rub. "I'm glad. That means a lot to me, you know."

"I know." It meant just as much to Kody, after all. He had found what he had been looking for: a sanctuary, a shelter away from judgment and expectations, a place where it was safe to open up. A place where the emasculated mouse was free to be emasculated. "I've never been happier."

"Really?" Keith's smile turned more mischievous. "And here I was, thinking next weekend will be even better. I could help you coordinate a new outfit, you know. You have the right idea with this one but nothing matches. Trust me; I'm a professional. I can get you a deal."

Kody's body tensed. "But what if—"

"If anyone asks? Why, it's for my girlfriend."

The mouse had no answer at first, except for a deep blush and a small whine. He then squeezed Keith, or at least tried to. "You're amazing," he finally said.

"Does this mean I get to dominate you *on* the court next time, too?"

"Hah! Are you kidding?" Kody broke the embrace and pushed off from Keith's chest, finally putting daylight between the two. He looked up at the bird with a confident smirk. "You think this is going to make it *easier* to win? I only had one weakness and you just freed me from it. I'm unstoppable now!"

Keith's laugh was deep and booming, perhaps ominously so. "Is that so? Should be an interesting game, then."

Kody leaned forward and planted a small, playful kiss on the tip of Keith's beak. "They always are."

CHAIN LINK

Slip-Wolf

"My eye might have an orbital fracture, fuck if I know. My knees are chipped flint creaking when they bend and my fur hides some wonderful bruises around the kidneys. Standing hurts, sitting hurts and my desk at the firm lets me do both. What I worry most about is under my tail. Fear lives under that which won't wag. I keep waiting for the right muscle to pull, for the right shift of skin against skin and have me feeling like a rusty bike chain is being dragged right through me. But there's nothing.

"I've seen three doctors and had every test and they tell me I'm clean, just minor infections from alley dirt or whatever. No rectal damage, no STI's, nothing. I just can't believe it. I was out for a couple hours. My pants were still on and I told myself they just pulled them back up. That made perfect sense. I'm luckier than I have a right to be, all things considered."

"But you don't feel lucky." Cilia raises a brow, her lapin ear cocks and lifts the frames of her glasses. She can see right through the wolf hunched in her severe leather guest chair. I take a moment to stare at the fern in her office's corner.

"Yes. No." A sigh bleeds out of me. "Even now, a tiny part of me is mad they just weren't cruel enough to give me what I wanted." I don't know whether I should laugh or cry at that admission. When I settle someplace in the middle, it hurts just the same and the wracking sobs take a few moments to stop lancing pain through my side. "Those wonderful, generous bastards."

"You were drunk."

"Very," I nod evenly, my muzzle up and down with a sniff.

"But what was it that brought you there in particular, Anton? We've been talking so long about safe outlets for you. Didn't you listen to anything I told you?"

No. I'll be regretting that for another four months. Still, she's been helping me sort through things for months. I may as well fill in the blanks. "It mostly involves a fox and a stag."

* * *

I'll back it up a little bit and address the lion who was briefly in the middle. Myself and twenty other sales pros congregated at the fiscal-end office party for Fitch and Stirwich investments, where enough lock and key alcohol was already flowing to do Olympic laps in. Mitch was there, my rival for top sales spot, mane coifed to static perfection and tail lashing as he dressed-down a stag waiter who nodded every so often. "If my chateaubriand was any more burnt I'd have a scotch coaster."

"Yes sir." The waiter said with a shallow nod of his antlers.

"Fix it."

"Yes sir." The stag turned away and met my eyes for a second. I caught that tiny fire deep down where he wanted to knock Mitch's teeth out, but control was maintained with effort and he stalked back to the kitchen.

"Cute ass on that one." Mitch laughed at me, just under the thumping music. We were both into the same things, but as the only two known gay mammals in a relatively conservative establishment, our dances were slow and wordless. We'd checked each other out and the view was just fine. His golden ass is pert under those beige slacks. Which of us started wearing biz attire that matched our fur? Was that in a magazine?

Never mind. As much of an asshole as Mitch could occasionally be, I couldn't help wondering through scotch fog whether his rump was as firm as it looked. Not to mention those shoulders, biceps and pecs. Vanity and a gym card made him a complete physical package. The band cleared and the rat and otter who were the key partners in our firm took the stage. Jenner Stirwich's naked tail whipped excitedly as he gave a lengthy speech on hard work and success and mastering the universe. Then came the award bullshit.

"Anton Fisher, top closer for two consecutive quarters! Come to the stage please!" Applause and whistles deafened the private function room. I stalked to the dais on which the rat and otter waited. I was congratulated with toothy smiles, handed a congratulatory plaque and the envelope that had my check. I plastered a smile on my muzzle like a Halloween costume as I thanked them for believing in me. The applause faded as I moved on and the next name was called. The worst part over, I chugged back two fingers of scotch and wrestled the check into a pocket. It was probably fifteen thousand crumpling next to my change and roll of mints and I didn't give a damn in the world. I responded to a back-pat with a raised glass, already being refilled, and didn't even turn around.

The air was getting heavy and I needed to get the fuck out of there. The smells had stirred into a morass and the buzz of scotch in my veins was mostly all I felt.

Mostly.

Mitch, sitting at my left, yawned wide enough to put a cub's head in his mouth. "Great, that plaque looks heavy enough to keep your scheduler from blowing away so you don't stand me up at squash again."

"Sorry Mitch. Had one of those nights."

"Smoke?"

I didn't smoke. Something in the way he asked…"Yeah, sure."

Passing the kitchen, Mitch put his arm low around me and grabbed my ass. The stir in my loins was immediate as a breath. Yeah, he felt it too.

"I'm in the mood for celebrating, how about you?" The lion's brows waggled above the rum-scented cage of his smile.

"We already went out for a drink," I teased. There'd been coy little hints all night that the lion was done stalking. Five drinks in, it seemed the right sentiment to have. "I think maybe we should go *in* instead."

Mitch took a swig of the glass I hadn't noticed he was holding. He set the empty on something without looking and ignored the sound of breaking glass when it fell. Behind him, that stag he upbraided glared, boring a cold 'fuck you' into the back of Mitch's head. "Your place is closer, right?"

My eyes left the stag to meet Mitch's gaze. The corners of my mouth said it's much closer.

Too soused to drive, we took a cab. We were close enough to make one another sweat on the elevator ride up to my condo.

Mitch was purring in my ear, tail tip tapping my shin. "I could tell what you wanted. At lunch yesterday, last couple weeks. You were really dodging around it, which was strange from somebody who seems to get what he wants from people, but I still knew."

"You were right," I breathed.

Mitch grinned. "You're gonna be mine up there." He said it unambiguously and I felt a thrill jolt through me. "I don't bottom."

"You won't have to." Minutes later we were wrestling one another's neckties off as the apartment door slammed. The lights stayed low as clothes came away, our scents filling the foyer, then the kitchen and finally the bedroom, a trail of designer labels trailing civilization behind our ragged pants. I hadn't known Mitch for long, but had become intimately familiar with what the lion wanted from me, or from anyone really. The stories of his conquests wouldn't have needed circulating. The golden cat simply radiated domineering power, certainty rooted in his stance, his glare, the musk trapped under the elastic waistband of his Emporios. I resisted a belch as I grabbed at the silk briefs and dragged them downward. "I want to see what you're going to take me with."

Mitch smiled daggers. "Doggie, you're in for a ride."

"Tell me more." My cock was hardening as I felt the barbs of that thick cat-prod slipping free under my paw. Pre-cum wet the black undergarment as he let me shed it. "Are you gonna take me down?" I growled a playful challenge, ears rosy as I watched the cat's dick stiffly march from its sheath.

An assured nod. "I'll fuck your ass broken and make you my omega bitch."

Inelegant, sounded like wrestler trash talk, but it did the trick. My mouth hunted for Mitch's and we flirted tongues for a moment before I sank down, teeth and lips working the fur on Mitch's neck, nipple, each rock-hard roll of ab. We were naked now, toes digging into the carpet, Mitch's claws pricking deep through my shoulder fur. The slight sensation of pain as those arms pushed me insistently downward was as intoxicating as the view. Feline cock tickled my chin, nose, then tongue as I lapped it like cool cream in a high-noon summer before taking it in. The barbs on Mitch's cock slid along my cheeks as I started to draw off him.

"That's what I like," Mitch said approvingly, giving me a patronizing pat that brought a moment of shame. In that condescension was a trigger, something that hoisted deep into my one recurring fantasy and yanked it out squirming. Just like that, the membrane between what I really wanted and this moment broke wetly. In my mind, I saw a fox,

198

climbing over the detritus of a burnt out world, hungry for the wolf responsible. Shame settled over me like a sweaty fog.

Mitch's hips stopped thrusting just then. "I've had enough of that muzzle. I want your tail up," he growled.

I unsaddled my cheeks, immediately. The idea of that feline cock mercilessly parting my ass had me painfully hard. My tail wagged itself into a blur.

"Alright! I'm gonna fuck you like a force of nature," Mitch promised. "Pardon in advance for the property damage." He swigged his drink. I didn't remember pouring him one, but whatever.

"You can do whatever you want to me, even if it hurts," I moaned.

"You're into that?"

He could almost be my vulpine, or one of the avengers that attended him. "I want to get what's coming to me." It wasn't supposed to sound like the plead it was.

Mitch grabbed my tail, his other paw snapping a condom over his still-stiff cock. No lube. I didn't care. This made things perfect.

I hissed as the first inch forced its way inside. The girth making the cocktail of pain and pleasure that crawled after it even more potent. I stirred my hips around him, tail coming alive in the lion's fingers as my imagination kicked in furiously; I could feel the cold metal of a chain-link fence binding my muzzle, pressing diamonds into my chest, sliding along my testicles. This is the standing bed on which I was punished. Each member of the cast in my fantasy came to the fore, one by one.

"You're one deep dog," the lion chuckled. "Time to fuck the brown and grey right off you."

In my head, that promise came from other lips, a tabby cat's. They had me now, my captors, my masters, wingless Valkyries come to invade every part of me for the crimes I've committed. The sweet shuddering discomfort of the lion's invasion, taken one hot thrust at a time had me whining deep in the back of my throat, teeth bared and my tongue pressing through the gaps in that shaking chain link fence.

Then I did it. I fucked it all up. I just couldn't keep it in. "I'm so sorry," I breathed weakly, bucking at the rough paws around my hips. "I'm so sorry I took it all away."

Mitch's thrusts fell off stride for a moment. "What the fuck you talking about?" The lion hissed.

Mind dulled by the ecstasy of my fantasy and fogged by drink, I moaned pitifully. "Your wealth, all you had. I'm a bastard for what I did. I deserve to be punished!" The moan turned to a hiss as the lion's urgent thrusts pressed my face into the bed.

"You're being punished because that's what twinky wolves like you get. I'm your *god* little dog! Shut up!"

"I'm a thief, I'm a worthless parasite! I need to be punished, ground into the dirt! I've taken from so many and I know I deserve their contempt. Fuck me like the worthless mutt I am!"

"Shut up! Seriously God! Shut uuupp." Mitch groaned as he came. Hot liquid pulses of the feline filled the condom inside me.

Abruptly, the thrusting ceased. The lion glared down at me, cock still buried in my ass. "What the fuck is wrong with you? Are you sick or something?"

I turned one baleful eye on the lion. "No?" I said it like a question.

"What is all this shit about you being a parasite? Is that a joke?"

Now I'd done it. "I'm...I need to, uh, dammit Mitch you wouldn't understand."

The lion pulled out, barbs hurting with the surprise. Mitch was furious as he stalked around the bed. "This whole time, breaking every single sales record, making the bosses look over all our heads at you like they're gonna make you partner and you're what, a goddam socialist or something?"

"No. That's not it! I've just got...issues with what I do."

"Issues with what? We take money from people too stupid to hold onto it because stupid people shouldn't have money. None of it's illegal. They didn't want risk, they shouldn't have sat in the chair should they? Some funds fail, so what? We're masters of the fucking universe. That's what I thought brought both of us here tonight!" Mitch winced in disgust.

I looked down into the sheets on my bed. No sense going half way. "I haven't felt pride in any of this in a long time, Mitch. It's all habit, nothing more."

Mitch swore a stream of profanity as he wrestled his clothes back on. "I'm not gonna stand here and listen to you tell me I'm some kind of asshole for taking what I want in life. I can *rent* a better ass than yours. I'm celebrating elsewhere."

I hunted for the right words as he got dressed. "You won't tell them at work, will you?"

"Who would ever believe you're this sick? Wise up to how good you have it you embarrassing mess." My unit's door slamming was all the punctuation the lion needed.

I had another drink in my hand in minutes, not bothering to dress just yet, swearing up a storm. Goddam it, I was getting nowhere with this. I had to act.

* * *

"You probably want to know what that was just now, especially as it was just two hours later that I found myself almost dead."

"I think I know most of it." Cilia coughs politely. If any of this is exciting to her she has a clinical wall thicker than lead. Were she a guy, I'd find that just a little hot. "A little more context would help us unpack."

"You want me to back it up to the start."

"Was there a start? A first time you wanted…this?" Her eyes twinkle just a bit, in interest not amusement.

"Yes. That's where the fox gets involved."

* * *

Light scaled the glass flanks of buildings outside my office, illuminating the cable-knit sweatered badger with stripes crooked through worry. I wore one of my better suits, a sharp grey Brioni three piece, tie and shirt white as my throat fur. The match made me look pure, elemental and honest. Skunk-strength olfactory counters kept us both under a vanilla haze. The most effective hunters are never scented coming.

"I'm not sure I can move more than eighty into that fund," the badger muttered.

Show time. "Of course, if retirement means a trailer park in New Mexico and TV dinners till death then sure. Were those boat keys you just had? They had a float-ring on them I noticed."

The badger's paw went to a pocket and said nothing.

I didn't show teeth. "You have a lifestyle you don't want to surrender and why should you? That's why you're here."

The badger sniffed. "Any more would mean all I have. I'm not comfortable with that."

"But you aren't comfortable with taking next to nothing. What we want is always right there. It's just a question of stamping on that nagging voice that says you can't have it and taking what you know you deserve. Another forty thousand over twenty years parks that boat on the Amalfi coast. Have you seen Italian cats skinny-dipping? Beautiful sight."

The badger caved so slowly I could see the sun going down. "Are you sure this is the right fund for me?"

"*No. We're going to collect insurance when the fund fails, your wife will take whatever's left when she divorces you and you'll come down here to club and fuck my lying ass with my own golf putter!*"

"*Oh dear me!*"

Outside of my imagination; "It's the smart choice."

Triplicate signatures later I was alone. In just two days I'd collect my award at the restaurant. I had no boy or girlfriend, no travel plans, no toys I wanted. All I could do was dump the lucre into something safe and less reckless than the shit I peddled out of nothing more than habit. I felt heavier with the closed account on my desk, like I'd disgustingly gorged on a high calorie dessert that left me hot with indigestion. I deserved to feel that way.

I'm a hunter, true, evolved from pack structures that picked off the weak. Countless libertarian tracts clapped me on the back for staying true to that, despite the fact that I was becoming less and less successful about lying to myself that all were fair game.

Someday I would be called to account for that.

An hour later, after work was over, I took the same detour I'd taken for weeks.

The Beamer's engine purred as I scanned the derelict buildings, boarded up husks I passed every evening after work. My strong nose quivered instinctively, roving for a scent my AC had already scrubbed out before cool air ruffled my fur. My eyes sought a glint of red, behind a rickety shopping cart, or leaned against a doorframe. He was out there. He was my favorite.

I turned the muttering radio off with a manicured claw and swallowed. When I saw the vulpine again, I didn't know exactly what I'd feel, but the compulsion to find out kept me alert. In the shadow of a ruined tenement, my eyes picked out paw toes curling. Sparks came from flicking fingers and a cigarette shakily rose to a blunt white muzzle, a cat's by the nose.

The fox wasn't here. Too bad. Still I knew I'd remember the hobo cat, thin pinkish lips, dirty ashen pads on the soles of his feet. I'd imagine how my growing cast smelled, how the ragged fur bristled under the fabric, how the blunted claws were just sharp enough. I rolled on past picking up speed, imagination feeding me the tense anxiety of someone being chased. My loins were already tickling as I thought I could smell my own fear. I held that feeling, whatever it was, all the way past the light of a lone working gas-station, out of the city to my apartment on the burbs' edge.

An hour later, I poured a scotch and opened my laptop. Where to go first? Hobo porn or homeless porn always turned up nothing interesting. The best results always came when looking up nudism and feralism. Juicy stuff seemed to go with people who thought civilization and technology were mistakes and then said so on the internet.

But where was the porn? Past the social justice links about income inequality, deforestation and hemp, were the pics of tasteful, nude families at naturist camps offering gateways to the feral lifestyle and reclamation of nature. This was the part of the internet that commoditized feralism, right up to renting tent equipment for "feral" excursions into rainforests and jungles. I couldn't tell if sites like this were missing the point or seeing it perfectly and getting ahead of the game, but that was capitalism and who cared. I sipped my scotch again as I finally found an image set for feralism porn. Lots of images of naked mammals rutting outside, some cleanly, some muddy or wet that were kind of hot. It took a while to find something that stirred me, and while it wasn't gay, it was enticing to say the least.

A female cougar, naked except for a necklace of teeth, grabbed at the leash-like necktie of a twinkish corgi in a disheveled suit jacket who was naked from the waist down, hard little cock springing up at his attacker. The buxom, aggressive cougar, mouth roaring, bore a spear that dipped under the corgi's balls, examining her catch. The wide circle of terror on his face was comical, yet pathetic. The image had a caption that really did it for me. "When civilization fell and vines covered the earth, the Goddess stalked hungrily among the deposed masters of the fallen concrete kingdoms and took many slaves as her mewling toys."

Yes! This was more like it. I nearly spilled my scotch as my paw found my climbing cock and went to work. One handed, I sought more results, finding one gay-labeled feralism image which I anxiously clicked. In that photo, a coyote aggressively bottomed a wolverine, both naked except for thin grass skirts, and…riding on the back of a giant plastic dinosaur? What the fuck was this shit? I backed up the prior image, centered on it, drank in the raw violation promised by its vengeful narrative and the expressions of its participants. That worthless corgi was going to make a perfect slave for that sex-hungry kitten.

Ten strokes in, and I was already molding the fantasy, putting myself in the corgi's place. He was now on the sidelines and likely be forced to clean us both up with this tongue. The ferocious cougar lost her breasts, grew a weeping hard cock and was quickly surrounded by an equally insatiable tribe of hunters. Some wore the tattered remains of clothes representing lowly stations in life before the apocalypse. Others were proudly naked, smeared with pigments and jeweled with beads and bleached bones. The minions of nature's justice were all there to hold the captive lupine down as the king of the new jungle assessed his prey. I watched in terror as they threw my designer clothes on a bonfire piece by piece, a conflagration rising into the dusky sky. "I'm sorry!" I wailed. "I didn't mean to have your savings ruined! I didn't mean to leave you broke!"

The fox was the cougar's right-hand man, a leather harness binding his chest. He wore a leather biker's cap on his head.

Wait, no he didn't, that looked stupid. The feathers tied to his ears bobbed as he taunted me, kicking dirt over my bare legs. I was already filthy and would never be clean again. "You worthless wretch, thieving that which has no value in the new world. Worthless parasite!" His spit landed on my chest. The white tabby cat in ripped jeans grabbed at my arms while a thick-cocked stoat tugged at a leg. I squirmed and squealed and thrashed against my enslavers, managing to escape, racing through the ruins of a decrepit city as they gave chase, lustful whoops and screams echoing off the dead faces of empty sky-rises. Cackling taunts echoed on my heels. "We will catch you! For your crimes you will be spit-roasted on the cocks of every man in our tribe!"

I ran down an alley, hoping to lose them across a vacant lot, but it was blocked. The chain link fence rattled as I struck it, one paw reaching up to climb. Then they were on me. Growls and laughs closed in. "Time to suffer the consequences you insufferable mutt," someone breathed in my ear before a tongue dived in.

I didn't plead. I didn't dare. "I deserve this," I breathed. "I've had this coming for so long and I can't even beg for anything else."

Things moved fast at that point. A paw shoved my nose through a metal diamond of fence's chain, muzzling me. My filthy neck tie, torn in two, slipped around my wrists and was used to bind them, holding me spread-eagled. As the stink and musk and heat crowded in around me, claws digging into my flanks, my lengthening cock slid slickly against the cold metal of another link in that fence. Fingers wiggled in under my tail. I gasped as I felt my knot growing. The whole fence flexed against the weight my captors threw against me. "Do it, punish me. Please. I'll never be sorry enough."

The bodies parted briefly for the king, who wasted no time, invading me without grace or invitation, my tight ass a pliant conquest. "This is all you're worth, thief. A hot fuck under the sun of my kingdom," he purred. Languid thrusts picked up speed as the cougar growled, licks on my ear turning to tugging bites. As the cougar's hot lordly load popped off inside the christened slave, my eyes rolled back to see the hard stare of the savage hunter fox, grinning fiercely, stone-pierced ears flicking with impatience as he waited his turn with the tribe's new toy.

"Oh yeah," I gasped as I came, popping pearls of jizz on the space-bar and V-key. Breath caught in my throat in the real world as I gradually ramped down. My hooting captors departed but I said the words anyway in hushed whispers as the thread of release broke. "I deserved...that."

My libido quieted down, I sat in silence, pondering where I was going with this. How many circles could I twist in before this 'thing' I had drowned out everything else. I used a wet towel to clean the keyboard off before I logged in to an online haunt, Leatherdogs.com that I went to far less frequently than my derelict part of town. There were a few kinkster discussions going, a thread on ball-gag safewording. Somebody with a boxing kangaroo as an icon was suggesting that aardvark was a speak-able gag word. I hadn't been deep into any scene like this, feeling my fetish was something small that I could tuck away whenever I wanted too, but a souring worry tipped me off to the fact that my self-flagellation over my desire for everything short of flagellation was getting out of hand.

"What's up, brother?" Rack-thrill asked me in an instant message window.

I sat for a long time pondering how to answer that. "Honestly," I typed out. "I think I'm going through a dilemma." That was a great thing to call it. I reached down to shift my receding cock to prevent it from sticking to my thigh.

"Oh?" His icon was a muscular torso with beige-furred arm flexing in front of him. It was cut but not bulky, species indeterminate, and I was unsure if it was a stock photo. His icon was ringed by the rare red border of a self-identified Dom, while my wolf silhouette icon had the rare border of a sub's blue. Over two thirds of the people on this site had the green border that meant flexible.

"I had that fantasy again, that hot thing where I'm getting gang-banged. And it's awesome, don't get me wrong. Just wonder what it says about me."

We'd met months ago and chatted long enough on this site, never once having met in real life, to be unfazed by anything anybody said. Anonymity was so freeing.

I imagined I could hear a laugh in his reply. "It says you like getting fucked? Honestly, don't look too hard at what sends you over the falls, Janus." Janus was my online name. "I bring too much anger into my play I think. Not that I don't have reasons."

"Go on." Reading somebody unloading their own baggage let me put some distance between myself and my looming worries. For all my faults I was a great ear. Or was that eye?

"My boss got on me again. God I hate that fat civet bastard so much. And the customers, every one of them stuck-up, self-appointed royalty. They don't even see each other, all demanding attention, right goddam now. I'm so damn close to spitting on them, every single shift." Rack-thrill kept the description vague. He didn't like to talk about where he worked. I could identify with that. "My boss is the worst, inherited the place from his father. He's an idiot who thinks he's a higher life-form. I just want to flog him with a wet towel, just chase him naked through the place, snapping his jiggly ass over and over again."

The image made me laugh, a genuine, throaty heartfelt laugh. "How do you get him naked?" I typed.

"Put itching powder down his shirt and pants, lock him in the store room until he has no choice but to take it all off, then open up and herd him out. Really give those rich, greedy bastards a show."

And I was one of those very bastards, literally. The shame that tinted my ears was strangely welcome. Immediately, I wondered what a wet towel would feel like snapping my ass. "So have you…tried to live that fantasy?"

Long pause. "Once. I had somebody who I tried it with. The scene didn't work right. That kind of play has to be perfect."

I stared at the chiseled fur of the chest on his icon. It was entirely possible that he was a fox, not that it was being a fox that made the primary object of my attentions so enticing. All that raw musk, the raw essence of unwashed, pure vulpine. Just maybe Rack was… And just maybe if he wasn't that would be a good thing.

"Rack."

"Yeah."

"Wanna meet up some time?"

The pause was painfully long. I stared at the site, watching banner ads for a downtown dungeon meet recycle on my screen, sliding across bare furred backs and up leather cuffed wrists.

"I don't want to do that, yet," came the reply. "Listen though, I'd like to give you my number, maybe we could chat some time. I'm still not comfortable meeting somebody new yet. My last relationship was a bit of a mess and I want to keep this part of my life away from work. I'm a recognized face there."

I sagged. I knew the feeling, having only one person to talk to at work who even knew I was gay. I also could identify with relationship woes, having been alone for nearly three years. We just got bored… "I understand."

A phone-number came up. My phone was on the table so I scrawled it on a gas receipt. Another text came up while I was shoving the paper into the pocket of the pants I was sitting bare-assed on. "I'm gonna go offline now, gotta be at work early. Did you ever reach out to that friend I mentioned? The sex therapist?"

"Cilia Sparks? Not yet. I don't think I need that kind of help yet."

"She's just an ear, Janus. Somebody who has no competing interest or agenda. She runs her own scenes too, a workshop on master-slave discipline. She helps people process stuff that's hard to, well process. I've enjoyed our talks."

I scrawled that number down too. "Thanks."

* * *

I rarely bothered to talk about my predilections online anymore because while the fantasy of my deserved humiliation and conquest took different themes, the ingredients were the same. Whether back-country bayou or in a nuclear bunker, they always took me up against that fence, toyed with and fucked me until I popped. It was getting so I couldn't get off on anything else anymore. As days passed and I realized how poorly I'd buried my hatred for what I did for a living, I realized I didn't want to. A night of fantasy reckoning always reset me for the following day, ready to put on my mask and fuck more people over for their money.

Work dragged on. Accounts closed. Jenner Stirwich stopped in to find out if I'd moved inventory on the series six funds with all the junk bonds fattening them up and suggested I pitch them to an elderly raccoon couple coming in later that day before asking if I'd be early to the party. For the first time in a long time, listening to him, I actually felt a small wave of revulsion pass over me both for him and myself. Had I actually once been proud to work for this rat? To work here doing this? Who had that guy been who'd wagged his way in fresh out of college? The anger at my whole situation was sudden and invigorating, and while Stirwich droned on about white wines, I idly wondered how the rat would handle a post-apocalyptic jungle-fucking. The image wasn't as funny as I'd hoped it would be. We finished our exchange and he went to the next office. Disquiet turned to unease, and then became aggravation as my next clients fell under the block and signed what they were told to sign. I left a little early, hurrying to the car, sweat covering my back.

Once again my BMW rumbled past the same old haunts of bricks and trashed benches. I knew every detail of this place now like a studied work of modern art. But the people inhabiting it were different, idealized, purified to my self-disdaining purposes. The first time I ever saw the fox, I'd been startled by the juxtaposition between the vulpine's startling beauty and haggard state, two aspects that should have cancelled one another out. Since then I'd been compelled to drive by and seek him out, study him, covet his inexplicable potency.

Covet his judgement.

No fox right now. Today I spotted two people haunting this stretch, one rat in a dirty sweater and the cat again, smoking a stubby cig and leaning against a wall. I watched him look down awhile, then realized when he brushed ash away that he was reading a ragged book in his lap. I'd seen him a couple times now. He must be a regular. The cat stubbed out the butt on the cracked sidewalk and I felt a sudden surge of confidence as a frantic urgency welled up inside me. Fuck my internet and to hell with my chatroom.

I rolled forward, claw slipping to the passenger window button. "Hi."

The cat didn't respond until I repeated it and when he raised his head, his ears were going back. "What do you want?" His voice, spoken just loud enough to be heard over the thrum of my car had an edge, the words more a warning than a question.

The next words I wanted were syrup lost at the corners of my mouth. He just stared at me as I narrowly avoided asking him if he lived around here. I stammered a question straight to the point. "You know where I can find a…good time around here?"

"I don't sell drugs and I'm not buying any." His legs curled up defensively and he looked uncomfortable.

This was going wrong right off the bat. I frowned, wondering how I could recover the moment. The situation was so precarious, everything that chased my desires and loathing so close. The scent of the cat drifted over, dirt and musk and sweat in something primal my vacuous airtight world didn't know. I felt a slight stir in my loins and tried to drop my voice an octave when I asked him "Want to go somewhere?" I swallowed. "I have money."

He stared into my eyes for a moment, his blue ones narrowing. "Leave me alone."

"All I—"

"Fuck off." The anger came to his face and it was beautiful. It took all my effort to put the Beamer in gear and roll away, a tightness threatening to overwhelm me as desperation swelled. The fear was there of course, but subsumed under something deeper and more primal, the only thing stronger than fear I could feel. I went home and jerked off for an hour, but was wistful about the opportunity lost.

* * *

"So you were denied." Cilia says levelly.

"That time," I answer deadpan, feeling shame rise.

"Why didn't you simply accept what you'd been told and move on? Leave them be? Were you going to sexually proposition others on that block?"

I fidget in my seat. The bruises on my back make me wince. "In all honesty, I would have, given time. I don't know honestly."

"But you tried to find an outlet elsewhere."

I roll my eyes and remember Mitch. "My internet friend didn't want to play and nobody else drew my attention, so yeah I went for the low-hanging fruit. When that didn't work, and I was furious and horny and drunk as hell…"

* * *

"Get some help you embarrassing mess!" My condo door slammed and Mitch was gone.

I wanted to scream into the bedspread. I'd opened up, bared my soul to someone I'd thought a friend and that selfish bastard did what selfish bastards do. Wasn't enough that he could have me anyway he wanted to, he had to have his wolf in the state of mind that he chose. Goddam self-absorbed asshole.

So I downed another scotch and nearly spilled the next wrestling with my mouse as I logged on. The screen's ghostly light hurt in my temples, as I went to Leatherdogs. There were some handles online, but the one I sought was in away status. "Off getting fucked by the man" was Rack-thrill's 'at-work' signifier. I brought up some porn, flicked through a couple images, felt nothing. I needed contact. I needed release.

Cilia's number. She had a profile on this site and five others according to her listing on Leatherdogs. Her icon was a leather mask with two bunny-ears poking out, holding a framed doctorate diploma in gloved hands. Very tasteful, I had to admit. I finished another drink as I setup a DM contact request, mentioning Rack-thrill as a referral. I silently begged the rabbit to answer, nearly swaying from the accumulated booze in my system.

"Janus," the reply said, "I don't believe we've spoken. If you'd like a consultation, I will provide one complimentary hour by appointment or by chat."

"I need you—your help now. I have a fetish that…I'm in a bad place."

"I'm listening. And I'm not judging. All is confidential if you wish to trust me."

I bit back a sob as my fingers flew over the keys, creating a wall of text with more grammar and spelling mistakes than I could bother to count. My fetish, my desire for punishment. My work, my utter loathing for what I'd done and my outlet for release. I may even have typed in the firm I worked for, I don't know. All I knew was I didn't mention Mitch. I just couldn't bring myself to mention Mitch. All I wanted was a little sexually-charged abuse and that bastard left me dry.

"I understand the pervasiveness of a deep-seated desire you can't fulfill, Janus."

Can't fulfill. Reading those words hurt. They were right there, on the edge of town, broke, downtrodden by witless greedy slimes like me. And I had money to pay them to do it. That was the worst part. Scotch swished as I poured again. I could get my punishment, they could get a night of fun, treating some wolf's asshole like a stuffed animal and I could help them in their predicament, give them a step away from poverty with some of the lucre I accrued.

I saw the light through a beautiful alcoholic filter of total clarity. I could be their Robin Hood. Money taken from the rich and given, along with my willing hot little body, to the poor.

"I'm going to do it, Cilia. I'm going to get the scene put together tonight."

There was a protracted pause. "Really? You suggested a moment ago that this wasn't possible. You have partners for this scene that you've talked it over with?"

I could see the abandoned stretch of derelict lots and its derelict people in my mind's eye. The fox would likely be easy to find. Or hard. It didn't matter. "They're going to get the night of their life."

"Did you set parameters? Are we talking a proper RACK scene here?"

I stifled a fiery whiskey burp. "There aren't any racks in this deal. It's a fence, remember? I typed that, A chain link fence."

"Please note that I typed RACK, as in Risk Aware Consensual Kink. Discussed boundaries, tested bonds, third-parties not in the scene checking in on you. You need all that if you're setting up a rape simulation. There are essential resources on this that I've prepared." A list of links filled the next text panel.

Simulation. Drunk as I was, the word sounded dirty. My cock throbbed, knot refusing to budge and I touched it with a paw. It was going to happen, I decided with certainty and found my heart skipping with excitement. This was going to be my night.

"I know what my partners need. I know they know what I need. They're going to make me pay for all the bad ruthless shit I've ever done and fuck me down into the mud where I belong."

"I just hope you don't get hurt. Please, promise me you'll read these links and make sure you're doing things safely. I understand that risk is part of the attraction, but you have a responsibility to this community."

Holy shit, I thought she sounded like my mother. Quite wrongly though, I saw that later. "Thanks for the consultation. I'll let you know how it goes."

I logged off and disconnected.

The sun had gone down and the clock showed it was nearly nine p.m., the perfect time. I certainly hadn't planned this reckoning for the day time. I put my suit back on and shakily patted myself down for the car keys before realizing I'd left it valet parked at the restaurant not two hours ago. I called a cab, had the weasel driver stop at an ATM where I gathered my maximum withdrawal, a thousand in fifties. The weasel made me repeat the next and final destination twice to make sure he'd been heard correctly. "Just drop me at that intersection. I don't have a specific address."

"You're dressed pretty nicely for that part'a town. You'll be popular in all the wrong ways bud," the weasel counselled, scratching worriedly at one ear.

"Do you want this fare or not?" I slurred.

Twenty minutes later, streetlights blurring farther and farther apart, the cabbie dropped me off, and left in a huff when I declined a final opportunity to change his mind.

I was ragged with liquor and excitement, the sense of danger and vulnerability putting a thrill in me. My reckoning was coming soon and I anxiously began scanning and sniffing, looking for the essential ingredients of my quest. I found the cat first.

"Wanna get back at somebody who helped ruin your life?" I asked with a lump in my throat.

"Are you that guy from—" the cat's ears pinned back when I

dropped a hundred in his lap.

"Where's the fox?" I asked. "My height, really slim, fucking hot-looking." Should I have said that? The cat blinked and pointed down a long alley. I found a mangy-looking skunk further into the darkness, wandering towards the street, scent buzzing around him so heady it hurt. A waved bill and a beckoning motion was all it took. My genitals start to throb again as the inevitability of my actions started to set into my subconscious. This was going to happen!

Around a corner, past a dumpster that had long been unloaded and towards a glint of light that resolved itself into a small fire. A bear sat at it, and across from him, a white-tipped tail twitched.

I straightened my tie. Had to present myself just right. "Evening," I said, nearly stuttering under a bundle of nerves. The fox's muzzle turned to regard me and I saw firelight reflected in his golden eyes. "I have something for you."

I heard mutters at my shoulder and realized I was surrounded. This was it. My cock poked my briefs, and I hoped the dark concealed any tenting. The scotch was singing in my veins but I could still get it up. Here, on the doorstep of my wettest dream nothing could stop that. My eyes sought for but couldn't find any chain-link barriers.

"What is it?" The fox asked. By his voice, my age or a little older. The skunk's accumulated stink under his clothes blocked out much of the fox's musk, but I could still pick it out, potent and feral. This was the king who'd take the wolf as his prize.

The anticipation was too much. "I want to pay you to do something for me, all of you." The cash was in my hand where they could see it.

"And what's that?" the fox asked suspiciously.

The words felt so good slipping out. "I want you to fuck me. I want you to grope me, tear my clothes away, restrain me and fuck my brains out, all of you."

Silence was broken by the cat. "Fer God's sake, why?"

My salesman's forked tongue went to work. "Because I deserve it. I work in a job where I screw hardworking people out of their money and leave them destitute and broke like you all are. I lie to old and young alike, get away with bad deals and fudge numbers to make bad investments look good. I'm a slimy, self-serving soulless wretch who needs nothing more than to be treated as such by you, victims of people like me. I need to have you pleasure yourself in every hole in my body until

I'm raw and filthy and left in the dust to contemplate what I've done."
I hunched my shoulders in supplication, lowering my muzzle to abase
myself even as my cock started to rise. "And of course, for meting out
justice, I will pay you, each of you. One hundred up front, and another
hundred when it's done."

The bear had risen and come around to join us. I hadn't imagined
a bear in my fantasy but I could roll with that. He had to have a coke-
can cock in there bigger than some toys I'd played with and I wondered
what it would feel like if—.

"What if I don't wanna fuck your preened ass? What if I just want
to bash your head in?" the cat yowled.

The bear, with patchy bald spots that shone in the weak firelight,
tracked my eyes to his crotch. He stroked it. "What if we do both?"

"I know you," the fox said abruptly. "You've been following us. I've
seen your car."

"Yes," I replied flatly.

"You were scoping us all…for sex?"

I nodded. My cock was rock hard at that point. The fox's golden
eyes narrowed at me. "And you thought that cause we're down on our
luck that we would do whatever the fuck pleased you for whatever
change you scrounged up?"

They just weren't getting it. "I imagined you'd do whatever pleased
you. To me. That's the point."

The fox growled low, hackles rising. I felt the same happening at
my shoulders like an alley full of angry static. The alcohol and my brav-
ery picked that moment to waver.

"So you think I'm a fox so I'd love to suck your dick or fuck your
ass, that you could have us all screw you dizzy, throw a couple bucks
our way and then head back to your mansion or whatever and watch
football? Is this how you turn over a new leaf banker-dog?"

"I just—"

"Shut up! You don't give a shit about settling scores or righting
wrongs. You don't want to help. You just want to scratch an itch."

He was right in my face, that raw musk and hot breath bathing my
nose and whiskers, tongue curling around his insults.

"Just fuck off!" he shouted at me, and when his mouth started to
close I was ready. I kissed him. My black lips wrapped around his, taking in fetid breath, the remains of scrounged take-out and the essence

of raw, furious fox. As his golden eyes widened and fixed on mine, as gasps rose like notes around us, I decided he was the sweetest thing I had ever tasted.

He shoved me back and a black-furred fist cracked my jaw. My shoulder was knocked by a shove from behind and spit hit my ear.

As the blows started to rain, my resolve collapsed entirely, arousal having fled like helium from a balloon and I ran.

They chased. Most of the epithets were familiar, some even from my fantasies, but in the night-breeze of stark reality, I realized I was in mortal trouble. I threw the money behind me. If they saw it they ignored it. A corner turned to double back to the street, one turn from safety, and of course I found my chain link fence.

They were on me before I climbed a single link. Blows and kicks landed on my head, back and side. The next few minutes were akin to that space in a car accident between the moment when an airbag goes off and the waving of an EMT's flashlight in your eyes, a whole slice of time erased by shock that you never would get back even if you wanted to.

When I rolled over, stripped of my jacket, cellphone, wallet and condo-keys, I needed several minutes to practice the art of drawing breath.

Eventually I got up. Agonized, eyes weepy, I wandered back to the street, limping to a streetlight, then another, unsure which direction I was even going. The lone living person, a rat with a knapsack, crossed the street to avoid me. Scrounging through my pockets, I found a few dimes, all I had saved for a crumpled receipt. I spotted a payphone, vandalized and spray tagged but functional. I crossed and pondered my options through a pounding headache. My parents lived two states away, I couldn't call nine-one-one and the only person who could understand my predicament here would be Mitch. I didn't want to phone him under any circumstances. The bastard was probably already going to leak what little he knew about me in some cowardly office back-channel. I unrolled the receipt, out of options and saw a number scrolled on it.

Rack-thrill. I had his phone number this whole evening and forgot about it. Feeding the phone change, I dialed him slowly. Three rings till a gruff, distracted voice answered. "Who's this?"

"It's me, Anton. I mean, Janus. From online."

"Oh hey, what's up? I'm just closing up work right now. Party thing."

"I need a favor, Rack. Its uh…kind of urgent actually."

A long silence ticked by before he said it. "I'm listening."

An hour later a Honda rolled up and the driver's door opened. A rack of antlers rose in view, then a slim deer's head and neck. Dark eyes narrowed and widened as he saw me. I recognized immediately the waiter at the restaurant whom Mitch had been castigating when I arrived and poured the first of too many drinks. My eyes widened too.

"Well," the deer said. "This is awkward." He looked me up and down. "You look like you could use a doctor."

* * *

Cilia sits back in her chair, adjusting her thick-framed glasses and sets her jaw, nose quivering. "So on my first consultation with you, you lied to me. You lied and then nearly got yourself killed." A cold flame lights in the rabbit's eyes and I see for an instance the Cilia Sparks that her slaves in training know, the kind who wields the bullwhip hanging on her wall and teaches Doms how to assert their roles and subs how to submit.

"I did. I'm an asshole for that. I'm sorry."

The clinical lid comes down on what she feels and the professional asserts her dominance. "What you need to understand Anton is that carefully negotiated kink is not just a responsibility for your own well-being. You have a responsibility to the care and comfort of other participants in the scene, who must be consenting, aware parties. The conduct you engage on reflects on this community and can cause far more damage to all affected far outside of and above the scene itself. It's not in my position as a therapist to exercise judgement of character within this room, but you need to be aware that there are consequences to acting as you have."

Something tells me that in another room she operates I would be hearing this told in another, less objective way but it has the effect required. The shame burns so close to the core I feel my bones toasting. "I was irresponsible, I admit that. But I've learned my lesson."

"I am willing to believe you think so."

"But I won't do this again. No amount of booze or drugs in the world could get me to try that again."

"There are still aspects to your situation I feel could benefit from further discussion. In the meantime, I have had an extensive discussion with your new friend Charles who has expressed concern for you."

"He's a good guy."

"He has your best interests at heart and has made some suggestions for how he may help you. He has shared with me that he has planned something, but in confidentiality asked that I say no more than that."

"Planned something?"

"Your time is up, Mister Fisher."

* * *

Charles drives me home. Up until a week prior, I'd thought his online name "Rack-thrill" referred to the torture device or the safe-play acronym. Now I know it refers to the majestic rack crowning his shapely head. "All healed up?" he asks.

"Almost, but not fully," I answer.

"Good."

I opened my mouth, but he shushed me. "We'll talk at your place."

I've had him over a couple times and he knows as much of my story as Cilia does. He's listened to me without comment and summarily decided I had to see Cilia professionally to get her opinion. I'm a mess in more ways than one.

"I've thought about where this could go," Charles says, out of the blue as he drives. "I haven't had a boyfriend in a while and neither have you and we're both worse off for that. But I don't know if we'd work out."

I stare ahead and just listen.

"I hate what you do. You are an asshole for it, screwing people over and if you deserve to be fucked for it, it's probably in prison."

Nothing I do is illegal, but I take his point. I feel the same way, and the loathing I've processed by putting myself through an erotic punishment will no longer work. We arrive at my condo and park. "Anton, there's a good guy in there, but you're just tearing yourself up by trying to deal with your shit this way. I really only have one solution for that."

He sees my questioning gaze as we walk to the elevator. "You let me water your plants for you while you were in the hospital. You never asked for your keys back."

We take the elevator up and he gives me my condo keys. I open my door and step in, my jaw dropping as I see the mess.

Work papers, all my expense reports, sales tracking and hundreds of sheets of raw data are jumbled and spilled all over my floor. Furniture is overturned and garbage is strewn along with the rest of my papers.

The door slams behind me and Charles' voice booms. "Welcome to the apocalypse you little shit. You're mine now. Strip."

"What the fuck—"

"I said strip! On the ground, now!" Charles pushes me and I slip on paperwork, falling on the floor. A rank smell rises from the sheets below me, as though something musky has doused them. "Do it!" Charles shouts again, and with a sudden rush of terrified excitement, I pull off my jacket. Deer hooves stalk past me, one of them roughly turning me over. I stare at the stippled ceiling as my paws go to my belt, loosening it. Above me, the deer slowly removes his own shirt, shrugging fabric away to expose chiseled abs rising to a lightly furred pair of firm pecs, a king in my concrete jungle. Fear from my encounter in the alley burns at my subconscious for a brief moment, but is quickly conquered by lust as the rack-crowned king unzips, lets his pants drop and then slides away his underwear to kick both across my living area. The cock that slips its sheath to dangle down at me is magnificent, sheened with moisture. My own cock hurts more than my fading bruises as I pull my own pants down and let them be kicked away. My shirt is torn at and soon I'm naked beneath my crouching king, who leans forward, an actual necklace of teeth bouncing at his neck. His hard musk drifts down upon me like a mist from the imposing manhood, balls and taint above me. It's intoxicating enough to have me panting.

"Taste me. Lick my cock you worthless slut."

Greedily I lap at it, each touch making that stiffening cock sway just a bit. He trails himself along me, fingers insistently pulling and pushing my pliant snout and tongue along his length, then his balls. The flesh star behind his taint dips low and I oblige him, burying my tongue in his dark depth. He stands tall once again and uses a hoof to turn me over, studiously avoiding where he knows my bruises are but insistent all the same. "Crawl. Now!"

I crawl across the torn papers and detritus of my destroyed work-world, toner smearing the light parts of my fur. I can see the papers are poorly photo-copied from my originals, but I don't care. The sticky, destroyed world spreads below me, papers gripping at my knees and elbows, making me slip. The stag's cold hoof against my balls urges me further, towards an array of metal on the floor. Past that is a box, overturned, covering something.

Surprisingly, the hoof turns me over again. "I hate listening to my slave's panting. You can release yourself from your bonds by calling me Emperor, but you are mine until that happens. Grab the rings over your head."

I reach back and feel around for two cold metal rings. Crouching over me, cock dripping pre on my chest, the stag fastens one ring around my muzzle, forcing my mouth mostly closed before shoving the cold ring around it. It's left open just enough for me to beg. The second, wrapped round my cock and balls, is so cold it almost hurts. I moan as he turns me over again, my cock stiff and proud.

"No link fence for you," he taunts gleefully. "Everywhere you run is my world. And I'm going to fuck my new toy until I grow bored of you."

Lube squirts on my tail, over my back, down my balls, sloppily and freely dousing my ass. I hear the snap of a prophylactic closing on stiff deer meat and then two fingers part my ass with a tickle. The stag's cock digs, then sinks, slipping into me with all the softness of a kiss. When he pulls out and thrusts again, roughly, I wince and hiss with delight. The stag fucks me like a toy, pushing my face into the printed ruins, my muzzle and cock warming the metal that bind me in the prison of my imagination, where I pay for my horrid crimes. The endless thrusts are pure heaven, small pains of bruises keeping me just grounded enough. My tribal master, my king, my Emperor rides me hard and long and hot, slowing only to bestow a final command as his hand winds under me and toys with my flush-knotted cock. "You get release only one way, with one action. Turn over the box."

I bat it over with a paw. There's a phone's handset underneath.

"Remove the muzzle." I flick it away as directed.

"You have been a slave to your guilt for too long, letting it eat at you and destroy you. Your emperor's final request, and this can only be a request, is thus: Call your investment firm, that palace of filth where your life is being squandered and do what you must do. Here you have a chance to do what you've silently dreamed of doing for as long as you can remember. I will not make you do this. It's up to you to decide if this is how you fix things."

It's mid-day, out there in the world. I crouch there, a cock filling my ass in frantic lunges and fingers bringing me right to the edge of bliss. Why do I have to hate myself to get here? Is there something else for me? There's only one way I can know.

I pick up the phone and dial Stirwich's office. Thankfully, it's taken by the answering service. There would be a record. "It's Anton." I try not to let my butt-fucking affect my voice too much. Let the old rat speculate. "I've done a lot of thinking and its official. I'm moving on. I quit. So…bye." I hang up, my whole world light as a feather. I come all over my own chest and the papers beneath, an ecstatic shudder that seems to move the building under me. I collapse to the papered floor and the stag nearly falls on top of me, pulling out at the last second. We both lay panting on the floor for a long while.

"Cilia's idea?" I finally ask.

He stroked my back and I could hear the smile in his voice. "No. But she endorsed it."

I laugh, feeling better than I had in years. I suddenly realize that I have a life in front of me, that one critical step has put the worst part of the past behind me. "I need to do more than this. Before I get another job, I need to fix things, maybe help out those guys I messed with in the alley. I could go down there and—"

Charles closes my muzzle with a firm hand. "I'll bring them all something, money, food, whatever. I really don't think you should personally go back there. Ever. I'm serious."

Silence falls for several minutes, our breathing slowing.

"I don't know how I can ever repay you."

Charles rolls me over and we gaze into each other's eyes. "Of course you do. This Wednesday after I get off shift."

I raise my ears in question.

"I have a boss who needs to be punished," Charles beams beatifically. "I'll bring home the right kind of towel."

THE BOOK OF PERIL

H. A. Kirsch

My name is Tomasz Dusicielski. I was born a human, in Mokotów, just
outside of Warsaw in Poland. Terrible things happened to me after we
moved to America. My family was deported. I became sick, and the
state fixed me.

Now I am a cat.

* * *

I am a photographer.

For example: a fox, in my living room. My apartment is my studio. He sat on the leather sofa and looked around like he had made a
terrible mistake. He waved his tail around behind him. He curled up
forward, clutching his black hands to his chest. He looked so scared.

"You look good like that," I said, and took a picture of him. He
whimpered. "Lie down."

Asking someone to pose is only good if you want to see a pose.
Maybe good for movie posters, but not sex. Sex is what I photograph
most. As soon as the fox began to move, I began to creep around, com-
posing shots as I went and as he leaned back.

I wore fancy leather pants, leather cowboy boots, a leather blazer,
and a white dress shirt. No tie. I did not even button the top collar of
the shirt. The leather squeaked against leather as I held myself at odd
angles, leaning in and twisting and hunkering down and stalking and
capturing moments.

I crept closer to the fox and he looked more and more nervous.
More ashamed. I took a good close-up of his face, of his pleading gold-
en slit eyes, of his tucked muzzle, of his flattened black ears. When my
studio flashes popped, he winced.

"Why not strip for me? Is why fox comes for pictures," I said, and squinted from behind my camera. He whimpered again. "Now to something else," I growled, and put the camera on a tripod. I reached into a coat pocket and took out a pair of black leather riding gloves. You must have very closely fitted leather gloves when riding a horse. I do not ride horses, but I must have leather gloves.

I looked at the fox while I fitted my hands into the leather. I have large hands, I am a big cat, and leather like this was only good while tight. It was impressive.

These gloves. Damascus makes gloves for law enforcement. They once were commissioned by a fetish company, a company that sells leather gloves to gay men, to make a special model. The D650HP, the Patrolman. They are rare now. They are rare for men like me: simple, authoritative, tough, tight, black, leather.

But as I put them on, I saw a crack in his facade. I saw, and heard, his breath catch in a way that was not any kind of terror.

The fox was acting. He had agreed to be my model. He even gave me a portfolio. Very nice and professional.

"I am not in picture, not my face," I said, and took something else out of my pocket. A remote control for the camera. "If you do not take off clothes, I do it." I put the remote control in my mouth so that I could bite on the action button. I composed a shot with the fox looking unsettled on the leather couch, then walked around behind it.

Then I started to manipulate him. He tried to cover himself up - he wore only blue jeans and black dress socks - but I dissuaded him by grabbing him by the mouth from behind.

Picture.

I clutched my gloved hand across his muzzle from around his neck, then slid it down to hold across as if throttling him.

Picture.

With both black, leather-gloved hands.

Picture.

He was a small fox, maybe only five-foot-six, slender, but he had some fight. I could feel his pulse start to race even through the leather. I leaned down further and unzipped his pants. I slipped my hand inside and my fingers slid so easily against his underwear. The fabric was so silky against my gloves.

I started to purr.

All the while, shot, shot, shot, shot. I stood up and pulled his jeans off, and finally! His shame, a pair of red satin panties and black sheer stockings. Why would a fox need black stockings? He closed his eyes and tucked his ears all the way back. It was not fear. It was lust. Arousal. It was how I felt, as I watched him, as I cupped him through the panties.

Then, even more: close-up of the fox's face with his hand covering it, close-up with my hand clutching his jaw, another grasp across the neck, another double throttling. It was only for the camera. I did not squeeze him. The second time, he struggled, but it came with such a groan and his cock throbbed so hard into that glossy red garment. Then I let go and stepped off to the side.

I told him to touch himself and he did, face almost tearful with his mock emotions. He was so hard. Big and hard. Skinny men always have such large cocks.

A shot of his rump. A shot of my gloved hand pulling his panties to the side, to show off his asshole. It quivered at me. I pondered putting my finger in, with a little spit, but hadn't even put it up to my mouth when he shuddered and let out a soft gasp.

"I'm sorry, shit, oh fuck," he hissed, then collapsed over to the side. The groan that followed was one of curt disappointment.

He curled up and I uncurled him with a hard pull. That red satin was stained dark now in front, throbbing as his cock bucked and squirted every few seconds. Glistening ooze pushed into the material and then spread to a wet patch.

He writhed and I let go; his cock slipped up out of its feminine prison and squirted his last shot onto his heaving abdomen, leaving a sticky mat of fur. "Whew. Uh, did I just ruin your photo shoot, dude?" The fox's speaking voice was very different from how he behaved. Deep, and almost stupid. He looked more irritated than concerned.

I looked just as irritated. I always looked irritated. There were very few moments when I did not have a feline scowl on my face. Those were very embarrassing moments. I had my shoulders up, hackles raised. I let my tail droop. "No. You make mess. Lick it from your hand," I chuffed, and quickly grabbed an instant-film camera. As soon as he made a timid gesture to lick semen from his hand, I snapped a picture. "Very good."

"Is there, uh, do I gotta fill out some contract or something?" Lick. Lick.

Yes, the time to ask that is after I take pictures of you, stupid fox.

I found the paperwork, he filled it out, and I sent him on his way. A fox in panties with a case of premature ejaculation? What magazine wants to have that for a spread? A fox in panties was just what I needed, not what some porn magazine or website needed.

I needed it for the hyena.

* * *

I was ready. I picked the best of the photos I took of the fox, and set them on a slideshow on my big television. I hate technology most of the time. Meaningless complex things, distractions and worries and advertising. But I like what it can do. No need to print anything out.

Sometimes I even use the television while I am taking shots. It faces my usual studio area. My subject can see himself as art, right away. I didn't do that with the fox. I was too caught up in worry about how they would come out. For him.

I did print one photograph, the perfect one, the required one, as an instant photo. I set it on the table in front of the television. It was a little shrine to tonight's… to what I had to do tonight.

Of course, there was a terrible storm. A perfect thunderstorm with rain that pattered hard on my high loft windows. It was a warehouse once. Now it was my studio.

The doorbell rang. I answered it. No, I reached for the knob, pulled my hand back. I was not wearing my gloves. *Ring, ring*, and then he started to pound on the door. I pulled my gloves out of my coat and slid them on. *Pound pound pound pound POUND*. I hissed.

I unlocked it and he pushed it open right into my nose. I hissed and spit, jolted backwards with my hands up to my face.

He was big, a little taller than me and I was already a few inches over six feet. He wore: a heavy olive green, rubber rain coat; matching rubber rain pants; black wading boots that came up to his thighs; black rubber gloves; and a black gas mask. Soaking wet, drenched, water was beaded up across the rubber. It was so fetishistic, but so raw, the rubber matte in some places. The gas mask was a respirator over only his muzzle; a separate pair of goggles covered his eyes. The rest: spotted charcoal and brown hyena.

He did not speak. He stepped forward and didn't even shut the door. I had to rush to close it, lock it, bar it, chain it. I had expensive cameras. I set the alarm system. I had lots of expensive toys, sex toys, leather, masks, equipment.

The wet rubber hyena stomped over to the flat screen and stared at it. I could not see his eyes through the goggles, but what else would he look at? He stood there and dripped on the floor. He took a binder out from under his coat, set it on the table, then resumed standing.

I didn't know what that meant. He just stood and huffed into his mask, and water drops pattered onto the floor, onto his boots, onto his pants. I crept close and went to touch him. No gloves, so I would feel whatever he wore. I loved to wear gloves. I hate seeing my cat-man hands with claws and fur and all that, touching things, filthy things, human things, stupid things. I loved seeing leather over my hands, but no.

Before I could touch the wet rubber, he turned and punched me in the chest. Hard, enough that it made me spin my head, muzzle smacked into his arm. Stunned, I tried to bolt away, but he just leaned forward and put his arm around me. My chest. Then my neck. A hard, solid chokehold. I barely had time to bring my hands up to pry him off before everything dropped to black.

I hit the ground and fell to my side. I stirred and there he was, straddling me, looming down. My pants would be scuffed. If he was too rough, he would tear my jacket. "No, no, I make what you ask for, why?" I howled.

He grabbed me by my shirt and pulled me up. The fabric ripped but held. I went to brush his hands off but he tackled me onto the table. He grappled with my coat and I shrugged my arms out. It was thousands of dollars, very fine leather, custom made for me. Alligator. Black.

I don't like anything. But I love leather.

Then the shirt, he just ripped that. He grabbed at my fur, felt my back and sides, then stroked down to above my tail. Shit, I arched and rowled, and started to purr, and I couldn't stop it. Of course he could do what he wanted with me. We had an agreement; I made things for him, he rewarded me with sex. I did something wrong, he punished me. He never spoke the agreement, but I knew he meant it.

The hyena could not speak. Sometimes visible on his head was a scar on the left side, over his ear. He did not speak so I didn't know where it came from, but it must have explained his dulled attitude and how he could only grunt or otherwise utter sounds.

Was this the reward? No. His rubber hands slid over my leather pants, reached in front, and unzipped. He pulled them down and I rowled again. Stupid cat reflexes! When someone stroked me, I could not help but purr and rub. I solved that by not letting anyone touch me. Except for the hyena.

Then he hit me. Spanked me, hard, with a paddle. No, not a paddle. My photo-tablet. It was all heavy glass and aluminum, fancy and electronic. I had no time to think that was stupid, because he hit me hard, again, again. Four times before the pain came and I screamed. He covered my mouth with his gloved hand. I tried to bite him, but he was too fast. Then he hit me again.

"I am sorry! I do better next time!"

Huff, gruff. He opened up the front of his rubber pants and pulled out... more rubber. His cock strained into a black rubber sheath with no hole. It was already glistening and slick with something. He pulled his gas mask off, muzzle sweaty and damp from it. Then he held it like a cup and spit into it.

He reached over and picked up the instant photo, then showed me. WHACK! Then he spit into the mask-up again. He set it down and held the photo in front of my face, and tore it in half. I was in it, looming headless into the frame, intimidating the fox into kissing sperm from his fingers.

Now I was alone in my half of the photo. WHACK! He set it down and picked up a black marker, then drew an X over my black leather puma self in the photo.

"Noooo! No I do better next time! I swear it! Don't kill me!" I tried to writhe away but he just grabbed onto my shoulders and held me down. When I settled, he reached over and spit into the mask again, then pulled it up over my muzzle. The rubber inside was cool and damp with sweat and breath, with a puddle of hyena-spit sloshing inside. I tried to keep it off me, but of course, when I inhaled, it sprayed up onto my lips.

I growled and chuffed into the mask, which made me so hard even if it was so disgusting - so much of his spit! It was slimy and smelled musky and acidic, a nice distraction from the terrible burn he left on my ass with that makeshift paddle.

Did the hyena fuck me? No, fucking was not punishment. He stood there and jerked off, watching me, drooling a little with his muzzle open, rubber glove squeezing and pulling at his sheathed cock. All of his wet gear made a racket, squeaking and slapping and rustling, and he grunted like a porn star who thankfully could not speak. Several minutes passed, while the hyena just stood and masturbated over me. I tried to push up to standing but he shoved me back down into place. Was my ass red? Could he see it through the fur? I never knew anything he could not make a gesture about or draw in a doodle.

His grunts turned desperate and strangled and his furious masturbating sounded extra sloppy, and then he stopped. There was no mess; it all stayed in that sheath. As his cock shrank, I could even see the mess of seed wobble like in a used condom, but of course it was all black.

He grabbed the gas mask off my face and without cleaning it off, put it on himself. Then he sat down with the binder and started to put the fox half of the instant photo into one of the picture sleeves. He had drawn a picture in the backing behind the photo sleeve; it was a yellow sticky note with a pen doodle of someone, male, wearing underwear and tall women's boots. It was a hybrid but I couldn't tell the species.

The hyena was not a very good artist.

After my punishment, I watched the hyena make a new drawing, this one complex. Some sort of creature, maybe a fox from its thick tail, was strapped to a table. There were wires leading to a stand. The creature was producing a fountain of piss, or cum, or both, from its cock. Then he drew in a circle, a cat face, and a thick slanted "NO" sign across it. He showed me the picture, then stuck it into the second-to-last slot in the binder.

"Yes, I do it right, no cat this time," I huffed.

The hyena closed up the binder and left it there on my table. I was its keeper.

He turned and stomped out of my apartment, again not bothering to close the door. I rushed up and shut it. It was like I had shut out a hurricane. Now I could breathe to myself.

* * *

When I got out of high school, I did not go to college. I could not stand anyone or anything, least of all school. Sometimes I was smart, like with reading and writing. Other times, I was stupid, like with math, or with speaking English aloud. Never did I enjoy anything I had to do. Instead of more school, I got a job as a janitor for a fitness center. I hated the job, because I had to clean up after mostly sweaty and rank humans at this particular gym, but it paid a little money. Enough money.

I first met the hyena there. I found him masturbating in a closet one day. He was wearing a gas mask and long rubber chemical gloves that went up to his shoulders. He stopped, looked at me, then just went back to his act. It stuck in my mind. Something happened to me at that moment that opened up part of my self. I still feel all wrong inside; I prickle my fur when I think about stumbling onto the hyena.

When I saw him another day, I worried that he would treat me differently. He took me into the same closet and made me wear the mask. Then he fucked me. Never did he treat me any differently, except for the part about fucking.

Later, once I had my own place, he showed up at my apartment unannounced. He had a black photo binder with him. He took out a small piece of paper and doodled something on it, a cougar sitting on a stool. A cat sitting on a stool. I assumed it was a cougar, because I was a cougar. He pointed over at my camera, then he left.

I had started doing photography as a hobby; otherwise I worked at a warehouse. So, I took a picture of myself. The hyena came back a few days later. When he came into my apartment, he ignored me and went straight to inspect the picture. He stared at it for a long time, slipped it into the binder, then made another drawing.

That was the beginning. Every week, the hyena gave me a new assignment. Every week, I had to complete it.

They started off simple; different portraits, different species, different clothing, different positions. His drawings were so terrible that it was hard not to laugh, but they got the point across with no words.

Portraits became pinups. Pinups became nudes. Nudes became sex. I had already started taking erotic photographs on my own; some of the first pictures I ever took were candid shots of a couple having sex in a park. They did not know anyone could see them. They did not know that I photographed them. That was also the beginning.

* * *

Over time, the assignments for the black photo book became extreme. A fox in panties is not that extreme. Maybe it is just a joke these days. Barebacking is not that extreme. A worn and loose asshole, maybe, but male porn is always so graphic and excessive.

Here is an example of more extreme: a generic animal stick figure, being spanked by a leather-daddy figure. I tried to get the hyena to clarify what sort of leather-daddy figure he wanted, but he just turned and left the room after making the drawing. Like always. The spanking looked violent, but perhaps it was the bad line work. The person being spanked looked like they were crying.

So, I needed someone who would enjoy being spanked. I also needed someone to do the spanking. I picked the top first, because with a bad top, it would all fall apart. I chose a black wolf friend of mine.

He wore a perfect outfit. Black leather riding breeches that flared at the hips, a black leather uniform shirt, a black leather motorcycle patrol jacket; black leather gauntlet gloves, a duty belt with handcuffs and a bullwhip and a frightening large hunting revolver.

"You are not cowboy wolf, you are leather-daddy," I motioned to the gun.

"You want me to spank some guy's ass for you? Then I'm gonna wear my gun," he said. He had a deep, growling voice. Perfect for a wolf. Very strong accent too. I think he was from New York City before moving upstate to this filthy place. "It's not loaded. Well, it's got one bullet, but there are six chambers in the way. If your little model plays nice, I won't have to use any of 'em."

"Ehh," I shrugged. No one threatens me.

Except the hyena.

The doorbell rang and I answered it. The bottom! He was half zebra and half pony, so he was not so tall compared to me. He wore trendy jeans, flashy snakeskin cowboy boots, a clingy tight tee-shirt and had his mohawk dyed blue. "Are you seriously going to pay me a thousand dollars to get spanked until I cum? Really?" He had an Australian accent. Why would a zebra be from Australia? Whatever.

I hissed in his face. "I take off one hundred each time you complain to me," I growled. "Go in there. You see leather things? Bare ass and tell wolf he has big dick. Maybe he plays with it instead of stupid gun."

The zebra walked into the main part of my studio and coughed when he saw who was there. "Oh Christ, you have to be fucking kidding me!"

I knew both of them. They knew each other. They just did not know they were going to be modeling together. "If you make fight I strangle each of you," I made the appropriate gesture with my hands, then started setting up. The zebra gave me a dirty look. "This is for camera you break!" He broke one of my cameras once. It was not expensive, I bought it as a shitty thing to take disturbing low-fidelity pictures for a project, but it was film and I lost all I had done. Plus, he was an asshole for breaking it.

"If you give me a thousand dollars right now, I might stay here," the zebra said. "Might. It depends on whether Mister Wolf here is going to call me names or not."

"You're a horny fuck-toy with a big horsey dick who'll do anything to get off, and you let your lion boyfriend bite your neck like he's gonna eat your prey ass for real," the wolf said, then disappeared into my toy room. "I'm gonna wear one of these masks. I don't wanna be too famous right now. Plus, you know, fucking masks." I could hear a tremble of excitement in his slobbery city accent.

Too many things happening at once. I took out my wallet and threw money at the zebra. A thousand dollars is a lot of money, but if I did not do a good job, what would the hyena do to me?

I could hear the rustling of rubber in the other room, the sound of a zipper, grunts, muffled breathing. It made me curl my tail, sent a tingle into my crotch. Such a distraction.

Then the wolf stalked back out, slapping a strap flogger into his hand. It was made of saddle leather, double-sided with a thicker piece inside of it, flexible but firm, well made, expensive, almost two feet long. More than the flogger, he had one of my gas mask hoods on, a model for a wolf. It made him glare, hid his yellow eyes behind dark lenses, turned his black wolf fur into angular shapes. I almost dropped my camera when I saw him in it, and he stared at me. Chuff.

I flexed one of my hands, shrank back, curled my tail around my leg, but I was so hard. I knew he could see it. If he couldn't see it, I could feel it, and that meant everyone could see it. "Him, hit him," I pointed to the zebra, who was leaning over some leather fetish furniture I had arranged. Leather seating blocks, two levels, and a pipe-frame at the higher end to hold onto. He had rolled his shirt up above the top of his pecs, and his jeans were scooted down below his ass. Despite complaining about the wolf, his cock hung out fully dropped and slowly rising.

The wolf grunted and stomped over, then delivered a swift whack to the zebra's ass. I barely was able to capture the picture; it was a dud.

"Heyheyhey! I need a safeword! You can't do that without a safe-word!" the zebra whinnied. Picture, picture, as he made a range of faces at the masked wolf. What a wolf. I wanted to take pictures of him all afternoon, doing things that would be a bad idea.

A malevolent idea popped into my head and I spit it out. "Hasselblad." The brand name of the camera he destroyed.

"Excuse you," the wolf said, then slapped the zebra's ass again. "Fair enough? That a good enough word for you? You're not gonna use that in a sentence while I'm spanking the jizz out of your pony dick."

I had suggested, years earlier, that the wolf should keep someone for a pet for some time, a prostitute zebra-pony he had just met. And he did it! Then he found out whose idea it was. That is why the zebra destroyed my camera and why he would have to say that word to get the wolf to stop beating sex out of him.

The wolf turned my way. "You got some kind of plan or you just want me to rail his ass with this?" Whack! I shuddered after the sound.

The poor zebra made such a groan and winced and tucked away and flicked his tail.

"Oww," he huffed, but then reached out for the pipe frame to hold on. Now he was fully erect.

"Whatever, is his ass and your hitting," I shrugged, then started my photographer creeping.

The wolf was brutal. There is a way to hit someone when you are flogging them, where you carefully work up from light to intense and ensure you strike varied places. Then, there is the way you hit someone when you are punishing them, which just hurts. There is a third way, which is how you hit someone when you enjoy punishing them. That is how the wolf hit.

As I said before, I knew these two. I think the word for them is "frenemies". They cannot stand each other so much that they have to be together sometimes.

Occasionally, the zebra looked at me with an alert, concerned glare as I moved lights and crept around in some odd position. Photography is exhausting for me. I nap when I am done. Most of the flogging, the zebra looked as if he was being tortured, about to sob, actually sobbing, and then swollen with the about-to-sneeze look of a coming climax.

"How, how can you just fucking *stand* there while he does this to me?" The zebra pleaded. He had an erection so it was just an act. It would just make him cum harder.

I shrugged. "I don't know." I am not like everyone else, I thought, but the words did not come to my mouth. The zebra and wolf and hyena and all the foxes, they were born well-adjusted into attractive animals. I was made into a mountain lion that can pounce thirty feet and who strangles his prey to death. You cannot pounce thirty feet and strangle people for a living. I settle for taking pictures of fantasies. "If you don't cum, wolf doesn't stop," I said.

"You took the fuckin' words out of my mouth, tomcat," said the wolf. I hissed at him. It was good enough; the sneeze look came back to the zebra's face.

I knew what I had to do for the final picture. The wolf wore the kind of outfit I wanted to see on someone, especially the mask. He was brutal and obnoxious to listen to. He was anonymous and authoritative. The zebra took it all perfectly, not only like it hurt for real, but that hurting felt good for real. I needed to capture the moment of climax again. That had been a thing for me lately.

I used a technique called "slow shutter sync". A camera flash is very fast, faster than indoor shutter speeds. With a shutter speed for indoor light, any movement will make a blur. If you combine them, you will have a blur of motion leading up to a definitive sharp picture. The ultimate action shot, like an illustration from a comic book without the sound word in bold letters, like tail lights on a car leaving trails at night. If you do it wrong, it looks impossible and stupid. I would not do it wrong.

I only had one try. "Hit him when he shoots," I told the wolf, with an angry winding hand gesture.

The wolf hit, and at just the right moment. The zebra was gaping his mouth apart like a horse caught whinnying, eyes terrified and wide, face wet with sweat and tears. The wolf had managed to stay bodily still except for his arm, which made a perfect streaked blur from shiny leather in my hot-lights that hit the zebra's ass with the perfect flash-lit impact. The colors were wrong from mixed lights, but I would make it black and white later. Dramatic, as it was.

At the exact moment, a massive squirt of semen had erupted from the zebra's cock and was well on its way to hit him on the chin. It was rendered perfectly by the flash lighting, a solid but wavy tube of creamy fluid that was almost two feet long. Almost unreal, like the way pouring water looks in those strange slow motion videos, or a science video from the space station.

I would post that photograph in the collection I kept around my studio as art. It was beyond perfect. It was the crowning achievement of this… project, so far.

The photo made it seem as if the mess would hit the zebra on the chin, but it actually hit my hand as he had flinched a split second later. I looked down at the mess, scowled, and wiped it off on his shoulder. "I give you money, now leave, I don't want fight," I said, to both of them, then turned and left the room. I think that walking out with the last word is called "dropping the microphone". It is a very cat thing to do.

* * *

I knew now one thing that the hyena would not like, which was including myself inappropriately in a picture for him. He punished me for that. I quivered when I thought of what he did to me. His spit, the mask, my face! But if he asked me to do it, if he drew for me to do it, then I would do it and it was okay.

I would still include myself, but not on film. Just with my subject. The Electric Fox.

Plus, I knew a fox who would enjoy electrical play. A very close friend. I would not have to even bribe him with money like I did the busy vicious wolf and the kept zebra.

"I'm surprised you don't have me, uh, in some kind of rubber suit or something," the fox said, as he undressed. "Very surprised. Very very."

"Photo is not for rubber fox. Is for cat. Is also not for, ahh, is not rubber photo. Is fox photo. With this," and I waved the electrical stimulation power box that he had brought over. It looked like an old piece of computer equipment, back when computers were beige metal boxes that made green text on a television set. It was heavy from some kind of lead battery inside. As I waved it his eyes followed as if it was the most interesting thing in the world.

This fox used to live downstairs from me in an apartment building. He was a silver fox, but he dyed his fur red, so that it made a red mohawk between his black ears and dusted him all over with a hint of the fiery color. It looked punk and aggressive but he was usually jovial, too outgoing about himself. He was a very big nerd about science fiction and fantasy, especially costumes. And, he was a complete masochist. I spent a lot of time with this fox for years.

I put the fox on a gynecological exam table. I had him sitting back, restrained only by his feet, legs spread apart. Nude, completely, with no other fetish gear or toys or clothing. We were in the mask room. It was not so large, cramped and hard for photography, and the walls were black so light was always so artificial. There was no way to take a picture without including some mask or hood or fetish toy or torture implement. That would be fine. Fox would love it. I would love it. Would the hyena love it? I fretted, even though him and masks…

"Do you know how to use that?" the fox said, voice slowly strangling upwards in pitch. "It's a little complicated, and not just techie complicated, like it's just a lot of button pushing, they don't give it a good user ex-ex-experience…" His eyes grew wide, turning from golden slits to big saucers. The fox in panties the other night had not ever looked so enthusiastic.

I connected the box to several wires. These led to the fox's cock. I put a leather cock-ring around the base and balls, so he would stay nice and thick. I put a rubber loop under his cockhead, connected to one of the wires. I put another loop on the base of his shaft, tight enough that the flesh bulged out around the black rubber tube. The third pole - I thought electricity was just two? - connected to a curved prostate massager toy in his ass, with a metal ball for a head.

I then turned on the box and twisted a knob until the screen read, "STROKE". I turned the "power" knob up to maybe nine o'clock. A blue light on the box flickered and swelled up, followed by another one next to it for the other pole of wires. The lights flicked off, then repeated their pulsating dance. Whatever the light did, the electricity did inside him.

"Oooh, that's just about right, that's just enough," the fox huffed and growled, voice dropping back down to a bedroom husky tone.

I turned it up two more notches. I watched him closely; when the lights were at full brightness, he squirmed as if someone had drawn nails along a chalk board, black hands clutching at the exam table, pulling against the unused restraints to strain against.

The fox huffed hard. "Aaaahh. Whew, hey, T-T-Tomasz, that gets twice, twice as strong almost when you go from one of those little tickmarks to another? You know?" His voice rose up to a tense pitch.

I took a picture.

"I know," I lied, and turned it up to the next level. He banged his head back against the exam chair pad with a thump and a loud, tight-jawed growl. I picked up my camera and framed a shot including my gloved hand about to turn the knob up again, and his gaping-muzzle reaction to the intense electricity.

Another picture.

The hyena used electricity on me once. It felt as if I had a vibrator stuck inside of me, but it was very strong, and would cause me to convulse at high enough power. It hurt, but when he turned it off, I wanted more, and more.

"More?" I turned towards him and approached, then pulled his arm over into the upper arm restraint. I took a picture of his wrist splayed back against the undone leather strap. Then I buckled it. He squeaked. I chirped, and he cocked his head, was about to speak, when another swell of that current hit his cock and asshole and he hooted and thrashed.

The fox looked terrified, wild-eyed and flat-eared and intermittently crunched up as if he had just banged his elbow. I took a picture of his pleading face. Then I took a picture of his straining, drooling cock as it bounced each time another 'stroke' electrical wave surged from the power box into him.

The panties-fox had been attractive but that situation was awkward, on purpose, and he had finished too early. I thought he was embarrassed, but it was just an act. He apologized like a confused college student but signed my release form anyway.

This fox? I could turn a knob and cause him to scream, and I knew he liked it. I knew how the wolf had felt with his zebra friend. I made the fox scream, but then backed the power way down so he could catch his breath. He stayed very, very erect. "If you do not like it, why so hard?" I turned it back up, and then changed the menu to say,

"INTENSE". The lights flickered fast, in alternating sequence.

More power, and this time, the fox looked much more pleased. He yowled and strained against the restraints, but he arched his body and tried to push into the electrodes. He only shied away when the muscle reflex moved him. I took another picture, this time of his lustful expression.

I flexed my gloved hand a few times, and he stared at it. Another picture. I turned the power knob up and the fox let out a chattering yelp. I turned the other knob up and the lights flashed faster, faster, until one grew steady and the other kept beating away. He jerked and his cock strained and spurted some clear pre-cum out onto his fur, his teeth chattered, one of his ears wilted down and trembled.

I really could get into this. I was going to make him cum. I was going to force him to cum. I knew what he liked. He told me, all the time when we would meet, even when it was not a good idea to talk about sex.

I picked a gas mask from the wall. This one had a rubber respirator face cup, like for a painting mask, but a long hose connected to it instead. It looked like something used for anesthesia, in a horror movie instead of a real hospital. I did not have anything to connect the hose to, but the fox could not see that far with his body pinned into the table. He saw the mask and started fighting for real.

"No, no no no, you can't do that, not like this, not while I'm s-shocked! You don't k-kn-kn-know how this f-f-feels, urgh!"

Picture, picture, picture—I snapped away with my other hand, while I approached him with the mask, my body bent to line up the impending mask into the shot. He hyperventilated to the point of looking suddenly drowsy, and then I made contact with the rubber cup of the mask and his slobbery, quivering fox snout. He screamed again, and this time he shot off, semen arcing up and splashing him across the face, again and again. Then another scream, and I remembered to turn the power down all the way. The rest of his climax pumped out and he gasped and groaned, then sank back against the chair. He looked at me, then sniffed inside the mask. "Hey, you didn't gas me or anything." He sounded like it was a letdown.

"Sorry, I don't have gas," I shrugged. I held up my camera and looked back through the pictures. I had managed to photograph him right with a huge streamer of seed about to hit his face, and my leather-gloved hand holding the mask approaching.

It was perfect.

But my arm was in it.

It was exactly what the hyena wanted.

But my arm was in it.

The fox was still here. I unstrapped him, then gave him a nudge. "Go." He did not complain like some do; he had known me too long for that.

I did not have an instant photo, but I printed something out after a little black and white processing on my computer. I put it on the table, and then started pacing. The hyena would be back.

The hyena would be back.

But my arm was in the picture.

* * *

I do not like it when people come into my bedroom. I sleep in it. It is a private place. There are things in my bedroom that are embarrassing. For example, when I had a new refrigerator delivered, I kept the box. I put it in the bedroom and put my spare blankets inside of it. I even left one top flap on. Sometimes, I crawl into it and look out, when I am feeling like a cat. If I do not indulge my cat feelings, I become angry at random things more than usual.

The doorbell rang. I did not answer it, because I was in the box. Ring, nothing. Ring, nothing. This proceeded for several minutes, until the ringer started to pound. The hyena. He always pounded the same way.

I burst out of the box and ran to the door. I opened it to the chain. The hyena was not wearing strange rubber rain and fetish gear, only black rubber farm boots, jeans that were too tight and almost threadbare, an old jean jacket. A pair of leather deerskin work gloves peeked out of the breast pocket.

I did not know how old he was, but he looked the same as he did when I met him years and years earlier. Gruff, dull and unfazed by anything around him. Completely silent. Of course he did not announce himself at the door. The scar on his head took that away. He was intimidating with the rubber fetish outfit from before, and he was intimidating without it.

"I feel sick, I have," and I tried to think of something legitimate to be sick with as I stuck my face out through the opening. "I have bad sushi for lunch."

If life was a comic book, I would be the angry cougar in it, and what the hyena did would have had a big sound bubble that read, "KA-WHAM!". He leaned back, rocked and twisted, and then heaved his shoulder against the door. The door chain snapped in half and the door knocked me backwards, like when I had done the other fox picture but so much more violent this time. I backpedaled, hissed, yowled, then smashed into the wall. I tried to scream but only crackled; I could not breathe. I sagged down to my knees, gasping, until the spasm went away. Even then, I had to sputter as if I had just been crying.

The hyena did not waste time. He did not act like a badass after bashing the door in. He simply walked in and went straight to the picture shrine. My handiwork was on display, a terrified fox about to be gassed (not really) and in the throes of screaming orgasm (really).

"I have to do it like that!" I whimpered. "I have to! Is what fox likes, to make him come for the picture!" This was true, but my arm was in the picture.

The hyena stared at it.

"Sorry," I groaned. I hung my head. I sulked.

He turned and came for me. He reached out with his arms and I knew for sure he would try to strangle me or try to tear me apart with his bare hands, maybe treat me like the wolf had treated the zebra. Instead, he embraced me and kissed me. His mouth tasted like meat and tobacco and acid, and he tongued at my lips and teeth. I tried not to bite him. It was disgusting. I did not like most intimate things.

Until I suddenly did. He held onto me as if I were a long lost relative, but he was so hard between his legs. I wanted to yell at him for not caring about my leather, my very expensive leather jacket, but then he reached around my back and stroked up the back. He felt the leather as much as he felt me. He felt it and groaned, desperate.

I started to purr. It was so loud, like when I was near catnip, and I couldn't stop it. Purring was embarrassing for me. Everyone else likes purring cats. You can buy a noise machine to lull you to sleep with the sound of a purring cat. I wished that I didn't do it, but it made me feel so good to do that I had to submit to it. The hyena knew this and rubbed at my face, brushed my whiskers back, rubbed above my eyes. Purr. Purrrrr. He began to undress me, big hands grabbing and pulling, jacket and shirt and boots and pants. I had to perch on the picture shrine table and even then I could not be comfortable.

I hated being naked but I did not want to make the hyena angry, and besides he was so forceful and matter of fact. He could not speak, so he made only actions. His actions pushed his cock against my ass, my tail, as he walked me forward. Towards my bedroom. "No, no, we do it out here, out here!" We reached the door and I put out my arms and legs to block my way through. He did not force me. He took the gloves out of his jacket pocket and slid them on. I could hear it. I did not look back; I just stared forward, at my room, at the pile of blankets and pillows and things I slept in, at the hiding box, at my racks and racks and racks of leather and rubber clothing and toys I used on myself.

My catnip sock was hidden. Very good. That made me feel relieved and I eased up. I almost fell forward and the hyena grabbed me. With leather gloved hands. He pulled my scruff and made me smell his hand. Leather, warm leather, vintage but cared for, musky with male smells, so many smells. Spit and cum and cock and sweat and hints of stale poppers and a little piss and so much else. So much. Purrrrrrrr.

The hyena was happy. He liked the photo. He was not going to punish me. He was going to fuck me. I was naked; he wore jeans and his rubber boots and took his shirt off. He was almost a little fat in the middle but still burly and strong. He worked with his body all day. He was still a janitor as far as I knew. He smelled like he had been at work all day, his own heat and all the sweat smells of others, human stinks and wolves and foxes and bears and cats. I chirped. Purr-rowrl!

He took his cock out, bare, from his button fly. I reached out and he held my hands back down against the cushions of my bed. He took a condom out of his pocket, ripped it open in his teeth, then unrolled it down his cock. I covered my mouth as I mewled and purred and gasped and huffed, my own cock throbbing against my stomach fur, teased by the stiff hairs. A cougar is not a housecat. We are rough.

He reached out for my face and I twisted it to the side. No, don't smother me, hyena! Fuck me and get it over with! I sniffed and pinned my ears back. Catnip. My catnip toy was probably underneath a pillow. Sometimes I brought it there in the middle of the night, like I am a cat owner and an insane house cat at once.

Catnip is like poppers for cats. Poppers give you a head-rush and they make your asshole loose. Suddenly, you want to fuck, be fucked. They can make you sick if you use them too much or eat them. On the other hand, catnip is harmless. A sniff of catnip and I am someone else, something else, somewhere else. I want to eat and fuck and bite things and kick them and strangle them and bury them under the dirt where no one will find them. And it makes me purr.

"Prrp?" I grabbed for the hyena's arm. He held me down. "Prrrrpt!" Then I chirped and lifted my legs up to kick at him. I did not black out. I did not put the memory away in my head. I would be ashamed as soon as the effect wore off, but I had no choice but to accept it.

He splayed my legs apart and tried to shove his black latexed cock into me, with whatever paltry greasy lubricant came inside the package. My asshole puckered up tight and I blurted out in Polish. "Nie, daj mi smaru! Nie można po prostu umieścić go w ten sposób!"

The hyena stopped what he was doing. He turned around, looked over to my nightstand where I had several bottles of lube and poppers, then grabbed one of the former and squirted it onto his cock.

I perked my ears. "Mówisz po polsku?" No response. "You speak Polish?" Nothing, not even a grunt.

Then he shoved it in. I do not let many people fuck me. So far, the number of people who have fucked me is one, and it is the hyena. However, I play with myself often, because nothing is more satisfying than probing deep. It feels like it is the only way I can squeeze every last drop out. So he could just shove it in, but it still hurt a little and I hissed in his face.

He covered my mouth with his gloved hand. I tried to bite it, and he just grabbed on with both hands, pinned my head back. I could barely breathe.

It only hurt for a few moments. He slid in until he hit my prostate, backed up, and slid in again. Over and over, hunched over, clutching my face while I clutched at his chest and arms. I couldn't pay attention to anything, not even his attempt at smothering me. All I could do was surrender to the prostate massage until my cock tingled and ached. I looked at it, as it bobbed while the hyena fucked me, and a thin whitish drool oozed from the tip. I felt like I was orgasming a little bit all the time, constantly, forever.

Too much! I ripped his hands off my face and gasped and then the real climax hit me. I probably screamed; he made a sour face but just kept grunting and pounding into me. I furiously pumped at my cock while my asshole clamped down on his shaft, and sent streak after streak of semen all over my chest. It felt disgusting and I could smell the awful acrid and chlorinated scent, and that embarrassed me, and that made it feel even better.

Still too much! I shoved him back and he pulled out. Then he yanked the condom off and started jerking off, grunting like he was having a medical problem. Splat. Just a dribble of semen. Then a huge, sticky gush that landed right on my own, leaving a glistening lump of it on my chest. I stared at it. Disgusting! Filthy! I hissed at him. He opened his hand and smacked me there, then ground it into the fur. Then he ground his hand around my snout again.

As soon as he was done, he stuffed back into his pants and climbed off me, then wandered around collecting his shirt and jacket. Then he just stomped off out of my apartment without even shutting the door.

He left the binder of photos on the tablet, with the latest one tucked into its slot. There was only one left in the book, a blank with no picture.

Now, every time I take a photo, I wonder, will that one complete the book? Sometimes the hyena visits. Sometimes, he punishes me. Sometimes, he fucks me. But every time, there is always one more picture to take.

ABOUT THE AUTHORS

Whyte Yoté
www.furaffinity.net/user/whyteyote/
www.twitter.com/WhyteYote
Whyte Yoté has been writing erotic furry fiction since 1995 when he was probably far too young to be doing such a thing, and he has been seriously pursuing his craft since 2000. His works have appeared multiple times in *FANG, ROAR* and *Heat* magazine, as well as the anthologies *X, The Fortune Teller's Poem, Holidays, Will of the Alpha, Taboo* and *Trick or Treat*. When he's not writing, he…oh wait, never-mind. He juggles personal work with anthology submissions as well as commissions and collaborations.

Kansan by birth, South Dakotan by serendipity and Californian by convenience, Whyte Yoté currently lives in Sacramento with writer/graphic designer Tym, his forever boyfriend since 2004.

BDSM carries a special burden in furry: not only must we work around taboos, but adding anthropomorphism turns concepts like the master/pet relationship and puppy play into unique challenges. What happens when the sheep becomes the shepherd? When the puppy really is a dog? These barely scratch the surface of the possibilities, and it is up to us to explore them, limitless though they may be, and have fun while doing it.

Salome Wilde and Talon Rihai
You can find the delectable duo at their website, www.salandtale-rotica.com, or visit them on Twitter, @salomewilde and @talonsage.

Salome Wilde and Talon Rihai enjoy the best of every world—real and imaged—as co-authors, co-editors, and loverboi/lovergrrrl. Together, they have published the hurt-comfort gay novella *After the First Taste of Love*, a group of erotic short stories reaching across the orientation spectrum, and the edited collection *Desire Behind Bars: Lesbian Prison Erotica*.

The origins of "Training Kane" reach back to the early days of Sal and Tal's lustful literary relationship in fandom, primarily in their mutual love of the dog demons of Inuyasha. Pushing the boundaries of power and pain-pleasure is another (related) shared fetish. With most of their published fiction in the contemporary and realist vein, they were thrilled to fulfill some of their wilder desires through the creation of the world of Master Alain and his servants. This is their first published furry story.

Friday Donnelly

Friday Donnelly is an otter writer, a sort of thing of which there are oddly many in the fandom. He currently lives in the NC area and attends a few cons a year; if you see him about, feel free to say hi! He won't bite. Well, unless you're a fish.

Friday is actually asexual, but has an interest in kinks. He finds the way they shape social and sexual interactions intriguing, and loves to examine them. He also has an interest in raising asexual visibility, and many of his stories (both erotica and non) contain ace characters. They tend to work particularly well in BDSM situations, he finds, where their disinterest can provide a tantalizing challenge for their partners...

Tarl "Voice" Hoch

A complete list of his works can be found at: https://www.goodreads.com/author/show/5759304.Tarl_Voice_Hoch

He can be found on Twitter @voicespider and on Facebook at: https://www.facebook.com/TarlWriter

Tarl "Voice" Hoch is primarily a writer of horror and erotica. From his lair in Alberta, Canada, he spends most of his time writing, reading, harassing his feline overlords (both 2 and 4 legged) or exploring the kinky side of life. The subject of BSDM is one of significant interest to him as it plays a part in his personal lifestyle. He finds it interesting due to the sheer variety and creativity one can find within the community, as well as the ability to play erotically without resorting to outright sex. It is something that you can let yourself go fully while in a safe environment with a person or people you trust. (none of this 50 Shades crap)

Tarl's works can be found in the original *Will of the Alpha*, *Taboo*, and *FANG* Volume 5, all published by FurPlanet. He was also head editor of the horror anthology *Abandoned Places*, also by FurPlanet.

Lafitte

www.furaffinity.net/user/Lafitte

robur.sofurry.com

Co-editor of the very tome you now hold, Lafitte spent many years studying literature in Academia and earned a Masters Degree in English. However, his primary interest is in less traditional forms of writing: genre fiction, comics, pornography, etc. He doesn't see any reason these forms and topics aren't worth serious consideration. Lafitte also dabbles in art on occasion.

Ross Whitlock

https://www.furaffinity.net/user/hengeworlds

Ross Whitlock is a longtime member of the furry community. He lives in Colorado with his boyfriend and ferret. His writing is fueled by numerous mugs of tea and daily walks, during which he meets many friendly dogs. Ross has been writing fiction since his tender teen years, though "Twins Apart" is only his second published story. He is hard at work on a series of very exciting furry fantasy novels.

Ross has always been a fan of BDSM, and is delighted to contribute to *Will of the Alpha*. He values interesting characters and compelling plot, even in the midst of steamy eroticism, and believes that the best erotic writing doesn't take itself too seriously. Sex is fun.

Tym Greene

http://www.furaffinity.net/user/tym/

Tym Greene is a writer and artist, particularly of anthro things, and aspires to work in concept art. In the meantime he fulfills his world-building desires with the crafting of fiction. Apart from a few entry-level college courses, he's mostly self-taught with regard to writing, and has to thank the pantheon of authors (both classic and otherwise), his editors, and his boyfriend for helping him to be the writer he is today.

He wanted to use the themes of BDSM (and role play) to explore the idea of species in a furry world, and how (just as with other differences in our own reality) that diversity can be played with within the reality. He also has always had a soft spot for pony play, and admires those who can slip into the "headspace" whenever they want. He used his story for this anthology, in part, to explore the feeling of that mentality.

George Squares

George Squares is a speculative fiction writer interested in fantasy, erotica, science fiction, mystery and historical fiction. He spends a lot of time thinking about how furry evolves as a genre and subgenre, and is interested in how furry grows and splits into endemic cultures around the world.

He is gay, engaged to be married August 31st, 2015, and graduated with a Bachelors of Science degree in biology from The University of North Carolina at Wilmington.

What interested him to write for a furry BDSM anthology is the question of why kinks might arouse us. He is interested in the question of how coping with a negative sensation or experience can turn into a positive one through arousal.

Kjorteo Kalante

http://kjorteo.net

http://www.weasyl.com/~kjorteo

Kjorteo Kalante is an aspiring third generation writer from New Mexico. New to the scene and hopeful, his aunt and grandmother are both career authors, and he seeks to attain that same success himself. His first novel, *The Afflicted*, is available on the Amazon Kindle store and Smashwords. A new revision is currently in development, which he intends to pitch to traditional publishers upon completion.

He has always enjoyed domination/submission themes in anthropomorphic writing and role-play, but only recently became aware of their connection to the larger BDSM scene. "Unmanned" is his first deliberate attempt to write a BDSM story, though some of his other works might also accidentally qualify. As with all his work, he wanted to take subject matter that he loves, explore it, and create something as appealing to the reader as it is to him.

Slip-Wolf

Three years ago, Slip-Wolf discovered that the funny animal people in his brain were whining so loud because they wanted a place to frolic. Discovery of the Furry fandom provided them with just the right place. While the angst and anger and melodrama were expected parts of Slip's character's repertoire, certain other things turned up that distressed and delighted this explorer of the trans-human condition.

They brought harnesses and muzzles, chains and leathers, whips for mutual taming and whipped cream for no discernible reason whatsoever. Fortunately, Slip found a proper dungeon within which to inter these voracious hedonists, and sends his observations on their behavior to anthologist moles for clinical assessment.

Slip enjoys exploring BDSM through a furry lens, exploring positions of power and subjection that can reinforce species' assumed natural roles or otherwise transcend them. The creature that wields the leash is not always the one in control, as Slip's many characters like to roughly remind him.

H. A. Kirsch

http://furaffinity.net/user/hawkwolf
http://www.hakirsch.com/

H. A. Kirsch has been writing weird furry stories since he was a child. Now an adult, he writes weird erotic furry stories. They're often dark, and almost always homosexual.

People often think of BDSM as 'give' and 'take', 'top' and 'bottom', 'dominant' and 'submissive'. You're one, or you're the other. Black and white thinking just gets everyone into trouble, though. Every dominant is someone else's submissive, and vice versa. What better way to illustrate this than with a neurotic, sociopathic cougar and his silent tormentor?

Rechan

http://www.furaffinity.net/user/rechan/

https://twitter.com/molewords

Rechan has been in his lab for the last year working on this book and its sequel, *Will of the Alpha 3*. The mole has organized a plethora of bondage and eroticism for your reading pleasure, and now that it's nearly done, he can nap.

In between engaging in the mad science of editing, the mole writes erotica, fantasy and horror. You can find his creations in *Taboo, ROAR* Volume 6, *Abandoned Places*, and Sofawolf's *Heat* magazine. In addition, he has stories on his SoFurry and FurAffinity accounts.

The first *Will of the Alpha* was started because Rechan has a deep interest in BDSM and wanted to see a publication exploring the many facets of the kink community and the stories that could be told from it. The enthusiasm shown to the first volume encouraged him to open the door for more. He is most intrigued by the power exchange and mental elements of D/s, humiliation and objectification, and many smaller aspects and kinks. This interest is all due to a wonderful accident during a Theatre Arts class, but that's a story for another time.

www.ingramcontent.com/pod-product-compliance
Lightning Source LLC
Chambersburg PA
CBHW051639050726
47502CB00011B/1337